At the same moment, a vehicle approached slowly up the road, headlights glaring, up higher and higher, up the hilly road it came. I suddenly realized it was not a car but a truck, a vintage Ford truck, driven by a long-haired cowboy-hatted person—man? woman?—with a dazed expression. Brakes squealed and the truck stopped.

"It's her," I hollered. "The one I told you about. Run!" I tried to move myself, but froze in panic.

Without a word, the three boys surrounded the driver's side of the truck. "Get out, bitch," one of them said.

"You been a bad girl, we heard."

I gaped, icy with fear as Glenda Mane slipped down from the Ford's seat and stared around her.

"You idiots, stand back. Get away from me." Her words pounded the air with rage. "Get back, I say, or I'll kill you."

She reached into the truck and I screamed. "Watch out, she could have a weapon." I was so terrified they'd be hurt I felt energy bound through my veins. "You!" I shrieked, and came running at her with the cane, swinging it wildly in her face. "Don't-you-hurt-these-boys." My blows at least caused the startled Glenda to lose her balance and slump against the truck as she warded off the attack of the cane.

The two bigger boys shuffled around aimlessly, paying close attention now, glancing back and forth at each other, but stunned, too, maybe, by my unexpected outburst. The brown-faced lad shoved us all out of the way and ran into Glenda, butting into her with his head bent down. He spun her around by her arm, then managed to get hold of both arms and twist them behind her back.

"Hey, good 'un, Brownie," the dog's boy shouted.

"Get somethin' to tie her with, you eejits," Brownie ordered.

Her fury rose, insulted as she must be to be manhandled by a much smaller person. "Get off me, you idiot. I killed a grown man single-handed, you think I can't hurt you and hurt you bad?"

That was all I needed to hear. I snatched up the foxy little dog, unbuckled his leash and tossed it to the boys. They looked up in surprise, saw what I'd done, and finally joined in the battle. Shouting obscenities at Glenda, they helped their friend subdue her while one of them tied her wrists together with the leash and lashed it to the steering wheel of her car. They made such a racket that lights went on in houses up and down the street, doors opened and people streamed out.

Other Works From The Pen Of

Eleanor Sulloo

Moonrakers, March 2002

Science and the supernatural clash head on in this Victorian mystery, aRomance of engulfing mystery and cruel betrayal.

Menopause Murders:

Hostage, February, 2010

Murder, Mayhem, Mad for love…These *Women on Fire* Turn Hot Flashes Into Hot Detecting and Sizzling Romance!

Harem, August, 2010

Murder in a nursing home, a streaking senior stud, an often-confused mother-in-law. Can *Women on Fire* solve it with a tea dance? Or will it take a trip to Italy and a new heart and brave beginnings?

Wings

MENOPAUSE MURDERS
HURDLES

by

Eleanor Sullo

A Wings ePress, Inc.

Encore L'Amour Mystery

Wings ePress, Inc.

Edited by: Jeanne Smith
Copy Edited by: Leslie Hodges
Senior Editor: Anita York
Executive Editor: Marilyn Kapp
Cover Artist: Pat Evans

All rights reserved

Names, characters and incidents depicted in this book are products of the author's imagination or are used fictitiously. Any resemblance to actual events, locales, organizations, or persons, living or dead, is entirely coincidental and beyond the intent of the author or the publisher.

No part of this book may be reproduced or transmitted in any form or by any means, electronic or mechanical, including photocopying, recording, or by any information storage and retrieval system, without permission in writing from the publisher.

Wings ePress Books
http://www.wings-press.com

Copyright © 2011 by Eleanor Sullo
ISBN 978-1-59705-509-3

Published In the United States Of America

May 2011

Wings ePress Inc.
403 Wallace Court
Richmond, KY 40475

Dedication

For Pat, a woman of spirit, faith and wisdom, who never fails to inspire

Page Of Appreciation And Thanks

I could not have written about horses and the horse scene in America and the UK without the help of many generous and wise equine professionals and amateurs. My thanks to them all.

ESS

Glossary of Heroines: Menopause Murders

Ada—Rich and powerful, owner of a travel agency, Ada manages by leaning on the men in her life and also by using her class and overwhelming wealth to buy her way out of difficulties. But recently she's been bitterly betrayed by some men in her life. Now, as the "queen" of a group of menopausal friends, Ada is learning that being vulnerable isn't the worst place to be, and generosity is life-giving. Can she wean herself from crippling attitudes and become both unselfish and independent after all?

Dorie—Skipping her way through life, this impetuous charmer's wacky logic and malapropisms often hit the mark. An accomplished artist, she's impetuous, impulsive, intuitive, and hungry for love, and, after leaving an abusive relationship, the tall and beautiful platinum blonde Goldie Hawn-look-alike is determined to become a mature and respected companion.

Meg—Small and gray-haired Meg is plain, stern and slightly stodgy, but beneath her plainness shines a quirky sense of humor and a luminosity both as a friend and a retired forensic scientist. Her sad expression betrays the scars of her youth spent in war-torn Bosnia and her unhappy childlessness, but she knows she can't hide her neediness behind her intellect forever.

Theo—Spunky and committed, some would say "bossy," Theo, a newlywed step-mom, is as dependable and respected as the former Mother Superior she was for three decades. She inspires the spiritual vitality of the group. Too bad everyone but she counts on ultra-serious, highly moral, classic-looking, groomed to a "t" Theo for her wisdom. And too bad she can't break from her old scrupulosity and throw caution to the wind, once in a while.

Hannah—The attractive, streaky-blonde journalist has been scared to death of flying since her husband died in a plane crash thirty years prior. Although smart, sassy and sophisticated, she lost her job because of this crippling fear, and faces older age with a dread of loneliness. Finally listening to her emotions, she's shaking the pain of her past by counseling grieving children, and allowing herself to face, instead of merely dazzling accomplishments, a future of relationships, and a sexy new lover.

Lucia—The warm, loving and charismatic "Mama" of the group, dark-eyed and frizzy-haired Lu feels everybody's pain and tries to "fix" them all. But as a reincarnated Demeter, chained to the forge, her nurturing Neapolitan heart sometimes feels too big for her small life. If she could "redo" her past and open her own restaurant, the stage of her life may stretch to hold her and her brilliant chef's skills—but only if her beloved Tony is at her side.

"Change of life is the time when you meet yourself at the crossroads and you decide whether to be honest or not before you die."—Katherine Butler Hathaway

One

Ada

"Awwrrgh!" I felt the scream vibrate through my throat, but still couldn't believe the horrendous sound had come from me.

My eyes popped open to a pulsating circle of blue sky, scudding clouds and—oh, staring faces. Lots of them. Something or someone had knocked me to the ground, and I was livid. But my anger was tinged with panic, and the panic did not match the silence all around me, with only the scratchy sound system droning on far away.

The sound system? Wait—what sound system, oh, oh, no—

"Ada, Ada dear, are you all right?"

Was that Devlin Doyle, with his handsome, reassuring countenance and smiling green eyes, inches from my face? My stomach coasted into quietude, but instantly went skidding again when I felt the breeze on my legs and realized my Anne Klein dress was up around my waist in this ridiculous prone position.

I let go what I hoped was a more lady-like scream, and pushed at the skirt as I struggled to rise, but Devlin's strong arms held me there, and other hands—Dorie's?—fussed with my skirt, pulling it down to my knees so I could finally assert myself. I've always maintained a woman is unlikely to assert herself with her thighs exposed in public.

"Devlin, you let me up this second. Dorie, enough now. I don't want to be fussed over." I squirmed up to my elbows, then half-sitting, until another man, someone I vaguely recognized from Board meetings at the hospital, came between us and eased my upper body back down. I was furious, but admittedly confused, too. Had I fallen, had a stroke? And that sound system static...

"Mrs. Javitt, did you strike your head any place?" This, this stranger was poking around in my hair, messing my latest Fifth Avenue do. I shook my head indignantly.

"I tell you I'm fine. I don't know how I landed here. Who hit me?"

"No one hit you, Mrs. Javitt. Apparently you passed out when the accident—"

It all washed over me then, and I clapped hand to my mouth to squelch another scream. Oh, Zeus, no! They'd missed the hurdle!

"The rider, is she okay? Devlin, is Sigourney...? And my horse, my poor—"

Memory returned in flashes of horror. I saw Fitzgibbons, my prize chestnut, about to leap, the rider bracing, and then suddenly flying forward over the saddle and into the air. I couldn't bear to think Siggy might be terribly hurt, or the horse might be lying in a heap at the foot of the hurdle.

He'd stopped. Fitzgibbons had stopped dead before the fence. And crumpled to the ground. I yelped again, then covered my mouth to still the raucous noise coming out of it. I made some effort toward an apology.

The doctor poking at me frowned. "I think she's all right. Help me with her, Devlin, let's see if she can stand."

I had no patience for their currying. I gently shoved the two-inch heel of my boot into the doctor's instep and yanked myself to my feet, nearly throwing Devlin into the crowd.

Quickly I grabbed him back by his corduroy lapels and gave him "I want answers" eyes. "Tell me, right now. What happened?"

Devlin shrugged, and wrapped an arm around me. As if I were a feeble, old woman. To hell with him! I squirmed away.

"I didn't see it, Ada. I was looking at you."

I grimaced. At *me?* In the state I was in? Dirty, disheveled, gawking stupidly? I shook my head and made a wish to disappear. But just then Dorie reached my side again through the assembled multitude.

"Sigourney's okay, I think, Ada. I saw her move. Theo's with her now."

"Let's go, Dorie, let's see for ourselves." I grabbed her hand and started toward the paddock, muttering, "Thank God, thank Yahweh. Oh, I couldn't have stood it if..." I scanned the field, saw the knot of horses and riders dispersing and the little group bent over the brown mass on the ground. In that second I finally understood the ceaseless static—the announcer was explaining the extent of the injuries of the accident over the loudspeaker. Of my horse and of my dear friend's daughter failing the jump.

Failing the jump...

The last thing I heard through the static nearly put me down a second time, and this time, I knew passing out would be a shoddy escape. I was a big girl; I had to face what was happening. I gritted my teeth.

The staticky voice droned on. "Ladies and gentlemen, it isn't looking so good for Fitzgibbons. This horse, champion and victor in so many regional shows this year, may never compete again."

I struggled for balance, allowing Devlin's arm around my waist from the other side, comforting and feeling not the least bit foreign, as if we'd been together, close like that, for years. More than old friends.

When actually this was the very first time the two of us had gone out together, in his car, on what minimally could be called a date. The annual Polo Club Event, where my thoroughbred was expected to carry home the blue. Oh, Fitzgibbons—

I was still speechless, my gaze alternating between Devlin and my pal Dorie when Danny reached me.

"Jesus, Mom, are you all right? I saw you go over when Fitzgibbons..."

"Shh, Danny. What happened, Ada?" His girlfriend Janet's usually stoic features had gone awry, her forehead wrinkled, mouth twisted. The two young people crowded close, their faces chalk white, eyes wide, more frightened than I'd seen them even in Alaska, when a man with a gun had been hunting them down. They tried to hug me, but I kept moving forward, gesturing them along with head nods and still trying to catch my breath.

"Fainted, I figure," Devlin Doyle said. "She'll be okay."

"Naw, not okay. Mom doesn't faint. Never loses a beat." Danny elbowed Devlin out of the way and grasped me around the shoulders as we walked. "She's the one who takes charge when something happens and everybody else is going crazy. Right, Mom?"

He was so totally right. I felt like a fool for having panicked. I know I blushed and scoffed. "Don't fuss over me, please. You know I hate that."

At that moment the screeching siren of an ambulance revived the image that had first sent me sprawling, the sight of my prize pony tossing poor Sigourney Rutledge to the ground as the half-ton of horse flesh, whinnying hard, stopped cold and crumpled a few yards before the final gate. The sight and sound and smell of where we stood not far from the gate now—scent of dust and grass and sweaty horse flesh, his hard whinnying—flooded my mind and returned my knees to mush.

Fitzgibbons hadn't made the jump. Hadn't even tried.

"Look, Mom. He's getting up." I saw the long, angular legs unbend, the brown mass heaving, tossing off his handlers, who scattered like flotsam in a writhing current. My breath caught in my chest.

"It's okay, Mom," Danny reassured me yet again.

"They have his lead. They're walking him to the stable. See?" Danny pointed and I'm sure I nodded, but I got sidetracked.

What about the rider, Sigourney? Something threw her upward, flying over the horse's head and... "Oh, migod."

I sank back against Dan before I could take a few more hesitant steps forward. I had to focus, to wake up from this horrible nightmare.

Devlin and Danny tried to hold me back, slow me down. Devlin's voice was anxious :"You need, Ada dear, you need..." he started.

"Stop it!" I dug in my heels, breathed deeply and stood as tall as my undersize frame would allow. "All I need... is to see... how Sigourney is, that's all I need." And to get back to the stables to check on Fitzgibbons. I squirmed away from the protective arms of both men but they held me fast.

In my mind I saw it again, backlit by the brilliant fall sun: Fitzgibbons on the ground in a heap, his rider, Sigourney, oh, God, Theo's stepdaughter. How was she? I heard myself whimper and felt myself shaking my head like a filly panicked at the scent of blood. Oh, Zeus, was there blood? Were they even alive? Then I remembered: oh, yes, Fitzgibbons was walking. Dorie saw Siggy move.

Thank you. Thank you.

I turned toward Dorie, who was trying to keep the crowd back by flailing her arms, her wispy hair trailing paths all over her panicked face.

"Dorie, make them let go of me." I forced the words out through my teeth.

Out in the field, the ambulance had pulled up close to the accident scene. We could hear them plainly now, opening some doors, slamming others, metal sliding against metal. The burst of activity out on the track distracted my captors, and as they glanced toward the course I executed a sly ducking motion to slip away and turn toward the spot where Theo's daughter lay. I tried to run, but my high heels sank in the soft turf and I wobbled again, then plunged forward, clumps of grass and soil stuck on my beige suede boots.

Dorie kicked at Danny's shins, then Devlin's, and grabbed my arm. I took another step, and another, then faster still while behind me, my captives groaned.

"Mom!" Danny hollered.

"Ada, wait!" Devlin called.

Dorie had kept up with me—she was smart and efficient, when she had to be.

"Let her go," she demanded. Grateful, I ran with Dorie the last twenty yards to where medical personnel and others were circling the fallen rider. Theo caught our eyes and, looking numb, nodded once and kept her mouth tight in a crooked half-smile.

I wanted to hug her, hold her close, say I was sorry, so sorry, but couldn't get near enough, so I hugged Dorie instead. My eyes burned from the dust still blowing on the track, and maybe from holding back tears that were pushing forward. Dorie was muttering something barely audible.

"No, you don't," I muttered, and Dorie glanced down at me, puzzled.

"What, Ada? I was just saying we should call the others. Hannah and Lu and Meg."

I shook my head. "I know, but later, hon, later." At that moment no one in the world existed except those here at the Polo Grounds, those especially who had been injured, who maybe fought for their lives at this very second. I ground my teeth, thought of all those who had fought for life and left me in the past few years: two dead husbands, a murdered gardener, my old friend Judith, my faithful Labrador...

Mixed up prayers spun through my mind, words of the Shiva service, about letting the dead go, about new life. I squirmed. Threw kisses as they closed the ambulance doors.

Once the ambulance pulled away, Theo at her stepdaughter's feet, her face a strained mask of calm, fingers clasping the small gold cross she always wore, Dorie and I collapsed against each other.

"How can she stand it?" Dorie whispered. "If it were Liza, if it were my child, I'd..."

I grunted, barely able to speak at the thought of Sigourney's ghost-pale face, panicky brown eyes trying to stare straight ahead, her neck supported in a Thomas collar, her body strapped to a board. I wanted to race closer, chase the ambulance and order the world aright again. I began moving. I had to move somewhere. Only after a dozen steps did I realize it was toward the stable and my chestnut thoroughbred. It was the horse who filled my mind now. I had to see Fitzgibbons, the sweet, dumb animal who'd so endeared himself to me, who was so perfect, had been so perfect and so faithful.

Until now.

"Fitzgibbons!" I yelped as I hurried across the paddock. The tight knot of my friends moved with me. Thank heavens, the horse's trainer, Mac, pulled up just then in the small Jeep he used at the track. I stopped, clutching at Dorie, who wavered in her three-inch consignment shop sandals. We all clambered in without speaking and let Mac deliver us to the stables. Squeezed in beside him, I blubbered my questions while Devlin handed me his hankie. I kept asking, though deep inside I dreaded the answers.

"Is he going to be—all right?"

"I sure hope so, Mrs. Javitt. Terry, that's my helper," he explained to the others, "called Doctor Ingmanson. He's on the way. Fitzgibbons seems calm, stable. They led him back to his box okay."

He pulled his cap down lower over his face, and I kept the questions coming, but Mac had gone silent, as I'd feared he would. I wasn't the only one who loved Fitzgibbons.

The engine whined as the jeep picked its way through parking lots and the back paddock, right up to the stable's wide doors.

"But what? Something you're not telling me, Mac."

The trainer shrugged, tried to yank the brim of his hat even lower over his furrowed brow and hazel eyes, his burnished skin, as if he'd like to disappear under my scrutiny. He knew something. Something wasn't so good. He wasn't about to tell me, just yet.

Okay, so Mac McClellan wasn't verbose. I knew it was why he loved working with animals. Horses, after all, didn't care a bit for conversation. An apple or two a day and a gentle currying, a chance to run once in a while, to be led into the various moves of an event—gallop, trot, canter, jump—and a good English thoroughbred was very much at home.

So why hadn't Fitzgibbons been at home today, on the final jump? Why didn't he strain to shine, to let his rider guide him, be one with him after they took the final approach?

Something in my heart snagged. It must be bad news, whatever the trainer wasn't saying. The thing that stopped the jumper, that threw his rider to the ground and sent him sprawling. It must be horrible, heart-stopping news.

As Mac pulled the Jeep up to the doors and tried to lead us into the stable, I clutched at the sharp pain in my chest with one hand and grabbed at his arm with my other hand. "Tell-me-now!"

He hung his head as he stepped away from me. "You'll see for yourself, Ms. Javitt, he's looking good, pretty darn good. Besides, Doc will know more 'n' me..." Still he hung his head. Why?

This time Devlin and Danny didn't have to slow me down. I know I slunk up the ramp, then practically crawled along the side of the indoor ring space between the rows of stalls. I caught a glimpse of Mac's assistant, Terry Bukowski and her gaunt white face as she worked over the animal, leading him through the cool down, unsaddling him, wiping him down. Terry's motions were abrupt, jagged. Like she had to hurry, as if rubbing Fitzgibbons down was a subversive action, as if she could hide what must be obvious to everyone there.

"Doc's here," a voice called from the entry behind us and I took a few quicker steps. I'd glimpsed the darkness on the thoroughbred's face and neck, the spot where Terry was hastily applying the wiping towels, and now I couldn't get there fast enough.

"Terry?" I called, my voice close enough to a shriek to startle everyone around me to a standstill. But I jogged forward, damn the old, nagging pain in my knee, dragging bits of shavings with the heels of my boots. I'd seen the blood Terry was trying to wipe away.

Blood? "Terry? Why is he bleeding?" *Oh, Lord, what's happened to my baby?*

I felt my stomach sink, my head go fuzzy. Blood couldn't be a good sign. It might mean he was badly hurt, cut somewhere, or maybe internal injuries, bleeding from the mouth, even though he was still standing, skittering around a bit as Terry toweled him dry. And coughing. Every few minutes he nudged his head up and to one side and coughed. I couldn't tell for sure, but it seemed he was standing a bit slumped, his back not arched as gracefully as usual, his head hanging low. Still, he was standing on all fours.

He nickered softly at the sound and sight of me coming closer. What beauty, what hope he'd brought into my life when he had been delivered to me just months after my second husband bought him and then died of a heart attack. He'd become my baby.

Fitzgibbons brought me hope, too, when my stepson had to return to drug rehab for the third time. Consoled me when my gardener was murdered a year-and-a-half ago. Stood patiently while I curried and combed him, weeping into his neck when my dear old friend Judith was murdered last year.

I could count on Fitzgibbons, always there for me, welcoming my gifts of apples and carrots, my visits, my soft murmurings and encouragements. Whinnying back at me. And once Mac had taken the skittish colt through his paces, over two years of training him to feel and sense and be one with his rider, I could count on him to win, to extend those classic long flanks and stretch that fabulous neck to take every jump they could manufacture for him.

And Sigourney, how she took to him, riding him at events all over the east coast before she left for college. And now, since she transferred back to the local college and prepared for this October classic, they were like one being: rider/horse.

I shook my head, my mind still clasped around a prayer for Sigourney, that she was okay, that there was no concussion, no major breaks, nothing critical. And now, Fitzgibbons, bleeding. I had to deal with this. I would. I must.

My brain spun.

Devlin and Danny stood respectfully a few yards back as I approached the animal. I heard their intake of breath when they saw what I saw. I took a fresh towel from Terry, close enough to reach out a hand now, and my fingers trembled as I held them below the horse's mouth and he lipped my knuckles and sighed out a breath. I rubbed his nose and held back a cry as the vet approached and moved past me.

"Let me work him over, Mrs. Javitt. It's really best if you're not here." When I didn't back off, he sighed. "We want to keep him calm."

I couldn't help but let out a snort of my own and lift my chin. The vet frowned, but drew back. I knew most men reacted to me, to my authoritative nature, even called it bossiness or worse. Ingmanson was no different. I didn't mind their scorn, when there was scorn, because I had the gift of being able to convince them I knew what was best, what path to take. And I only used my toughness and control of others for the best possible intentions.

Usually.

I didn't budge.

I'd seen the blood, and that could mean life was changed forever for beautiful Fitzgibbons. For me, too, with my wonder horse, who for over two years had seemed to be the new love of my life, the child I'd never had, the faithful lover I'd never been able to hang onto.

"Are you kidding?" Dorie shot out the words from Fitzgibbons's far side, where she'd been stroking his neck. "She keeps him calmer than anybody." I tried to keep a smile from softening my mouth.

"Yeah," Danny chimed in from behind me, "and don't even try to send her away, 'cause she won't go." I grabbed Danny's hand and stood firm, lifting my other hand to Fitzgibbons so he could once more lip my knuckles, gently, as he always did. Then I sighed, realizing my obstinacy would get us nowhere, and drew back a few steps to let the work begin.

Ingmanson huffed, stood face to face with my hurdler and told Mac to set him up in cross ties out in the center space to make it easier to control the animal while he worked. When he began his examination, I followed his every move. His fingers and hands ran up and down each leg, then did an extensive probe of the head. When Fitzgibbons coughed again, the veterinarian stiffened. He shone his penlight into the horse's nares, leaned to the side as if thinking, and then checked both nostrils again. Shook his head.

"What?" I demanded. "What are you seeing?"

The doctor waved an arm meaning to say hold on a minute, and carefully checked the horse's mouth and ears. He looked toward the trainer and his assistant, the young English girl who'd been helping out at the stables.

"Blood. Just coming from the nose? Or did you notice an injury when you first got him back here?"

Terry muttered something and held out the stack of used towels. Before she could speak, Mac stepped in front of her, eyeing the towels with shock in his eyes. He looked furious.

"Why didn't you say? For God's sake, Terry, you could have saved us all time. Where is he hurt?"

Terry shrugged so nonchalantly I wanted to shove the doctor out of the way and slap her face.

"Nuffin special 'bout it. Always had a little blood in the nose after practice. And coughs a bit, too, when he works hard. Lots of horses do."

Doc Ingmanson squared his shoulders and shook his head vigorously. "You should have said so. How long have you worked with horses?" He pressed against the horse's right shoulder, felt his neck, then palpated his right chest with gestures that seemed to soothe my Fitzgibbons. If Danny hadn't been hanging on to me I'd have tried to lurch forward to get closer.

"What is it, Doctor? What are you seeing? Was he injured today or is it something worse..." I asked through my teeth.

"Worked 'round horses six years," Terry muttered. "Seen some of 'em do like that and still do good work. Winnin' and all, anyways. Din't think nothing of it."

Shaking his head all the while, Mac gave Terry a light shove and told her to clean up. She gathered the towels and tack and skulked away.

"What do you think, Doc?" Mac asked." Any heat in those tendons?"

Ingmanson shook his head. "No leg injuries I can tell of."

He pulled out his stethoscope and listened to Fitzgibbons's chest. Then swallowed hard. The poor animal began to paw the shavings at his feet and flick his head tremulously as he coughed again. All this activity and talking around him were making him skittish. I tried to lean closer to soothe him, but this time Devlin helped Danny hold me back, their warm hands on my shoulders. I had the crazy thought that this must be a bit like being sane but kept in a straight jacket.

"Anything internal?" Mac stood across from me

beyond the horse, but I could feel the heat coming off him.

"Too soon to say." The doctor again rode his fingers along each leg to feel for damage, then unbent his lanky form, stroked the long skull of the horse down his nose and turned toward our worried crowd behind him.

I clutched at his sleeve. "What is it? What are you finding?"

"Too early to say, Mrs. Javitt."

I put my face close to his. "I understand. But I want to know what you're thinking, Dr. Ingmanson. Please. Has he been injured in the fall or, or, is this bleeding a sign of something he's already had? Could it hurt him, cut short his—" I started to say "life," then caught the soft brown eyes of the animal turned in my direction—"career?"

The doctor's sigh was quiet, but I heard it all the same and it scared me, a sigh of resignation, maybe, or of fear. "Mrs. Javitt, it could be something chronic. Or not. I'm going to need blood work, get him over to UMass for x-rays, maybe even insert a tube down his throat to see what's going on down there."

"Whatever you need to do. I want him to have the best. Call in any experts, get him whatever help you think he needs." I closed my eyes tight and swayed a little in place. Dr. Ingmanson took hold of my arm this time.

"Look, Mrs. Javitt. Let's give Fitzgibbons some quiet time. He needs more cooling down, maybe because of the trauma he's been through or maybe the stimulation of all of us around him. Anyhow, he's still sweating."

I grabbed for a towel, nearly tripping in my

ridiculous small-heeled boots as I did so. "I'll do it, I'll—"

"No's" from several direction s peppered my ears.

"We'll take care of it, Ms. Javitt," Mac said. "Terry and I will be working with Fitzgibbons every minute."

I shook my head, clenched my jaw. *"If you'd done your job—"* I wanted to say, but didn't. I'd known Mac as long as I'd known Fitzgibbons. I'd trusted him. Terry was another story, but I'd never had any reason to think her incompetent, or worse, stupid.

Mac saw the rage teeming on my face, I'm sure, because he came close and spoke softly. "Ms. Javitt, Ada, I hold myself responsible for this. Remember I asked if we could have a meeting on Monday? I still want to talk with you about something."

I nodded, frozen, having not the vaguest idea why he wanted to meet me, but recalling he'd mentioned a meeting before today's events. Was it about Terry? Her incompetence? "Call me," I said, feeling numb, and rocking where I stood. "I suppose the poor boy will calm down a bit when I'm out of here. And then there's Sigourney to check on."

Mac blew out air and shook his head. "Let me know how she is." I nodded.

"Let me take you home now, Ada, dear. I'm sure the doctor will call you as soon as he can." Devlin's voice stood out, assured, confident. I wanted to turn against him and rest my head on his chest. It was exciting, and somehow comforting to have Devlin there, a man I'd always admired, felt drawn to. Yet I couldn't think straight, fearing something might be horribly wrong with my thoroughbred. I couldn't walk away from him right now. How dare anybody think so?

My hand covered my mouth. "A treat. If only I had a carrot or something, some kind of treat for him before I leave so he'd know, he'd remember the one who loves him is still here," I muttered.

Doc Ingmanson spoke up quickly. "Not a good time for him to be ingesting but a little water, Mrs. Javitt. We don't know how he is internally yet."

I sulked, then put my hand under Fitzgibbons's chin. To my rattled brain it seemed he almost smiled at me. That was what I focused on, tears burning my eyelids, as my little group turned and left the stables.

Doc Ingmanson, Mac and the skittish Terry, back from her laundry errand, still had much work to do.

"Call me, please, with anything at all, any news, good or—" I called back. "And thank you," I said, eyeing Mac and the doctor and purposely ignoring the young English hand who kept herself half hidden behind Mac with her limp hair hanging in her face, her eyes downcast.

I breathed deeply and clung to Devlin's arm as we left the stable, watching a man in denim steer away a crowd of curious onlookers from the ramp. We crossed the lots to our cars. Anger still topped my fear.

"That young woman is totally useless. I don't know why Mac hired her. Imagine not telling them..."

Devlin whispered, "Hush now, let it be 'til we know what's happening. Okay?"

I couldn't nod, but let myself focus on the sounds in the distance, where the final events of the day were drawing light applause from a crowd still stunned by the huge accident in the arena. The Master of Ceremonies' voice was still a muffled buzz of static, and I tuned him out before I could hear his words. I have to admit I didn't care about the rest of the events, the winners, the losers. That cup had been Fitzgibbons's to win; everyone knew it.

But something brutal had happened to keep him from it. I choked back a rebellious cry in my throat.

Dorie asked if she should go to the hospital to check on Theo and her injured daughter. "Absolutely," I said, sorry I hadn't thought of it myself. "I'll come with you."

Devlin groaned, and Danny spoke up. "Mom, please let Mr. Doyle take you home. Janet and I will take Aunt Dorie to the hospital and see how Sigourney's doing."

"Oh, yes, Ada," Janet said quickly. "Please let us go. Sig's our friend, too."

I shaded my eyes against the bright sunlight in the west, barely able to keep them open; they were so raw, perhaps from the dust on the course, or from holding back tears. I did have to get home, rest my eyes, take an ibuprofen, have something cold to drink, just sink into oblivion. I also knew Janet and Sigourney had become fast friends since they'd met taking courses at Tunxis Community. I couldn't blame the young people for wanting to go. The state I was in, trembling and torn with emotion, I'd be useless to Theo. Let Dorie and the young people handle it.

I nodded, and waved my arm at them to go ahead.

"Devlin, make her rest," Dorie called out as the three turned right for Danny's little Corolla.

Beside me, I felt Devlin Doyle wave back, then take firmer control of my elbow as he guided me into his Land Rover without another protest. He even snapped my seat buckle for me, and I sighed gratefully.

I did need a break. I wasn't a young woman anymore. That was the cruel truth. And my bum knee ached with every step. I didn't even begin to know how to handle Fitzgibbons's accident, Sigourney's injuries. I who always felt competent and in charge suddenly felt my age, not just in the slump of my shoulders, the ache of my arthritic knee, the soreness of my feet.

An allover hurt, but mostly deep in my heart.

Devlin sidled close to me when he got in and patted my leg, then started the engine. Its roar echoed inside me. I pushed thoughts of my beautiful thoroughbred chestnut to the back of my mind with a conscious effort of will. He'd be all right. I had to think so.

"Take it easy, dear. I don't want you worrying about anything. It's all going to be fine. Now rest." Devlin's words were soft, his voice deep and floating so close it seemed to wrap me up. How comforted I felt. I relented, and to my surprise, his hand on my thigh warmed parts of me that had lain dormant far too long.

Is this me? I wondered to myself. By then we were on the road home and my eyes had closed against the salt in them. I think I dozed until we pulled into my driveway, and woke blanketed in a shield of warmth and a welcome sense of numbness.

"You'll get through this, Ada. You're a strong woman, and Doc Ingmanson is going to make Fitzgibbons well again. I just know it." Devlin had drawn me close to him, his strong arm around my shoulders. The crazy thought veered through my mind: for a Social Security recipient, the man had plenty of sex appeal.

Before I could file the thought away, I was focusing on his mouth, inches from my face, and his neatly sculpted features, his narrow but deep green eyes When we kissed, it seemed like the most natural thing in the world. When we stopped, it didn't.

Two

Dorie

At the hospital, breathless and too frightened and confused to say or do much to help, I felt my legs go numb when Danny located the Rutledge group in an alcove of the emergency room: Theo, Siggy's younger sister Shannon and her boyfriend. I froze where I was, wondering why I had offered to come; I was useless in an emergency, never had the right words, and, as usual, would probably say something totally berserk when I opened my mouth.

Dan and Janet hurried ahead, spoke to Theo, then moved quietly with Shannon and her boyfriend to the glass-windowed treatment room, where they were working on the injured rider. Shannon seemed to be explaining something to the young people, as staff within ran to and fro in a kind of well-practiced dance.

Even from where I stopped, six or seven yards away from the cubicle, I could see Sigourney was conscious, because her hand lifted in a sort of wave when she saw the others at the window. She may even have smiled, but there were so many people working on her, and so much equipment attached to her, it was hard to tell if she was badly hurt, or improving each minute, perhaps even coming 'round to "okay."

I hated to intrude on this family's tragedy, but I'd promised Ada. Theo hadn't seen me yet, and was standing there like a pillar, strong and dauntless, her arms crossed over her chest, fingers of one hand clutching her cross, her large, dark eyes directed to the window where Dan and Janet were signaling thumbs up to the girl in the hospital bed.

Theo still intimidated me a little. Of everyone in our Women on Fire group, Theo seemed the most distant, and I hadn't known her long. Sometimes she seemed judgmental, and other times, filled with a kind of peacefulness that seemed to say "I've got it all over you."

I, on the other hand, never felt that confident, that peaceful inside. I fiddled with my clothes even now, adjusting the chiffon top over my rainbow-colored handkerchief skirt, poking strands of hair back away from my face. It seemed to me there was always some adjustment to be made, some correction to my person as much as to my art, adding a dab of color here, smoothing out a brush stroke there. Though I was the tallest of the group and had, I'd heard tell, a good eye for make-up and clothes, even ones from Goodwill, Theo, with her straight back, sturdy body and neat, dark bob with every hair in place, made me feel small and unkempt.

Or maybe it was because Theo had spent about a zillion years in the convent, part of it as the Superior Mother or whatever they called it, something I couldn't imagine doing, even for a day. Locked up, alone, serene, responsible for everyone and everything in any situation?

Not.

Like today, with her stepdaughter lying there like a pie being portioned out and served.

A small squeak left my lips before I could choke it back and Theo turned and saw me, dropped the crucifix she had been fingering and spread her arms wide.

I ran to her. We hugged. And the way Theo clung to me, making little swallowing noises and drawing in little shudders of breath, I knew something had changed.

Theo was glad—relieved or something—to see me. Me... mindless, confused, incapable Dorie.

"Dorine, oh, I'm happy it's you. When I saw Danny I thought his mother must be right behind him, and I could see at the showground, Ada's such a wreck, so filled with guilt or something. Though there's nothing she could have done differently... this was not her fault. But she'll never believe it."

I nodded and grinned, still speechless.

"She'd be rattling on and on, needing assurance, and I just couldn't handle the drama at this moment. Ada's, well, you know, outside of my Sisters, she's been my dearest friend since high school, but I am too scared myself to console anybody else at this moment."

I tried not to let my shock over Theo's vulnerability show in too wide a grin. Uttering wordless murmurs that couldn't mean anything, I helped Theo ease into one of those plastic upholstered loveseats they furnished ERs with, and plopped beside her, not caring how my skirt twisted or my chiffon top flew up around my waist. I put an arm around Theodora's shoulders, wishing I could say something consoling. But my mind went almost totally blank.

"You know how Ada is, Thee, feeling like she should manage, oh, I don't know, the whole world or something and, and..."

"And get it right the first time," Theo said, and her lips turned up in a grin. Without knowing who started it, we clutched each other again and laughed, scattering tension like birds on a sidewalk abandoning their crumbs at the sound of a backfire.

I straightened my back and took a deep breath. "But how is she? How's Sigourney? She looked so beautiful out there, as if she and the horse were one, so graceful, so..."

Theo nodded. "That's the strange part. She said Fitzgibbons seemed absolutely fluid beneath her, anticipating every jump, eager but leaving control to her as he should, as he always does, and then, then, he seemed to falter, to make a sound like a cough or something..." Theo dabbed at her eyes. She breathed in and out consciously to steady herself, one hand on my arm.

"They don't know much yet. She seems to have movement okay in her limbs, but also probably a concussion, so they're checking for brain swelling now, that's the scariest thing, and they've just done x-rays of everything. She's complaining about pain in her left shoulder, thinks that's where she hit the ground."

"When the horse just stopped at the what-do-you-call-it, the wooden thing?"

Theo nodded. "The gate. She's being very brave about it all, but when her father gets here, oh, he's going to be so upset, and she always breaks down and cries in front of him when something's wrong. I mean, she can hold up when it's just me."

I started to correct my friend, assure her the girls felt very close to her now, even if she was only their stepmother, when footsteps sounded behind me. Theo looked over, too, and we saw her husband Wilson rushing toward us. He was wearing golfing clothes, a sharp tan polo shirt and umber slacks and cardigan. Theo jumped up and went to him, and they hugged briefly, but his face was twisted with worry and pain.

I patted Theo's arm and moved across the room so the two could talk. Just then a doctor came out of the exam room, his mask dropped down around his neck, his scrubs marred with what, I didn't want to know. Theo and her husband went right to him, and Shannon came running, too. In the small space I could hear the news in bits and snatches myself.

"Concussion, yes, but no severe brain swelling. Not at this time." Wilson's shoulders quivered when he sighed. "No paralysis anywhere we can see. And she's responding well to questions."

I watched Theo's knees dip and nearly give way as she exhaled. "The shoulder pain... due to a fracture at the top of the humerus. A good size one... bit of bone floating around in there. She says she landed on her shoulder."

Wilson Rutledge rubbed his fingers over his eyes. The doctor put a hand on the man's arm. "...if that's the worse thing Sigourney takes away from this fall... lucky girl. ...don't mean to minimize... it'll require surgery, but we'll call in an orthopedist when the swelling's gone down." They talked further about who to call in, then Wilson asked if he could go see his daughter. His face was red, and the muscles of his neck tight, but there was something like relief sparkling in his gray eyes. His daughter Shannon gripped his arm so tightly they walked like two people in a three-legged race.

I waved to Theo as she went toward the exam room following them. "I'll let the others know, Thee," I said. "Ada will be so relieved. Call me if you need—"

Theo threw me a kiss, nodded, and, smoothing her purple blazer, followed Wilson and Shannon in. Danny and Janet clustered around me, and I told them what the doctor had said. They both cheered and ran back to the window to give Sigourney another thumbs up, and then followed me down the corridor on the way out.

"Can't wait to tell Mom. She'll be glad Siggy's okay," Danny enthused as we made our way to the car.

"Well, I wouldn't call a broken shoulder *that* okay," Janet said. "I mean, it's better than a brain injury, but heck, she won't be able to ride again for months. The doctor said she'd have to have surgery, then months of therapy. Wonder if she'll be able to go back to classes this semester at all."

I watched the way Danny smoothed Janet's long hank of black hair as they walked, concern palpable on his face.

I tried to brighten for their sake. "Oh, sure she will, hon. After a few weeks, maybe. She's young, and you guys heal fast."

Danny scuffed some small pebbles off the sidewalk and shook his head. "She's right, Jan. Just idiots like me that take a long time to heal."

"That's different," Janet said, punching Danny teasingly on the bicep, reminding him he'd been drug-free for nearly a year, and his "aw, shucks" grin got them hugging by the time they reached the car and climbed in. I was still muttering about how lucky it was Sigourney's injuries weren't any worse.

"Now if only Fitzgibbons is okay," I said, settling in the back seat.

"Mom's a wreck about them both. I don't know why she always blames herself. There's nothing she could have done. I mean, jumping came naturally to that chestnut from the day Dad bought him. His father was a British champion steeplechaser, his mom had great records down in Virginia for all kinds of events. Mom hires the best trainer, pays for an assistant to Mac, and gets a terrific rider." Danny shifted the car and turned into the Avenue, heading for home. "What more could she do?"

"Yeah, Siggy says she's been riding Fitzgibbons long enough so they know each other's every move even before they make it! What could have gone wrong, so miserably wrong?" Janet mused.

I thought about what she said, and wondered if the Women on Fire would be of any help in solving this mystery. Why had the horse suddenly stopped dead in his tracks at the last whatever-it-was called, letting his rider shoot forward over his neck and land on her shoulder fifteen feet away? Then I realized I'd failed to call any of our group, and took out my cell phone. While Danny and Janet drove and discussed the possibilities of why the accident happened, I dialed Lu's number at her restaurant. She'd be busy, making sauces or something, but she'd never forgive me if I didn't call and tell her about the accident.

Lu's husband Tony was on phone duty. "Hey, Dorine, how are ya? Good time at the horse show?"

"Not really, Tony. I need to tell Lu about it. Can she spare a minute?"

Lu took up the receiver in seconds. "Hey, what's wrong? You okay?"

"I'm okay," I said. "It's Ada."

"What!" Lu's gasp exploded over the wires.

I rushed my answer. "Well, no, I mean not really Ada. Not physically. It's just, well Devlin took her home and I don't know how she is at this exact moment but—"

"Dorine, Dorie honey, take it slow and tell me what the hell is wrong. Go ahead, now, I won't interrupt."

I liked that. I hated interruptions, because it was hard enough to hold my track, or was it train, of thoughts, anyhow. I took a breath.

"Okay. Well, Ada's horse was doing great, and everybody was cheering, you know. Theo's daughter was riding him. She looked so tall and fine in the saddle." I heard Lu take in a gulp of breath.

"No... don't say it."

"Yes, the horse just stopped. He wouldn't go any farther and they were at one of those white wooden things in the path where he's supposed to jump, and instead, well, he stopped. And Sigourney didn't. She flew over his head and then over the white thing, too, and Fitzgibbons kind-of fell to the ground." I couldn't believe I had to brush away tears just from telling the story.

This time Lu's voice was deep, heavy as the heaviest suitcase. "How's Theo's daughter? And the horse?"

"That's the good part, Theo's daughter. We just left the hospital. I'm with Danny and his girlfriend, and I was with Theo and Wilson when the doctor came in. He said Sigourney's head is okay, except for a concussive thing, but nothing real bad so far. Though she hit her shoulder hard when she landed and broke it. She'll need an operation." Lu mumbled something but Dorie couldn't tell what. Maybe a prayer.

"When it first happened, Fitzgibbons got up, too, and walked back to the stable okay. But there was something about blood. He was bleeding and coughing, and that English girl who helps the trainer said it was nothing new, so that's why she hadn't told them. But the trainer wasn't too happy about it, and Ada was furious."

"How's Ada doing?" I could hear voices in the background, people hurrying Lu like they needed her.

"We're headed there now to help calm her down. She'll be so glad about Sigourney not having a worse head injury. We're almost there, Lu. But I wanted to call you. And Meg and Hannah, too."

This time I could hear the prayer Lu said aloud. "Holy Mary, mother of God... Dorie, thank you, sweetheart. Be strong. She needs you. Tell her I'll call after dinner service. I'm down three people, one up front and two in back, so it's crazy here. Later." She hung up and I thought to myself I still didn't understand all the new words Lucia was using now that her restaurant had opened and she was so busy with it. I missed Lu, and would have loved to leave all this running back and forth and calling people up to her. She was so much better at it.

Trying to be a good mama to everyone like Lu was, I next tried Meg, but there was no answer. I left a message for Meg to call me back. Being retired, she and her husband often went off on little trips and forgot to mention it to any of us. Meg claimed it was only Women on Fire who had gotten her and Arthur up off the couch long enough to enjoy their retirement. One week they even drove all the way to Maine to study seashells at some conference. And another time Arthur entered his Africans in a show in New York state somewhere. The violets, I mean.

I was happy for Meg, and thought seashells and violets at least were better than dead bodies, which Meg had been studying for years as assistant dead body examiner of the state, I couldn't remember the exact title.

Just before we turned down Ada's road, I dialed Hannah, hating to bother her, because I knew Hannah and her boyfriend, the sexy detective, were on a date. Hannah answered so quickly I didn't have time to wonder if they were having a good time.

"Wow, you must have had your phone in your hand," I said.

"I did. I was trying to decide whether to call you or Ada. Not sure if you were together or what."

"No, Ada went home with..." I hesitated as a smile played across my lips. "...your dad. I'm with Janet and Danny. Hannah, something bad has happened."

"Yes," Hannah said. "I know about the accident with the horse, and I spoke to Theo just now at the hospital. But Dorie, something else has happened. Bernie got the call during dessert and we hurried right over."

I frowned. "What do you mean Bernie was called? Was it a crime for Fitzgibbons to fall and throw his rider? Or what? Why did they call police? What's happening?" I could tell Danny and Janet in the front seat had heard me as they suddenly grew quiet, and Janet half turned toward me as if to say "What?"

Hannah's voice was choppy, like the connection was bad, or maybe she was talking to someone in the background. "Hannah?" I yelled. Danny had just pulled up in Ada's driveway and turned the motor off. And suddenly Hannah's voice came through loud and clear.

"It's not about the accident. Listen, Dor. I'm heading over there to tell Ada, but if you have to tell her, do it nice and easy like. She's had enough to deal with today. Make her take a Valium or something first."

"What is it, Hannah? Is it Fitzgibbons, is he worse? Tell me," I asked, but I didn't want to hear, really. I wanted to block it out, to pretend I was dreaming and would wake up in a minute. "Hannah?"

"No, no, Fitzgibbons's okay. The doctor trailered him out right after we got here. It's Mac, Ada's trainer. They found him in Fitzgibbons's stall. I should say the veterinarian found him when he brought some equipment in for testing the horse."

"What do you mean 'found him'? Geeze, Hannah, not—"

"Yes, that. He was... hanging by some ropes rigged up in the beams. It could be suicide, but the way it looks, Bernie thinks maybe not..." Her voice drifted off.

I hadn't been a full-fledged member of Women on Fire for almost two full years without learning a thing or two. I choked back the words muffled in my throat. "You mean..."

"Yeah. He's dead. And he might have had help getting that way," Hannah said. "Tell Ada, Bernie's on it, the Crime Scene Unit's on the way, and we'll get back to her as soon as we can."

I shook my head by way of a goodbye and felt myself turning a very hot shade of pink. No, not this, not again.

Not murder.

Three

Ada

I slipped out of the skirt of my lightweight houndstooth suit, and pulled the cerise knit shell over my head, not caring for once if I totally destroyed my usually impeccable hairdo. Recalling those strong male fingers rifling my hair not minutes ago gave me a tiny thrill I worked hard at putting out of my mind. And why the dickens had I worn a skirt that could fly up to my waist when I fell down, so inappropriate at a horse event? Was it just because I would be with Devlin, with a man for a change?

What had I been thinking?

Oh, Ada, I said to myself as I glanced at the mirror. You think you're so strong, so, so authoritative. But you weaken like underdone gelatin when a man's involved. I shuddered when I saw before me a woman getting closer to Medicare every day, with skin slightly sagging despite twice-weekly gym stints and once-weekly facials, and occasional more drastic treatments, and pocked with tiny liver spots and under-the-skin hemorrhages not even laser treatments could erase.

A woman who'd known a lot of life, and had a wonderful circle of friends, and yes, who'd had plenty of bad luck, but a woman on her own. Independence used to seem like a goal, an achievement. Now I had to admit it: I was, bottom line, a lonely woman.

I slipped off my earrings and ran my fingers across my lips. Until very recently I was also a woman who hadn't been kissed or held by a man for two whole years, and not for many times in the six years of a rocky marriage before that. Would Devlin have been horrified at this sight of me in bra and panties? Would he have turned away and made excuses?

Somewhere deep inside I felt he wouldn't. After all, he was more than ten years older than me, and his chin drooped, too, and sagging little patches above his eyes obscured part of his irises, too. His face was weathered more than a seventy-year-old's should be, what with the work he did, photographing the great outdoors all over the world.

And anyhow, should I care what Devlin Doyle thought? What made him so great?

I growled at my image. Then laughed. Devlin *was* one heck of a man, that's why. His arms around me had felt strong and reassuring. His eyes were deep with compassion and his muscles were hard, and probably still quite capable in other more private body areas. I braced my hands on the dresser and moaned.

Then why-oh-why had I sent him away? Cut off any further comforting, cuddling or whatever else he had in mind? When we'd entered the house, the first thing I did was step out of my Manolo boots and sink onto the sofa, wondering what to do with the swirling feelings left over from our tender kiss in the car. Devlin immediately had gone down on a knee and massaged my stocking feet until the thrills I felt threatened to give me amnesia—to forget the horror at the track, forget about Sigourney and Fitzgibbons and that snippy young girl trainer.

When I stopped him with a request for a beverage, he went dutifully to the bar and made me a drink and we'd sat side-by-side sipping Long Island tea.

I'd made an effort to focus on him, on lovely Devlin. After all, hadn't I fantasized a moment like this a hundred times? But the scene at the Polo Grounds kept rumbling through my brain, the pounding of hooves, Fitzgibbons coming up short, his rider hurtling through the air, then the big animal folding up his legs and collapsing on the ground. Then later the ambulance, Theo's pale face and clasped hands as she stood over her wounded daughter, and the blood on my horse, his slump, and weakened nicker.

I'd put my restless legs out before me, making to rise, and Devlin Doyle had gently pulled me back, drawn my legs up on the couch so I had to turn and face him.

"Try to relax a bit, Ada," he said. "You've been through a tremendous trauma. Now we've got the doctors and their helpers doing everything they can, and you need to try and let it go."

"I prayed to be able to do that, would you believe it?" I'd laughed, more of a snort that put me in mind of my horse again. "Letting go isn't in my lexicon, Devlin. Dorie's a dear, but I don't know if she'll get everything straight. I need to call the hospital, see how poor Sigourney is doing, and call my friends. Hannah, on the other hand, could surely think of something we should be doing right now and aren't. Meg's a doctor, she should be there, too, helping Theo get through—"

I had tried to swing myself forward but Devlin ever-so-gently eased me back. Two hands cupping my face, he got me to place my back against on the couch pillows, the same pillows, I remembered bitterly, the gunman had shot when he'd held me and my friends hostage not so long ago. This time Devlin leaned forward so he was looking into my eyes, smiling gently.

I did so admire the man's strong but soothing way. That was putting it mildly. My insides thundered, that's the truth.

I studied his laugh lines and approved, brushed a lock of silver hair from his forehead and saw such deep concern—or could it even be caring?—in his narrow green eyes I'd had to catch at a breath not to moan aloud.

"But I need to—I need..." I tried hard to say what pressures were on me, always on me to do the right thing, to put others first, to manage and organize and arrange. He wouldn't let me finish.

Instead he asked if he could kiss me again. "I don't want to seem bold, but you are so dear. I've thought so long about what this would be like..."

I remember staring. "You, you have?"

He nodded. "Ever since we danced together at the old age home party months ago. You sparkle, Ada, you're a gem, but a warm one. So warm, so perfect and petite..."

I gulped. Devlin had been wanting me, too? I closed my eyes in astonishment and I suppose he took it as a signal to bring his mouth to mine. This time I let myself sink into his kiss, and it was warm, and moist, going in the direction most such kisses go. I forgot to inhale and he sensed it, but the minute he drew back I surprised us both by pushing toward him again and naturally our arms and hands followed our feelings and I shivered to feel the utter strength across his back, then his fingers in my hair, tracing the curves of my ears, finally sliding down my arms and up under my silky knit shell. The one I'd bought to go with the black and white houndstooth suit which, except for the skirt, was so perfect for the horse show as it was a fall suit but light...

The horse show. The horse. The girl.

I yelped. "No, oh, dear Devlin, no." I straightened my clothing, then pulled myself up off the couch.

"I can't. It's way too selfish of me, Devlin. I don't even know if Sigourney's paralyzed from her fall off my horse. I don't even know if Fitzgibbons is deathly ill himself. I can't, Devlin, I'm so sorry. I have calls to make, research to do..."

Devlin stared at me, blank-eyed. "Research?"

"You know, about the bleeding Terry says has been going on."

"But the veterinarian is checking." He reached out a hand toward me.

I tried to shake off the molten feelings still tumbling inside me from Devlin's touch, and, even more, my response. I turned away and walked toward the parrot cage, lifting its cover so the bird would stop his incessant mumbling.

"You don't think I'm going to trust one ordinary equine vet with this, do you? I have to consult the experts, get busy on it right away. Be an advocate for the poor animal."

Devlin rose and took me by my arms. He nodded, looking glum, hurt maybe, but as my eyes pleaded with him to understand, and Ramon cut the tension by squawking, "Hello, goodbye," he eventually smiled that wonderful crinkly-eyed smile of his. "I just wanted you to relax, forget it for a few minutes. Feel how much I care... But you're right, Ada, the timing is bad. I'm the selfish one. I took advantage. I shouldn't have pushed. I mean, we hardly know each other. Right? I shouldn't have. I'm sorry."

Ramon ducked his head beneath a wing, a familiar gesture whenever he heard the word "sorry." I laughed a little, and so did Devlin. Before I could argue with him and end up sounding desperate, I looped my arm through his, turned and walked him to the front door.

"Research, huh?" he said with a grin still on his face.

I said, with a forced air of nonchalance, "Hannah showed me, you know, how to Google things on the computer, follow links and all. She's so good at it." I tried not to let out another little laugh imagining Devlin's daughter as my girlfriend. The irony of it.

Devlin cleared his throat. "But will you rest, then? After you do your research?"

"I promise," I said, staring at my stockinged feet on the marble floor. "I'll see you later. I'll call. You've been so—kind." He'd left then, and finally the parrot began to chide me as I slunk out of my jacket and took a step onto the thick Aubusson carpets. Alone again.

"See ya later," the parrot squawked.

"I hope so," I whispered as I went up the stairs to change.

Now, slipping on knit slacks and a warmer jersey top and soft tennis shoes, I worried I'd been a fool to let Devlin Doyle go. Back in my twenties and even a few times in my forties, I'd have fallen into such a man's arms with abandon when an occasion presented itself. My dear first husband always said I was a bit over the edge on sexual appetite, and I'd reveled in that, when I had willing partners. Not that any of my woman friends would have guessed it.

After all, back then I was young, I felt sexy, and brought up as a rich girl by a doting father, I got used to having anything I wanted when I wanted it.

With a tiny frisson of embarrassment, I thought of a certain stable boy I'd caroused with when I was in college, and later, that very sensual friend of my father, an older man, who'd seduced me, or I him, and, well...

My reminiscences dried up when I recalled what Devlin had said: "We hardly know each other," he'd said. And left without an argument. That in itself was hard to swallow, that he hadn't made more of an effort, so when I heard a car pull up at the door, I took a deep breath and ran down to the foyer. Maybe he'd rethought it; maybe he wanted more of me now. Wouldn't take no—

I pulled up short as the door swung open.

My stepson Danny had used his key, and held the door open for Dorie, then Janet. He followed them in, head down, feet dragging.

Dorie took hold of my hand without looking me in the eye and asked me to come sit at the dining room table.

I took a step forward, and felt the energy inside me fizz away like stale champagne. I gulped hard. Something must be wrong, really wrong to make them look so straight ahead, avoiding my eyes. Even little Janet, who tried hard to be cheerful around me, so kind and sweet, yearning to earn my favor.

I touched Janet's arm lightly. "Dear, there's iced tea in the refrigerator. Get some glasses. You three look parched."

Janet nodded and went, clinking glasses together softly in the other room as we took our seats.

I folded my hands in front of me. Stay strong, I told myself. Keep the others strong. You can do it.

"So—it's bad news about Sigourney?" I eyed Dorie but got a confused head-tossed look from my artist friend. It reminded me of Fitzgibbons when he wasn't in the mood to be let out, or bothered at all. Before, that is, I gave him a treat. "My God, is she..."

Danny jumped in. "No, Mom, not all bad. Siggy, Sigourney's doing okay. She waved to us from the exam room, though we couldn't talk to her just yet. But the doctor doesn't think there's a severe brain injury, just a, well, a shoulder injury."

"Spell it out, dear," I said.

"Broken, at the top of the humerus," Janet offered as she rejoined us. She'd taken courses in anatomy; so she could well explain the break and how they'd be operating to repair it in a day or two, removing some bone fragments. Followed by lots of therapy.

Dorie drank some of her iced tea, then nodded, a little more enthusiastic. "Theo's relieved. I mean, you can deal with a bone injury. Wilson was there, her father, and he said it will take a lot of work on her part. Theo thinks her stepdaughter ought to be able to ride again at some point."

"If she wants to," Danny added.

I exhaled with a prayer of thanks speeding across my mind. Other thoughts came unstuck like cars in gridlock suddenly coming apart when a traffic light changes. Why on earth was Dorie so fluttery? And Danny so crestfallen?

If not Sigourney, then the horse. My Fitzgibbons.

Danny seemed to read my mind. "Fitzgibbons's good, too, Mom. I called. Doc Ingmanson's got him on the way up to UMass for x-rays. They're opening up special for him, even though it's Sunday. Then after the tests, Doc will take him to his animal hospital."

Dorie jumped in to join the wave of optimism before the clearly waiting ax must surely fall. "Yeah, Hannah says they had him on a cross or something—"

"Cross-tied, she means," Dan said. "Like before, only

in the truck, so's they could keep him stable and move him around better."

"He's not bleeding anymore," Janet added, then stared into her tea. Dorie nodded.

I tapped the table with my iced tea spoon.

"Okay, sounds good, so why are you three looking so glum?" Something suddenly occurred to me and I nearly jumped out of my seat. "Wait. What do you mean Hannah said? Why is Hannah involved? Why is she at the barn? My God, people, tell me!"

The guilty parties exchanged worried glances. Danny drew his glass to his lips and shifted his eyes to Dorie. Janet clamped her lips shut and stared at her hands.

"Dorine. Talk!" My heart raced, I could taste the metal of fear along with my tea.

Dorie tugged at the errant strands of platinum hair that always fell across the side of her face. "Oh, Ada. This part's not good. It's Mac. Your trainer." Her last word was inaudible. She shrugged and tears burst from her eyes.

I shuddered. What was wrong with her? Couldn't this darn woman keep herself together? Ever?

"What? What did Mac say? What did he do? Dorie?" I tried to take a deep breath but my diaphragm felt locked, too tight to budge. "Something's happened to Mac?" The silence in the room wrapped its cold digits around my throat.

"They found him later, when Doc got back with his equipment. And Mac was, was..." Dorie covered her mouth with her hand and again mumbled something inaudible. Danny coughed. My eyes darted from one to the other, my heart raced. Finally it was Janet who reached out and placed a hand over mine on the mahogany table.

"He's dead, Ada. In Fitzgibbons's stall. They found him..." She gestured upward at the brilliant Williamsburg chandelier. "I'm so sorry..."

"H-hung? Omigod, he hanged himself?" I know for once my voice was a feeble whimper. I couldn't stop shaking my head. "No, no, it's a mistake. No." Danny got up and stood behind me, pressing his cheek to mine. Dorie pulled out a tissue and passed it across the table. Something turned inside me and suddenly I crumpled the tissue in my fist.

"The bastard!" I said. "He must have had something to do with Fitzgibbons's accident. Knew he'd done wrong, and would be found out." I pounded the table with my fists, only vaguely aware of Danny slipping away toward the front door.

"The weasel," I said, my voice now rising to a shout. "To kill himself to avoid the recriminations for not properly training my Fitzgibbons." As soon as I said it, I knew it was wrong, I knew no matter what Mac had done it shouldn't have cost him his life. Mac loved Fitzgibbons, too.

There was the sound of a door opening and closing, and, then, footsteps. I bowed my head and my body shook with unshed tears. "Suicide, how awful."

Hannah's voice came through to me like hail stinging a metal roof: "Awful, yes," she said, coming closer and grasping my hand. "Ada, I'm so sorry. But it might be worse."

My voice came out like a tolling bell, low, and final. "Murder."

Hannah nodded, and let Danny provide the hug.

Four

Hannah

While I pulled up a chair and Janet poured me a glass of tea, everyone was all questions. Everyone but Ada, who just stared, as if frozen.

I held up the glass of amber liquid and peered through it. "Nothing a little gin couldn't fix."

Ada snapped to and tried to release a ragged chuckle. "That's what Devlin said..." She stopped short, then recovered. "I'm sorry. How can I even think of such a thing? My nerves are frayed... Tell us, Hannah. Who found him? And what on earth do you mean about murder?"

I patted her arm and briefly closed my eyes trying to mentally reassemble the gruesome details of the violent death. "Doc Ingmanson found him, cut him down, said his body... he was still warm. He tried to revive him, did CPR until the ambulance came."

"Why do they think it could be murder?" Dorie asked

softly, her eyes pleading for something, anything other than murder. I understood Dorie's sweet, innocent soul never did enjoy solving these homicides that had strewn themselves across our path. We Women on Fire had turned out to have a real knack for helping to solve some big cases when we put all our talents together, but Dorie was the one most reluctant to get involved in the first place. Always ready to believe the best in people, not the worst. Or maybe because in the past she came so close to being violently mishandled by her ex-husband.

I set down my glass and tucked my hair behind my ears. "So far it's just a guess. Bernie spotted a lump on Mac's head, a blow that may have knocked him out, or even killed him. The way he was... arranged... signified that someone did that, then hoisted him up with some old ropes that had been lying in the tack room. There was a ladder fallen to the side, perhaps also arranged just so. Too perfect, Bernie said. The girl, what's her name?"

"Terry?" Danny asked.

"Exactly. Terry had left with the laundry, then came back to find Doc Ingmanson trying to cut Mac down. She assisted as she could, then called the police while he tried giving CPR. After a bit I guess the vet realized it was hopeless. By then there were other riders and horses all over the place, and Bernie got Terry to send them out while they waited for the forensics people."

"That smirking, nasty girl. She ignored Fitzgibbons's possible chronic problems until they nearly killed him," Ada snapped. "How do we know she was in the mud room doing the towels? Could it have been Terry?"

There was a low hum of negatives around the room. "If they do ascertain it was not suicide, I'm sure the police will consider it, but she's such a wisp of a thing. Could she have lifted Mac's body up like that?" I took a slug of my tea, trying not to tremble at the possibility.

Dorie said, "No way," clearly still wishing someone's evil actions had not killed yet another person we had all known and cared about. I frowned into my beverage, then took a big swallow and shrugged my shoulders.

Ada sighed. "Then who? Who would have wanted Mac dead? I just can't believe it's happening again. A murder, and so close to home."

Danny passed his stepmother a stack of paper napkins Janet had brought to the table and she sniffed into them while we all studied our hands or our drinks.

"There wasn't anyone else around until the event ended, right?" Dan said at last. "They were keeping people away after the accident. You know, the rubber-neckers."

My eyes got wide. "Who's 'they'?"

Danny shrugged. "I dunno. There was some guy we passed on our way out, remember?"

Janet joined in. "Yeah, shouting at people to get back from the barn."

"Don't know his name," Dan said, "but he looked vaguely familiar. Even yelled at Charity Finch who took the blue today. She and her dad were leading Vixen into the barn after her cool down and he yelled for them to take the horse to the paddock for now."

"I remember the guy you mean," Dorie said. "The one who sort of took charge. All dressed like a cowboy."

"Dark denim everything," Janet added. "Shiny new tooled paddock boots."

"Do you think he works there?" I asked.

"I suppose that's what we all thought," Ada said. "Though I don't remember seeing him before. But then, I wasn't there every day. I didn't see Josie Hand, the barn manager at all. I suppose she was up in the judges' booth."

"That Mr. Finch had a few words with the cowboy guy and kept on going right into the barn until the guy barred his path. I saw the girl, Charity, you say? Leading her horse. She had tears in her eyes and looked real upset." Janet offered refills on the tea and Ada gave her a smile and a nod.

"She and Siggy been riding together all their lives," Danny said. "No wonder she was upset."

"Come to think of it, Gus Finch always seemed a little jealous to me," Ada muttered into her tissues. "Everybody knew Sigourney Rutledge was a better rider than his daughter."

Janet swallowed a gulp of her beverage and spoke up. "I doubt Charity ever expected to win today. She was in awe of Sigourney. Me, too. I've seen walls full of trophies at her house."

"Finch was always asking about Fitzgibbons, where I'd got him, what his genealogy was and so on. Very intense. And very curious." Ada dabbed her forehead with the wad of napkins. "I wish Doc would call and let me know what he's discovered about my horse's prognosis. I can't stand the waiting. Or these awful heat waves I thought I was done with." Ada smoothed out the paper napkins before her, then used them as a fan beneath her chin. "Oh, poor Mac. I can't bear this."

I drained my glass and rose. "I'm going to pass all this information on to Bernie, folks. He'll appreciate it, I know. Even though he hates having us get involved in his murder cases. And look, Ada, Doc said to tell you they've left for UMass to go through some tests and things. He's going to spend the night up there with Fitzgibbons. Might have information for you in the morning, but nothing tonight. You ought to get some rest."

Ada nodded. "Do you have a way to get home?"

I shook my head and looked toward Dan. "Could you?"

Danny grinned and jumped up. "Sure, Aunt Hannah. I was going to take Aunt Dorie home, too. Janet, want to come?"

The gentle Inuit girl put him off with a gesture that said no. "I'll help your mom get cleaned up here and see she gets to bed. You look exhausted, Mrs. J."

I thought how lucky my friend was to have her son home and with a very sweet girlfriend, too.

Not to mention a new beau—my own father.

Ada pushed herself up from the table with difficulty and stood wavering through our goodnight hugs. "You're all too thoughtful. Thanks, dears. Dan, be sure and take Sancho out before you go to bed. Poor pup hasn't had a bit of attention today."

Dan said he would.

"We'll see you tomorrow, Ada. Keep in touch," I said. Dorie echoed me. From over our shoulders we watched Janet follow our friend up the stairs.

When Danny led us out to his car, he was smiling. "Janet treats my mom better 'n' me. And Mom really likes her. Loves her, I guess."

Dorie squealed with delight. "That's one good thing about today, how nice Janet treats your mom. And it's about time Ada has you two around to help her and keep her company. She does so much for everyone."

Danny nodded, grinning silently as he turned the wheel and slowed down in Dorie's neighborhood.

Dorie leaned forward and messed Danny's short hair. "Keep it up, Dan. She's so happy to have you back and staying with her. Especially now, with all this terrible mess happening."

After we dropped off Dorie, I questioned Danny further. "You think anybody at the stables has an issue with your mother, Dan? Wants to get even with her over something?"

Danny shook his head. Even with darkness falling, I noticed how much more manly his profile was becoming—a little like his uncle's, but I hoped the resemblance ended there. Judd Javitt was not my favorite person.

"I honestly don't know, Aunt Han. I know she can be pretty firm about wanting things her way. But I've never heard her say she had trouble with anyone there. Fitzgibbons's brought her nothing but happiness. I just hate seeing her get tangled up in this horror. She's had a tough couple of years, mostly with me."

Danny had been in and out of several rehab programs but I thought he seemed to be doing so much better, especially with his girlfriend Janet coming back with him from Alaska. She was surely a stabilizing influence.

"I worry about Ada, too, but she's not alone in this, Dan. She has you and Janet and us, her women friends. And apparently my father, now."

"Yeah, Mr. Doyle was great with her today. I think I might have hurt his feelings a little, 'cause I kept stepping in and trying to take charge of Mom. You should have seen her when Siggy went flying over the gate and the horse just crumpled. She passed right out."

I shivered, longing to light up a cigarette but figuring I'd wait until I was out of the car—no point being a bad influence on a kid who's struggled as much as he had with addictions.

Danny down-shifted and turned his neat Subaru toward my apartment in the new development center in town. "I was whacked out thinking *Mom* had got hurt."

His voice trembled.

"Danny, I'm sure my dad is okay with you wanting to console your mom. It's natural." With a sinking in the pit of my stomach, I had a brief memory flash of Devlin trying to protect me, when my husband and brother had died in the same plane crash thirty years ago. He was a gentle giant to me then. I shook my head to bring me back to the moment.

"But how about you, Dan? You seem pretty rattled by the accident."

"Well, sure. Siggy's our friend. And Fitzgibbons's been a real pal for Mom. And now she's worried about what happened to Mac. I just hope she can chill. Not get all, y'know, depressed again."

Now it was my turn to nod. "Yes, and start popping those pills of hers like around the time your dad died and you—" I stopped short, as Danny let loose a low growl in his throat.

Darkness was heavy on us now, and streetlights and headlights had gone on, as Danny swung into the Avenue where my condo was.

I drew a deep breath. "Sorry for bringing that up, but I guess the big question is, does she have anything to worry about with you? Are you going to be okay?"

Danny's chuckle was quiet but hard-edged. "If you're asking will I go off the deep end again, naw. I can handle stuff a lot better. Janet and the others up there in Alaska, I learned a lot from them. I'm better, Aunt Hannah. Maybe never cured, but a lot better. I still go to Narc-A-Non." He pulled into a parking place a few down from my door and flicked the key off.

"Funny, Jan and I were going to tell Mom we're thinking of getting our own place, a little flat over in Oakwood, y'know? My friend at school has his third floor empty and will rent it to us cheap. We shouldn't be a drag on Mom in her, well, her later years. But now, cripes, it's probably not a good time to leave her."

"I think that's true. Janet's a big support for Ada. You, too. And she could use that right now."

"Well, there's not much we can do being in school all day and both of us with part-time jobs. But at least we're there at night."

I laughed as I opened the door and swung my legs out. "Don't let daytimes bug you, Dan. Your mother has her Women on Fire friends to keep her busy. And if I know her, in another day or two she'll be hauling our asses around town, or who knows where, to solve this damn crime."

Danny chuckled but put up a hand. "I don't want her to be in any danger. I know you guys have taken some pretty wild chances..."

"Never mind. Hey, she's the one who gets us into trouble." Danny laughed. I told him thanks for the lift, and to call me if he thought of anything else Bernie should be looking at.

As Danny pulled away, I realized it must be odd for him to be considered someone who could help the police, when only a few years ago he was avoiding them at any cost.

I bounced up the stairs in a hurry to catch my dad before he settled in for the night. I'd love to hear about the events at the Polo Grounds from his experienced and more objective view. But he was in his room, with only a dim light still on, clearly seeking privacy, when I got in. So I placed a call to Bernie whose machine was on, then checked my messages and got Meg's.

"I can't believe what happened at the Polo Grounds, Hannah. Theo's poor daughter injured, and that lovely horse being looked at for possible internal injuries. Call me first thing in the morning and we'll get together to do our visits to our friends. Something sounds fishy about the whole thing to me."

Obviously Meg didn't know yet just how fishy. She didn't know the Women on Fire had possibly another homicide staring us in the face, no matter what Bernie's bosses determined. I had investigated crimes—and suicides—for *The Courant* for years on their crime beat. Instinct, call it intuition, had always been a pretty reliable guide for me. And I had to concur with my sweetheart: there was no way the death of Ada's horse trainer was a suicide.

Oh, yeah, we'd be meeting tomorrow all right. And probably every day after that for a while. I showered to rid myself of the stink of manure and worse from those hours spent in the stable, then went to bed trying to chase away images of poor Mac McClellan, his life cut short by a noose of rope around his neck.

Or by something earlier and even more sinister.

Five

Meg

I met Hannah for bagels and coffee hoping to get a more detailed rundown on the Polo Grounds accident. First thing she did was spring on me the fact of Mac McClellan's death.

"Looked like a simple suicide at first glance," Hannah said, spreading her cream cheese thickly on the poppy seed bagel.

I smiled inwardly, recalling Hannah's former passion for "everything" bagels, you know, onion, seeds, garlic, the whole nine yards. But a woman in love would be willing to forego the garlic and onion, I thought, and only a slender woman currently indulging herself in the sensuality department would spread the cream cheese on like it was going to be rationed tomorrow. Good for her.

Not fitting into either category, I spread my own cream cheese thinly, and, with a sigh of appreciation, bit into the fragrant, savory half that reeked of garlic, onion and all the other tantalizing flavors they fit on the four-inch toasted round. Although I was a woman in love, it was love with a sixteen-year history, not to mention a dangerous cholesterol level, to boot.

"There's a but there somewhere," I said.

Hannah nodded as she sipped her black coffee. "Bernie's idea. Why'd he want to hang himself so high up, on some of the highest beams, he wondered. And why in such a public place? People around there said Mac kept to himself, very focused on his work. Doing anything dramatic or unusual was way out of line for him. Especially dying. The girl who worked with him even said so. Terry her name is. Totally shattered by it all. I guess Mac got her the job here. He'd known her family over in England and has been pretty nice to her. No wonder the kid is wiped out."

"Any possible reason *she'd* want him dead?" I asked, working the sheen of cheese onto my second pungent circle of breakfast bread.

Hannah said no, not that she knew of. She'd checked with the other Women on Fire and passed a bunch of possible suspects' names over to Bernie early this morning and he thought it looked promising. She asked why I was so interested. "You thinking we ought to pool our brainpower and get in on this one, too?"

I shook my head, but Hannah laughed. "I hear you. You're slitting your Slavic eyes at me and tilting your head while you chew. I suppose that means we've done pretty well in the past, especially you with your pathological talents, and this, well, this hits pretty close to home. Though Bernie will have a fit, since it's his case."

I swallowed and drank some coffee. "Imagine, another of Ada's people, the third in a row, you could say, and the poor woman's probably teetering on the brink of deep depression," was all I could answer.

Hannah finished off her bagel and slugged the last of her coffee. "Did I tell you my father is trying the personal approach to forestall that very event?"

I almost choked on the last crumbs of bagel. "What? They're seeing each other? Like romantically? Wow! I knew Ada had the hots for him, and I remember they flirted at the nursing home dance fiasco last year but your dad seems like such a self-satisfied, no-nonsense kind of guy. I can't picture him getting involved with someone as Sarah-Bernhardtish and bossy as our beloved Ada"

Hannah's laugh was tinged with something I couldn't name. Melancholy? Pretend nonchalance?

I remembered Dorie saying Hannah looked like a young girl when she tucked her hair behind her ears, as she did now under my stare. Especially true when she blushed, as she did now, too.

"Oh no, Daddy's not so self-satisfied he doesn't still take notice of an attractive woman in the right age bracket. And he's been known to generate *some* nonsense over the years. Let's see, there was a Ghanian woman who led a poverty campaign in the eighties, and a triple divorcee in Oregon who tried to get him to move in on her marijuana farm about five years ago."

It was my turn to grin. "But, Hannah, it's wonderful. Do you have a problem with it? Because I think whenever two people can console or interest or enliven one another, in *that* way, whatever their ages, it's a good thing. Don't you think?"

"Jury's still out," Hannah said. "Ada's been my very good friend for eight or nine years, and I'm not ready to classify her as something different just yet."

"You mean, like step-mom?"

Hannah pfished at me and hooted. "Oh, quiet. Go scoot along and do your business, Meggie. I'd love to hang out with you but I'm needed at the Mary-Martha Center this morning, and I'm already late for a meeting."

"So good of you to help Theo counsel those children, Han."

She uh-huhed and stood to gather her purse and I said it again. "But you are, and it's a task not everyone can do." She waved and kept moving. I tried to grab her jacket tail as she slid out from behind the table and stepped away, but then gave up, laughing to myself as I watched her go. Ada and Devlin Doyle. What an interesting match-up. Maybe it would help Ada get through yet another disaster. Or maybe it would be a disaster itself.

I wiped my fingers on the paper napkin and crumpled it up alongside Hannah's. I'd better go spend a few minutes with Ada and try very hard not to mention the budding romance. Ada liked her secrets kept, and this was no time to taunt her.

~ * ~

Finding Ada relatively in control and busy communicating about the accident by phone and by e-mail to various veterinarians and other experts, I chatted with her only briefly, then drove to St. Peter's Hospital. I figured I'd spend my morning hanging out with Theo during her daughter's surgery.

She seemed to feel comforted by my background as a physician, even if what I mostly had done for a career was to work with dead people as a pathologist for the state. I was able to get a few moments on the inside track with the surgeon just before he went up to the operating theater, and then I was able to explain to Theo and her husband in everyday language, and drawing diagrams on the backs of envelopes, exactly what they faced with the girl's injuries.

"Treatable, fixable, and in a young woman like your daughter, there shouldn't be any complications. She'll probably sail through."

Wilson Rutledge grumped through a haze of moisture in his eyes. "My daughter's never even been in an emergency room. Though she's ridden since she was seven years old!" He shook his head and angled his face away from Theo and me, no doubt embarrassed over his emotion.

Theo reached out for his arm and squeezed it. "You've taken wonderful care of her and Shannon, Wilson. Just amazing."

"But accidents do happen," I said, hardly realizing what I was saying. Suddenly I fell into a chair behind me in the waiting room. With a hand over my face I tried unsuccessfully to avoid the flash of twisted metal and screeching sirens in a corner of my own mind. And the heat wave that followed it today.

An accident that haunted my own nightmares.

"Why, though?" the distraught father snapped, ignoring the emotion on my face. "Why'd this happen? She was used to this horse, has ridden him for two years. He was used to her. I swear the reason she left Skidmore was to be closer to home so she could continue to train and compete with Fitzgibbons. I didn't object then, especially since she transferred to U of H. and she's been doing well in her studies. But I have to tell you that now I'm going to lay down the law. Have her make other arrangements for next semester. Go back to her school, and quit this dangerous event riding."

Theo tried to hug him to get him to stop, but her new husband was adamant.

"No, Theo. This is just too damn much. She could have been brain-injured, killed, for God's sake. Someone's got to pay for this tragedy..." Wilson stormed away a few feet and noisily blew his nose, and I rose again and put an arm around Theo, who was casting worried looks her husband's way.

"We're all paying, Wilson," I said, my voice suddenly hoarse and tired.

Theo took a deep breath. "And we'll do so cheerfully, if we possibly can. Sigourney will go through her surgery and her rehabilitation with our encouragement and plenty of positive thoughts. I know she wants to ride again. Not that it will be Fitzgibbons. We don't yet know enough about his condition..."

Wilson coughed and turned back to us, his face red, his jaw chomping on words he was trying to control. "I don't give a damn about the horse."

"And the trainer?" I asked. "He's dead." I bit my lip. I'd only met Wilson once before, and I was surprised and a little shocked to find him so overwrought over his daughter, and so bitter. But then, I'd never known quite what it was like to have a child, especially one in jeopardy. To me it seemed logical Sigourney would want to take up riding again. Maybe it was a parent's job to limit the dangers a child passed through. Hadn't my own father...

I let the thought drift away.

Wilson caught my eye and ducked his head down. "I know. I know. It's just... it's awful to consider it might have been Sigourney whose funeral..."

Theo ran to him and shushed him, placing her fingers across his mouth, and he reached for her, his face twisted in anguish. They hugged tight, and I slipped away to the far corner of the waiting room. I'd best be quiet until Siggy was back from the surgery. Then I could help translate the results and prognosis if I could, and head out for my main assignment of the day: a trip to the Medical Examiner's office, where I'd bribe one of my old friends into letting me see the deceased Mr. McClellan, one guy who wouldn't be giving me any lip today.

If there was a crime involved in this tragic bloodbath, studying it should start there, with Mac, where it had begun and ended. If it truly were a suicide, there were questions about Mac to be answered. And if it weren't a suicide, well, the questions mounted.

Maybe at some point I'd even have a chance to talk with the vet about Ada's horse.

Ada was counting on me, and so, obviously, were lots of other people.

Which was why, when I later found the front office empty at the state facility, after my cheery chat with the security guard at the front door, I dared to take a few quiet steps down the hall toward the door marked, "No Admittance: Morgue." My footsteps resounded far more loudly than I'd expected, and I regretted not wearing my new soft-soled Mary Janes or my favorite Reeboks.

At the door, I stood trying to breathe normally, afraid of hyperventilating. I let my fingers trace the black lettering on the translucent glass top half of the door and gradually let them slide toward the knob. How many times had I been in and out of that room with full authority—hundreds? More?

And never shirking the work load, staying late when needed, coming in early or even in the middle of the night if necessary. My breath blew out in a jagged huff. I forced myself to stay very still, the way, I mused, I had never been when actually employed here. In those days, not too long ago, I was always in a hurry, or the ME was, and I'd followed every order, gone the extra mile, done the dirty cases more times than not, as well as the accident victims, the elderly who'd died away from their homes or hospitals.

A flood of them passed before my eyes as I again fingered the black letters: dead drug dealers, shot through the chest, women raped and beaten to death, children, even. My heart clenched, and I shook my head. Let the past go. An old dictum I'd had of necessity mostly followed.

I needed some details about Mac McClellan, details the police would be hesitant to reveal. Why shouldn't I seek out the privilege of extra information, for all I'd done for the state before they gave me the bum's rush, as Arthur called it, and let me go a few years early to lower their budget? I'd cared, dammit, even if my patients were only dead people, bodies whose spirits had departed. Yes, I cared, and if I could have, I'd have healed people, made them open their eyes and breathe again.

Oh, yes, I would have. Starting with my father in 1989.

Suddenly a hum of voices broke the silence. Voices within the morgue's laboratory, in the inner sanctum of "No Admittance." Hopefully, I prayed, not one of them being the chief.

Quickly, before I lost my nerve, I turned the knob and went into the viewing foyer, so the people in the lab beyond could see me through the glass wall. I mustered a smile, a wave, and gestured for one of them to unlock the door that stood cold to my touch and triple-locked beside me.

~ * ~

An hour-and-a-half later I wobbled away from the facility, passing a receptionist I didn't know in the lobby, and a different security guard out front. I spoke in a high-pitched, almost girlish voice, "Good afternoon. 'Bye now," to each. Made it to my car only scuffing the toes of my dressy black low pumps twice, and got in. There I exhaled, started the engine and backed out of my spot. As I pulled down the quiet road away from the state facility I let out a very un-ladylike whoop.

"I did it, Ada. I got in, and got a look at your old buddy," I cried. "And just in time, as he's being released to the undertaker tonight for tomorrow's service. Why the hell was I scared in the first place?" In the tight jumble of my throat, I knew why: I'd always been the good girl, the follower, the one to go by the book. My fist whacked the wheel of the car as I headed toward I91 and West Parkford.

"But you no-good, brilliant, wonderful Women on Fire have sparked me and lit me up, ladies," I crooned to the imaginary faces around me, Ada, the queen, and Dorie, the flake, and Hannah the whiz kid, Theo the mother superior and Lucia the earth mother. They'd all combined to make me a rule-breaking, terrified and terrifying, pretty smart investigator. The police might not admit it yet, but with the help of my old friend Frankie and his new part-time assistant Jan at the state facility, it was pretty clear the equine trainer Mac McClellan had not committed suicide at all. The ligature markings were wrong. There was a bit of epithelial and dried blood under his fingernails, indicating defensive wounds, And the small knot deep in the thatch of his reddish brown hair had all the right signs for a killing blow to the skull. Mac had been struck and killed before he ever got his neck put in a noose.

Blunt force trauma.

I almost giggled with relief. Then stopped at the exit ramp stop sign and took a deep slug from the water bottle I carried in the car. "Why in Allah's name am I so happy?" I wondered aloud. "Maybe because Ada will feel better that poor Mac hadn't done something to himself because he felt responsible for Fitzgibbons's fall, or guilty of anything." But now it was up to me to find out what blunt force had given Mac the death blow.

In other words, to find the murder weapon. And the one guilty of using it. I swung west instead of east on Route 4 and made my way to the Polo Grounds on a hunch. It was still early, kids weren't out of school for an hour yet, and the place might be fairly deserted. A good time to drive up there and have a look. And I felt so spiked with adrenalin—and maybe also with the three cups of black coffee my friends at the ME's had given me to keep me standing during their show-off of the body on their slab—quite possibly it was a perfect time to sniff out the stables, too.

I felt a tremor of nostalgia as I parked my car under a blazing maple tree and slowly approached the grand red barn at the Polo Grounds. In my home country of Bosnia, most farm families had a barn sheltered by a tree. Ours had been a gnarly old apple over a faded brown barn that once housed a few heads of livestock, chickens and ducks for eggs, a pig at times. Before the heaviest bombing, Grandpa had had a mule, a flock of feathered creatures, a brown and white goat. I remembered it all clearly.

Now I found myself literally sniffing out the animal and hay scents, and smiling even at the whiff of animal waste, as well as the heavy mix of dust and leather as I passed the turn-out ring and walked up the ramp. Most of the horses had been put out to grass on this beautiful October day, but there were some still in their stalls on either side of the practice ring, and as I passed them, many nickered softly, or shuffled their feet in a nervous dance.

There was a woman working with a horse at the far end of the barn, and, engrossed in her currying, she paid me no mind.

I breathed a sigh of relief and then another when I discovered each horse's stall was identified by small plaques. I quickly scanned for Fitzgibbons's, and entered it, its emptiness clutching at my throat. I wondered how the young thoroughbred was doing in Dr. Ingmanson's care, and once again felt a pang of sadness for Ada, still so pent up today over the accident that had injured our friend's daughter and perhaps put her horse on the retired list for good. I gave an unexpected grunt myself—retirement wasn't much fun, except for my escapades with the Women on Fire and the little trips Arthur and I took.

I was glad to have something to interest me.

But it was even worse for a badly injured horse who had nothing to look forward to but the end of suffering.

As I stepped through the bedding material, for the second time today I yearned for my sneakers. Everything was clean and tidy enough, but stepping through two or three inches of shavings in even little heels was awkward. The bits of wood cut into my nyloned ankles, and I couldn't help but worry about what lay beneath the surface of the nicely raked bedding material.

I paused for a moment in the middle of Fitzgibbons's stall, enjoying the beam of sunlight coming through the high window. I wondered if I should drive home and put on clothes and shoes more appropriate for the task at hand. It was at that exact moment that I looked back toward the rafters of the barn just outside the horse's stall and noticed a dark mark on the bottom edge of a rafter, where, I guessed, the fatal rope had been knotted. The rafters were pretty high, maybe two feet or more above someone tall like detective Bernie Cascone. And late in the day yesterday they would have been in deep shadow.

But I was known as eagle-eye Meg, and when I pulled out my little penlight and focused it on the spot where clearly something dark had rubbed against the wood, I wondered if Bernie and the other investigators may have missed the dark smudge altogether. I walked up exactly beneath the beam and stared. Excited now, I flipped open my giant sized purse and yanked out an old pair of latex gloves I kept tucked in a side pocket and found, as well, a clean folded paper towel, reminders of the work I'd technically retired from almost two years ago.

While I rummaged for a clean plastic baggie I knew was there, I felt my heart beat faster, my mouth go dry. Finally, gloves on, I shone the light at the spot and stretched my right arm above my head to touch it with the towel. Of course, I couldn't begin to reach. Minor problem: my other nickname was "Shorty."

Muttering, I launched myself on the most direct route to the spot on the rafter. If I climbed up to the top of the smooth fencing separating Fitzgibbons's stall from the one beside his, and held onto the vertical metal bars on the top half of the separating wall near the barn's rafters, I could maybe, just barely—reach the suspicious spot.

Or die trying.

I pushed the silly words out of my mind and began easing up the smooth wall, gripping the penlight between my teeth and trying not to catch my latex gloves on splinters as I climbed. It was a slippery ascent because there was nothing to give my feet purchase, no slits or breaks in the wood at all. With a prayer to Allah, I angled upward and finally gripped the metal bars near the top, sliding a foot through two bars to hold me there. I took a deep breath and leaned to my right to scrape off the bit of dark material I had seen from below. My heart sank. What I had suspected might be blood was nothing more than a jagged piece of the rafter hanging like a thick splinter.

My shoulder felt wrenched, my neck ached, but there was no way I was going to give up so close to the spot where Mac had been found hanging. My body felt stretched apart as I glanced below and realized I was a good eight or ten feet off the ground. I shuddered all over, clinging for dear life.

How I regretted not calling Hannah to meet me here. My younger friend was taller, more agile, to be engaged in such youthful gymnastics. Even Dorie, whimsical and clumsy as she was, had six or eight inches on me and could have easily surveyed the area around the hanging beam if she didn't fall into the bedding first.

Down the aisle a horse nickered loudly, another snorted, as noisy human laughter cut the quiet of the barn. Kids arriving after school.

I was not about to be beaten. I stretched, reaching to my max, trying visually to scan the entire area. When I felt my right shoe go tumbling off on the other side of the metal bars and into the next stall, I yelped. With only my slippery stockinged toes gripping the bars to keep me in place, the realization hit me hard: if I didn't let my twisted right foot slip out from between the metal bars I could break my ankle trying to let myself down. Wincing, I slid my foot out from between the bars and, as I knew I must, went tumbling into the wood shavings, backside first.

That's how Hannah and Dorie found me a few seconds later, flat on my tush just outside Fitzgibbons's stall, eyes popped open wide in total shock, and missing a shoe. Whatever I'd landed in sent up noxious fumes of a clearly barnyard nature.

And though I wasn't feeling the least nostalgic now, even earthbound, I know I looked triumphant. Because scrunching over sideways, I was staring at the clear wood of the barn floor where my landing had disturbed a particular patch of bedding material. Before I could think twice about it, I reached with my paper towel into the dark spot a few inches away from the animal excrement.

"Yes," I tooted.

In my purple-gloved hand raised high over my head, I gripped the towel smeared with a huge splinter of barn rafter drenched in dried blood.

Hannah was quick, but never as quick as this moment. "'Murder, she wrote,' Dorie. Our Meg has done it again."

Dorie only whooped. And then frowned.

"It could be horse blood. Fitzgibbons's."

"Oh, Dorine, shut it!" Hannah yipped, chasing our friend down the aisle and trying to whack her with her pocketbook. "You know Meg has found the telling clue."

Dorie surrendered, covering her face from the attack and mumbling, "Okay, okay, but telling what?"

I calmly lifted myself, tucked the towel with its treasure into the clean baggie, retrieved my purse and shoe and followed my friends out. I could barely whisper as I went, achy from my fall, breath shallow, but still keeping up, "Telling us the whole story. Mac's story."

I'd have liked to have been more excited, more Hannah and Dorie, but I was Slavic after all, and wasn't I supposed to hide my feelings on all occasions?

This time it took real effort.

Six

Ada

Without Chantal, my friend and daily helper, I fussed around the kitchen feeling more than a little *verklempt*. Just making the coffee, and, of course, herbal tea for Theo, who'd recently "gone green," as she put it, made me uneasy. I'd never in my entire life had to manage the food preparation of a home; in fact, my skills didn't go beyond boiling water and making toast. Running the Women's Hadassah, or organizing travel arrangements for thousands of people over the years, even holding political office in this vibrant community I called home was as nothing to me, compared to grinding up coffee beans and figuring out how to put together the new-fangled drip-pot. Naturally, in this case my emergency two-cup coffee press was completely inadequate.

They were on their way, all my Women on Fire friends, and I mustn't appear helpless in the kitchen, even though they all know I am.

I never minded being my cook's right-hand woman in the kitchen, the helper. When I was a child, the Polish woman who cooked for us let me help her twist bits of dough together to make fabulous fried cookies we ate with powdered sugar. Sometimes she taught me Polish songs, like the one for Happy Birthday—I can still sing it. And I always enjoyed helping Chantal, especially arranging the flowers, choosing the wine and the china and helping to plate things prettily—but it took years of experience around food and hearth to be the one in charge. I knew it was too late for me.

But no matter how much I missed dear Chantal, she'd recently had the chance to join her sister-in-law in a wonderful new fabrics business they'd started in town, so how could I object? They already employed three sales clerks and two seamstresses, and women were coming from miles around, crazy for their designs and products. Good for them. How many times in my life had I wished to have a career, a profession, other than planning people's fun trips after my first husband bought me the Travel Agency to play with.

Even then, I was no expert. I just knew how to get people together with what they really wanted. Come to think of it, that's what I always enjoyed doing most. Like seeing Danny and Janet's love bloom, and my menopausal friends come together with astounding skills at solving crimes, and showing my thoroughbred with his brilliant rider...

I choked, remembering why we were gathering today. And why I felt so awkward in the kitchen. For three days now it had taken so much effort getting involved with the details of daily living. Since the accident, I'd spent hours on the computer doing research as Hannah had taught me over the last couple of years. I knew more about horses, their provenance and medical shortcomings, than ever. Not that it did me much good, except to keep me tuned in, so to speak, until Dr. Ingmanson called with the final verdict on Fitzgibbons's condition and prognosis.

But then, there was my trainer's death, which I assumed was mainly why we WOF, Women on Fire, had insisted on a meeting at my house this morning. It helped that Lu was bringing go-withs from her rave-reviewed new restaurant. How moronic of me to complain about the simple, menial tasks of setting out cups and measuring coffee and water.

Especially since I needed my friends more than they realized. Lu and Dorine had joined me at Mac's memorial service yesterday afternoon, and had helped me hold my emotions together and save them for a private time. Theo, of course, had been in devoted attendance on her stepdaughter following the girl's serious shoulder surgery, and Hannah and Meg had been, they told Dorie to pass the word on, harassing the police and other agencies regarding Mac's death. Until now, only sweet Bernie, Hannah's darling detective, would even admit the possibility of something worse than suicide.

And I felt I must know, and know soon. If Mac had killed himself, what was he trying to cover up? Had something he'd done caused the accident on Sunday that injured sweet Sigourney Rutledge and my stalwart jumper? On the other hand, if it were murder, who, and why on earth, were big questions.

While I placed a bowl of vivid fall leaves for a spot of color on the dining room table, I shook my head and resolved not to let this horrible new disaster get me down. I'd had two or three miserable years of massive hot flashes, and enough memory loss, dry skin and depression to last a lifetime. I had to keep my chin up. My boy and his sweet girlfriend were living here, doing their best at college and at work, and it would be ungrateful of me to spoil things by acting like a baby over the accident at the Plantation Valley Polo Grounds.

And although he had called daily from wherever he was traveling, I also missed a certain gentleman who was much on my mind, with his pale green eyes and considerate manners. And very hot lips.

Actually I wished Devlin Doyle had not taken me so seriously when I told him I wasn't up to having dinner with him before he left for a work-related trip, that it was best to let me be with my grief for a few days after the accident. I could hardly wait to meet him tomorrow when he returned briefly, before flying overseas again this weekend. I missed him mightily. More than I felt was appropriate for a woman my age.

Maybe I was too hung up on "appropriate."

I stood at the dining room window and felt a smile soften what I knew were my too harsh and aquiline features, as I watched Sancho, my new black Labradoodle pup romping about in his fenced play yard, leaping at falling leaves, sniffing the ones that lay in small heaps. Sancho was very aware of my moods, and I didn't want to depress the puppy who seemed so leery of other people and other animals. I'd rather neglected him this week, poor dog. After the meeting I'll walk him and toss a ball with him.

A squawk from my macaw Ramon startled me. I'd forgotten to remove his night covering! I ran to the living room and flipped off the bright cloth, cooing at the bird to apologize and soothe his upset. I fed him and checked his water dish, sang a little song to cheer him up.

I sighed. Good thing I'd never had children—I'd have been a poor mother indeed. I'd been so wrapped up in Gibby, my injured horse, I'd neglected the other two babies.

Car doors closing in the driveway took me out of my self-recriminations. I took a deep breath and tried to stand tall enough to overcome my shrinkage to five feet-one and my arthritic knee. So many counting on me. And I wasn't doing a very good job for any of them.

When the doorbell rang, I hurried to the foyer, heard my friends chatting away on the other side of the door, and caught myself smiling in the hallway mirror. In truth, this meeting with these wonderful women was just what the doctor ordered. It was time the Women on Fire started solving this new disaster in our usual dramatic way.

Then, too, there was my little secret in the romance department. Maybe soon, when things sorted themselves out, I could tell them all, and my new beau and I could launch our future together, whatever that might be, whatever was "appropriate."

"Oh, damn, here I go again," I said aloud, taking a deep breath and drawing open the door.

Glaring at each other, mouths clamped shut, stood Hannah and Meg. Indeed, Meg poked Hannah hard in the shoulder before either one of them would turn and look my way.

"What on earth..." I started.

Hannah slid past me and stomped across the foyer muttering. Meg set her fists on her hips and watched her go, still glaring. "You could have stood up for me a tiny bit!" she said.

Hannah whirled around. "Oh, sure, and have the guy I love hate me? Or watch him get fired? Honestly Meg, you had no right..."

Meg swore in Bosnian and Hannah answered back with a groan. I figured I'd best step between them before fists flew.

"You two. Come on, sit and be civilized and tell me what's going on."

Meg stepped inside and shut the door behind her with a defiant bang. "I spent half the day, I risked my life, Ada, I found a clue the police missed, and gave myself an injury in the process, not to mention ruining my new skirt, and she's blaming me for making trouble at the police station. I just don't understand you Americans sometimes. You're so, so—"

"And you, and you—" Hannah was sputtering so hard she couldn't form words either, outrageous for a gifted writer like her.

I put a firm hand on the backs of the necks of my two feuding friends and guided them into the dining room. "Sit," I ordered, in the tone usually reserved for Sancho.

They glared at each other a moment longer and by the time they settled in their chairs, across from each other, Dorie and Lucia had come in together, bearing huge boxes of sweet-smelling munchies. The fragrances of cinnamon and freshly baked sweet breads filled the air. I snatched up the boxes.

"You two sit here, one by Hannah and one by Meg, before they take a swing at one another." I chuckled at Lu's and Dorie's blank expressions, then hurried to the kitchen to place the goodies on platters and in baskets. Sesame sweet buns, apricot turnovers and rugelach that looked as flaky and crunchy as crusty snow iced over on a winter's day teemed from the boxes. The rugelach was still warm, almost hot to the touch. My stomach growled and I nearly swooned tasting a few crumbs that had fallen on the counter.

"I'd better get these back into the dining room to break up those bad moods," I muttered to myself. I picked out the closest basket standing against the backsplash and arranged the pastries to their best advantage. Suddenly I realized I didn't really mind the more physical tasks of hosting after all. So hosting was a way to make people happy!

By the time I came back, Lu had let Theo in, and the group was peppering Sigourney's mom with questions about her daughter's health. I placed the basket-platter on the table and hugged Theo tightly. She patted my cheek and we hugged again. It was the first time we'd met since the accident.

Behind us at the table our friends let loose little sobs and sighs, and Hannah blew her nose loudly. When Theo and I had taken our seats at table head and foot, I looked around and saw all was well with the Women on Fire. Bubbly and bitchy, tempestuous as ever and warm as the rugelach and those sesame buns in the basket, they were my Top Five List and I loved them.

"Order of business," I declared over the lump in my throat, "will be, first, Theo's full report on Sigourney, and then Hannah and Meg will in partnership reveal what tied them in knots—"

"With the police," Hannah snapped.

"—this morning." I continued. "And then I'll report on Fitzgibbons and the meeting will be open for plans and ideas." I reached for a rugelach and passed them on.

"Police?" Dorie muttered. "The police tied you two up? For heaven's sake, why?"

The meeting began with laughter, and stayed on the edge of hysteria for the next hour.

Theo's announcement about Sigourney's condition even met with applause. "The surgery went perfectly. They put a pin in her humerus, at the head where it was fractured. There was a tearing of the rotator cuff, too, so the doc repaired that while they were in there. He insists if she rehabs compliantly—and she's just raring to get started—she'll be back to normal, maybe even better than normal, in eight or ten weeks."

I swallowed the lump in my throat and asked, cautiously, "Will she ride...?"

"Absolutely! Though her father's not happy about it, Siggy says that's what will keep her motivated. She can't wait to ride Fitzgibbons again."

There was a twitch of tension in the group, and Dorie snapped it. "Assuming Fitzgibbons wants to, I mean if he *can* ride again, right?"

She sipped her coffee peacefully while the group laughed again. I dabbed at my eyes. "Right, Dorine. Dr. Ingmanson promised to call me today, which may give us a hint of that possibility. And I'm just praying he'll have good news."

"We'll keep our fingers crossed," Meg said, reaching for another rugelach. "Now I suppose you all want to know what travesty happened this morning at police headquarters." Hannah interrupted her as soon as she could swallow her most recent mouthful of apricot turnover.

"I'm the first to say it, you have to give Meg credit for finding what she did, but I thought she was going to have it checked it out at the state lab, not at Bernie's own police department! I mean, it's a pretty sure sign Mac McClellan was murdered, and did not commit suicide. But when I walked into headquarters this morning to have coffee with Bernie, there she was with her evidence bag and her authoritative tone..."

There was a group murmur registering shock and awe.

Meg cleared her throat. "I had called Detective Cascone last night when I got home and told him I'd bring the evidence in. Besides, for almost fifteen years, remember, the police came to me for answers about evidence. Of course I'm authoritative."

"Well you never told me you were going to do that. I

figured you were heading out to Farmingville to have it checked."

Meg dropped her pastry and her eyes shot angry arrows Hannah's way. "I made one brave call suggesting that route yesterday, and was told if I brought the sample to my old lab I would probably be arrested for withholding evidence in a felony murder. You'd have liked that, wouldn't you? Come visit me in jail and bring me one of Lu's rugelachs then, wouldn't you? How sweet." I caught the welling of tears in Meg's eyes and started to jump up, but Lu had already put her hands out to quell the harsh words going both ways.

Lu's vibrant alto rose above the hum of protesting voices. "Sweethearts, come on, tell us about it from the beginning. What evidence, Meggie, and where and how did you find it?"

Hannah's clamped teeth and drawn in lips made a harsh line in her jaw and she rapped her knuckles on the table a few times while Meg explained her trip out to the stables the afternoon before.

"I didn't tell you, Ada, because I wasn't sure what it meant, but the state lab people had already told me they'd found a suspicious but inconspicuous head injury on Mac, plus some residue under his nails that indicated he may have tried to fight off his attacker. So it seemed more possible than ever his death was not a suicide. I drove right to the barn from the lab to find something the police may have missed. There I inspected every surface of Fitzgibbons's stall I could reach, and the place right outside the stall where they, you know…"

"Found the rope," Hannah interjected. "You should have seen her, Ada, she was hanging onto this sheer wall with just one foot hooked into the metal fencing..."

Dorie took over. "With a flashlight in her teeth and her fancy rubber gloves on, and she was peering at everything about fifty feet up in the air when suddenly—"

"She dropped to the ground like a dead fly," Hannah said, and as she said it, her eyes rounded in wonder and she looked across the table with pride and astonishment on her face. "I couldn't believe it, you were absolutely intrepid, Megan, going after some tiny clue without a regard for your own welfare." She turned to Lucia beside her. "You'd have cheered for her, Lu..."

"Which we did," Dorie interrupted, "even though she landed in—what's the polite word—I guess equine fecal matter, and then rolled over right on it and found what she was looking for."

The group's giggle level stopped abruptly when Meg filled in the blank.

"Blood. My fall had sent the sawdust on the floor flying, and right there beside me I found a smear of blood stuck on a huge splinter from the rafter. I bagged it and brought it to Bernie this morning, along with what might be a bloody paper towel from wiping off the beam overhead."

I felt my face droop. "But Meggie, heroine that you are, that could just be Fitzgibbons's blood after all. It seems he was bleeding from the nose after the accident and..."

This time it was Hannah who settled down the

rumbling. "I doubt he bled upward, Ada, onto the beams. We'll know soon whose blood it is, thanks to our Spiderwoman here." She turned to Meg across the table, and blew her a kiss. "Sorry, hon, I shouldn't have got so vicious."

"Forgiven," Meg said, "and your handsome detective may well save the day."

Hannah beamed. "True. Bernie calmed right down when he heard Meg's story and sent the sample out for testing. He's had a hunch all along Mac did not kill himself. Finding Mac's blood outside the stall would prove he had received that head injury before he was, sorry, strung up. Of course, Bernie's bosses were furious 'those nosey biddies' were getting involved in their homicide case again. And Lieutenant Ketry, of course, assumed I had put Meg up to it."

"Us, nosey old biddies?" Dorie was horrified.

We all shook our heads commiserating with our youngest member. Fifty-four was too young to be called old for sure. And none of us liked being called biddies, although there'd been a worse "b" word we'd occasionally heard ascribed to us, making biddy seem mild to me.

"But Hannah was a dear," Meg said, with a sly smile growing as she lifted her coffee cup, "and gave me full credit. So now I'm the only one who's been told to keep my itchy fingers out of the case once and for all."

"Good for you, Meg," Theo called out, toasting Meg with her own cup, and we all joined in with a cheer. "We know that won't particularly slow you down."

It dawned on me Meg had been walking with a limp

when she came in today. "Oh, heavens, were you hurt, Meg? And what on earth were you wearing, hon, that you could climb all over that stable and sit in a pile of—waste, and not just utterly collapse?"

Meg blushed. "I've sat in worse, Ada. Though it was a new wool pants suit and of course it had to go right to the cleaners. No problem, though. I did twist my back a bit as I fell, but Arthur gave me a good back rub in the shower when I got home. A rather healing and intimate moment for two old geezers."

"Well, even better," Lucia cheered.

Dorie and Hannah chuckled, having been witness to the fall itself. But before any more evidence could be discussed, the phone rang, and I snatched my cell phone from the sideboard and headed for the kitchen doorway to speak.

When I returned to the table I'm sure I was pale, and the phone in my fingers was shaking.

"The test results are in," I said, barely above a whisper.

"Well, hurry and tell us, dear," Lu demanded.

"Let's hear it." Hannah set her coffee cup down with a slight clang and I choked back my emotions, then nodded.

"E-I-P-H," I said. "Exercise-induced pulmonary-something. I can't tell you very much about it. But it's basically caused by blood leaking from the pulmonary artery into the trachea and bronchi, making it difficult for the afflicted horse to breathe during or after running."

"The 'h' must stand for hemorrhage. Why, I wonder,

did no one diagnose it earlier?" Meg snatched her notebook from her haversack and jotted something on the pages.

I shrugged. "Remember that girl who assists Mac said she'd noticed blood in his nares after he'd sprinted in the past? She said she thought lots of horses did that and so never mentioned it to Mac. But why didn't Mac himself ever notice?"

"What will it mean for Fitzgibbons's future?" Hannah asked, her features as grim as mine felt.

"Doctor Ingmanson says there are a couple of different treatments, but all horses respond differently. He also said the condition should have been evident when we bought Fitzgibbons in England three years ago, and the seller was wrong not to tell us."

"If he knew," Dorie chimed in.

Lucia's cocked eyebrow and curled lip said she was too cynical to think he didn't know. "If it happens when they exert themselves, why wouldn't the sellers have known? Surely they had this horse running or galloping or whatever they call it before they sold him."

I was able to confirm it. "He was a big winner at Cheltenham, where the best horses race, steeplechase and all."

Meg cleared her throat. "Will the doctor let him resume training?"

I shook my head, almost afraid to picture the future for my thoroughbred. "Wants to treat him gingerly for a week or two, extra grub, especially protein, and only walks. No mounting, no galloping. Apparently there's no sure treatment, except using water pills at the start of a race. I don't want to have to push Fitzgibbons to perform like that. I couldn't."

"What are the symptoms, besides the nose bleeds?" Theo asked, her mind no doubt still in medical mode after spending three days at the hospital with her stepdaughter. "And the prognosis?"

I sank back into my chair and shuddered. "He wasn't too hopeful. Speed may well be a permanent problem for Fitzgibbons. Doctors at Ohio State have proven horses with this EIPA or H or something don't tend to recover, and many do poorly competing. Sometimes they just stop and refuse to run, or crumple to the ground as Fitzgibbons did."

Hannah brightened. "But Fitzgibbons's done great on the circuit, right? Besides, he's not a racehorse. He's an eventer, a what-do-you-call it?" Her fingers did the table tattoo again.

"Dressage competitor, jumper, too, where the hurdles are important, and the form," I said. "But speed can be important, too, and we don't know how much stress eventing of any kind may put on the poor animal." I couldn't help but bury my face in my hands. Dorie got up to give me a half-hug. I patted her pretty cheek, and sighed.

"At least he's ready to come back to the stables, so I can go see my poor baby."

Lu came over to hug me, too, then, and the room was quiet. In all that silence nobody could miss Theo's huffing.

"What, Thee? What is it?"

"Maybe that'll shut my Wilson up. I'm sick of him blaming you, Ada, and the trainer and even the stable management people for Sigourney's injury. And warning us all he's going to—"

She covered her mouth with her hand just as I looked up. I know my eyes were wide with shock, my face a mask of horror.

"Oh, Theo, no. Wilson blames me? He, he wants to... sue me?"

Now it was Theo's turn to look up through eyes glazed in moisture. "I'm so sorry. I never meant to mention it. I'm certain he won't. He's just been so upset about the accident. Every time he thinks about what might have happened to his little girl, he just explodes. But Siggy and I don't want that, see no reason for it, and we'll keep talking to him..."

Hannah fidgeted with the crumbs remaining on her plate and bristled with irritation. "Tell him for us it's a ridiculous idea, Theo. Ada didn't cause the accident. It hardly seems Mac did either since he's the one who paid the highest price for the damn thing."

Lu cut in quickly. "No, Theo. Don't tell him that. The man's upset. He needs to grieve his way through this and he will. You and the girls will keep him going until he sees litigation is not the answer here. But meanwhile, let's not condemn him. A parent's love is a powerful thing. Sometimes you go a little crazy." I suspected she was thinking of her recent reunion with her long absent father in Italy.

Hannah started to retort, but Dorie let loose a strangled sob and her pouty face nearly exploded with upset. "I know what Lu's saying. She's right. But let's not all of us start fighting with each other. We need to solve this mystery, and when we have the answers, everybody can be happy again. Please."

Not all the tension left the room, but I sensed the Women on Fire as a group wanted to grab onto what Dorie was saying, and after a brief moment of quiet and inhaled breaths, the buzz resumed, more urgent than ever.

"My plan is that I'm going to push Bernie to get quick results on that blood sample." Hannah pressed her fingers to her temples and shut her eyes tightly. I hoped it was enthusiasm and not one of my friend's debilitating headaches coming on.

Meg was about to beat them all out the door. "I'm headed out to the UConn animal labs in Storrs to look further into this EIPH for you, Ada."

"And I'm going to wrestle Wilson to the ground if I hear one more word about lawyers and blaming!" Theo blew kisses around the room. "Thanks for the tea, love. And Lu, your treats were out of this world."

"It's all of us together who are out of this world. I'm back to 'Lucia Mia' for the noontime rush, but call if there's anything I can help with. Ada?"

I lifted my arms in a gesture of solidarity and softly said "Amen," then added, "Before I go out to see Fitzgibbons I'm going to get on the computer and Google this ailment. I need to know more right away."

"What can I do?" Dorie asked. "I don't have to be at

the Warren's house for the wife's portrait sitting until three."

"Help me clean up the mess, sweetheart," I suggested. "And play with the puppy. Poor thing needs attention and my bad knee is killing me. I don't think I'm up for another half-hour of kitchen duty or ball tossing."

Dorie's face dropped. "No problem. But then can we go together to see how Fitzgibbons is doing?"

I brightened. "You'll come with me? Oh, Dorie, thank you. Exactly what I was going to suggest. Dr. Ingmanson thinks we can move him back to the stables from his place today. You can drive the truck." Absently I rubbed my right knee and watched Dorie grin and fluff out her gauzy blue peasant top and hobbled navy skirt.

"I love driving the truck," Dorie said. "Maybe I ought to change on the way. You know, after seeing what Meg got into at the stable and all."

"It was a very fortunate 'getting into,' Dorine," Meg squawked. "Don't knock it." Once again laughter punctuated our goodbye hugs. A sense of purpose seemed to energize each woman as we dispersed. And for a few moments even the pain of my aching knee faded as I went toward the entry to say goodbyes.

There was a breath of hope in the air. I just prayed we hadn't manufactured the whole thing ourselves.

Seven

Hannah

I stood in the doorway letting the crisp fall air blow into the space we'd all so recently warmed with our activity and conversation. Tragic as it all was, I sensed my friends would poke and pick their way successfully through yet another disaster. I could almost feel the air clearing in my head, too.

Ada caught up with me at the door and while Dorie went out in the yard to play with Sancho, I grasped her hands to say goodbye.

"I'm truly sorry I was such a jerk when I arrived, Ada. I really wasn't blaming Meg. With what she did out at the stables, she's my hero. It's just, well, Bernie has asked me so many times to keep the Women on Fire out of police business. It makes it really awkward for him, since he's still the new guy on the force."

"I know how they tease him. I understand his reluctance for us to get involved. But we gals, we're good at this, don't you think?"

I nodded. "When we put our heads together we're pretty amazing. But I'm always so torn. Wanting Bernie's, well, love and affection, but having to be true to my friends, too."

Ada bent to rub her knee and nodded. "That I get completely, sweetheart. It's very comforting to have a special man in your life. Someone to turn to when you don't exactly feel like Superwoman or Spiderwoman or whatever."

I searched Ada's eyes. Clearly my old friend wasn't giving up her secret about her love life just yet, and I wouldn't bug her. Well, maybe not too much. As I dug into my purse for my car keys, I thought I'd leave one tease in the air.

"Especially today," I said as I straightened, armed with my keys, "I'm kind of depressed because Dad told me this morning he's accepted an assignment for a shoot in Ireland soon. Seems he'll just get back from Columbia and he'll be off again."

I could see Ada's legs go weak.

"Oh, Ada, what is it? Your knee? Are you okay?" I reached out to grab her elbow and help her to a chair. "Is that arthritis getting worse?"

Ada hugged herself hard and gazed up at me, surrender in her eyes. "Oh, no, I—oh, Hannah. That's the worst possible news. Devlin going away. I... I didn't want to tell you yet, didn't know how you'd feel..."

"About what?" I couldn't keep from grinning.

Ada stood and poked her journalist friend in the ribs. "Darn you. You know. You knew all along, didn't you?"

I tried putting on a blank face but a laugh snuck out anyway.

We screeched each other's names and hugged.

"Are you okay with it?" Ada asked, holding me at arm's length.

"With you and my father being an item?"

Ada nodded, and blushed to her throat.

I exploded again in mirth. "You do realize you're dating an older man?"

Ada shook her head. "The sweetest, kindest man I've ever known. Devlin's so smart, knows everything going on in the world, and a hunk, too. I never quite realized until this year what a hunk your father is."

Now it was my turn to blush. "I've got to tell you, Ada dear, it's tough to think of your own dad wrinkling somebody's sheets. Oh, not that I'm saying you two— But, anyhow, since he also seems to think very highly of you, I suppose my best position regarding this budding shall-we-say, friendship, is at neutral. At least I assume it's budding."

Ada frowned. "Yes, you tease, just budding. He was wonderful the day of the accident, but because I've put off seeing him since then, everything's kind of in limbo. I felt it wouldn't be right to be having a good old time dancing the night away with Devlin while Sigourney and Fitzgibbons are suffering, and poor Mac buried..."

I patted Ada's cheek. "About the neutral part, Ade, I just meant, don't be using me as a conduit or anything between you two. And in this particular case only, I don't want to know the details of your love life."

Ada laughed. "Guaranteed. Let's not ever go there!"

"Okay. That settled, enjoy yourself. Now I've got to get to Bernie by lunchtime. Maybe he'll have a half-hour for me." I started down the steps and out on the walk leading to the driveway.

Ada called goodbye and bent again to rub her knee. I threw back one last retort before tugging open the door of my Volvo and sliding into the driver's seat.

"Just be warned: whatever happens, however blissful you two get together, I will never, absolutely never, call you 'Mom!'"

From the looks of it, Ada nearly collapsed with smothered laughter as I backed out the driveway and swung up along Mountainview Road for the trip into town. When I was out of her sight, I reached for the cigarette I'd unearthed and lit it with the car lighter. I'd just have time for most of the smoke before I got to police headquarters and used my mouthwash tabs. None of my pals, not even Bernie, knew my efforts to quit smoking had failed miserably. And I wasn't about to admit to a weakness to any of them.

So Ada and Devlin Doyle were pursuing their crush. It made me shiver, but I wasn't sure why. I loved them both, liked them both even. Just hoped no one would get hurt.

I blew out smoke toward my already fogged up window and thought of Bernie, how thrilling it still felt to cuddle beside him, to experience a man's strong, taut body beneath me, beside me. Come to think of it, I'd gladly take a chance on getting hurt for the sweet rewards

I felt every day of being in love with him. I was surprised to hear a very throaty laugh rise up in me. Bernie's love was changing me, that's for sure.

As my next pouf of smoke cleared, I nudged myself to get with it and focused more intently on the roadway. At the same time, the puzzle pieces of this latest homicide we had stumbled across began to adjust and fit together in my mind. Meg was sure to find something to help with the horse disease that seemed to have caused the accident. And the blood she'd discovered on the stable floor might even be the horse's. But if it was human, and could be traced back to Ada's trainer, Mac McClellan, or some guilty culprit, it meant the man was murdered for sure. Then finding the source of the residue under his fingernails was the next step.

I had no idea what sort of person we were looking for. Who'd do that to a man in the prime of his life? Who'd have a motive? Or an opportunity? And did the accident itself have anything to do with Mac's death?

After I saw Bernie, I'd go home and start outlining an article, maybe a series on the horsey set in town, a color piece, which would enable me to interview certain people involved in the case. One was the young gal who had been Mac's assistant. Then there was the dad of the competing rider. The manager of the stables. And the stranger in denim witnesses had mentioned.

And while I was at it, I'd love to give Wilson Rutledge a piece of my mind, too, for blaming Ada, hating Mac so terribly, and considering litigation.

As I pulled up beside Bernie's squad car at the

station, a nasty dilemma crossed my mind: should I have mentioned all these candidates for investigation to Bernie early this morning? Maybe I shouldn't have, and yet, maybe he'd respond by suggesting some suspects of his own. If, that is, he was still speaking to me after Meg's unbidden participation in the case.

I squished out my cigarette and dropped it into a plastic bag I kept tucked in the door pocket, used my instant mouthwash, and wiped my fingers with an anti-bacterial hand-wipe. Then I freshened my lipstick and ran my fingers through my hair so my highlights weren't buried under a flattened, uncombed do. I was just stepping out of the car and smoothing out the wrinkles in my ancient chino slacks when Bernie and Lieutenant Ketry burst out the door.

Bernie waved and kept moving.

I was dumbfounded, but also quick enough to catch him as he yanked open his car door and slid in. I leaned in after him and brushed the side of his face with my lips.

"I'm sorry about this morning. Can we talk? Can we have a cup of coffee?" I watched Ketry pause, his hand on the opposite side's door handle before getting into the car as if to give us a few moments to speak. I waved my thanks.

Bernie stared straight ahead. "We're in a hurry. Had a call. No time. We'll talk later."

Something jiggled deep in my gut. I couldn't stand that he wouldn't even look at me. "But I have info that may help on the case. We don't want to steal it away from you guys, we just want to help."

Ketry looked like he couldn't contain himself any longer. "Let's go, Cascone. This gal could jump."

"Who? What gal? Is this about Mac's death? Aw, c'mon you two. Let me ride along. I'll fill you both in on our stuff." I let go of Bernie's door so he could start the engine and snatch at his seatbelt. Meanwhile, I slid into the back seat as Ketry got in the front and turned to glare at me.

"'S'that Agatha Christie with you?" Ketry asked, his face one big scowl.

I huffed. "No, she's off to UConn to investigate the horse's problem."

Bernie was already backing out of his spot and swinging the car around to exit the lot on Faymont Road. I grinned, then remembered my cigarettes and purse on the seat of my car and gulped hard. I still had the remote car keys in my hand, and it took less than a second to aim them out Ketry's front window toward my Volvo as I clicked the "lock" button. I sighed with relief as the lights in the car flicked on and off, meaning the doors had locked.

It didn't dawn on me until much later I'd left the car window wide open, something I could never have been accused of during my days as a police reporter when I'd move too quickly and efficiently to make mistakes. When it came to keeping close tabs on police investigators, I was known to be fleet of foot and sure of step, and if truth be told, a pain in the posterior to some. Persevering, I called it.

So maybe not much had changed, except my

decreasing post-menopausal memory.

That and being in love. I sighed. And maybe later today, a missing purse.

"So where are we heading? What's the call you got?" I asked, my stomach tightened up to high gear.

"You first," Ketry barked. In the rearview mirror I caught a glimpse of Bernie breaking out in a small grin.

"Okay, tit for tat. One, Ms. Javitts and the people who were with her that day saw a guy they did not know helping to keep people out of the barn when the doc was working on her horse."

"Description?" Ketry asked.

"Just average height, average build, wearing dark, like new denims, jacket and jeans, a western hat of some kind, brown boots, hardly scuffed up at all. Dark brows and sideburns. Wearing sunglasses."

Bernie and his lieutenant exchanged glances.

"Your turn," I snapped.

"Got anything else besides the cowboy?" The lieutenant wouldn't even turn in my direction and I was getting ticked. Now that I was retired from crime reporting, the boys just didn't treat me the same. What was I, invisible?

Bernie sensed my irritation.

"We had a call, a tip, that some guy's been spending lots of time around McClellan's house. The property manager has seen him a couple times."

I calmed down and hit him lightly on the back of the neck.

"Thank you, officer. Think it's my denim guy?"

"Dunno. Never heard what he was wearing. We asked the Bukowski kid about him, she said he might be a parent of one of the riders. Looks familiar to her."

I told them about Charity Finch's dad, his pushiness, and the way he always asked too many questions of Ada. "Could be him, or the denim guy."

Up front the lieutenant was jotting everything I said in a vest pocket notebook. "Good one, Ms. Doyle. Finch might be the one. Heard he knows his way around and mucks out one of the stalls on weekends. His daughter's horse, I guess."

"So aren't we heading to the stables?" I asked as we missed the I-84 entrance and scooted up New Britain Avenue.

"Naw," Bernie said. "Miss Terry won't talk to us there. In case anyone who shouldn't see us is hanging around. We're going to her house. A mobile home up by the lake."

"In McClellan's backyard." Ketry waved a folded paper at Hannah. "So we can conveniently execute this search order at the same time."

So they were going to interview Terry, the trainer's aide. I tried to hide my grin. Sometimes life handed you roses, when all you expected was briars on the bush.

Eight

Theo

I faced the empty bed in my stepdaughter's hospital room and wrapped a hand around my throat: Oh, God, how awful the unoccupied bed looked, as if, as if...

No, surely she was fine, she was off doing a test or therapy or something.

"Calm down," I told myself. Sigourney might even be in the rest room. But no, the door to the private bathroom was open. I placed a hand on the sheets and grinned. Still warm. She'd be back in a moment. Hopefully.

I thought of Wilson, my husband, and how panicked he was over Sigourney's fall at the horse show on Sunday. If anything worse happened, Lord, the poor man would surely go into cardiac arrest.

I sensed myself holding my breath, and when I heard the lilt of Siggy's laughter and another voice blending with hers, and coming closer, I managed to exhale, breathe deeply and smile.

"Oh, honey, it's so good to see you up and around," I told my daughter, pretending I hadn't been alarmed at all. I hugged her gingerly, avoiding the right arm in its splint and bandages. Then said hello to Glenda Mane, the girls' former instructor in riding, who was aiding Siggy in her ramble about the hospital corridors.

"Hi, Theo," Sigourney said, grinning. "Isn't this a surprise? The nurse let me walk first thing this morning, then Glenda came for a visit and they said she could walk with me if I wanted."

"And, oh, boy, did she want to," tall, sturdy Glenda Mane said, with a chuckle. "And I could hardly keep up with her!"

"Oh, silly. Not true. I'm walking on eggshells, like afraid I'll break something if I stumble."

"Well, you're motivated," Glenda said. "Especially when you saw that cute intern." Glenda and I helped Sigourney settle on the edge of the bed and Glenda propped a pillow under Sig's elbow to hold up her injured arm.

"You know it," Siggy said. "Wow, this feels good after three solid days in bed. And the doctor says I can go home tomorrow if the x-rays later today look okay."

"Oh, Siggy, that's great news." I smoothed the sheets around my teen-ager to cover her bare knees, then was sorry I'd fussed like that. It's not the convent anymore, Theodora, I reminded myself. "Tomorrow, huh? I'll bet your dad would love to pick you up, and I can meet you at home at lunchtime."

"Morning meeting?" Sig asked, a trace of disappointment in her face.

I nodded. "Oh, but wait, he's in Boston on business for the night." We'd have to work this out.

"Maybe Shannon could drive me. I know she just has her learner's permit, but I'll technically be the licensed driver with her..."

Before Theo could answer, Glenda jumped in. "No problem. I'll be happy to drive Sigourney home and stay with her until you can get home, Ms. R. Help me to feel useful. I don't like seeing my old champion laid up one bit. I want to see her get started on her therapy right away."

"I'm afraid I'm not ready for that, Glenda," Siggy said, curling her legs up and twisting around so she was fully reclining on her left side. "She wore me out running all over this floor, Mom, can you believe it? And tried to get me on the elevator so I could walk around in the lobby. Fortunately the head nurse stopped us."

I inhaled sharply. "Oh. I think that's a bit much for your first day..."

Glenda waved us off with a big wave of her arm. "Nonsense. This is one strong gal, and the sooner she gets moving, the sooner she'll be riding again."

"You're the one who's strong, Glenda. Can you believe it, Thee, when I stumbled a bit in the hall she practically lifted me up by my elbows to keep me from falling, until I screamed at her that she might hurt my shoulder."

"Did she hurt you?" I asked, feeling myself go weak

inside. *What's the matter with people? Don't they realize what this child has gone through?* I said nothing but cluck-clucked in my old Mother Superior way. I'd never warmed to Glenda, who always seemed a bit self-focused and rough-and-tumble for a thirty-year-old woman. But apparently the girls were fond of her since their younger days when they'd learned everything about riding, currying and loving a horse from her.

Siggy shook her head. "I'm okay," she said.

But I still felt myself frowning, and let the conversation about transport home dribble away. Soon Glenda, her cheeks pink with embarrassment, was taking her cue and saying goodbye.

"You let me know if I can drive you home, kid," she said to Sigourney. "Nice to see you, Ms. R. Don't let her get lazy, now. I've got a great horse for her to ride if she can come back by early spring. Might even make the Grand Circuit." She punched a celebratory fist in the air and turned, taking two or three long strides to leave the room and disappear down the corridor.

Siggy's face twisted in some conflicting emotion and I gave her a few minutes of quiet, then settled at her side and placed some new magazines on her bedside table. When I turned back to her, Siggy was dabbing at her cheek where a lone tear had moistened the surface.

"What's wrong, honey? Are we rushing you with this rehab business?"

She shook her head firmly. "No, Mom, it's just... I get a little confused by Glenda sometimes. She really hurt me when she grabbed me. I guess she's always been like that, rough, you know? Even when Shannon and I took lessons as little girls, she'd kind of push and pull at us too harshly. Teased us for being softies. I'm just remembering it now. I think back then I figured it was because she's such a big woman, she didn't know her own strength, or our weakness, as little girls. I hope you or dad can take me home tomorrow. I don't want to go with her."

I nodded and took a moment to consider what my daughter had said. "You don't feel safe with Glenda right now, do you, Sig?"

Sigourney shook her head. "I guess not. Or it's just me, being gun-shy after the accident. Anyhow, I don't want to get, what's the word, beholden to her to ride her horse she's raving about, because I want to ride Fitzgibbons again. Only Gibby. Is he doing better? Have they found out what happened to him yet?" She squirmed herself into a comfortable position and lay back to rest and breathe deeply.

I perked up. "Well, they have a name for it. Ada just found out from Doctor Ingmanson. They believe it's a disorder called EPH, or is it EPI? It involves bleeding from the lungs when an affected horse exerts himself too much, and when it's severe, sometimes they fall, or just decide to stop running. Maybe because it hurts. Although no one mentioned any pain."

Suddenly Sigourney was bouncing around in her bed. "I don't believe it. EIPH? No! I don't believe it. That's what my professor thought all the time, and I never even mentioned it to Mac, or to Ada. Oh, I feel like such a fool." She covered her face and I worried she was about to burst into tears and make herself sick.

I placed a gentle hand on Sigourney's uninjured arm. "Siggy, honey, what didn't you mention? Tell me. No one seems to know much about this disease, and Ada is up to her eyeballs doing research, and Meg has gone out to UConn to study it. So if you know anything..."

Siggy took another deep breath and propped the pillow under herself more securely. "I don't know a whole lot, but Mom, Fitzgibbons always had these little nosebleeds, sometimes when we worked out, sometimes after an event. I asked Terry about it, Mac's assistant? And she said lots of horses get that, it's no big deal."

I curled up closer beside her. "Apparently that's what Terry said in the barn when Doc Ingmanson was examining him. But Mac didn't seem to know a thing about bleeding. He was furious at her for not saying anything before."

Siggy blanched. "Oh, God, I feel so awful. I should have mentioned it."

"But you said you mentioned it to your professor?"

"Yeah, at Skidmore. I had only been riding Gibby a month or two, but I'd noticed. He was such a trooper, he *is* such a trooper, it didn't seem to slow him down or bother him. At least 'til now." She rubbed her neck above her injured shoulder lightly with her other hand, "Oh, wow, was I stupid."

I started to object, but Siggy waved me off, and bolted upright to make her point. "No, see, Mom, I mentioned to my Equine Sciences instructor the horse I rode had these little nosebleeds. He said it might be exercise-induced, which could cause the lungs to seep a little blood. Pulmonary hemorrhage. EIPH. He said lots of horses have it. Some owners never know it, if the horse isn't racing or being pushed into competitive eventing." She lay back and stared at the ceiling. "And, oh, boy, did we push poor Fitzgibbons." Before I could speak, she was bolt upright again, tugging at my arm. "Is he going to be all right? What did the vet say?"

I tried to recall just what had been reported at Ada's house a few hours earlier. "Well, there's a treatment, giving the horse a diuretic before an event helps, because it lowers the blood pressure in the lungs."

Siggy nodded. "Dr. James mentioned that. He also said there are newer, better treatments, even some training facilities in England and Australia that promise a cure, using some new medicine and a carefully structured rehab program."

"Well, there you go, honey. If something exists to help Fitzgibbons, you can be sure Ada Javitt will find it. And do it. You'll both rehab and get back together before you know it." I leaned forward and pressed my cheek to Siggy's, fully aware this disaster had brought stepmom and stepdaughter much closer together. I was grateful for small favors.

Siggy sniffled. "I was wrong not to talk to Ada or Mac about it, Mom," she said softly.

I started to argue with her about that and Siggy pulled away and clenched her teeth.

"No, Theo, I was wrong." I felt myself tense when she switched back to my first name.

Siggy's face had turned bright red. "The reason I didn't say anything was because my professor told me there was something odd about this pulmonary hemorrhage thing: it may hurt the horse in the end, but for a lot of them, it seems to improve their performance. They run harder, better. The doctors don't know why, but..."

I reached out for my stepdaughter and Siggy leaned into my arms, gulping back sobs.

"I wanted him to be a champion. A champion with me on his back. Oh, damn me. I'm an idiot!" She jiggled her wrapped shoulder as she cried and winced with the pain. "And look what I've done, Mom. Look what I've done!"

Nine

Hannah

A patrol car with two eager young uniformed policemen met Bernie, Ketry and me at McClellan's place, a small but tidy log home with a narrow view of the lake, and the pleasant scent of pine growing behind and around the cabin. When Ketry produced and used a key that had been found in the pocket of the deceased, he flung the door open, eyes alert. Bernie sidled up to me, drawing me close to speak quietly on the front porch after the lieutenant and the two patrolmen had entered and divided up their duties.

Ketry stuck his head out the door. "You take the basement level, the little shed back there and the outdoors, Cascone," he called down to Bernie, "And tell her hands off anything."

"I know, I know, Tim." Bernie tried to keep the irritation out of his voice. "Damn," he muttered. "It's my case and I get the goodies in the garbage."

"Garbage is good, though, isn't it? You can find interesting stuff in garbage."

Bernie gave me look. I grinned up at him. "Sorry, I guess it's because of me. I'm a handicap to you in your business, huh?"

He ran his heavy fingers across my face, and let his smile reach his eyes. I got that intense pull toward him that always happened when we were eye-to-eye.

"No, don't you believe it. You're my guiding light, the star in my ..." He glanced around him, then up at the cloudless October blue above. "My sky," he said, dropping his hands. "But Ketry's right on one thing. Please don't touch anything, sweetheart. Let's not complicate this search with civilian interference, okay? You can look, but don't touch. And if you see anything interesting, or offbeat, something out of place or unusual, let me know. Me or Ketry."

I nodded, and as we walked up the four or five steps to the front porch, I promised to behave.

"I know you will. And you have a good eye. You may spot something we never thought of."

"Thanks for your confidence in me, Bernardo. It's your most endearing quality."

Bernie gave me a quick kiss on the cheek and we entered the building, where Ketry was rifling through every drawer and cabinet in the kitchen area, and the two patrolmen were trooping up the stairs to hassle the second floor.

I wandered around the sitting area trying to absorb everything at once, thinking of weapons, mail, illicit magazines. I spotted a laptop and moved toward it with one hand reaching out only to hear Ketry roar, "Uh-uh. Don't even think about it. That we'll take with us."

"I'm pretty good on computers, Tim. I could maybe save you some time."

His mustache twitched when he said, "Thanks, but no way."

I put both arms at my sides and Ketry relaxed. I sighed, and watched Bernie descend to the lower level. Cobwebby cellars didn't appeal to me, so I simply roamed around the living space, all one big room, and tried to imagine the life of the man who'd lived here. I found myself not only looking but also sniffing; there was a scent in the air just inside the front door—something heavy, sweet, almost spicy, but plant-like. I couldn't place it. Wished I had Dorie with me—her senses were more acute than mine.

After a few minutes of frustration for not locating the source, and wanting to touch and explore what I did see—an ancient saddle, some clothes thrown across a chair, a book with a bookmark stuck halfway in it, a wall calendar with lots of scribbles in the date boxes—I turned and went outside. I checked the porch and found nothing but a wicker rocker turned to face the water view, and quite a bit of soil stuck on a boot scraper by the front door. I had been trying to think of a lead-in image for my free lance story on horse life in West Parkford, and something about the boot-scraper seemed to capture it. The dirt, the boots scraping along the wrought iron, the earthiness of riding, both English and Western as we had in the area.

The boot scraper would be a great image, the dirt a

metaphor for the crime, for evil that could work its way into any sport, any activity... I'd definitely work on it tomorrow.

As I walked along the porch, I glanced up at a smaller cabin of wood siding painted red, across and up the driveway another thirty yards.

I saw the curtains at the front window of the cottage flutter, and then the door opened, and a young woman, thinner than she should be, with thin brown hair pulled back tight in a pony tail and eyes that darted everywhere and nowhere, was staring across at me.

I gave a little wave, and stepped down off the porch. I hoped Terry Bukowski didn't recognize me from our brief encounter a few days ago. Trying to look nonchalant, I headed at a casual pace up the slight incline toward the cabin. As I walked I wondered about the relationship between the deceased trainer and this young woman who assisted him and lived a stone's throw from his home. Were they closer than people realized? Had the police questioned the female assistant since Sunday at the barn, and if so, what had they learned? Bernie hadn't told me anything about Terry Bukowski. But then, why should I be privy to everything they learned in the investigation? Just because two of my friends had had a traumatic experience involving this woman? Well, duh.

I had to admit it, I'd like to write about the mystery unfolding in my hometown rather than a general feature on the whole horse scene. But then I'd surely alienate Bernie even more. I wouldn't close the door on the possibility just yet. Maybe I could interview Terry

Bukowski, find out where she fit in, both in the local horse world *and* in the accident and murder at the Polo Grounds.

I decided to play innocent, and as I approached the walkway to the red cottage, I looked up with bright eyes and a friendly smile.

"Are you Terry?"

The girl nodded, twisted her hands together in front of her and backed up slightly toward her door.

"I'm Hannah. I'm a friend of Mrs. Javitt, you know, Fitzgibbons's owner."

The girl's face relaxed a tiny bit. "Oh." She seemed to take a breath. "I thought you were here with them." She gestured with her chin toward the police vehicles.

I was a few feet away now, and stuck out my hand. Terry Bukowski reached out, but her thin hand felt like a jittery damp crab claw, and she drew it back rapidly, as if she were protecting herself.

"I am with them," I said, "but only because one of them's my boyfriend, and he said I could come for the ride." I turned to survey the glimpse of water and the surrounding pines in brilliant sunshine and breathed deeply. "It's so pretty out here. Wow. I'd love to live in a place like this."

Suddenly the young woman squatted and sat on her haunches, offering the top step of her porch to me. If I weren't mistaken, a small smile had cracked the sober surfaces of her thin, wan face.

"Yeah, I'm, I was pretty lucky Mac let me stay here. I couldn't afford anything else, either."

"So you knew Mac back in England?" I asked as I sat and angled myself to watch Ms. Bukowski's facial expressions. Her voice had a peculiar bend in it, something European, Slavic maybe, colliding with the British.

"No, my parents fixed—" She stopped short, made an offhand "whatever" gesture with her hand.

I nodded as if I understood. I didn't. "You been working with Fitzgibbons long?"

The girl nodded. "'Bout a couple years. D'you know how he's doing? 'E coming back to the stables?"

"Yes, today in fact."

Terry's face lit up.

"Then I should get over there." She popped up from her squatting position and yanked up her jeans around her too-slim hips. "I mean, with Mac gone, who'll take care of him?"

I put out an arm and tapped Terry's arm. "There's no hurry. Mrs. Javitt was just heading out with the horse box when I left her, and they'll have to drive all the way to the vet's and back."

The girl chewed her lower lip. "Mrs. Javitt's mad at me. Because I didn't say anything about Gibby's bleeding. I didn't know. I never worked with horses much, except my own pony and a neighbor's, doing the grunt work, y'know, back in Gloucester. Other people, someone very experienced, said it was no big deal." She gave me a solemn look, a defensive look, and hurried on. "Mac was right to be mad, though. He always was, you know. He thought I was stupid. He harped at me to tell him anything that might be wrong. I just didn't know the bleeding could..." She studied her boots, new ones that looked way too big for her. "Is that what they think it is? Was the accident because of his nosebleeds?" She grew wide-eyed, anticipating the answer.

I shrugged. "I don't know much about horses either," I said. "So, who told you it was no big deal? Who was the someone you mentioned?"

Terry seemed to freeze in position. She gazed across and down the lane at the activity around the doorway and yard of Mac's house and swallowed hard.

"I dunno. Just someone. Anyone, really, that I mentioned it to." Her foot tapped a tattoo on the porch floorboards. "What are they doing over there? What are they looking for?"

I lifted one shoulder. "Don't know. It's what they do when someone, you know, dies unexpectedly."

Terry grew more taut, a coil about to spring. "But no one's there. Told them I'd seen a guy wanderin' 'round once, but never again. There's been no one there since Mac..." To my surprise the girl's face suddenly softened, and tears gushed from her eyes. She wiped them off with her bony knuckles in a panic.

"Sorry. Din't mean to do that. I gotta go call Ms. Hand, see if I should come in. I want to. I want to help with Fitzgibbons."

"But the police are going to ask you some questions, aren't they?"

Terry Bukowski didn't answer. She slid into her house, slippery as an eel, and let the screen door bump closed behind her.

Right then, like a punctuation mark added to the girl's hurried move indoors, Bernie called loudly from the front porch of the log cabin.

"News," he said. "C'mere." He was smiling, and holding his cell phone.

I ran, slipped on the carpet of pine needles, got my bearings and loped on down the hill. I'd needed another three minutes with the waif. Just three. It could've been important.

Bernie was gazing up at me with affection. He reached out a hand to help me up the sloping walk to Mac's cabin.

"What?" I laughed, then gathered my face into a serious question mark. "What's the big news? You find something in there?"

Bernie shook his head. He led me up the steps to Mac's empty house. "Nothing. But we just got the report on the blood sample Meg came across on the splinter in the barn."

"Human?"

Bernie nodded. "They don't know yet if the DNA looks a match for Mac's. The matter under his fingernails is positive for human epithelial and blood, too. I told them to try and match the samples each to each. Still, the evidence is pointing real clear already. He was killed before he got hung up on those rafters, Hannah. You and your friends were right."

I whoopeed and wrapped my arms around his neck.

"Fantastic, detective. So *you* were right, too."

Bernie started to say more but I pressed my fingers across his lips. "Wait. This is important. That girl is going to scoot out of here in a second, Bernie. You've got to talk to her. Ask her who owns these cabins, will you? As well as who's been coming around here that looks familiar since Mac died." Bernie motioned to Ketry and said he'd pin the girl down before she left. Ketry nodded.

I walked back down the sloping walk with him. "She also said Mac was always mad at her. Why, I wonder. She's pretty scared, and if she runs..."

The sound of a light engine starting up behind the red cottage made us both jump. Bernie left me behind and ran down and out into the driveway barely in time to yell at the young woman on the motor bike kicking up the dust and about to zigzag past him.

His yell got her to stop. She stood shaking for a minute, then unhooked her helmet, though she wouldn't look up from the handlebars of her ride.

"That's better."

Bernie's voice was firm but gentle. I loved that combination in a man, but was glad I wasn't the frightened girl on the bike.

"Ms. Bukowski, as you know we're here to interview you about something to do with the death of Mr. McClellan. It wouldn't be a good idea to run away from police officers trying to question you in regard to a homicide, Miss."

The girl glanced up at me and toward the doorway of Mac's cabin where Ketry stood like a sentinel, hands on hips, expression threatening. Her eyes flicked back and forth over the road ahead and the people beside her. Finally she turned the engine off and set the bike in its stand.

Ketry stepped out and tried not to grin. "Atta girl. Now, up to your place, let's go. The detective and I have some questions."

Terry sulked away from her bike and walked up the hill, defeated. I wished I knew what caused that look of desperation, and how I could help her.

On the other hand, from what I knew of the day of Fitzgibbons' accident, Ms. Bukowski might have been the last one to see Mac McClellan alive.

If not, she might know who was.

Ten

Ada

When my thoroughbred finished munching on the carrots I'd hand fed him, I pulled up the small farrier's stool Dorie had brought me from a corner of the stables, and parked myself just a few feet from my pretty boy. I just wanted to gaze at him and feel a smile take over my insides. He was alive, his gait was good, he had even put on some weight with the light exercise schedule Doctor Ingmanson had him on.

Dorie jigged happily studying the horse from first one side, then the other. He nickered softly, seeming grateful for the attention. "I'm just so thrilled he's okay, Ada. He doesn't look sick at all. His coat is so smooth and sleek, his—"

I shook my head. "He is sick, Dorine. They fed him well, and limited his workouts, so he's filled out a little, that's all. But if we should put him through his paces today, he'd be in another crisis as bad as last Sunday's.

Right now I don't know what we can do to help him, other than the diuretic the vet mentioned. But the vet doesn't know if that might have bad side effects."

I rested my head on my hands, and my elbows on my knees, then sat up straight, rubbed my right knee and huffed out a long breath.

"Hurts, huh?" Dorie asked.

"Like the Dickens. And don't ask me what that means, sweetie. I'm out of answers for the day."

"I'm not," piped up a voice from behind Dorie. It was Meg, who had learned her lesson about stable visits and was wearing some old, dark twill slacks and her Reebok sneakers. "I stopped at home to change and came right here. Ladies, my three hours at the university proved very enlightening. Thanks to Sigourney Rutledge."

Dorie gaped at her, and I rose with difficulty, and leaned against the post beside me.

"What on earth?" I asked. "Sigourney?"

Dorie tugged at Meg's tan over-shirt. "Spell it out, girl," Dorie said. "I was just about to leave to keep my appointment with the bank president's wife, I mean Mrs. Warren, and I can't be late for our sitting. But I've got to hear about your research first. Tell us, tell us."

Meg took a moment to greet the handsome chestnut and admire his coat and his bright eyes.

"He's surely looking in good form today. And, Ada, I definitely think Fitzgibbons will be a winner again. There are treatments, there is more we can do to make him well." She gave a thumbs-up signal and grinned from ear to ear.

Meg's smugness was deserved, I thought, if what she said was true.

"What? Oh, Meggie! Talk. Tell us." I made a come-on, come-on motion with waggling fingertips and Meg laughed.

"Okay. I learned a lot about EIPH, how it's more prevalent than you'd think, and some of the treatments they've tried for it in the past. The sad thing is that horses with it untreated have been known to succumb right on the track—two in one race just last year in Virginia."

Dorie squelched a squeal. I moaned and looked over at my sleek gelding to reassure myself he was not close to that happening anytime soon.

"The irony is that some horses with EIPH actually perform quite well, better in many instances than horses who don't have the affliction."

"But how does that affect their health? And where does Sigourney come in? Are you saying it's something about the way she rides Fitzgibbons?" I fidgeted with the buttons of my chambray shirt, and sank back down on the stool.

Meg took a deep breath. "No, no, no. Here's the funny part. Theo called me on my cell phone while I was at the Animal Sciences library. It seems last year already Sigourney thought something might be wrong with Fitzgibbons when he had more than one nosebleed after she worked him, and she feels ever so guilty for not telling you or Mac. She did mention it to Terry once, but Terry said she'd been told it's nothing, most horses have it."

"Oh, poor Siggy. I hate having her feel responsible

over this."

"But that's not all. She also mentioned the problem to her Equine Sciences instructor up at Skidmore; he's an expert on the thing. He says there's been very little real research into EIPH, and only now is the equine community gearing up to do a major study of how to prevent or treat the ailment."

"That's wonderful, that's super," Dorie said. "And on that note I've got to run, but I'm so happy we've found an expert to guide us. I'll be sure and tell Mrs. Warren. She's on the board here, you know, and very concerned about Fitzgibbons. I'm off, you two, I'll catch the rest later. Thanks for letting me drive the truck, Ada."

She blew a kiss and hurried out to her own car parked in the shade by the visitor center.

Meg and I watched her go and took time to chuckle. For me it was a laugh of relief to hear there was some hope for my Gibby.

I sank back down on the stool exhaling a pouf of air and stretched my legs out in front of me. "Tell me more, Meg. Tell me."

Meg squatted against the post opposite me, checking the ground beneath her first, and Fitzgibbons nickered again, turning his head from side to side at us.

"Well, thanks to Theo and Sigourney, I got Siggy's professor's telephone number and called him in upstate New York. We had a long chat. He's very sympathetic, Ada dear, and wanted your name and number so he can keep track of what happens with Fitzgibbons."

"Sure, that's fine, Meg."

"And best of all, he told me about someone who's apparently miles ahead in the research and treatment of EIPH, too. An equine center that claims to have developed a system of rehabilitation for afflicted horses. They use some simple medications, nothing radical, and a carefully structured program of therapy to get the animal back where he should be."

Meg stopped for breath and a big nod at me. I nearly fell off my stool in joy. Suddenly my knee didn't hurt, my waning spirits surged and I couldn't wait to ask.

"I want Fitzgibbons to go there. If this professor says this place has a good record, and a decent success rate, I'll take him there whatever it costs."

Meg nodded. "I knew you would, so I got all the details." She pulled out a small notebook from her breast pocket and opened it to a page she'd book-marked. She rose and handed the notebook to me.

"Oh, I'm so excited. I can hardly believe it." I caught my breath and came close to Fitzgibbons, resting my head against his neck before I glanced down at the pages before me.

I stepped back, lifted my glasses to my eyes and read. "Amber Hill Equine Clinic, da-ta-da-ta-da..." I read, and came to the address.. "In... oh, Meggie, UK? This miracle place to make my Gibby well again is back in *England* where he came from?"

Meg frowned at me. "Problem?"

"Are you kidding?" I reached out to scratch Fitzgibbons' neck, and smooth back his ear. "We're taking you home for a visit, you rascal. We're going to England."

~ * ~

I left Fitzgibbons in the care of Josie Hand, who explained she had the doctor's instructions for feed, watering and exercise, and that Terry Bukowski would be in shortly, to resume her duties in the barn, particularly with Fitzgibbons. Nothing could dampen my happiness over what I had learned from Meg, though I felt slightly squeamish about the young woman taking over the horse's care and said so.

"I'll be an angel on her shoulder, Mrs. Javitt. Don't you worry," Josie said.

For once, I didn't. When I pulled into the driveway on Mountainview, I saw Dan's car was already there, and faintly heard his and Janet's voices and little Sancho's yipping, hopefully playing together in the play yard. I breathed a sigh of relief. I could hardly wait to tell them the good news. But with everyone taken care of for the moment, I rushed, limping a bit, to the living room couch, phone in hand, to call Theo and thank her for the help she and Sigourney had given Meg, only to find my old friend in tears on the other end of the line.

"My dear, what is it? Not something gone wrong with your darling daughter? Not Sigourney."

"Nothing about her physical condition, Ada. But yes, it's Siggy. I'm so angry and so full of regrets. I should have known better."

I steeled myself. "Tell me. I'll do whatever I can."

"I'm afraid there's nothing you can do this time, love. It's the shock of the whole thing, how she found out." Theo's ragged breath caught on a sob.

I reassured her I'd wait, told her to take her time. At that moment the young people came in from their romp with Sancho and I covered the mouthpiece. "It's Theo. Something's upset Sigourney, and I'm trying to find out what." My stepson and his girlfriend shot each other glances.

"We ought to go to her," Janet said. Dan shook his head and shushed her.

"Let's find out what it is, first," he said. "C'mon, Jan, let's see what we can pull together first for dinner." They left the room as Theo began speaking, more surely now, but the anger barely bitten back.

"Ada, I see now I was wrong, but I hadn't told Sigourney about Mac's death yet. I knew how terribly upset she'd be and I didn't want to hamper her wonderful progress at the hospital. Maybe turn her hopefulness to depression or something. I figured when we got her home... It was all Wilson's idea, and he's been pretty devastated by his daughter's injuries, as you know. I don't like to argue every point with him."

"I can understand that, Theo. Go on."

"We had mentioned it to everyone, her sister Shannon, all her friends, Janet and Dan and Glenda Mane, her old instructor. Everyone. Told them we'd tell her about it once she got home when she couldn't avoid hearing about it. TV and papers, all that." Theo let out a great sigh.

"But someone told her."

Theo's voice came out almost a screech. "Can you believe it? And tomorrow, God willing, the doctors are releasing her. We would have told her tomorrow. I'm so angry I could simply slap her face."

"Sigourney's?" I snapped.

A bitter laugh blended with Theo's retort. "No, no, of course not. I mean Glenda Mane. She had seen Siggy this morning and was a little rough with her, trying to get her to walk around more than she wanted to. Offered to take her home tomorrow because Wilson's off tonight on a quick trip to Boston and I have appointments in the morning. I thanked her and said no, but can you believe it? She came back this afternoon and told Siggy what we were keeping from her. That Mac was dead, and everything they've written about it in the papers, and tried to make me out to be the enemy because I withheld it all. And that Cruella still expects to drive her home tomorrow from the hospital!"

"Glenda told her about... the hanging, the gruesome details?"

"Everything. She said Siggy had a right to know. That she shouldn't go back to those stables at all, that she wanted her back at Glenda's own academy, riding Glenda's horses."

"Oh, glory. What did Siggy tell her?"

"She was shocked. And very angry. Asked her to leave, then called me at the agency and wept on the phone for three minutes before she could say a word. I locked up early, Ada, I hope you don't mind."

"Of course not, dear. You couldn't leave her in a state like that. How is she now?"

"Well, I talked my heart out to her, and we both cried for an hour off and on. She's asleep now, because I asked the doctor to give her something. And she absolutely refuses to be picked up in the morning by Ms. Mane. She's furious at her."

"Understandable. How crass and unfeeling."

"But the worst part is she still doesn't quite forgive us, Wilson and me, for not telling her about Mac. She dearly loved the man, Ada. You know that. He was so good with her and Fitzgibbons. She felt it was a match made in heaven." Theo's voice got whispery again.

"Are you still at the hospital?"

"No, dear, I've come home to Shannon so we could have a bite to eat together, and then Shannon's going to go back alone and spend the evening with her sister. She thinks it's best if I stay at home tonight."

"If she'd like company, I'm sure Janet and Dan would come by to sit with the girls."

Janet had just poked her head out from the kitchen and was about to tell me something about dinner. Instead, she caught the drift of the conversation and nodded. "Sure. Whatever," she said softly.

Theo thought Shannon would appreciate that, and it would give Siggy a chance to process everything out with her friends. "Thank you, dear one. You're so good. Have them pick Shannon up if they could. She only has her learner's permit to drive."

"Of course. They'll be there in an hour. And, listen, Theo, I'm going to pick up Sigourney tomorrow myself. If Shannon can come with me, it would be perfect."

"Oh, Ada." Theo was speechless.

"Tell Shannon I'll pick her up at your house at ten,

and we'll go right to the hospital. Have her bring whatever her sister needs for the ride home."

Theo soughed a little non-verbal thank you, and soon we'd ended the call.

I started to rise to meet the young people in the kitchen but my knee gave way, followed immediately by a cataclysmic hot flash—damn the arthritis!—and I sank back into my chair. Dan and Janet came running.

"What, Mom? What's wrong with Siggy?" Dan asked, Janet clinging to him in worry.

I explained what had happened, listened to their cries of fury at the old riding instructor. I said I'd offered their help, and apologized for not asking first.

"You know you can count on us," Janet said. "We've put the makings of a nice omelet together, and as soon as we've cooked it and you've joined us for a bite, we'll head over to pick up Shannon. Something's hurting you, right, Ms. Javitt? Is it that knee again?"

I nodded. "Silly thing, always acts up just when I most need my two legs working. And my darlings, I won't be having your lovely omelet with you." I put a trembling hand to my brow. "I just remembered Mr. Doyle is picking me up for dinner out at the country club tonight. He's leaving soon for overseas, so it's a kind of a..." I gulped back a little lump in my throat, "bon voyage party."

"Can I help you get ready?" Janet asked.

I grinned. "No, but you're a sweetheart to ask. Dan, why don't you find that old cane of mine? I think it's in the hall closet."

Dan nodded. "Sure, Mom, and I'll get you a couple of ibuprofen and a glass of water first. You sit there and be comfortable. Give your knee a rest before you go upstairs."

I agreed, and my heart warmed to have these two so lovingly nearby during this difficult moment. I ached inside for what Theo was going through right now. Ever since she'd married Wilson after an online dating service match-up, Theo's hardest job had been to get his teen-age daughters to warm up to her, to accept her as a sort of substitute mom. Their own mother had died three years back, and was just the opposite of Theo—fair-haired and feminine, always home caring for house, husband and children, a sweet woman who wrote poetry in her spare time.

Theo, on the other hand, with her no-nonsense brunette good looks, page boy hair cut, and quick hustle to be everywhere at once, including her practice as a psychological counselor at the Center for Grieving Children and her part-time work at my travel agency, was her own person first. Several decades in the nunnery had given her an independent, take-charge nature she often had to guard against abusing in her new family situation.

But you only had to look into her warm brown eyes when she was around Wilson and his daughters to see how much love she had to spend on them.

I sighed, took the medication and drank down the cool glass of water Dan delivered and kissed him on the cheek in thanks. I lifted my leg up on the ottoman he'd slid up to my chair and lay back. "Dan darling, I've forgotten to tell you the good news with all this happening. I think we've found a place for Fitzgibbons, where they practically guarantee good results with his disorder. I'll tell you the details later."

"Aw, Mom, that's great. That's perfect. We'll tell Siggy, and maybe that will help cheer her up."

"Absolutely. Do it." I smiled, and felt my energy restored.

Maybe, with a little instruction, Janet could pick out my clothes and jewelry for tonight and bring them downstairs so I wouldn't have to stress my knee any further. Something told me that, as the doctors had predicted, the cartilage in the knee joint was worn so badly now, that my orthopedic surgeon was right: the time had come for at least a partial replacement. I just prayed it could wait until I'd gone to England and back for Fitzgibbons's care.

As if reminding me how important my family is, including my assortment of creatures, little Sancho came running and vaulted himself up to my lap. When I laughed, Ramon laughed with me, a parrot's raspy squawk only a mother could love.

I had a lot to do, hobbling around on one leg. But I'd be damned if I let it slow me down. A half-hour rest was all I asked, and all I'd get.

Eleven

Hannah

While I put the coffee on in the kitchen, Dorie capped her paints and stood her brushes in turps, then wiped her hands well on a color-splashed rag.

"You mean you've already been working this morning and with nothing to eat or drink?"

While she washed up at the kitchen sink, Dorie giggled. "Have to iron while the strike is hot, or whatever. Sometimes I forget to eat when I'm just getting started on a painting. Eating never seems important when you're doing something you love, know what I mean?"

I rolled my eyes and nodded behind Dorine's back. With the memory of last night's marathon in the arms of Detective Bernie Cascone fresh in my mind and stamped onto my body's more tender spots, I had to agree. In fact, we'd intended to go for dinner first and then watch the Red Sox at Bernie's apartment, but got into an athletic game of our own and never made it to

Franklin Avenue or the flat screen.

As I recalled our hurried and urgent need for one another, I pictured us, at our age, well, my age anyway, racing each other up the stairs to Bernie's second floor spread, and undressing each other just inside the door. Who needed boring baseball games when that man definitely knew how to pitch strikes and hit homeruns of his own, I mused. His hot breath on me, the look of derring-do in his eyes when we came together, were memories to warm my colder nights—if I'd ever get any after these hot flash years.

"Hannah? Hannah!" Dorie said. "Did you hear me? Do you agree? When you have a passion, food doesn't seem important. Right?"

Feebly lifting mugs down from the cupboards, I nodded.

"'Course Lucia might disagree since food's her passion, well, food and Tony, especially since that trip of hers to Italy. Oh, kind of like you and Bernie." Dorie faced me as she dried her hands, then pointed, chuckling, at what I suppose was my blushing face.

Or was it another hot flash?

I stiffened. "Ms. Boulé, don't even go there."

Dorie covered her mouth and laughed again. "Oh, sorry. I didn't mean to imply..."

"Pour the coffee, Dorine. And find us something for breakfast while we catch up on the sad case of Mac McClellan, etc."

Dorie found an old box of Cheerios in the cupboard, provided bowls, spoons, milk and sugar, and set them by the coffee mugs in front of us. "There might be an old yogurt in there," she gestured toward the refrigerator. "Check the expiration date, though."

I huffed. "You're helpless, woman. I'll check *your* expiration date in a minute. We should have had this meeting at Lucia's. At least she has edible accompaniments in her cupboards."

Dorie grinned. "But this way, you're the first to see my new sketch of Ms. Warren. Do you like it so far?"

I creamed my coffee and milked my cereal and nodded. "I'm absolutely amazed how such a quick sketch, based only on one sitting, already captures the woman. You're amazing, Dor. By the way, it's 'strike while the iron is hot.'"

"Oh, 'course. And we had a really nice chat while we worked, too. She's on the board at the Polo Grounds, and is very interested in Gibby's condition. I told her about Meg's research, and how there's actually someone Sigourney knows who thinks he can cure the horse's condition, that EPIS thing. If I have it all right."

"EIPH," I corrected, hating, for once, my school teacher voice. "That's marvelous, Dorine. Who is this person? And how did Sigourney get involved? Dad told me Ada was going to be making plans to go to England for the treatment."

"I didn't know that part. I left partway through Meg's story to meet Ms. Warren." Dorie threaded her way through as much of Meg's report as she knew as we munched on our Cheerios. "I just know it has to do with Sigourney's professor, and Ada is thrilled to bits."

"Bless Ada. This morning she's taking Sigourney home from the hospital because Theo has appointments and Wilson is in Boston, and Glenda Mane, who offered to take her, upset Siggy by telling her about Mac's death when Theo was planning to do that at home."

Dorie's eyes went wide. "Oh, how mean of Glenda Mane. Who's she anyway?"

"Siggy's old riding instructor."

Dorie tilted her head to one side. "Hmmm. Yes, I remember seeing her at the hospital one day. Theo introduced us, and Ms. Mane left then. A big gal, broad shoulders, but attractive, too, in a, well, jockish sort of way. I remember even I had to look up to talk to her she was so tall."

"Anyhow, apparently she's trying to get Sig away from Fitzgibbons and riding for her at Rosemont Farms. Although, I talked to that Terry Bukowski yesterday, and she didn't say anything about a competition for Siggy going on."

"I think it's so exciting that Officer Ketry and Bernie let you go along for the search at Mac's house. What did you all find?"

I paused to try and recall if anything had stood out, other than the laptop which they'd carried back to police headquarters. "Don't really know, hon, but they have learned the blood smears Meggie found are human blood, and so's the residue under Mac's fingernails, not the horse's, so, sorry dear, it does look like the trainer was killed and then strung up on the ropes."

"I feel so bad about Mac. At his memorial service

everyone had something nice to say about him. Even that grouchy Mr. Finch. And of course, Ada, too."

"Sorry I didn't go with you all, but yesterday I had that good chat with Terry, and I'm certain she knows more than she's saying."

Dorie drained her coffee and set down her mug with a bang. "Well, then, let's us go interview her again. You know, casually, like we're just there to see Fitzgibbons. Ada can't go this morning because she's driving Siggy, but we can go in her place. We're her friends."

My mouth twitched. "And Fitzgibbons', too. Great idea, you spook. I'm free until after lunchtime, then I have a small group of kids to counsel. But you were working." I nodded toward the easel set-up in what used to be Dorie's dining room.

"Mrs. Warren will wait. That's the nice thing about my job. No punch in, no punch out."

~ * ~

A half hour later we pulled into the Polo Grounds.

I parked my aging Volvo in the shade outside the stable and tried to cover up my nerves so Dorie wouldn't panic. Every time I thought of what had happened here, I wanted a cigarette. But this wouldn't be a good time or place to smoke.

"How peaceful it is here today," Dorie said, as we walked from the car to the stable entrance.

I grinned but guessed it came out a grimace, so I turned my face away. With school in session on this crisp fall morning, and most instructors and students missing, the barn *was* quiet. Within, we could see a couple of feed men had done their rounds of distributing each resident's morning meal, and were now sweeping up. One older woman was currying her horse, and Terry Bukowski was leading a bay pony out to the paddock.

We walked by the outside path and met her coming back up to the building.

"Hi," I said cheerily. "We're here to check on Fitzgibbons as Mrs. Javitt is otherwise occupied today."

"And anyhow, we're Gibby's friends, too," Dorie said with a sunshine smile.

Terry Bukowski nodded and led the way back in to Fitzgibbons' stall. While we greeted Fitzgibbons, and I rubbed his neck lightly, the girl stood silently by.

"Doesn't he look great?" Dorie asked.

Terry stared at her feet, which I noticed were not stuffed into what had seemed like very large paddock boots, but instead in tall, green rubber boots. "You don't have your nice new ones on today."

Something in Terry's face cringed. "Mucking boots. I have to do a couple of stalls for Ms. Hand today."

Dorie tried to catch her eye while her gaze was lifted from footwear. "You remember me, right, Terry? I was here with Mrs. Javitt and the others the day of the accident."

Terry gave her a sulky glance. "You want something?"

We shook our heads. I jumped in. "No, but we were worried about Fitzgibbons, _and_ you. You doing okay? The police didn't treat you badly yesterday, did they?"

"Police are always slugs," Terry muttered. "But your

boyfriend, the cute one, he was okay."

I held back a giggle. "Uh huh. Terry has the nicest cottage on the lake, Dorie, near Mac's old house." I watched Terry's eyes cloud over.

"Not anymore," she said.

"Why, you moving?" Dorie asked.

The girl shrugged. "Police said I hafta. Mac's rent's only paid up to Friday, and the landlord wants me out."

Dorie's eyebrows shot up. "Are you planning to leave the Polo Grounds? Going home to England?"

"Don't want to. The manager, Ms. Hand, she wants me to stay on, take over some of Mac's duties."

"That'd be great." Still thinking of my piece for the newspaper, I wanted to question her about her background, how she came to be here in the States as Mac's assistant. But Dorie wasn't through with the topic of Terry's residence.

"But that's awful, kicking you out of your place. Who's the landlord there, do you know?"

"Yeah, some bank, I heard. 'First something.' Mac just always paid my rent for me as part of my salary. He always made out the checks." She was folding Fitzgibbons' blanket and pulled the folded parcel to her thin chest.

Dorine broke into a wide grin. "Wow."

"What?" I asked.

Terry looked up, interested. "Yeah, what?" she asked.

"I think I can help," Dorie said with a mischievous grin. "Hannah, do you have your cell?" I nodded. "Let me borrow it."

Terry pushed her limp hair out of her face and stared as I turned over the phone. Dorie backed away toward the front of the barn.

This time it was my turn to shrug. I asked Terry about Glenda Mane.

"She was Ms. Rutledge's old instructor. You know who she is? Seems to want her to come back to Rosemont and ride her horses when she's better."

Terry moved away and looked around Fitzgibbons's stall. "Darn," she said. "My regular shovel's gone. Disappeared since Fitzgibbons went off with the doc. Have to get me a new one from Ms. Hand." She began wordlessly setting up the horse to be turned out to pasture and ignored any future questions I asked.

Until Dorie returned and nudged me in the hip as she turned over the phone.

Terry eyed her and went back to fastening the horse's bridle.

"It's good news," Dorie said. "Terry, would you like to continue to live in your cottage at the lake?"

The girl glanced up sharply and shrugged again.

"Couldn't afford it, if I did."

"But how about if the landlord will let you stay there rent-free for six months, until you decide if you're staying or going?"

My eyes were probably as round as Terry's. The girl fastened Dorie with a cynical glare, then made a face saying it couldn't be possible.

"I mean it," Dorie said, coming closer and offering a little one-armed hug. Her enthusiasm was contagious. "I know the landlord, well, the wife of the landlord. Mrs. Warren," she explained to us both.

"But how?" Terry asked, beginning to be drawn into Dorie's excitement. "Why'd they do that for me?"

"Because Mrs. Warren's on the board here, and always tries to help out the stable. Josie Hand needs you to stay on, with fall and winter on us and lots of the helpers gone back to school, so they're making you this offer. Are you going to accept?"

This time Terry's face when she looked up at us was twisted with a mix of emotions neither Dorie nor I could identify, yet.

"Well, sure, yeah, if it's real. I can keep working here and living there, like starting now?" She pulled the leather straps up to her face and pressed the fists grasping them into her thin cheeks.

I gasped. "Dorie, that's fabulous." My grin triggered a faint one on Terry Bukowski's face, and Dorie whooped.

"See?" she said. "I told you I could help."

Terry clearly had to force herself to hold back from returning Dorie's earlier hug. Instead the girl turned and gazed up at Fitzgibbons, and softly stroked the gelding's mane.

"Thanks," she said softly. "No one's ever helped like that before, except Mac." Her voice caught on a barb of emotion and she twisted away as moisture formed in her eyes.

"You're welcome," Dorie said. "Later I'll give you this lady's number and if you need anything at the cottage, or have any questions, you can call her."

Terry nodded. "I have a cell phone," she said. "Mac made me get it in case he needed me."

I said that was great. Then pursued my earlier line of questioning, no doubt hoping for different results.

Terry answered right away. "Yeah, that Mane lady, she's the tall one, right?"

I nodded.

"She been here a few times, talking to Siggy, uh, Ms. Rutledge, after she'd ridden Gibby. I heard her say Siggy'd do better at her place, she had better horses. Siggy could win championships there. Siggy just laughed at her and didn't seem to take her seriously. But I saw her—"

She paused and Dorie and I moved closer, right under Gibby's nose, where Terry had begun organizing the bridle and its lead to walk him out.

Dorie touched Terry's arm as she worked. "It would help us to know about this, Terry. Might help us find Mac's, well, you know, how he died."

Terry stared at her boots for a moment, then looked up, her eyes darting everywhere but landing nowhere.

"I saw Ms. Mane's face. She was serious. She waited until Siggy left the stall one day and whacked her hand on the rail there, in front of Fitzgibbons. She said, 'Damn you,' and then she went out making a racket with her boot heels, even on the shavings." She nodded to the ground, waved the women away and opened Fitzgibbons' gate. "Turnin' him out now," she said, leading the horse out into the wide space at the center of the barn and toward the rear doors. "Thanks again."

I slapped Dorie on the back. "Brilliant, girl. You were brilliant," I whispered.

"Now we should go and visit Glenda Mane," Dorie said.

"Or I could call Bernie and tell him to—"

Dorie laughed as we swung out of the stable, arm-in-arm. "Sure can tell who's always on your mind."

I clapped an open hand across my mouth and tried in vain to keep the grin off my face. We climbed into my Volvo and called Theo at her office, putting it on speakerphone so we both could hear.

"I only have a second, someone's waiting for me," Theo said.

"We only need a second," Dorie answered, and I grinned at her new assertiveness. "Can you tell us where Rosemont Farm is? Hannah and I are doing a little stable tour this morning."

Theo's laugh was brief. "Yeah, I'll bet. Now don't you two go getting into any trouble. Be careful with that woman. Turns out she's not such a nice person after all. Anyhow, her place is down by the river in Torville. You can reach it by Route Five-sixty-six. I remember Wilson saying he rode that route so many times getting his girls back and forth to lessons he could do it blindfolded."

"Thanks, Thee," I added.. "Any news how Siggy's making out on the trip home?"

"They're on the way now. Poor Ada stumbled and nearly fell walking down the corridor, though. Her ortho doctor was in the vicinity and he absolutely ordered her to make an appointment and come see him. He's worried about that knee of hers. Now I've got to go. See you."

Dorie hung up, repeated the directions and bemoaned Ada's knee problem.

"That's all Ada needs," Dorie said, as I turned onto I-84 and eased into the traffic. "With a trip to England on the books."

"Yeah, England. That's right. Wow, is that funny or what?"

"What?" Dorie asked.

"My dad's leaving for Ireland soon."

"Well, that's bound to turn up the heat on those two."

I know I blushed.

"Oh, boy. Oh, boy." Dorie rocked in her seat with giggles.

It was my turn to ask "What?"

Dorine had suddenly grown very serious. "Do you realize, I'll be the only one without a man in my life by the time this case is over?" she sulked. "Even Lu's mother-law is sharing a room at Golden Haven now with her boyfriend Mr. Angelis, the two senior lovebirds."

"I'm happy for them. Love shouldn't end just 'cause you grow old."

Dorie sighed and ran a hand across her forehead and down both sides of her face. "But something tells me I have another problem besides an empty spot beside me on the sofa when the late show's on. I think that mental pause thing is starting for me, too."

"It's menopause, Dorine. C'mon, you know better."

"Let's face it, Hannah Doyle. You've seen what that thing has done to all of the Women on Fire. Lucia gets red in the face when she's cooking or eating. Agile Ada gets arthritis, and you exhibit that dazed, worn out look you get whenever you've been with Bernie doing who-knows–what the night before. Psychologically perfect Theo cries a lot, and law-abiding Meg's wild as a criminal breaking every law in the books to find her answers to things. We all go weaker in whatever our weakest area is. And for Dorine Boulé, who could deny it's going to be up here?"

She tapped her head, and knew she'd made the point when I leaned over the steering wheel choking on the laughter I refused to free from my throat.

Twelve

Lucia

Though the dining room was humming and I was about to toss some lightly battered oysters in my sauté pan, I had a hunch I'd better take this call. Tony said it was Ada, and her voice sounded weak and weepy. Not *our* Ada, Queen Ada, stalwart and in-charge Ada.

Yes, Tony said, the same. I lobbed a prayer heavenward as I slid the wide sauté pan off the burner, wiped my hands on my apron and took the house phone from my husband, who was sending me hopeful eyes and a grin of support as he backed away to the dining room.

"Ada," I said into the mouthpiece, "what's wrong?" I moved out of the line of fire of my sous chefs, salad makers and servers frenetically criss-crossing my gleaming kitchen at Lucia's Ristorante and snuck into a quiet corner by the delivery door. "Tell Mama."

Ada always teased me for filling in as everyone's mama, and doing a good job of it, too. I remembered

Ada's mom had died under tragic circumstances when her daughter was young and I welcomed every chance to mother her, even though we were the same age.

"Oh, Lucia. Have I caught you at a bad time? Are you busy?"

At high noon on a Thursday, most popular payday in West Parkford? Naw.

"Thank God I'm busy, dear, or we wouldn't put up with this daily grind on our feet and at the hot stoves. What's going on? You sound, I don't know, not yourself."

"I'm myself, which is a wreck, lately. At least I got Sigourney Rutledge home from the hospital, and she's doing better surrounded by her dog, cat and television set. I left her in her sister Shannon's care. Theo had left them lunch, a lovely Cobb salad with chicken."

"Did you eat?"

"No, I couldn't touch a bite. I'm heading home, but Lu, I don't want to go home. So many things are up in the air, unsettled, and I don't know what to worry about first."

I was sure I heard sniffles on the other end of the line. A delivery man barged in and hoisted some large meat parts toward the cooler with a nod. I scrambled out of the way. My assistant manager called out that he was busy putting out a small fire—oh, not a real fire, I knew what he meant, a customer totally dissatisfied, or a filet charred too much—and could someone else take care of the incoming orders. I wanted desperately to dash back and take charge, make everybody calm again, but the sound of my old friend's shaky voice turned me completely around and toward the door. I stepped outside and breathed in the crisp October air, felt the blessing of the sun on my face and nodded.

"Gotcha. Well, Mama Lucia is an expert on worrying, so suppose we spend some time together?"

"When, you mean tomorrow, or tonight, or something? I don't know."

I laughed. "Hey, I haven't abandoned the Women on Fire ship quite yet. No, I mean right now. You get yourself over here to the restaurant and I'll take my afternoon break with you and we'll have lunch together. We got some beautiful seafood in today. You're going to love the clams or the jumbo shrimp or something. What do you say?"

"I am hungry when you put it that way," Ada admitted.

"Then turn yourself east and come on. Tell Tony when you get here we'll take that little table in the corner by the bar. It'll be quiet as a dormouse over there in about twenty minutes when all the guys in shirts and ties get back to their offices. Meanwhile, I'll go fry oysters 'till I'm drooling."

Ada thanked me, and, as I'd predicted, twenty minutes later, we met up and exchanged hugs in a surprisingly quiet corner of the new bistro. I had Tony bring us some very chilled Pinot Grigio, and asked him to keep an eye on the mixed temperaments of the staff.

"More like an ear out, she means," he told Ada. "They speak about five different languages back there, and all of them want to be heard in his or her own. I don't know how Lucia handles our Babel."

I blew my husband a kiss and he trotted off for our orders. Ada had hardly cracked a smile.

"Wow, you really are on another planet when you don't succumb to my Tony's charms."

Ada took a huge gulp of her Pino and nodded. "But I was thinking how sweet he is. I'm so glad you two ironed things out last year and are like lovebirds again. Sorry I'm being so self-centered."

I put a hand on my BFF's trembling fingers wrapped around her wine glass. "Ada, look. We all have times when we need to minister to our selves, as Theo would say. You are simply taking care of business, important business that's clogging up the works so you can't be all you can be to the people you love. Now what's up?"

Ada sighed. "So many things I don't know where to begin. Not all bad, either." She drank another sip of wine, while I slugged mine.

"Okay, so why don't we start with any good stuff that's going on?" I watched a tiny smile try to break through on Ada's tense features. It crossed her lips but left the rest of her face anxious.

"That's it, dear. What you call the good thing, actually, the best thing, I can hardly talk about. I certainly can't tell Theo, she'd judge me. And you'll soon see why I can't tell Hannah. As for Dorie, she'd giggle, and Meg would stare me down and warn me about old-age dryness and all that clinical stuff."

I tipped my head to the side and studied my bud. This wasn't like Ada. She was usually bubbly with good news, practical with bad, and knew a dozen solutions for everybody's problems herself.

"Ada, what on earth? Is something going on with Fitzgibbons? What...?"

Ada was staring into her wine glass. She rotated it a little until the remains in the glass swirled 'round and 'round.

"He's just so fine, Lu. I can't resist him—" Her gaze left the wine glass and went far, far away. "Those eyes—I just melt. And the strength in his shoulders and legs. I never dreamed... I just absolutely go all wet and mushy when—"

I choked on my current swallow of Pinot Grigio.

"Omigod, you're not talking about the horse, are you?"

"...he's with me and I feel like a tender and beautiful flower opening wide to the sun." Ada sported the queen of blushes, and a bell rang in my mind.

"*Mama mia*! It's Devlin Doyle, isn't it? You have the hots for Devlin Doyle." I leaned so far forward I nearly slid off the chair. I drained my glass and waved to Tony to bring the bottle, while Ada's whole face bloomed into a smiling, sun-warmed sunflower. One, I suspected, that had been recently well-watered.

Tony brought a wine chiller with the rest of the Pinot and stepped away without a word at my hasty fingertip across my lips.

"He's really quite incredible, Lu. I don't know how he's remained single all these years since his wife's death. And for his age, quite, well, energetic. Ever so kind and solicitous of me. He's put up with my delaying tactics because I've been so preoccupied with all my other worries. But I just can't resist any longer. Do you think I'm mad?"

I laughed from my depths, drawing the attention of some late diners across the room. I pushed my face closer to Ada's and whispered. "Are you kidding? I think you're just finally catching up to yourself."

Ada poufed out a big breath. "We went to dinner last night, then dancing, even though my knee was throbbing, I couldn't resist. I'll tell you more about the knee later. Anyhow, we were the only couple on the floor most of the time. He wanted to come in for an Irish coffee, but Danny and Janet are there now. I don't know how they'd feel, having their old mom carousing..."

I poured Ada another generous glass of the white wine and poured a half-glass for myself. There were still dinner specials to prepare, and red sauce to make. I needed to stay on top of things.

"Besides, I feel I should still be in mourning. I am in mourning, Lucia. I want Mac's killer caught, to solve this mystery about why Fitzgibbons threw Sigourney, and what I'm going to do about his illness."

"Meg told me something about that. That there's a place in England?"

"Which is also good news, wonderful news. She's going to make arrangements for me to take Fitzgibbons there as soon as they can see him." A stutter caught her next word and she giggled like a girl. "That's another nice thing. Devlin's going to Ireland on assignment soon, and when I said I might be in England he said why don't we meet up and take a few days for ourselves? I know he means overnight days. I got the message when he touched my cheek and I felt myself melting inside."

Ada drank and pressed the cool glass to her cheeks for a moment. "I must be mad. I am mad. It's this damned menopause—" She looked up at me with a blank stare as if she hardly knew who or where she was. Her Fifth Avenue coifed and colored bob trembled when she did, and despite the premier botoxing she'd experienced more than once, the lines around Ada's eyes seemed more deeply imprinted. Even her fine sharp features with their perfect proportions seemed somehow twisted and out of whack.

I got up, went to her side and squeezed her in a no-nonsense hug, our cheeks touching.

"Ada, Ada, you're not mad." My whisper came out all husky. "You're in love. You're alive and in love!"

Ada stared back at me speechless. I almost chuckled. For the forty-plus years of our friendship, Ada had always needed to be right. Although I often bowed to the power she wielded with her very sharp mind, her millionaire status and her deep need to be in control after a shattered childhood, sometimes I had argued her to the wall to make an important point, or just to hold my own. My own childhood had had its rough spots, too, and no one could say I wasn't an independent and capable woman, with my own new restaurant, thanks to the support of my family and my own Herculean efforts.

But this time I wasn't even going to let Ada argue. I placed my work worn hands flat on the table, uncowed by

Ada's hoity-toity French manicure. "Enough of those wide eyes, m'dear. You're in love and it sounds like Devlin's head over heels, too. The evidence is in, and you of all people should know love like that cannot be stopped whatever our age. In fact, that love, and your nourishment from it, can get you through all the other problems you're worried about. You're a religious woman, Ada. Isn't there some Hebrew saying about not accepting God's gifts?"

She started to open her mouth, but I snapped, "Think about it," and waved to the waiter standing by, and we were suddenly inundated by a barrage of exquisite dishes—oysters on the half shell, fragrant steaming lobster bisque in stay-warm mugs, an arranged salad of Bibb lettuce, plump salmon-colored shrimp, vivid red chunks of roasted peppers, artichoke hearts and slender, oily, green beans. A basket of spicy foccaccias was placed in the center of our table and Ada nearly swooned at the array.

"There's dessert, too," Lucia said, "so save room. Now, *mangiare,* and while you eat, chew over what I said."

By the time our slivers of almond mocha mousse had disappeared and Tony had brought us steaming espressos, Ada had undergone a transformation. Sated, pleasured by the elegant little lunch I'd engineered, she sat back, tapped her lips with her linen napkin and sighed deeply.

"What can I say, Lucia? You've outdone yourself. And I realize you're right about Devlin. I will not procrastinate with him another day. He wants me, Lu. That is a gift, and the thing that's so amazing is he wants me for our sake, not his." She stirred a bit of sugar into her cup and sipped the drink with gusto. "But, oh, Lu, what will Hannah say?"

"She'll say she's a damn lucky woman to see her widowed dad find someone like you, at this or any age. Would you say Hannah's one to live on convention and what people think?"

Ada laughed. "Are you kidding, the way she smooches with that detective sweetheart of hers? I wouldn't be surprised to see them tie the knot one of these days, and him eight years younger than her, too."

I gave her an I told-you-so look over the rim of my cup.

"Okay, okay, and you're also right to say I'm up to it, a romance with dear Devlin. Mentally maybe I am. But the question is, am I physically? I nearly took a fall at the hospital today when I was picking up Siggy, and who's staring at me from down the hall but my orthopedic surgeon. He says I've got to take care of that knee, before it requires total replacement."

"And what's the problem with that? People are replacing joints every day, Ada Javitt. Half my friends are bionic women. You're no baby, go for it."

Ada tapped her fingers on the tablecloth. "I know I must do it, and I'll be the better for it, better dancer, better partner for Devlin. Maybe I could even ride Fitzgibbons again. It's just the timing, Lu. I want to get my horse to England quickly, see he gets some good years left to do what he loves to do. Racing, jumping."

"Can your doc do something temporarily, a shot or something, until you get back?"

Finally, Ada smiled. "I hadn't thought of that. Maybe that's why he wants to see me in his office on Monday. He'll do an x-ray..."

"And help you decide what your course of action will be."

"Right. Okay, I can handle that. Lu, you've been a big help." Ada drained her espresso and waved off an offer of more. She glanced at her watch.

"Relax, you're not going anywhere until you tell me what else is bothering you." I settled back, even though sounds from the kitchen echoed the first preparations of the afternoon for dinner, and they'd be hollering for me soon.

Ada nodded. "Are you sure? Don't you have to go pound veal cutlets or something?"

"Not 'till I'm through pounding you, sweetheart." We laughed together, and I could tell it was a relief for Ada. I realized with a pang I'd missed my friends because of putting so much time into Lucia's in the last six months. That would have to change. Life was too short, as I'd learned through the loss of my father this past year.

With a glance at her watch, Ada settled back a bit, too. "Honey, it's this accident Fitzgibbons had. I know Sigourney is going to get better. She'll start physical therapy soon and she can't wait to ride Gibby again. But when I think about what happened to Mac, I wonder if any of us are safe. Why was he killed? And would whoever did it try to hurt Sigourney, or that Terry who's still at the stable, or any of my friends who are helping?"

"Or even you, yourself? Are you safe, Ada?"

She shrugged her shoulders. "I'm more worried about, say, Meg, who's dug around at the horse barn, and is researching and arranging for me to take the horse to England. Or about Hannah and Dorie. Theo told me Dorie and Hannah were at the stables this morning to see what else they could find out, and now they're heading off to visit Glenda Mane, Siggy's old instructor, who's been bullying her to change stables."

"Wow, kind of insensitive of Ms. Mane to be doing that right now."

"Guess she's been doing it for a while. And yesterday Glenda threw Siggy for a loop by telling her about Mac's death. Theo and Wilson were hoping to keep it from her until they got her settled at home. Poor thing was hysterical when she heard. Theo had to close the shop and run to the hospital. And she'd asked everyone to keep quiet about Mac."

"I know. She told me to keep it quiet, too, though I haven't had a chance to see Siggy yet. Tomorrow afternoon I'll take my lunch hour to bring her something tasty. So, is this Mane woman dangerous, or just callous?"

Again, Ada shrugged. "I'm not even sure if Terry Bukowski is dangerous, but they have her working with Fitzgibbons again, now he's home from the vet's. Bernie hasn't reported in to me from the police for a while, though Hannah told me they didn't find anything much in Mac's house to point to a motive. I think it has to be someone from England, someone who knew him a long time ago and had to settle a score, as they say."

"Interesting thought. Do you know much about Mac's past?"

Ada folded her napkin and laid it across her dessert plate, then took out her lipstick and reapplied it. "I seem to recall something about him being in trouble with the Jockey Board or whatever they have in the UK. But he also had three very fine references, one from Gibby's owners, one from the stable where he worked last, and I forget where George said the other came from. I should look it up in George's old papers. I doubt the police have looked at that angle, as no one has asked me for any of those old documents."

Both of us rose together, and I encouraged Ada to keep on digging. She thanked me "from the bottom of my heart" for the wonderful lunch, and mostly for the wonderful talk, and told me to go manage my troops who were getting noisy in the kitchen.

I laughed. "I will. Do you know it's my favorite time of day, when the plans for the evening start to get fleshed out, and everybody's on edge, and excited, and throwing meatballs or something across the kitchen? Just like we used to at Pop's..."

I grew quiet, caught in a moment of sad reflection. My father had died less than a year ago, but not before he'd been swamped with photos and DVDs of the new *ristorante,* "Lucia Mia's," his dream for his daughter, and hers for herself and her family, come true.

I walked Ada to the door and planted a noisy kiss on each cheek. "Don't you worry about your Sherlock Holmes' friends. We'll all take care, if you will. And give Devlin a kiss for me."

"Fat chance," Ada said as she walked off, bearing a

crooked smile. "Only for myself." I stood watching as she stepped down the street. No wonder Devlin Doyle was taken with her. With her petite loveliness, slim hips and confident stride, Ada was perfect, and her expensive clothes just amplified her beauty. True, there was a slight limp in her walk today, but her back was straight as ever, her shoulders squared, and I had every hope love was about to brighten her unsettled world in every way.

I turned around to find Tony staring at me, and clearly thinking amiable thoughts himself about his own wife. I smiled a come-hither smile, and felt the old tingle of appreciation down my spine. What a relief to feel so loved after the upside down year we'd had, me thinking I was about to lose him. Instead, he'd given up his own business, everything, for me to open the restaurant I'd always dreamed of. Tony gave me a quick kiss on the lips and a pat on the backside as I passed him, and whispered something in my ear that kept me smiling all through dinner prep.

Thirteen

Hannah

I soon discovered Glenda Mane was even less hospitable than I expected. It was obvious that, when Mane heard our car, she'd come quickly out of her barn and swung the heavy doors shut behind her. It was a newish barn, a walk-through type, expensively made with fine siding and windows down each side at horse eye level, as well as light-casting curved windows high above the front doors. In the paddock, eight or ten horses were turned out, their coats shiny and thick, all looking well fed and well financed.

So I commented.

Dorie agreed. "But I have a feeling we're not exactly going to get much out of Ms. Mane."

The trainer took a few aggressive steps toward the Volvo, squaring her broad shoulders and adjusting her wide-brimmed Western hat. As she came closer, she frowned, and stared suspiciously at the two of us emerging from the front seat. She gestured first at Dorie.

"I know you. You were at the hospital with Mrs. Rutledge."

"Yes, I saw you there. I'm Dorie Boulé. Nice barn you have here."

"I worked hard to get it built. What do you want?"

"I'm Hannah Doyle," I said. I put my hand out and started to smile. Ms. Mane gave me a dismissive nod.

"Yeah, the one who works with the police and pokes into everybody's business."

"I beg your pardon," I snapped back. I was slightly distracted by a scent in the air, and it wasn't just horse leavings or hay, either. But more a purposeful scent, a sort of earthy sweetness I'd certainly never smelled near a stable. I pushed myself to pay attention. "I'm a friend of Sigourney Rutledge, for your information. I'm curious to know why you treated her so badly yesterday. And why you've been hounding her to come ride for you."

"She say that? Hey, she deserved to hear the truth about that so-called trainer of hers. A good friend looks out for you. Like I did for Siggy." The woman planted her hands on her hips and jutted her big chin forward. Something in the gesture shot up my adrenaline level. I kept an eye on Mane's hands and decided she didn't have a weapon, though her welcome left a whole lot to be desired in the friend-making department.

I stepped closer, trying to look my most ferocious. "Look, we're here to try and find out why Mrs. Javitt's horse threw Sigourney, and while we're at it, to check out anybody who might have a grudge against Mac

McClellan. You know anything that can help us?"

Mane's cheeks colored, and her chin seemed to grow and jut further forward. "Who the hell are you to be asking me any of that? You're not the police. Let them talk to me if they want information."

Dorie eased forward, her innocence shining in her limpid purple eyes. "No need to get upset, Glenda. We're all friends of Siggy and we're just trying to help. We know you taught her to ride, her and Shannon, and you did a great job. Would you mind showing us your horses?"

"Yeah," I said, "especially the one you've been asking Siggy to try out. A real champion, she said."

Mane wasn't accepting any softening up. And she wasn't about to show us anything. In one swift move, she drew a hay fork from a nearby hay wagon and stuck it firmly into the gravelly earth at her feet. "There's nothing for you here," the trainer said, looking Valkyrian in the pose. "Siggy can see the horse anytime she wants. Her so-called friends are not welcome."

Dorie eased backward, but I stayed put, feeling like I had a big one on the hook. My Irish temper was also up, and that made me stubborn as that Greek god who rolls that boulder up the hill for all eternity—Sisyphus, is it?

"What are you afraid of, Ms. Mane?" I tried again, hands on hips.

"I'll tell you what I'm afraid of. I'm afraid of two *civilians*"—she spat the word out and turned the fork upward one-hundred eighty degrees, its long curved and pointed tines facing us—"taking a quick tour of this very modern and well-equipped riding academy and having a terrible accident of their own."

I felt Dorie shiver, put a hand on my arm and draw me back toward the Volvo, but in my head I was making arrows out of every thought I could muster and sending them toward Glenda Mane. Once Dorie was safely inside the car, I stopped beside the driver's door and narrowed my eyes at the woman a dozen feet away. "You don't scare us, you brazen bully. But I feel sorry for the kids who are learning how to ride from you. I think we'd better pass the word around to the parents who use your services, Glenda. Your techniques have seen better days."

"Let's go, let's get out of here, Hannah," Dorie pleaded But I shushed her and took my time doing a two-point turn and cruising slowly down the driveway. In my rearview mirror, I saw the fury rise as more red blotches on Mane's face, and the hay fork trembling in her fist.

"Rosemont Farms, huh," I said. "I can't imagine a rose growing anywhere near that witch."

"What'll we do, Hannah? That woman's so mean she might have had something to do with Fitzgibbons' accident."

"Or worse. Look, Dorie, I've got to get in touch with Bernie and compare notes. I know he hates the fact we're running around trying to help on the case. He's afraid it'll look like we've scooped him, or something. But think about what we've learned in the last couple of days. Bernie ought to put these facts into the hopper."

"What's the hopper, Hannah?" Dorie asked. "I mean," she said, looking jittery again from my steely-eyed glance, "I agree we should catch Bernie up on everything, but where can we put it in a hopper? All the information. And how can we find out what he has in there already?"

"Hmmm. We passed a dairy bar on the way in. Let's stop for a bite to eat and make a list of what we've learned. Not necessarily key evidence or anything, but just brainstorm some stuff."

Dorie was thrilled with the idea. When it turned out the dairy bar had only ice cream, she wasn't disappointed either. Any day was a good day for a lunch of ice cream. We bought double cones, vanilla for Dorie, peanut butter chunk for me, and sat at a picnic table in the shade of a huge maple whose leaves were drifting down around us.

I pulled out a notebook and pen from the glove compartment and while we demolished our ice cream, we talked, and jotted.

"Well, we know what disease Fitzgibbons has, which could be why he fell, and Meg has found a place in England where they might be able to cure him," Dorie said. "That's the best news."

"Yes, as far as the horse is concerned. What about Siggy, though? She took an awfully hard fall."

"And her old riding teacher is not very nice. According to Terry Bukowski, she's been pressuring Siggy to change to her horse farm again." I made quick notes on the pad, doing a double lick on my ice cream to keep it from melting.

"Plus she upset Siggy by telling her about Mac's death when she was still awfully sick. What kind of friend does that?" Dorie smeared her face with vanilla ice cream as she considered further.

"And Terry Bukowski was kind of odd when I went with Bernie and Ketry to talk to her and check out Mac's house."

"Odd how?" Dorie asked, mopping her face before attacking the vanilla mound again.

"Well, for one thing, she almost left before the police talked to her, after having agreed to meet them."

"Did Bernie tell you what she said to them?"

I shook my head, then attacked my cone by whittling it down to a neat geometric spiral. "Ketry was with us, so I didn't want to pry, and I haven't talked to Bern since then. About the case, anyhow." Her eyes got misty. "I'll ask him tonight when we meet for dinner. But thinking about Terry, her hands were all red and rough that day, and she yelled ouch when I shook her hand, and she yanked it back and shook it. And she had on these nice new riding boots. But today she had on ugly old mucking boots."

Dorie nibbled on her cone. "But she said she had to clean out some of the slots—"

"Stalls," I corrected.

"And actually she wasn't very nice until I got Mrs. Warren to get her husband to let her live at the cabin free for six months. Oh, I forgot to tell her, she has to pay her own utilities."

"I'm sure she won't mind. She's very grateful for what you did."

"Which reminds me, I'm due at Warrens' at three for our sitting."

"I'll drop you off in plenty of time. Please thank her for all of us."

"Whatever." Dorie got quiet, serious about devouring her ice cream before it melted. After several minutes, a light came into her eyes. "Did you get to search the house, too? Mac's house, I mean?"

I chewed and swallowed before answering. "They wouldn't let me touch a thing, like papers, or the computer, or anything. All I saw was this calendar filled out with dates or something, probably Mac's schedule, a couple of books open to pages he must have been reading, and, oh yeah, this nice new jeans suit he must have bought, you know, jacket and pants? They were folded on a chair by the door."

Dorie paused in slurping down her cone. "Wait. You mean, like the dark blue denim with the white stitching, before they fade out and you break them in a little?"

I nodded. "Exactly." I was about to demolish the rest of my own ice cream when Dorie jumped up, plastered both her hands with vanilla ice cream and squeezed most of it into her mouth before she squeaked, "I know'th... ts... oot..."

"What?" I asked, laughing. "Dorine you're a mess, here have another napkin." While Dorine chewed and mopped up her hands and face, she was jumping up and down and nodding.

"What do you mean you know that suit?"

She stopped jiggling, crumpled all her napkins together and threw them up in the air.

"The new jeans, Hannah. I saw the very outfit, dark,

like brand new, jeans and jacket, and a pair of cool-looking hand-tooled brown leather boots. The day of the accident. I think we're talking about the same suit. I saw a guy, we all did, Ada and Danny and Janet and your father, too, at the doorway of the barn, keeping people out. That's how he was dressed. Hannah, were there boots with the denim outfit at Mac's house?"

I popped the bottom of my cone into my mouth and nearly choked, whooping as I got the point. "No, Dorine," I said as I swallowed. "Not there, not at Mac's, but across the lane, I saw the boots you're describing. Hand-tooled, medium brown, shiny new. I saw them on Terry Bukowski."

Dorie stooped to pick up her paper napkins and looked deflated. "Naw, these were large boots, on a guy. Terry's too little for these boots."

I grabbed my notebook and started writing again. "Cinderella factor, Dor," I said. "Who, then, was wearing those boots and the denim outfit when you first saw them at the barn?"

"A guy, I'm telling you, an average, medium-size guy. With sideburns and dark hair."

"Dorie, wait. Something is clicking in my head." I shut my eyes and sniffed, then popped my eyes wide open and laid my hands flat on the table. "Is it me, or did you notice that awful perfume Ms. Mane was wearing today?"

"Yeah, I noticed. Heavy, sort of spicy. Why?"

"Honey, I smelled that same smell at Mac's house. Maybe on the denim jacket and jeans lying on a chair."

Dorie shrugged. "I think it's Musk. It was popular in

the Seventies. Wasn't it called Musk?"

I nodded. "Let's check it out. You didn't smell that smell when you saw that sideburns person at the barn, did you?"

Dorie looked weary, tired of thinking about it. "No, we weren't that close. Just noticed the guy, helping out, keeping people away. An average sized guy, dark hair under a cowboy hat."

I gestured with a flick of my wrist for the two of us to get back in the car. Once I had the engine running, I turned my own peanut-butter smeared face to Dorine and said what I was thinking.

"Or a large, oversize woman, dark hair stuffed under a cowboy hat."

Dorie woo-hooed. The woman parking her toddler-filled station wagon beside us looked up sharply.

"Don't mind her," I said sweetly. "Sugar high. It's how she gets."

Fourteen

Meg

I called Arthur on my cell phone as I got closer to Ada's, where we were to meet in late afternoon.

"Is there a chance you could do frozen something tonight, old dear?" I asked, a bit of fatigue creeping into my voice.

"Why of course, Majidah. You sound tired."

"I haven't had a bite of lunch, so maybe we can eat early? Although I'm pulling up at Ada's now, and she'll probably smother me in snacks, which will keep me fine until I can get home to you, my darling."

Arthur laughed. "Take what you can get, Dr. Dautrey, and give me a call when you're heading home. I'll turn on the oven. And set up the CD player with some very acceptable Dvorzak. We'll relax this evening. Did you have a productive day?"

I laughed softly. "Productive but exhausting. There's more paperwork to getting a horse overseas than half a border country emigrating to the U. S. of A."

"I can imagine. Shots, quarantine, the whole thing, yes?"

"Exactly. Arthur, I've just pulled up in Ada's driveway. So be at ease until I call you, and then fire up the grill."

"Will do, sweet one. I'll be pruning my violets while I wait for my tulip."

"You, you poet, you," I cried, laughing. Who'd have ever thought the stodgy old university botanical researcher I'd met in my first months here in the States would have such a sensitive inner nature? I hung up the phone, hoisted my briefcase and went to Ada's door.

I found my friend propped on the sofa with plenty of pillows, right leg elevated and an actual box of bonbons by her side. "My God, woman! You're a cliché."

Ada laughed. "No steamy romance novel in my grip, though."

I harrumphed. "Probably have enough romantic fantasies in that head of yours these days to supplant that!"

Ada blushed.

Danny, who had come to open the door for me, offered me a snack and a drink.

"Janet and I are putting together some hors-d'oeuvres for the three of us. We have plenty."

"Don't tell me they're caviar and crackers, dear boy, or I'll go weak in the knees."

Danny laughed, nodding. "Exactly that, among other things Janet cooked up. Join Mom, then, it's rest time for her, too. I'll be right back."

"Aren't they wonderful?" Ada said, shifting to keep me in view as I collapsed into a matching loveseat across the creamy carpet. "Those kids are becoming very adept in the kitchen. Though I shouldn't be eating a thing after the lovely lunch Lucia treated me to at Lucia Mia's."

I reached over for the candy box and snatched it away. "Then grant me the leavings," I said, chuckling and picking out a couple of chocolates. "I haven't had a drop to eat since I left my house at 9 a.m. and I am famished."

"Oh, poor Meg. What a day you must have had. Was it awful going through all that red tape?"

"I'll live," I told her, knowing my too serious Slavic face would have Ada worried if I didn't stop exaggerating. "These chocolates are fantastic. But first, tell me, did Sigourney make it home all right? Any pain?"

Ada nodded. "She was in terrible pain by the time Shannon and I got her onto the couch in the den. She liked resting her back against the couch, though, said it helped, and Shannon gave her two of her pain pills before I left. Those girls are very responsible, Meggie. I like them so much. Though Siggy is still very angry at her father and Theo for not cluing her in about Mac's death."

"I don't blame her, but I do see their side of it. She's been through such a traumatic experience, and they didn't want to shake her up emotionally any sooner than they had to; your emotions can affect your rate of healing, y'know. Though I'm one for whom the bitter brutal truth always seems the best prescription. And I've paid for that, I suppose."

Ada reached a hand in my direction as if to console me. The Women on Fire had each heard a bit of my Bosnian horror story, the death of my family members, the bombings even of the hospital where I worked. They knew it still haunted me, and perhaps always would, but I resisted speaking of it almost always.

"Thank you so much for putting aside your own needs and doing this legwork for me, Meg. The doctor saw me today and wants me to have that knee surgery soon. But I have to get to England with Fitzgibbons first. That's tops on the list. So, when can we go? What did you find out?"

As I was about to start, Janet brought me a glass of chardonnay, and Danny set down a tray of appetizers on the coffee table between Ada and me.

Ada groaned. "I can't eat a bite, dears, I'm still stuffed from lunch, but they look wonderful." She sipped her already launched glass of wine and waited for me to snack.

"More for me." I whisked a caviar topped cracker into my mouth. "Luscious. You two will be joining Mrs. Catamonte in the business soon if I'm any judge."

"Naw," Danny said. "We're happy enough to have Mom's full refrigerator and see what we can do with the contents."

"Beats camp food like I'm used to," Janet said.

"And frozen everything, like I'm used to," I replied. The young people said they had their own tray and were taking it out in the yard where they could nibble while they tossed the puppy a Frisbee for a while. When they left, I sipped my wine and took up my report.

"Better," I said.

"So it was a hard day, Meggie?"

"No, actually it's been a good day. The best part is Amber Hill Equine Center is happy to take on Fitzgibbons's case. I called them first thing because of the time difference, which gave them time to call Dr. Ingmanson and verify the horse's condition. They compared notes. Bottom line is they're both confident Amber Hill's treatment for EIPH will benefit Fitzgibbons. It's very expensive, and there's no guarantee, of course..."

Ada beamed across the coffee table. "None needed. Just to know there's a chance for him. That they'll take him on. When, Meggie, when can they see him?"

"They're pretty busy, just finishing up with a Dutch Warmblood this week, and in two weeks they have another thoroughbred from northern England coming in, and they close down for the winter. But if we can meet the requirements for shipping a horse from here to the UK quickly, they'll take him by next weekend. They'd fly him to Amsterdam first, then box ship him across the channel by ferry."

"Nothing quicker, dear? How about the chunnel?"

"No live horses or cows allowed. But their route seems pretty efficient. From Dover it's an easy half-day transport to Devon, where they're located. They'll help make reservations for you and your party, if you wish, also. I have all the paperwork to explain to you." She pointed to the snacks "Will you..."

Ada declined. "But you go ahead, dear. You must be famished."

I munched for a few moments on cheese and grapes. Ada watched me, smiling affectionately.

"Do you remember when it all started in this very room, Meggie? All of us held at gunpoint except for you and Theo, and your ring on the doorbell sent that son-of-a-gun running."

I paused before my next big bite. "Seems we had a big snack of something delicious that day, too, after we got rid of the criminal."

"Some of us barely knew each other then. I don't think Dorie had met Theo, and you hardly knew Lucia yet. I'm so grateful for all your friendships. And to think it all started because some of us were fed up with hot flashes and memory lapses..."

"Insomnia, dry skin and loss of interest in, well, you know..."

"Thank Yahweh, that symptom's gone!"

"Ada Javitt! You have something going on you haven't told me yet. Though I have my suspicions"

Ada blushed a deeper shade of crimson. "Back to us girls, Meg. Do you realize we've become like a sisterhood?"

"A sisterhood that does plenty of eating, talking and solving of mysteries. Though I don't think we have a clue on this one yet, on Mac's death I mean."

The ring of the doorbell and a rush of someone into the room brought us to high alert.

"Hannah!" we both said at once.

The slender, frosted blond in the red faux suede jacket hurried forward, accompanied by her own verbal drum roll, and headed for the snacks. "Mmm, delicious. Caviar after ice cream." She reached for the delicacy after pecking Ada on the cheek

"Sounds like you at least had lunch," I whined, returning to the snack tray for another look. "Uncover any criminals?"

Hannah planted her feet in the middle of the plush carpet, nodding vigorously and pointing to her mouth. She finally swallowed. "Possibly. Plus counseled a family of four through some pretty tough stuff at Mary-Martha, God bless them. They have an inner strength I know will get them through."

Ada was excited enough to sit up from her reclining position and drop her ice pack on the floor. "Wonderful. Now do you think you found out something important, Hannah? Tell us, Oh, please tell us, I can't bear the idea of some wicked man out there perhaps about to hurt another friend."

Hannah was coy. We knew her act and waited patiently while she pirouetted, popped a grape or two in her mouth and pulled up a slipper chair to join us.

"How about some wicked woman, Ada? Or maybe even two?"

Fifteen

Ada

I couldn't stop trembling. So much to consider, so much happening so fast!

Both women had left, Meg home to Arthur who had supper waiting, and Hannah to prepare for a rendezvous with Bernie when he got off work. She'd tell him everything the women had learned and ask him to fill in any blanks. They'd call me later. Meanwhile I ate a light supper with the young people on the back porch; they were stuffed, too, from the elegant hors-d'oeuvres they'd put together, and then I had Janet bring down my aqua pants suit so I wouldn't have to do the stairs.

Once changed, I took a much-needed pain pill and went to the den supposedly to study the documents Meg had delivered but more likely to ponder my options learned on this worrisome, but invigorating day. Fitzgibbons would need blood tests, a series of shots, the long, rigorous journey, and then a short period of quarantine before he was accepted at Amber Hill. Meg had said they could make arrangements for me and my party to be housed. But who would be in my party, I wondered.

With my knee so pained, I'd surely need some help getting around. How I'd love it if all the Women on Fire could join me in Devon. Maybe some of them could. Hardly Lucia, who wasn't well-enough established at "Lucia Mia's" yet to leave and delegate management. And how could Theo desert her ailing stepdaughter who needed all that therapy and driving to and fro?

Dorie had just started with a new client, and they were so few and far between, but perhaps Meg could get away, and maybe Hannah. They were both so competent, I'd really prefer them, though Hannah was not likely to agree to fly for five or six hours. And it would take days on a liner. She was in a definite panic on a plane, even though she'd made it now to both Florida and then California, once to save Dorie's life, and then to see her new baby grandson, accompanied by the sturdy and sexy detective. Maybe Dorie, who was such fun to be with, could get time off, but Theo, so emotionally solid, and such a fearless traveler I could hardly ask. I remembered last year when Theo had accompanied Lu to Italy, just dropping everything for our friend. And then Lu coming home to help solve that awful death at Golden Haven Healthcare and getting back together so happily with Tony.

I wondered what else my friends and I could do to help solve Mac's murder, here and now. Did Glenda Mane really have something to do with it? I still suspected

Terry, or perhaps some stranger from England with a score to settle with Mac.

Once we got to England to put Fitzgibbons in this rehab facility, would the others left behind continue to unravel the case? I counted on them. And I hoped and prayed the treatment for my thoroughbred would work, and he'd be his old self once again, or better. Maybe if I got my knee fixed, I could ride once more, too. The thought was delicious..

Or perhaps I'm getting too old. A twinge in my kneecap answered yes, maybe I am. But the more optimistic part of me snapped to attention. Hadn't I just read the United States was sending its oldest ever Equestrian team to the Olympics? I'd read the names and their ages, and all but one of the athletes were in their forties and fifties—even late fifties. One was a youngster, thirty-three, if I remembered correctly.

But then again, memory hadn't been one of my strong points all through this malicious old menopause.

As I relaxed in my recliner, I let my eyes drift closed. I was thinking back to the days when my second husband George had Fitzgibbons sent home. Maybe it was a last ditch effort to save our marriage, after all his partying around town, and it had helped keep me with him until he died from a heart attack a short time later.

I had gone out and bridled Gibby every day, sometimes turning him out, or walking him, and then after George's death I'd begun to ride him two or three times a week. The fluid motion of his body, the silky feel of his neck, the whinnies and jostling he gave me when I tried to turn him toward home and he wanted more. I would never forget those days. Then as my depression settled in—menopause mixed with grief, the doctor said—those rides with Fitzgibbons were the saving graces of my weeks.

I could almost feel him under me as I remembered the rhythm of his canter, the lazy way he'd meander toward the barn when I insisted we'd had enough, or I had, anyway.

The phone jangled me to wakefulness. I reached for it, knowing Dan and his girlfriend had gone off to the college library.

"Ada? I've been thinking of you, and damn it, I can't work with you on my mind."

I gulped, popped my eyes open wide.

"Devlin. You're calling from Vermont?"

"Right. The publisher I came up to see wants me to put together a proposal and I'm having a devilish time concentrating."

"Oh, sorry, Devlin. I hate to say it, but it comes with age."

"Damned if it does. It comes from caring too much about someone, and letting your feelings go all over hell."

I nearly choked. He was as much as saying he loved me, "caring too much," he'd said. Me, a widow twice in my life, a year or two away from Medicare, and this darling man is saying his world is affected by his feelings for me!

"Are you there, my lovely Ms. Javitt?"

"I am, and I'm touched by your words," I said haltingly. "But I should tell you I'm not so sharp this evening. I took a pain pill for my knee a while ago and

I'm practically drifting off where I recline."

Devlin chuckled. "Does the pill make it better?"

"It does, and so does your call. I thought this might be the first day we didn't have a phone conversation since the accident at the Polo Grounds. By the way, your daughter and our Dorie are hot on the trail of a couple of suspects for the crime. Hannah's passing on the word to Detective Cascone tonight. And Meg made the arrangements for us to take my horse to England pronto. So even if my doctor insists on surgery, I'm going to insist he wait until I return."

Devlin cleared his throat. "Not a good idea if you're suffering so much, Ada."

"I can take it. Honestly, the pain's not that bad, though I may have to use a cane. Ooh, Devlin, won't you be embarrassed to be seen with an old woman with a cane?" I tittered.

His voice deepened. "As a matter of fact, I'll get one for myself, so we'll be a matching pair. I would be thrilled to escort you anywhere at any time, Ada Javitt, cane, walker or roller skates. I also wouldn't mind staying home with you anytime, if you'll have me."

I felt a tug deep inside and rocked a little in my chair, liking the sensation.

Devlin cleared his throat, and there was some sort of message in it. "In fact, I'll be home this weekend, and I know for a fact Hannah is going up to Boston to see her youngest in some sort of show up there. He's a singer, you know. So I'll have my place to myself. I could put together a little repast for us on Saturday evening. What do you think?"

I didn't know what to think. I was feeling plenty of clues from my body, wishing Devlin were here at this very moment to hold me, stroke me where I hurt, and elsewhere. Remind me of how much a woman I still am, arthritis and all, a woman very much alive...

"But aren't you flying out soon?" It helped contain my feelings to be practical.

"Mm hmm. Sunday night I'm off to Ireland. But I have to tell you I'm planning to curtail my long distance assignments from here on."

"You should, it's too hard on you, traveling all the time."

"I didn't mean that, Ada. I mean I want to stick around wherever you are. I want to get to know you through and through. I want to be closer to you. Very close. I want..." I could almost see him shake his head and correct himself. "No, that's too much about what I want. What do you want, my dear? That's why I called, really. What do you want of me, a gray-haired, old working stiff who's been collecting from Medicare for years."

Your love, your strength, your body, your breath mingling with mine, darling Devlin, I wanted to say. But I'd been raised to be a lady, with poise and discretion, and I couldn't throw it all away on a physical impulse now.

"Ada?" Devlin said. His voice was husky, earnest. He wasn't joking. He cared, he'd said so.

I smiled drowsily into the phone, wishing he could see me, could read my mind. My eyes grew heavy, and in that moment just before sleep comes when your will weakens and everything seems a dream, I answered simply.

"You."

Silence wrapped us around. A soothing, loving silence.

"What next?" I asked myself soon after, as I practically crawled up the stairs to my bed.

Sixteen

Hannah

It would have hurt me less if Bernie hadn't laughed maniacally when I told him what Dorie and I suspected about Mac's murder.

"That little wisp of a girl overcoming Mac and stringing him up? There isn't a thing we've learned about Terry or from the guy in England we have working with us that would remotely give her a motive to do in her boss. She was grateful to him, he gave her a place to live. C'mon, honey. Be real."

He'd laughed so hard the other patrons of The Steak Barn craned their necks to see who in booth number sixteen was having such a wild time.

"Oh, shush, Bernard Cascone," I said, using my newly validated grandmotherly tone for emphasis. "You're not listening. I didn't say Terry Bukowski could have killed Mac on her own. But she did say sometimes he was mean to her. How mean, I don't know. But you should follow that up. Besides, he didn't give her the place to live, he took the rental out of her salary. It's only because Dorine is painting the wife of the bank president who manages the property that she's still in there, and for free this time."

"You women do get around," he answered before he bit into another roll.

"I'm just worried we shouldn't have helped her hang around the Polo Grounds, Bernie. And working so closely with Fitzgibbons. She may not be the innocent she seems."

"Hannah, have you looked at the girl? She probably weighs ninety-five pounds soaking wet. She's petite, she's bashful."

"And you're naïve. You don't think small, bashful people ever committed murder?" My voice had risen and I made an effort to keep it down by popping a chunk of buttered roll into my mouth. Though that didn't entirely stop the flow of my entreaty.

"Suppose there was another person, even another woman, a big, strong woman, and they conspired together to string Mac up after knocking him unconscious, as you say." She pouted while he sipped his red wine and pondered my idea.

"And this woman would be who?"

It scared me that Bernie didn't seem to be in a joking mood anymore. His lips had tightened, and the frown, dug into his forehead from years of chasing bad guys and suffering life's ills himself, deepened.

I studied my own wine and sipped it, than patted my

lips dry. "That's what I wanted to report to you, officially, as police business."

"I'm listening," he said, but he was so focused on frosting his roll with butter he seemed to forget I was there.

I rolled my eyeballs and breathed deeply. "Okay. Now wait 'til you hear this. We learned from Terry, and it was later confirmed by Theo, that Sigourney's former instructor is trying to get her back to her stables, and away from Fitzgibbons. I don't know why. Maybe she just admires Siggy's riding. Or maybe she has other motives we don't know yet. I still think it's worth..."

"Are you speaking of Glenda Mane out at Rosemont?"

I nodded. "How did you know?"

"She phoned the house today. Made an official complaint about two whacko women who were harassing her about her business with Siggy Rutledge. Wanted to be sure you weren't working on behalf of the police. I said you were not, and she said in that case she would keep on guard, in case you returned. I checked, and, Hannah, she has a licensed firearm. If I didn't know better, I'd think she was threatening you."

I shivered. "There! There you go. See? Meek little Dorie and helpless little me harassing her? We were just asking why she'd been harassing Siggy. As to threatening, she's the one who poked a great big sharp hay fork at us, Bern. Scared Dorie half to death. If she's not guilty of anything, why was she so adamant about closing her barn up tight when we got there, and not letting us look around?"

"You weren't the police, Hannah. You had no right. See, it's things like that you and your Women on Fire get everybody all irritated about. She's a private citizen, and she has a right to privacy. She also said you threatened to phone all her clients and malign her. You know that's a prosecutable offense."

I sputtered, trying to put together a response while the waiter placed our sizzling steaks before us and served our sides. Shaking his head, Bernie lifted his steak knife and was about to dig in when I put a hand on his and the knife dropped to the table.

"Hey," he said, startled. "What?"

"Not if what we tell them is true, Bernie. And I think it is. I don't know for sure why, but I think this very tall, very strong, broad-shouldered woman might have, could have, dressed up in men's clothes and kept people out of the barn just before Mac McClellan met his early death."

We both held our breath, equally startled at the ramifications of what I'd said. Before Bernie started shaking his head again, I hurried on. "You need to check her out. And you need to check out the suit of denim clothing that was lying on a chair in McClellan's living room the other day."

"Check it how and why, Hannah, my sweet? You think it'll have fingerprints, blood?"

"You never know. But I can almost guarantee it'll have Musk perfume still permeating the fabric. That's definitely the scent Glenda Mane wears, and plenty of it. Dorie and I smelled it to high heaven, and stopped by the perfume counter at Macy's to verify the brand. Promise me you'll look into it. Please."

When he wouldn't look up at me, I let out a big sigh and picked up my own knife and fork. I was about to cut into my T-bone when Bernie rubbed a hand across his frowning face. My dear, sexy, clearly hungry Bernie, aggravated to death with me.

"The hell I'll promise anything," he said. "You're not running the police, Hannah Doyle. You can run me all you want—run my social life, my wardrobe, run me around town dining with you, meeting your pals, checking out the boudoirs in your place or mine—that especially—or run me down in the street, if you want—as long as it's nothing to do with solving my cases. Now eat your steak."

An inner shock wave of queasiness stilled me where I sat. I tapped my feet on the floor and shifted in my seat. I thought I had lost my appetite. But as Bernie enthusiastically pursued his own grilled meat and vegetables, I kept eating, maybe out of an instinct for survival. In between bites I thought of a way to pursue my interest in Glenda Mane.

"You know I'm writing a piece on equine life in the area for *The Courant*, don 't you, Bern?" I asked after a swallow. "We could say I'm interviewing you for that and minimize the murder thing. But surely knowing more about Rosemont Farm would be relevant to my piece. I mean, it's either you or Ketry who get to fill my feedbag. What do you say?"

"I'll pass," Bernie muttered with a mouthful of salad, looking vulnerable as greens poked out from his teeth and tomato juices and olive oil dribbled down his chin.

I could barely control a chuckle, but at the same instant realized how much I had fallen in love with the local detective. I wanted to kiss away his dribbles, feed him from my hot and trembling fingers. I couldn't imagine a life without him anymore.

Then I thought of Mac McClellan's body lying in the sawdust, the ropes that had possibly quenched his life heaped around him. I thought of Ada, wrecked by her horse's near demise, and Siggy Rutledge's dangerous fall.

I didn't want to lose Bernie's affection, but Dad always said I was a risk-taker. "But I need to know tomorrow—I'm leaving for Boston on Saturday, you know, for my son's concert."

Bernie washed down his steak with a hearty gulp of Valpolicello.

"Have a wonderful time," he said, and his face closed down on his own thoughts.

"Damn you," I muttered as I speared another hunk of medium rare beef, then glared at my dark and handsome stud-bud across from me. I've never known a more stubborn guy, I thought as I chewed. But then, he hadn't seen the strange, ominous looks—different from one another, but ominous still—in the eyes of Terry Butkowski and Glenda Mane. I had.

Bernie might hate me by the time the night was over, but I wasn't giving up, not yet.

Seventeen

Ada

I swung the Town Car as close to the barn as possible. No point walking extra yards if I didn't have to. Besides, it might rain before the morning was out. I yanked my cane from the back seat and hobbled across the lawn and then the gravel walkways toward the doors, remembering with a shudder this was the first time I'd been here alone since before the accident. My knee twinged as I stepped up on the ramp to enter the barn and I muttered to myself, "How strange I should feel as nearly physically battered and affected by that awful day as poor Sigourney and poor Fitzgibbons must have felt. It's like my body, too, is reacting to the horror of it."

I limped down the quiet center aisle of the huge stable amid some soft nickerings and snortings of the horses, most of whom had not yet been turned out, no doubt because of the chancy weather. When, because of prior commitments, none of the other Women on Fire could make the morning inspection with me, I decided going alone to the Polo Grounds was but one more opportunity to prove I was still capable, and thus, could make the trip to England. Vulnerable as I felt tottering along through the sawdust by myself, I had to admit doing this was a moot point: I had to get moving on my own. Without my independence I'd feel half-dead.

Halfway down the alley, I paused for breath and to rest my knee. Some stable hands were mucking out stalls and a couple of owners were currying their animals, giving off that earthy, woody and warm-animal smell I'd learned to attach to my Fitzgibbons. We waved to one another.

Suddenly enthused, eager to see his progress, I hurried on, feeling at the same time for the pair of apples in my canvas jacket pocket. I approached Gibby's stall with a smile and heard him nicker a gentle greeting. But my smile turned to a big question-mark frown when I found half his feed in the bottom of his bucket.

"What? Not finishing your breakfast? What's wrong, Gibby-boy?" I looked around for Terry Bukowski who ought to be looking after such details, and spotted her returning from the wash and tack room. I hailed her with a wave and the slender young woman hoisted the load of rags and towels against her chest and hurried over.

"Terry, what's going on with Fitzgibbons? Is he off his feed? I should have been told." I felt a panicked fury rising up in me. The horse was sick, he had a special diet, why wasn't someone looking after him?

Terry craned her neck to look into the feed bin and tossed her unkempt hanks of hair.

"He finished up yesterday's allotment, Ms. Javitt. I think with a lower level of exercise he just in't hungry as before. I been busy with chores Ms. Hand gave me and hadn't got to him yet this morning."

"That's pretty obvious," I said. I thought of retorting with the details of how much I paid for my horse to get first class care, but instead picked at some dried leaf bits and grass on Gibby's coat and bit my tongue. "You planning to turn him out?"

Terry studied the bundle of laundry in her arms and shook her head. "Rain coming. But I'll walk him here, in the indoor ring, ma'am. Just let me put this stuff away and I'll work him out."

I shook my head. Fitzgibbons had poked his neck forward and was trying to nestle his head close to my pockets. I roughed up the fur between his ears and stroked his neck.

"Thanks, but no," I said. "I'll brush and clean him first. Myself."

Terry stared at my cane, then glanced quickly at my face and looked away.

"You sure, Ms. Javitt? I don't mind. I can do that, too, in a bit. I need to poke out his hooves, too. The ground was a bit damp when he was out yesterday."

I shook my head again. "Go do your other chores. I'll get him started. You check on how much he was given today and make sure it's the right amount. I've got to build him up before we take him to England and leaving his feed won't do it."

Terry started to back away. "You shipping him over to Amsterdam and then England?" she asked.

I nodded.

"You be needing a helper to travel with him?"

I stopped in the middle of opening Gibby's door and turned back to the girl. "Why, are you interested in making the trip?"

It was Terry's turn to shake her head. "Not especially so, ma'am, unless you can work it out with Ms. Hand. She needs me here, I think."

"I'd have thought you'd welcome a trip home."

Terry's face seemed to blanch in the gray light of the day. "No, ma'am. I'm all set here for now. One of your friends got my place paid up, and Ms. Hand's paying me okay, too. Unless you need me real bad, I'd rather stay."

I shrugged and turned back to the work ahead of me. Mac, I thought, would have wanted to be by Fitzgibbons' side every minute of such a long, harrowing trip. Shaking my head, and trying to keep my balance, I brushed and curried Fitzgibbons from all sides until his coat shone as it had on the Sunday he was injured. He nickered softly throughout, cherishing the attention. I had taken the hoof pick from the wall, and was about to begin cleaning his feet, when Terry returned, seeming in a hurry.

"No, don't you mess yourself up, ma'am. I'll get that. I do it nearly every day, just missed yesterday is all."

She appeared so nervous, I backed away, letting her squat by Gibby's right front foot, facing the back of the stall, and watched as the girl began picking out the debris and soil caught in the grooves there. She worked unstintingly, and I was impressed. Maybe she was not such a bad assistant trainer after all.

Meanwhile, I continued to brush Fitzgibbons gently, loathe to walk away when the horse's warmth and vigor was so comforting. I felt a tenderness for him I could barely express. If anything bad happened, on the trip over, maybe, or while there, I'd never forgive myself.

Terry seemed about to move to the next foot, and was suddenly distracted by someone coming down the alley with a heavy step. From the back of the stall I couldn't quite see who it was, but someone definitely stopped beside Terry at the front of the stall, though I heard no conversation.

"I'll get the other side, Terry," I said, taking the pick from her and squatting down with my backside braced against the sidewall. But before I could even lift Fitzgibbons's left rear leg, I collapsed into a sitting position, and yelped softly in pain.

"Mrs. J? You all right?" Terry called, trying to see around the bulk of the thoroughbred. I tried to laugh, and I swear Gibby snorted in laughter himself, but I was having trouble pulling myself up to standing.

As I struggled to stand, retrieving my butt from the bedding, I saw that between Gibby's legs the person standing by Terry had moved, spun around and was heading back down the alley.

"Who's there, Terry?" I called when I finally regained my footing and inched toward the front of the stall.

"No one," Terry said. But I made it to the stall opening by the horse's long, finely sculpted head and leaned out of the stall for a good look toward the doors. I saw the large, square person hurrying off and heard their boots clomping hard on the stable floor.

"What do you mean, no one?" I demanded.

Terry's face was white, and yet she seemed to force herself to shrug nonchalantly. "Just looking for someone, I guess."

I wasn't taking that evasion for an answer. Though my knee by now was screeching pain, I staggered to the doorway just in time to see a large pick-up truck begin to move from the entrance.

"What on earth..." For an instant, as I stood there trembling against the barn door frame, I shook my head. "I'm just being crazy," I muttered aloud. "Why should I feel so frightened?"

Then I realized there might well be reason to fear the strange visitor. For a second I strained to read the license plate numbers as the vehicle peeled away, then realized I didn't have to do that.

The name on the truck's side told me all I had to know: inscribed in neat italics across the door in gold paint, highlighted in red were the words, "Rosemont Farms Equine Center, G. Mane, Proprietor."

~ * ~

Hannah was at my door when I got home, and gave me a bit of a hand to get into the house. I was embarrassed and still trembling, but tried not to show it. I asked her to make us some coffee and sat in the kitchen while she did. Sancho jumped up on my lap for some stroking, and I welcomed him with his velvety hair. Just then I realized I'd never fed Fitzgibbons his apples, and I'd left my canvas coat in the stall. No loss. I'd go back tomorrow and retrieve it, and have another talk with Terry

Bukowski. Why had the girl lied to me, I wondered, saying she didn't know who had stopped at Gibby's stall to speak with her? And why was she so hesitant to travel with Fitzgibbons for a visit to her home?

I told Hannah all about it when she poured our mugs full and got the creamer from the refrigerator. We sat together, me with my leg resting on another chair.

"Huh! This is getting really serious, Ade," Hannah answered. "I don't like the idea of Glenda Mane anywhere near Fitzgibbons. And I'm a little leery of that meek little whippet of a girl, Terry."

"Who acted a bit strange today herself. Didn't want to accompany Fitzgibbons on the trip overseas. But anyhow, I don't think it was Glenda, Hannah. Looked more like a man to me, though I only saw him from behind and a quick profile shot as he drove away.

Hannah was silent for minute and I could almost see her phenomenal brain clicking away. "Okay, but did the guy remind you of anyone you've seen before? At the stables, I mean?"

It was my turn to pause. "Well, maybe the build and the cowboy type hat, though the clothing was different and there wasn't as much hair around the ears, no sideburns I guess..." My voice drifted off, because I just plain didn't know what to think.

"So you're saying the driver of the Rosemont truck looked like—"

A light flashed in my head and our voices joined up and spoke the same words in a rush: "The guy in denim!"

Hannah clucked. "That's what Dorie and I are trying

to tell the police—because of her size and craggy facial features, Glenda Mane could perhaps disguise herself as a man, and we think she did, and we think..."

A jolt of recognition made my voice hoarse. "If that man in denim were her, she stayed when we left, she kept the people out. Oh my, *she* may have been the one to kill Mac. Oh, Zeus. How awful. What's she doing hanging around my horse? And that poor little Terry?"

"Remains to be seen if Terry is so poor and little, after all," Hannah said.

I gulped. "Hannah, look. I've got to get on the phone to Josie Hand who manages the stables. I'm going to see if I can hire a security person to make sure that woman doesn't come near my horse again." She handed me her ever-present cell phone and I dialed the stables.

"Great idea. Tony Catamonte can help you with that, Ade. He still has friends in the business. He'd know the best people to call."

I muttered, "Thanks," and was so distracted I was about to hang up.

"Hey!" Hannah said, and my hand on the receiver paused. "Talk to Josie!"

I nodded, feeling panicked. Here I was forgetting important details again, like at the peak of my "'pause."

Hannah grinned and patted my knee. "It's okay. Also, I just wanted to remind you I'm heading off to Boston in the morning, dear. I won't be home until Sunday, just in time to drive Dad to Bradley."

Like I don't know that, I thought, waiting for Josie to pick up the phone. "But won't you and your sweetie pie be missing one another too much?"

Hannah made a scoffing noise. "I doubt he'll be missing me. Probably relieved to get me out of his hair for a while." Hannah still sounded snappy and unbothered by her ongoing argument with Bernie, but I felt certain if I listened to my journalist friend any longer, I might hear some sadness—or even worry—creeping into her blithe voice.

I knew how I'd feel if it were Devlin who was angry with me.

Josie Hand answered my call and I explained my concerns without mentioning names. I said I'd be sending a security man every evening. She agreed with "no problem," and when I hung up, my gutsy girlfriend was looking for her cigarettes in her big purse.

"Oh, Hannah," I said, "do try to make up with Bernie. You know he loves you. Somehow we have to make Detective Cascone understand we mean no harm in our efforts to solve Mac's murder, we just want to help, and help before anyone else is hurt."

There was a soughing sound in Hannah's throat. She stopped looking for her Carletons and I knew I'd touched a chord.

"Thanks," Hannah said in a little girl voice. "Meanwhile, you be very careful. Hang out with Dan and Janet when you can and, and go somewhere, do something, don't be alone over the weekend."

"Oh," I said, with a low chuckle, "don't worry about me. I'll be," I gulped "just fine." *You'll never know how fine, or just where I'll be and with whom. And what I might be doing.* My stomach flip-flopped as I tried to blink away the image of myself in Hannah's father's bed.

I cleared my throat noisily and forced myself to drink my coffee. And shift to another topic.

"Oh, and Hannah, when you're back, say, Monday lunchtime? I'd like to have a meeting of Women on Fire, all of us, to help plan the trip to England, and figure out where we are with the case."

Hannah agreed. "Good idea. I'll call Lucia and ask her to host it at the *Ristorante*. You'll be done with your surgeon's appointment by then, right? And you can give us a full update."

When she'd left, I thought of calling the rest of the Women on Fire, but decided that could wait. First I had to call Lucia's husband Tony about a security guard. Then I needed lunch, a pain pill, and maybe a stretch on the couch to ease my leg. Later I'd plan my activities for the next day: a little shopping to buy a tasteful gift for Devlin, appointments for having my hair done and, of course, a facial. Maybe a full body massage.

I tried to picture myself heading up to Devlin's apartment tomorrow evening for our "date," but the thought made my heart race in an unpleasant way. If only I felt worthy. If only my damned knee didn't ache so continuously I felt like an aged train wreck. "If only," I burst out aloud, "I hadn't landed on my backside in the stall today, and run like a maniac through the barn to further irritate my arthritis."

Sancho leapt off my lap and tilted his head to study me. Feeling a bit forlorn, I chuckled.

Maybe I should call the whole thing off. It was a

fiasco, anyhow. Imagine, romance at our ages. Then the sight of Devlin sparked before my eyes, his warm and sincere smile, his strong arms reaching out to hold me, the scent of him—clean clothes and fresh, piney air—and I simply crumpled back on the kitchen chair again.

No, Ada, my inner voice said. Don't be a wimp and go back on what you've committed to. Take what you can, and give back what you can. Live. You told Lucia you would. Hell, you told yourself. Don't say no again. Be good to yourself.

I breathed deeply and rose, putting nearly all my weight on my left leg. "Half good, anyway," I mumbled aloud.

When I called Tony, he was quick to recommend two fellows still on the job and said he'd make the arrangements. Grateful, I hobbled to the kitchen and poked around for leftovers.

"That's me," I said aloud to Ramon and Sancho, who were my only company, "I'm nothing but leftovers, and for such a brilliant, charming, virile man, it's just not right."

Sancho leaned against my legs and from the living room Ramon squawked, "Not right," at the top of his croaky, inhuman voice. "Not right."

"Don't remind me," I scolded, then sighed as two little tears of remorse slid down my cheeks. No, it wasn't right and I could not do it. Who was I kidding? I'd have to call it off. I couldn't go to bed and reveal my aging tush to Devlin Doyle. I'd call him tonight and lose him forever.

Eighteen

Theo

I brought the three girls hot chocolate and a plate of the biscotti Lucia had brought for Sigourney the day before. Imagine Lu taking the time from her full-time duties at the restaurant to spend an hour visiting with them. But today's visitor was not such a consolation.

I would not leave my daughters alone with their particular guest, so I hunkered down at the far end of the family room organizing magazines, DVDs and board games while Siggy, Shannon and Charity Finch sipped cocoa and talked about everyday things: who'd win *American Idol*, what current movies they wanted to see, and what schools Shannon and Charity planned to apply to. I wasn't exactly in spy mode, but Siggy's emotions were so tender right now, I wanted to protect her, make certain she was okay visiting with her eventing rival. When talk turned to horses, Shannon excused herself to study for a history exam, and I wandered away to get myself a second cup of coffee.

Returning, I heard Siggy say she had been surprised to hear from Charity.

"It's nice of you to... well, drop by. I guess I should congratulate you on winning last week." Siggy's voice was soft, strained, Theo thought. That must have been hard for my step daughter to say.

From a corner of the room where I couldn't be seen, I paused and ran my fingers along the books lined up in the built-in cases.

"S-sorry I didn't get to see you ride." I stiffened when I heard Siggy's voice go muffled with tears.

Charity's light, girlish voice, on the other hand, got choppy like light surf on Long Island Sound. "No, no, you couldn't of, and I don't deserve congratulating. I mean, it was yours, it should have been yours to win, Sigourney. Everyone knows you're a better rider, and Fitzgibbons, wow, he's just—"

She stopped short and at that point Theo heard sniffles, maybe from both girls. Finally she heard Sigourney respond, her voice shaky. "No, you did great from what I hear. It wasn't your fault Gibby had that spill." She laughed awkwardly. "At least I get to legally miss classes for a couple of weeks."

"I'm... Sigourney, I'm just so glad it wasn't worse. For you or your horse. I heard they're taking him to England to get rehabbed?"

Silence. Theo hoped Charity didn't take her daughter any more deeply into the details of the tragedy, or she'd have to come break it up and change the subject. Siggy muttered something, and Charity went on, her voice renewed and stronger than before.

"We tried to get in to see him after, my dad and me, but some guy wouldn't let us in. And then we heard about Mac. How horrible. He was nice. I think I'd have liked him as a trainer for me, too, eventually. But Fitzgibbons, Fitzgibbons was the best."

Theo could tell Siggy was trying to change the subject; it still hurt her so much to talk about the accident. But Charity was on a roll.

"My dad says if we could get a horse like Fitzgibbons, I could be a champion, too. Well, I don't mean like you. You're way better. But a better horse would, you know, help me. That's why Dad keeps asking Mrs. Javitt who she bought him from. He wants to go to England and shop for a better horse for me. I'm really too tall for my pony, now, and she can't learn new stuff as easily anymore."

The room was as still as a cloister. Charity nattered on.

"Dad says he'd kill for a horse like yours. Also, we're kind of worried about who's sneaking around the barn now. Afraid someone might hurt my pony or me or whatever."

I heard Sigourney take a deep breath. "Then maybe you should change to Rosemont. I hear Glenda's looking for new riders."

"Oh." Charity sounded confused. "I... we... never thought of that. Dad said the fall was a lucky break for me, getting me the blue ribbon and all, and now people will take notice of me as an up and coming rider. Oh, crap, I shouldn't have said..."

More silence.

Charity giggled uncomfortably. "Do the police know, I mean are there any suspects?" she asked. "Gee, it's like a murder mystery on TV."

When I heard Siggy whimper, I knew she'd had enough. I burst back into the main part of the family room.

"You girls want more cookies, or cocoa?"

There were negative responses though neither one had touched the biscotti. I swept them up with the half-emptied mugs and smiled at our visitor. "It was so nice of you to come, Charity. But I make Siggy take a rest at this time every day, so..."

Charity got the hint. She nodded and stood. "Oh, sorry. Hope I didn't tire you out. I better go. I'll wait for my dad outside."

Siggy muttered her thanks and lay back on the couch pillows, managing a grateful smile as I walked Charity toward the door.

When I opened the door and saw the Finch's SUV parked close by, I was a little startled. I waved to the man in the front seat who gave a nod of his head, and then watched his daughter climb into the vehicle.

I closed the door soundly behind me and went back to perch on the sofa with wan, pale Sigourney, her eyes red-rimmed with distress, her hair tumbling over her forehead. I leaned across, pushed my stepdaughter's hair from her eyes and gently rubbed her bandaged shoulder.

"I think she meant well, hon."

Sigourney nodded. "But if any of my other friends want to come and see me, tell them I'm too sick. Except Janet and Dan. At least they have a heart and don't keep drilling me about the details. I'm scared of Gibby going to England, all the things that could happen, I'm... scared of everything right now."

"It's okay, Fitzgibbons will be okay, hon. And so will you. Just going to take time." Theo nodded and patted her uninjured arm. "I think Charity has some heart, but it hasn't had much opportunity to grow being shadowed by that nasty, one-track minded father of hers."

As I cleaned up the cocoa things, I wondered just how serious Charity's claim might be. Was her father so desperate to get his daughter a better horse? Would he really "kill"? Maybe Detective Cascone ought to hear what Charity had said. Just in case.

Nineteen

Ada

The lunchtime bustle at Lucia Mia's had barely begun at eleven-forty-five a.m., but as I strolled in I saw a flurry of activity mostly revolved around the large circular table being fussed over by wait staff at one end of the dining room. Lu was supervising the placement of water, flowers, and a healthy basket of *foccaccia* bread, her chef's hat and apron abandoned in the kitchen.

We hugged, Lu beaming. "It looks fabulous, Lucia. I'm hungrier just seeing this beautiful table. And look at the chrysanthemums in that rich, red color!"

"Hey," Lu said, in that husky Italian alto she reserved for such moments, "when the boss eats, it better taste great and look good, too!"

"I'm so glad you could take time from your busy lunch hour."

Lu waved her friend's comment aside. "Ah, Mondays are no big deal. Never a full house. And having all my beautiful friends in here gracing the premises will only make people want to come back more and more. Besides, what's going on with you? You're absolutely glowing. Good news at the doctor's?"

I cleared my throat, trying not to blush. There was no way anybody was going to hear the details of my night with Devlin Doyle. I would keep it as a precious secret like a locket hidden near my heart.

"Yes, Doctor Hardy is brilliant. I can hardly wait to tell you." I eased into the chair Lu indicated. Almost immediately the others started to arrive and I was thankful I didn't have to expand on the reasons for my giddy smile and trembling hands.

First came Theo and Meg, chatting seriously as they approached, Meg in her fuchsia pillbox and a slimming gray sheath dress with bolero jacket, and Theo vibrant in her South American poncho over slender black pants, bright red and yellow jungle birds dangling at her ears.

By the time they were seated, Hannah and Dorie, the ones Lucia called the babies because they were a few years younger than the rest of us, came strolling in, Hannah, street-smart in a tawny new-look pants suit with a gorgeous pendant in amber and gold setting off her streaked, bobbed hair under her stylish green beret. Dorie, as usual, looked like she was about to fly away at any second, with her lavender silk two piece dress with handkerchief hems and long, breezy panels at the waist. The purple depths in her eyes were highlighted by the modest amethysts she wore at her ears, and draped around her neck was the fabulous pink boa she'd bought for our special Women on Fire meetings.

Dorie noticed my state of relative undress immediately. "Your hunting cap, Ada. Have you forgotten it?"

Ada tapped the top of her head. "Oh, darn. I didn't want to wear it into the doctor's office, and now I've gone and left it in the car." I shuffled in my purse for the car keys and started to rise.

Dorie popped back up. "No, no, our queen. Let me go and get it for you." She snatched the keys and ran out giggling.

"While she's gone," Lucia said, I'll just go change my shoes and we'll be officially in order." The others laughed, and watched Lu slip off her chef's coat, to reveal a stunning cherry red tunic accented with jet beads. It looked sharp, even with her checkered chef's pants.

"Wait until she returns with those luscious red Manolo Blahniks she wears for meetings," I warned. "I'll have to give up center stage for sure."

"Never, Ade," Hannah snapped. "Lu may be 'da boss' but you 'da queen.'"

I spluttered into my water glass. *Yeah, queen of the boudoir—if they only knew.*

Laughing, the other women toasted me with their water glasses. Tony Catamonte interrupted, held up a just-opened bottle of something amber, cold and sparkly, and poured. "Orders from headquarters," he said.

Meg opined this must be pretty tame work for Tony, who had enjoyed being the president of an up and coming security company before the opening of "Lucia Mia's."

He put an extra head on Meg's glass and chuckled. "Are you kidding? Those road trips and sales calls and paperwork can't compare with being around my Lucia all day. There's never a dull moment, and always a great glass of wine or plate of fettuccine to try out."

"Good for you, Tony," Theo said. "I wish Wilson and I had more time together."

I grabbed Tony's hand as he filled my glass. "Thank you, Tony, for the security recommendations. I haven't heard anything, so I assume all's quiet."

"We spoke last night, Ada," Tony said. "Your hired guard enjoyed spending the weekend around the stables. Watching the riders, the workouts, etc. I told him it would get quiet during the week, but he's happy with the job. Has another fellow spelling him late nights."

We both watched Dorie nearly trip her way through the restaurant bearing my Day-Glo orange hunting hat with the silk camellia pinned to the side. Just seeing it made me, and probably everyone else, recall the urgent business that had sent me to Alaska a couple of years back on the trail of a killer. It was a sobering, but hopeful sight.

I placed the hat on my head, not nearly as careful of my hairdo as usual, and observed Lucia come toddling toward us in her stiletto-heeled sandals. She sat, as well, threw her husband a kiss and asked him to have the servers start the meal.

Lu leaned forward to announce, "I've arranged for everything to be served family style, so you can pick what you like best to eat. The menu is on those little cards by your wine glass."

"Oh, my dear, you've fussed too much," I said, glancing at the delectable items on the calligraphied cards. "We shouldn't have had this meeting here when you're so busy."

"Nonsense," Lu said. "I may have to excuse myself once or twice to tend to some culinary crisis, but if you hadn't met here, I couldn't have been with you at all."

Theo held up her glass of bubbly. "Then I think it's a fabulous decision made by all of us. Here's to Hannah for suggesting it, Ada for calling it and Lucia for hosting it."

"And to all of us for being here," Dorie interjected as they drank and giggled at the bubbles rising up to their noses. "Cheers."

"Cheers!" five voices echoed, just as the waiters brought the platters of antipasto, brilliantly colored with vivid red roasted peppers, huge glistening green olives, creamy yellow and white cheeses, and more.

"Cheers again!" someone said. "To the cooks!" The meal, and the meeting, had begun.

"What's first on the agenda?" Meg asked. "I for one am dying to know how you made out at the doctor's."

"Oh, Meg," Hannah teased. "You're always so—medical."

"No, no," Theo interrupted. "She's right. Ada's health is our top concern at this crucial moment. What did he say?"

I put down my fork and pressed my napkin to my chin. "Well, I suspect he's a miracle worker. He said I need to have the surgery for sure. There's not a bit of cartilage left to cushion my bones in that knee. But he has no problem waiting a month for surgery, if I can tolerate the pain."

"Can you?" Dorie asked, popping a rolled-up slice of salami into her pretty, usually pouty mouth.

"Absolutely. He gave me an injection this morning that has already taken away at least half the pain. I'm amazed. And he said he'd give me an additional one just before I leave for England, if I like."

"Perfect," Lucia proclaimed. She'd finally finished filling her salad plate with mushrooms, eggplant, provolone and hot capicola. "That's a relief, hon."

We munched while we wondered what would be discussed next.

Meg, who had made all the arrangements with the English Equine Center, was most anxious of anyone for details. "What date shall I tell them at Amber Hill, then, Ada? It has to be finished by mid-November when they close for the winter. Do we have a timeline yet?" She reached for the foccaccia and tore off a piece to enjoy with her pickled vegetables and *sopressotta*.

For one second I held my fork in midair, trying to concentrate with all this delectable food overwhelming us. "I suppose that's one of the main reasons I needed to talk with you all. Planning the trip is my goal today. Except for us all sharing the progress in the case of Mac's murder. We definitely need to fill one another in on what each of us knows about that."

Hannah spoke with half a mouthful, her mind always ruminating on the case. "Good idea, Ada. I'll start. Does everyone know Dorie and I met up with Glenda Mane, and because of her very negative attitude toward us—"

"She wouldn't even let us look in her barn," Dorie interjected. "Slammed the door right on us, and poked at us with a legal-looking hay fork." She popped an olive into her mouth and snapped her lips closed to mimic the effect of the slammed doors.

"Lethal-looking, you mean, Dor," Lucia said.

"Yes, and it was sharp, too."

Hannah sipped her bubbly, grinned and continued. "Anyway, her attitude toward us, and her size, which to say the least is manly, and her—"

"Smell," Dorine popped up again. "Musk perfume. Overpowering. She must bathe in it. And, after a day of mulling it over, I remembered smelling that very scent when this so-called guy was keeping people out of the barn after the accident You know what a great sensor I am with smells and such."

I toyed with a luscious, tangy eggplant relish and nodded. Dorie was highly gifted in the five senses, though slightly under par in language skills. We loved her as she was. "And to think I was grateful for that person's involvement that day."

Theo covered her mouth with her napkin, then sat back trying not to jump on this news. "So you really think Glenda Mane, the one who hurt Sigourney so with her tattling of what had happened to Mac, might be his... killer?"

"No one said no yet," Hannah retorted, and poked in the platter for the tiny curled up anchovies, her favorites, as the others burst out with uncontrolled exclamations.

Dorie blushed. "Ooh, are we too loud, Lucia?"

The restaurant had begun to fill with customers, but Lucia shook her head. "Not at all. You should hear some of these tables when they've all had refills of wine or beer." She glanced up, saw someone enter the restaurant and gave a little wave. "Oops, my appointment is early. I'll excuse myself and get back before the pasta, I promise." She wiped her hands on her napkin and stood to straighten her beautiful tunic.

We watched her hurry off as well as she could in those spikes, and continued passing the antipasto platter while we chatted.

Theo took up where she had left off. "But somehow I can't believe Glenda could have pulled that off. Don't go shrugging your petite shoulders like you've already convicted her, Ada. Why on earth would she?"

"No, no, I'm not at all sure she's guilty. But maybe because she *is* trying to get Siggy back to Rosemont."

Theo bit off half of a spicy Tuscan pepper and shook her head. "I can't imagine why she'd be so desperate to do that. Siggy's good, but not great enough to kill for, for heaven's sake. By the way, did I tell everyone Charity Finch came to see Sig? She offered her condolences and left a bouquet of flowers. But said a couple of funny things."

Hannah looked up wide-eyed and placed her fork on the table. "I hadn't heard. What exactly did she say?"

"That her father still wants to know where Ada's husband bought Fitzgibbons. He'd kill, she said, to have such a fine horse. And that in itself could make Charity a champion."

Meg made a non-verbal throat-scraping sound. "How crude and tasteless. What a thing to say to someone who almost gave her own life..."

Dorie jumped in, a piece of *foccaccia* covered in strips of scarlet roasted peppers in her long, delicate fingers. "Did she mean really kill, or just a, what do you call it, speech of figure?"

"Ha!" said Hannah, forgetting her plate in her excitement, "that's the big question. You've never given Gus Finch the information he wants then, Ada?"

I shook my head and swallowed a tasty morsel of sharp, salty cheese. "I don't even know the answer to it until I look it up in George's papers. And anyway, why would I want to help such a nasty man?"

Theo nodded. "Don't tell him, ever," she advised. "I don't trust that man as far as I could throw him. Do you know he didn't even ask after Siggy when I met him at the door of my house delivering his daughter? And Charity seemed, well, nervous, like she'd been sent to third-degree Siggy, and couldn't wait to get out of there."

"Detective Cascone should know this," Meg said, using her napkin on lips and hands.

Theo nodded. "I called him on Saturday afternoon. He was very interested. Said he was swamped with leads, and was checking out the new security guards at the Polo Grounds Stables first."

I jumped in. "What? Why? Tony helped me set that up, after I saw that vicious Mane woman there trying to talk with Terry Bukowski. You know, I can't figure that young girl out. I asked if she'd like to assist with

Fitzgibbons on the way over to England and she said no, thanks. Said she's needed at the stables. And also said, by the way, she had no idea who Glenda Mane was."

"Not what she told us after Dorie saved her cabin," Hannah snapped.

"You'd think she'd welcome a vacation home," Dorie mused. Taking seconds on firm, oil covered artichoke hearts, she cooed, "Ooh, these are yummy."

"Save room for pasta and what all else Lucia has planned." Meg glanced at her menu card and hooted. "Like tiramisu at the end. Whoa. I can't believe it." She patted her waistline.

Theo laughed. "Forget the diet today, Meggie. You're looking great with your new exercise program."

"Arthur and I are both watching our cholesterol and waistlines," the laconic Meg replied, pushing away her plate. Yesterday he suggested we have leftovers for dinner and not bother with a big meal. The dear's really trying to learn to cook and keep up the kitchen for me, but I swear the cold pizza he tried to serve me yesterday looked like a forgotten scientific experiment."

Theo patted Meg's hand on the table. "Then eat, dear, eat. This will be a small glitch in your overall progress."

Hannah had finished chewing, and pushed her salad plate away as the waiters approached. She had clearly been thinking something over. Now at last, the plates and platter cleared, she spoke.

"There's kind of big glitch in my progress with Detective Cascone, too," she said. Her green eyes seemed more moist and greener than ever underneath the retired army beret she wore.

"Oh, no, Hannah, what?" I asked. "Because of our snooping into the case?"

Hannah lifted her shoulders up around her ears and slowly released them.

"Maybe. Or maybe I'm just too intense for him. He doesn't seem to get it, that I'm worried about my friends, and hurting for them. For you, Theo, with your injured child, and for you, Ada, with all this trouble over Fitzgibbons, and then Mac's death."

"And for all of us, 'cuz somebody's still out there maybe waiting to kill again," Dorie blurted.

We nodded as one, and I shivered. "You mean, this weekend away in Boston was really a break in your relationship?"

Hannah gave a short nod. "Not meant to be, it was just time for me to go to one of Kevin's concerts. It was lovely, he's such a great kid. I don't know where he gets that voice." She crossed her legs and glanced at her purse on the floor and I knew my friend was longing to light up a cigarette. "But it's kind of working out that way. We haven't spoken since last Thursday."

A mournful hush came over the table, just as Lucia returned, looking as joyful as a second-grader on the last day of school.

"What?" she said. "Did somebody die?" She studied each face at the table, but all eyes were on the centerpiece. She reached out and poked at the flowers. "Something hidden in there? What on earth has happened?"

Dorie couldn't restrain herself. "Bernie and Hannah..."

Lucia grinned, probably thinking it was time for a big announcement, an engagement, or a live-together plan or something. But the faces of her friends said "Not."

She eyed Hannah. "True?"

Hannah seemed to shrink into herself. "Maybe. We may grow through this. But I'm not going to be someone other than myself, though. I can't be who or what he wants me to be and let this case go."

Inwardly, I cringed. How could Hannah be so blasé about possibly losing the love of her life? Since I'd just cemented my own relationship with Devlin, I couldn't picture ever walking away from him. In fact, although he'd only been gone a day, I already missed him horribly. I closed my eyes to picture his neat, sculpted face framed in thick silvery hair, and almost felt his arms around me.

I felt a tremor go through my body where it met the fine, upholstered seat of the restaurant chair that made my eyes pop open.

Theo had leaned forward, a pleading look on her face as she pinned Hannah with her urgency. "Honey, I know you feel a responsibility for Ada and Siggy and all, but maybe if you could be just a little less intense. He loves you so much, Hannah. Anybody can see."

Lucia started to argue with her. "Being passionate about something is how Hannah lives, it's who she is. Bernie's got to love her for *that*." The whole group joined in with opinions, and Hannah's face broke into such rapid changes of expression it was like the looks of the television screen when the digital picture is breaking into waves of tiny squares.

I reached across Dorie and touched Hannah's arm. "She doesn't want to hear anymore, right?"

Hannah nodded, lips pressed together, eyes watery.

"Besides, here comes the pasta," Lu said. "And the special sausage we make here, and the broccoli rabe dish, and the eggplant parmesan."

I smiled at Lu's bright, proud face. "Okay, then,' I decreed, "let's leave Hannah alone."

"Wait," Hannah said. "Thank you everyone for your compassion, your ideas. I already have a plan to get through this, and if Ada will agree, it just may work."

I know my eyebrows raised and mouth gaped open. What now? "Anything, Hannah dear. What can I do?"

Hannah tucked her napkin onto her lap as the waitstaff moved away and the women paused in the passing of the serving bowls. She breathed deeply and resettled her beret on her head.

"Take me to England, Ada. Let me help with Fitzgibbons over there and get out of Bernie's hair for the moment."

There was a rush of breath being sucked in around the table. "Hannah," Theo chimed, "you'll fly?"

She had turned a little pale, but Hannah snatched the sausage platter from Dorie and served herself as she said as nonchalantly as she could, "You better believe it."

I nodded and grinned, beside myself with joy. "Of course, of course. I'd hoped..."

"But Afghanistan," Meg reminded her. "You won't

fly there for that fabulous assignment."

"Don't go there, Meggie," Theo warned, passing her friend the pasta to keep her quiet.

Hannah shook her head. "No, it's okay. I was thinking I might do that, too. Set it up while I'm in England, then fly there when Ada and Fitzgibbons go home."

"Wow," someone said, and was answered by Lucia's "*Fantastico.*"

Then they all held up their glasses and toasted Hannah this time.

Twenty

Hannah

I was happy to burrow in my pasta—we had our choice of *fettuccini* in a lightened *carbonara* sauce, or *putanesca*, which Dorie and I selected while asking for the translation of the term. When Lu told us it was an ancient recipe the street women of Rome concocted out of whatever was on hand when one of their "clients" grew hungry after "partying," we could hardly keep from chuckling.

"Wow, Rome," Dorie said. "I've never been across the ocean. I wish I could come to England. But I could never afford it." She twirled her noodles disconsolately.

"I plan to raid my 401K to make the trip," Meg announced. "If you'll have me." She leveled a look at Ada as she scooped up some of the broccoli raab. "I'll be with you, kiddo. I'll handle all the housing details, if you like. Just give me dates."

"No reason I can't handle the housing reservations

and flights. I am the resident travel agent, even though I can't be on the trip." Theo let sauce dribble on her chin for one flinty-eyed glance at Meg, then wiped at her face with her napkin.

I swabbed the red sauce of the eggplant parmesan from my lips and reached out hands to both Meg and Dorie, then waved two hands to Theo across the table.

Ada looked like she'd burst. "You're all dears to offer. "And of course there'll be no expense for you. Unless you want to buy souvenirs. I'll pay for plane fare, lodging and dining for anyone who accompanies me and Fitzgibbons. The more the merrier. And Meg, why don't you handle Fitzgibbons' transport and let Theo do the housing for us women, but do pass on to her everything you have from the Equine Center."

Meg chewed unceremoniously while nodding, but Dorie made happy, wordless noises. "Wow, thanks, Ade. You know I'll do anything I can to help, even brush down your horse every day."

I chuckled. "You won't have to do that, Dorine. Meg says the shipping people will have someone aboard to care for Fitzgibbons. But are you sure Mrs. Warren won't mind you putting off her portrait?"

"Oh, I won't have to put it off. I'll just work extra hard on it now. She won't mind taking extra sittings, as she's very worried about your Fitzgibbons getting his rehabilitation. She'd do anything to help."

"Perfecto," Lucia said. "As exciting as it is, sometimes I wish I didn't have the millstone of this restaurant around my neck." She glanced up at the door and excused herself again. "Sorry for the interruption. This should be the last one." Lu walked up to a young woman striding toward her and guided her into the bar area where they chatted.

"I hate to see Lucia call this place a millstone. It's absolutely perfect, and what she always dreamed of," Theo said. "We all just need to remind her to take sufficient time off. Everyone needs to relax and recreate for good mental and physical health."

"Yes, Doctor Phil," Meg teased.

But Theo wasn't laughing. "Seriously. Even the children we counsel at the Mary-Martha Center often need to be reminded they must have time to play, have fun, relax, so they can handle their serious moments better. Right, Hannah?"

I nodded vigorously, mouth too full to speak, so Theo went on.

"Ada, I so wish I could come with you all. But I just can't leave Sigourney..."

Ada paused in forking up her *carbonara* to shake her head, "Don't you worry one bit about it, Thee. I understand completely. I wouldn't leave my child either. And soon you'll be bringing her to therapy every other day—"

"And protecting her from possible suspects," Dorie said. "You need to take care, Theo. She's been through enough."

Theo nodded.

"Besides," Meg said, "with four of us gone, you're going to have to keep tabs on the police and make sure that pain-in-the-arse detective friend of Hannah's keeps on the job."

Everyone agreed. Ada practically inhaled her last bite of eggplant parmesan and sat back to relax after putting down her fork. I noted she seemed almost giddy. Was it from being sated with a fine meal, or thrilled that three of her friends would accompany her to England? Or had something mischievous gone on over the weekend involving my paternal parent?

Suddenly the music of "Hello Dolly!" rang out and Ada went scrambling into her purse. She snapped open the cover of her cell phone and answered. Her face went white, then dark with shock, or anger or something we couldn't decipher.

"I don't believe it. Okay, okay. Here's what to do. Call my lawyer... And I'll be there in half an hour." She snapped the phone shut and dropped it into her bag.

Alarm prickled in the air like a lightning strike.

"Ada, what?" Dorie asked.

"Our favorite detective friend," Ada growled. "He's been questioning Danny and Janet in the parking lot at the college. Now he's asked them to come down to police headquarters to make official statements. I'm furious!"

I clapped a hand to my chest. "I don't believe it. Bernie's questioning the kids?"

"But why on earth?" Meg asked.

"What is wrong with that man?" Theo shook her head mournfully. "He should be talking with Gus Finch, or Glenda Mane or somebody nasty. Does he suspect them of something or what?"

Ada was mumbling in disbelief. "Says they were witnesses to almost everything from the get-go, and it would help him get a clearer picture—other than the one all 'those women' have been presenting. Wait until I talk to his boss."

I leaned across the table. "Oh, don't do that, Ada. Please. Let's see what Bernie wants exactly from the young people before we go blaming him for something. I'm sorry Danny and Janet have to go through it, but at least it shows Bernie's not leaving a stone unturned."

Ada shook her head. "But they're upset, Hannah. Janet says she's fine, but Danny's almost crying every time he retells the story of the accident and about me passing out and all of that."

"Poor kids," Dorie moaned. "I can't believe nice guy Detective Cascone is doing that."

Suddenly something made Ada squint toward the restaurant's large windows, crinkle her eyes, and tap Dorie on the arm. "Tell Hannah, without being too obvious about it, that particular 'nice guy' is standing outside the restaurant staring in, with his hand on the door handle."

Everyone at the table jumped and twisted around in their seats, except me. Instead I rose nonchalantly, and placed my napkin across my clean silverware. "I plan to be back for tiramisu," I said as I turned away.

"Better take your purse, Han," Meg called out, tossing it to her. "You may be about to be arrested."

Dorie tittered, but everyone else was quiet. Again Lucia returned to a morgue-like atmosphere. I could hear my friends explaining to Lu in snatches of conversation. I heard Lu tell them not to worry. They'd feel better after dessert and coffee.

I grinned. I felt strangely imperturbable as I marched to the front door, straightening my beret as I went. He was here, he was looking for me. That was a good sign.

Maybe. My stomach did a double flip.

Outside, Bernie asked if we could speak. I opened my purse, took out a cigarette and, with a twisted grin of defiance, lighted it.

Bernie choked on the first flow of smoke. "I thought you quit them."

"You thought wrong. Now what can I do for you, Detective?" I tried to keep a smirk off my face, but he caught it and I was surprised to see him grin back at me, light from the noonday sun sparkling in his eyes and turning the soft brown to amber. As for my heart, it was hopeless. I let it palpitate until my eyes had soaked in enough of his broad shoulders, his crooked nose, tender mouth and broad forehead trying hard now to form a scowl.

I wondered idly how he'd look when he'd turned sixty-five. I was willing to bet he'd still be a heartbreaker, to me, anyway. Depending on how things turned out.

"I'm, uh, getting statements from Dan Javitts and his girl. You know, a kind of objective look at the accident at the Polo Grounds and some of the stuff that went on afterwards. I didn't want anyone to worry they're suspects or anything." He ran a fist across his mouth, as if wishing he had something better to do with it than speak. His eyes never left mine.

"Well, people are worrying. And insulted that you don't think any of us are capable of objectivity. And also wondering why you haven't got Gus Finch on a short leash, or Glenda Mane being checked for DNA. There's still the matter of blood samples under McClellan's fingernails. Am I right? You have some likely candidates." I took a deep drag on the cigarette, coughed and deposited the butt on the sidewalk where I crushed it with my shoe.

Bernie nodded. "I interviewed Mane yesterday. She's in a snit, says she has friends in the governor's office and is going to have my ass for supper because she had to leave her horses unattended for a couple of hours."

"And?"

"She admits she was at the Grounds when the accident happened, but cleared out with her two horses and their riders soon after Fitzgibbons' fall. Everyone was too rattled to compete after that, she said."

"You got names? DNA samples?"

Bernie's face twisted in some sort of mix of emotions. He skittered to the left and then the right like a worked up stallion and finally put his hands on my arms. I felt myself tense. My friends staring out the restaurant window would surely think we were about to make up. But close up, I could tell Bernie was definitely not growing more affectionate.

"Don't do that, sweetheart. Don't check up on my police work. See, that's what I hate. I don't need someone looking over my shoulder. They have police brass getting paid to do that downtown."

I let myself go limp in his grip. I even eased closer to the warm body that loomed over mine. And I smiled.

He wasn't finished. That busy slash of a manly mouth kept going.

"I mean, I like that you're interested in what I do, but we have more than that, more than these screwy cases your gang keeps getting involved in. Look, let's take a couple days off together and go look at the foliage in Vermont or something this weekend. I have time coming. We can forget..."

"No," I said, "but thanks. I can't forget—anything. I'll be getting completely out of your hair for a while anyhow, maybe as early as this weekend."

"Why?" His eyes darkened, smothering all the sunlight in West Parkford in their shadows. "Where are you going?"

I tried to move away and toward the front door, but his grip had tightened. I stamped my foot and slapped at his hands.

"Let me go, Bernard. I'm helping Ada take Fitzgibbons for therapy in England."

"You're, you're flying?"

"And then on to Afghanistan where I've been putting off a plum of a story for almost two years."

"You're flying, Hannah? You?"

"No, I'm vaulting over. What do you think, Cascone?" Even while I tried to make light of daring to fly again, my stomach was the thing vaulting inside me. Too much eggplant parmesan.

Or not.

I stopped struggling against him and watched the progression of feelings on his face.

Just when I yearned for him to pull me closer, his arms dropped to his sides. His eyes narrowed in his handsome skull with its short brush cut going silver at the sides. I tried to breathe.

"I don't want you to go, Hannah. Not to Afghanistan. They got a war going on over there. Let's be together this weekend and talk more about it. Please."

I took off my beret and tossed my bobbed hair loose, running my fingers through it to help clear my head.

"I got to think about that one, Detective," I said at last. "You're a puzzle. You want me out of your case, practically out of your life, but you want to control mine. Pfftt!" I gave him a little wave with the fingers of my right hand like I'd seen Ada do when dismissing someone. "Gotta go."

I turned and my heels clicked their way to the restaurant door. I could hear Bernie taking two steps toward me.

"Hey."

I stopped midstep. "What?"

"I checked, by the way. I don't smell anything on her but a swamp."

I couldn't control the laugh that bubbled out of me. He took advantage of the moment and leaned in for a small, but pleading kiss.

"'Musk,' they call it, Cascone," I said as I slipped through the door and let it swing shut behind me. "Musk."

Back at the table, Lucia had everything cleared and

the staff serving coffee and dessert, and, as they stirred and sugared, the owners of five pairs of eyes studied my return. Dorie was barely controlling a giggle, Ada was nodding toward the window.

"He looks like you punched him in the gut or something, Hannah Doyle. Why were you so cruel?" Lucia asked.

"I'll explain to you later," Theo said behind her hand.

"What about Danny and Janet? What's his excuse for getting them involved?" Meg demanded to know.

"Yes, what?" Ada echoed.

"You two are like a whirlwind," Dorie said. "Or whatever." Everybody nodded. "And that kiss. What was that about?"

"Well, duh, Dorine," Theo said. "They're in love. They have that look, even when they're upset with each other." She looked around the table and fastened her gaze on Ada and frowned.

"Come to think of it, you have that look, too, Ada Javitts."

I nearly fell into my seat, sighing heavily. "I don't want to know, Ada. Thanks for not mentioning what's going on with you right now."

Ada made a Mona Lisa smile. "Okay. So what's with the detective?"

"Doesn't want me to go overseas. He says Danny and Janet are not suspects. Did interview Glenda Mane and thought she smelled like a swamp. I told him it was Musk. I think he'll check it out now. He's not hopeless, I guess. And I'm really sorry he upset Dan. But honestly, Ada, he means well. He's got to cover all the bases or he's not doing his job properly."

"You told him four of us are going to England?" Meg asked.

Lucia called for a point of order. "Hold on, everybody. Who's going to England?"

"Ada, Meg, Hannah and me," Dorie piped up.

Lucia sipped her espresso and set it down carefully. "What about me? Am I chopped liver?"

Ada gulped hard. "Oh, darling Lucia, I never thought to put it to you directly. I guess we all assumed you wouldn't be able to get away from your responsibilities here."

Lu laughed. "Before today I couldn't have. But I just interviewed two new possible assistant chefs to lighten my load, and hired them both. One's been an executive chef for thirteen years, and the other I've heard tell is a genius with Italian cuisine. Bologna born-and-bred. So why couldn't I go? Isn't it about time Tony unchained his Hera from the forge?"

The entire table cheered Lucia's news.

Ada had tears in her eyes. "Lu, I could kiss you, darling. I'm so thrilled to have you along."

"We'll need a big enough place to stay that Lucia can cook for us once in a while," Meg said.

"Hurray," Dorie shouted, then looked around and slumped, distressed for having drawn the attention of the entire dining room. As one, we picked up our dessert spoons and dug into whipped cream and chocolate.

Only Theo look disconsolate, though she obviously

was trying with all her heart to keep the flow of energy going. "I'll get to the office this afternoon," she said, "and book you ladies something for London pronto."

"Excellent," Ada declared. "Let's try for next Tuesday. That was the first available date at Amber Hill, right Meg?"

Meg nodded with a mouthful, her eyes round with delight. "I'll start the shipping process for Fitzgibbons later today. He may arrive a few days after us."

Feeling butterflies slide down my throat along with the tiramisu, I tried to focus on the arrival in London, and not so much the plane ride over. I wondered if Ada still had her supply of Valium. Or if I should get my own. I hoped I'd have the courage to call my old editor and commit to the second leg of my journey before I got cold feet, hands, and everything else.

And then there was my story on the Polo Grounds and the horsey set of West Parkford and Corrington. I'd better work on that today.

Maybe Bernie would keep me warm enough over the weekend so I wouldn't even feel the chill.

From him.

Twenty-one

Theo

I was the last one of the group to give Lucia a goodbye hug as the Women on Fire drifted out of Lucia Mia. I told Lu I was thrilled my hard-working friends could take a whole week off for the trip to England. I remembered how happy I'd been to help Lu out last year when we traveled together to Umbria to visit her dying father, and how much had changed in Lu's life as a result of the reconciliation she'd experienced.

"But I'm going to miss being with you."

"Oh, Thee, I know." Lu snatched my hand and squeezed it "We can't all afford to be gone, though. It's good you'll be here, keeping an eye on the police and letting us know what's happening with Mac's case."

"Yeah, that part's good. But a little dangerous maybe, too. I have to watch over Sigourney, first off. Keep her safe, and healing." I turned away in a rush before I spilled some tears, and in my haste bumped smack into a group of businessmen coming in for a late lunch. Jostled, I threaded my way through and hurried to the parking lot.

My friends were just pulling out, and waved cheerily. But I didn't feel cheery as I poked along toward my Lexus off by itself in a far corner. It occurred to me that if Wilson hadn't married me, he'd have had to take time off to get Siggy to her doctors and therapists. Or, I thought, a little distressed at the idea, maybe he'd simply hire someone to do the job.

That's cold hearted of you, Theodora, Wilson tries hard. He's been a single dad for years and he lives for those girls. Can't you do your part? Since when are you reluctant to put yourself second? So you can't travel with the Women on Fire this time. There'll be other times.

"Yeah," I said aloud. "When I'm seventy-five, maybe. Hmph!"

As I aimed my remote toward the car door, the sun seemed to slip behind a cloud and a sudden chill blew through the clear October day. And stopped me cold.

"What the..." I cried.

The hand gripping my arm was steel-strong and unforgiving.

I spun around, still trapped. Gus Finch was staring me in the eye.

"Always talk to yourself, Ms. Rutledge? Must be all that money in the bank your husband's salted away over the years."

I squirmed away and straight-armed the nasty fellow in the business suit and western hat. Where did he think he was, Texas?

"Get your hands off me." I pressed the palm of my hand against his ugly tie and sloppy dress shirt. Gus Finch pulled back, but barely.

"How's your little girl doing? Any permanent damage? What a shame that horse threw her just as she was about to win the gold. And to think people respected that trainer she had. Must have been a fraud all along, guilty of something. Killing himself."

"I don't know what you're talking about, Mr. Finch," I said, sliding my finger on the remote to the alarm button, just in case. Why I should feel so threatened in the middle of the day in a public parking lot in West Parkford center I couldn't say. But this man with his squinty eyes and loose lips beneath a drooping mustache gave me the creeps.

"If you wanted to ask about Sigourney's health, why didn't you do it when you were parked in front of our home on Saturday?"

Finch made fists of the hands at his sides and bristled. "I hear tell Ms. Javitts is going to take her horse to England for some cure or other. She taking him back where they bought him?"

"I don't know, and if I knew I wouldn't tell you," I snapped.

"Where'd she get that horse, anyhow? Newmarket? Cheltenham?" His eyes narrowed to cruel slits and I sidled up closer to the car.

"Goodbye, Mr. Finch. I suggest you pay more attention to your sweet little girl and her horse than someone else's. Say hello to Charity for me." I focused on my remote, unlocked my door and was just sliding into my Hybrid Lexus when Finch darted toward me.

"I don't see what the big secret is. I could buy a dozen horses like that Fitzgibbons. What is it, Ms. Rutledge? You and your kid afraid of a little healthy competition?"

I forced myself to start the engine and hit the door lock button.

"Don't worry, Charity'll be back," he shouted through the window. "Visiting the sick at your house, that is. Maybe I'll stop in, too."

I almost screamed aloud as I backed out and swung as close by him as I dared in order to pull out toward the exit.

"Yeah, sure, just try it," I whispered to myself, trying not to notice the trembling of my hands on the wheel and the shortness of my breath.

~ * ~

I headed for the travel agency office as planned. Though I felt more like collapsing at home in bed or screaming hysterically, I didn't dare go home and let Siggy see me so upset. Instead, I unlocked the door, opened a few windows to get more air into the office, which had been closed since Friday, and went to the women's room to splash cold water on my face. In the mirror over the sink, my usually smooth and untroubled face looked lined and haggard.

"That damn fellow aged me ten years," I told the face staring back at me with gaunt dark eyes and pale cheeks. I brushed my hair, added fresh lip color and put tea water on. I dangled a green tea bag in a mug and took deep breaths. At my desk I tried hard to banish the image of nasty Gus Finch and focused on taking phone messages and returning calls and e-mails.

Once my tea was poured and fragrant, I called home and asked Shannon how her sister was doing.

"She's great, Mom. Ate a really big lunch, wanted seconds of potato salad and turkey sandwich, Mrs. Iliano said. But I think the big meal made her sleepy. She's been napping on the porch on the chaise since the housekeeper left."

I breathed a huge sigh of relief. I could talk to Shannon without Siggy poking her nose into it.

"What's wrong, Mom? You sound, I don't know, out of breath or something."

"Shan, I am. But I'm okay. I'm going to tell you something but you're not to tell Sigourney, okay?"

"Sure, but what..."

I explained about Gus Finch's verbal assault on me in the parking lot of Lucia Mia's.

"The man's a kook. He said Charity's going to visit Siggy again, and I think it's because he's trying to get some information about Mrs. Javitts' horse. Shannon, I don't want Charity coming over under any circumstances. Okay? If Siggy argues with you about it, you'll have to tell her why I don't want the Finches anywhere around, but I'd rather she not get upset again about the accident and all that."

"Weird, huh, Mom? That whole Finch family..."

"No, I don't think they're all weird, but Mr. Finch is a definite borderline case. He kind of threatened me, hon.

So keep the doors locked and stay inside today, all right? I have to stay at the office late, because all my friends are going to England with Mrs. Javitts, and I'm to make the arrangements for their flights this afternoon, flights and cars, and lodging, I guess."

"But you're not going to go, Mom?"

I said I would not go. "You and your sister need me right now, especially with this Finch family and Glenda Mane acting so strangely after the death of Mr. McClellan."

"Mo-om," Shannon whined, "Daddy will protect us. You should go. If Women on Fire are all going, you deserve to go, too. We can manage, honestly."

There was a flurry of activity and angry sounds at the other end of the line. My heart raced until a voice came on, clear and throaty, Siggy's after-a-nap voice, amplified by her emotions.

"Theo Rutledge, don't you dare stay home to baby us! If you're going over to Europe to help Mrs. J. with Fitzgibbons and his therapy, I'll at least feel like our family is doing our part."

"Honey, it's not like Ada is desperate to have me along. The others are all going, Mrs. Catamonte and Meg Dautrey and the others. Everyone else. Besides you and I have a ton of appointments."

"We can get Mrs. Iliano to bring me to appointments. And Shannon's going to be with me after school until Dad gets home. Mom, you absolutely have to go. I couldn't bear it if you didn't go because of me."

Sigourney's voice was rising. She seemed almost hysterical.

"It's going to be my fault again, Mom, don't you see? I let Fitzgibbons collapse at the gate, I didn't hold on to him or lead him correctly or even tell anyone about his nosebleeds. My fault Mac is dead, too." She started to sob and I tried interrupting, saying I'd be right home, not to worry, they'd talk about it then.

"No," Sigourney shouted. "Don't come home. Who needs you anyhow? You think I can't bear having you chauffeur me around and make me cocoa and help me with my Psychology class notes? After all, we didn't have a mother for five years, did we, and we survived. But this, you can do this for me, Theo, don't you see? You can help Ada and the others get Fitzgibbons well, and help solve the mystery of Mac's death while you're at it."

"Sigourney!" I snapped. "Calm down."

The girl on the other end let loose an out-of control burst of laughter. Or was it weeping? "Okay, okay. You know it's bad enough to sit here helpless, but I can bear that." Suddenly her voice softened so I had to strain to hear it. "The only thing I can't bear is that you won't take my place. I thought more of you, Theo. Your generosity, your caring. But you not going to England is what I cannot bear."

I exhaled and felt my heart rate settle as I smoothed the papers on my desk with a flat palm.

"I hear you, Sig," I said quietly. "I'm going to call your father and tell him the plan. Then I'm going to order six roundtrip tickets for London."

There was a choked back sob on the other end, and a whispered, "Thanks, Mom," before I set down the telephone.

"Thank you, too," I said into the silence.

Why hadn't anyone told me what parenting was really like?

What made me think I could start off as an amateur mother in the middle of menopause—sleepless nights and dry skin and hot flashes and craziness everyday—and make it work without a few unexpected challenges?

I slipped out of my Bolivian poncho and wiped the perspiration from my brow. What I was about to do could cost me my marriage, but solidify my parenting.

How the devil would that work?

Twenty-two

Meg

"Oh, Meg. Good to see you!"

I paused in Ada's doorway to study my flushed and slightly frantic friend. Usually implacable, Ada was twisting her hands together and pursing her lips in the way she often did when she was feeling out of control of her emotions or a situation at hand. There was a sheen of perspiration on her face and neck, and she wore gym shorts and jersey, something she'd probably never been seen in except in the inner sanctum of the women's gym. I soon learned the specifics.

"Hurry, come in. I've been working out. Not the knee, but the abs and upper body, these flabby arm wings everyone gets at our age. They're such an embarrassment."

I was about to object to Ada's negative appraisal of what seemed a perfect sixty-year-old body. But suddenly she turned and grasped me by my own arm wings. "I'm in such a panic, I don't know what to do first. The security people called first thing this morning. C'mon, dear, come in and sit with me at the breakfast table. Do you want coffee?"

"I'll get it for myself. You sit yourself down; you're limping again. Isn't that knee better after the injection?"

Ada nodded. "But stress makes it worse. I swear, Meg, if someone hurts Fitzgibbons I'll—no, I won't say 'kill him, or her'—but I'll surely feel like doing so."

I poured my coffee and lightened it with a dash of cream, then came to sit with Ada in the breakfast nook.

"Tell me what happened."

She took a deep breath and spread her hands on the oak surface of the table, as if to give herself strength to continue. "The very thing I hired them for," she squeaked out, then took another breath. "Thank God they were there. Someone came spooking around Fitzgibbons's stall last night. The fellow on guard was on the outside of the building, but after a few minutes suspected whoever had gone in might not be just another horse owner come to work on their animal at ten-forty-five at night. At that hour, the overhead lights were out, just a couple of security lamps along each wall, so it was pretty dark in there and as he headed toward Fitzgibbons's stall, he heard someone muttering something. He flicked on his flashlight and whoever it was scampered out through the rear doors." Ada took another deep breath and sipped her cooled coffee.

"They obviously knew their way around."

She nodded. "Before he could even get to the doors,

he heard the roar of what he thought was a small vehicle. Out in the yard, with no moon last night, the vehicle had already gone past him and out of the driveway before he spotted it."

"Was Fitzgibbons okay?"

"Yes, he checked him out and called Josie Hand, the manager, who came and inspected everything. They didn't want to bother me so late, but I wish they had. I swear I'll go over there each night and sleep outside my boy's stall if I have to, to keep him safe."

I reached around and rubbed Ada's back. "You don't have to do that. We'll get your thoroughbred out of there ASAP. I spoke with Dr. Ingmanson this morning and he's going to give Fitzgibbons all the required immunizations before his trip to England. I'll give him a buzz and ask him to do that tomorrow at the latest. And we'll ask the transport people to pick him up on Friday, instead of Saturday. They have a group of animals going out on Sunday. This means by the time we get to England, he'll be ready to be released from quarantine, and we can drive him ourselves to Devon."

Ada exhaled heavily, pulled the small gold Star of David pendant from her neckline and gave it a squeeze. "Yahweh be with him, then. Only two more nights at the Polo Grounds. They promised to put two men on the stables tonight. But, oh, Meg, I hate to have him traveling alone."

I set my coffee mug down and smiled broadly to give Ada heart. "But he won't be alone, love. They have a groom, a trainer and a security person all the way to the

Netherlands and across on the ferry to England."

Even sipping the last of her coffee, Ada moaned. "Still..."

"Enough," I said with finality. "We aren't going to go and get all tentative about this. I've made the arrangements, the company is highly reputable. God willing, they will deliver your horse to us in Dover, and Fitzgibbons' treatments will begin pronto."

Ada set her own cup down with a decisive bang. "You're absolutely right. If we can just get through tonight and tomorrow night. Meg, will you come with me to the stables? I want to see my horse. And talk to Ms. Bukowski. One more shot at trying to get her to come."

I started to huff and puff and Ada put up her hands as a stop sign. "I know, I know," she said. "He's going to be fine. But Terry's been okay with him, he's used to her, and I don't think she could hurt a fly, really. Let me give it one more try." While she'd been talking, Sancho had leaped up on Ada's lap and now cuddled into her warmth. She petted him distractedly.

"But you don't even like the girl, Ada. You thought she was careless for not telling Mac about Gibby's bleeding."

"I know, I was in a fit that day. But now I think she's just an inexperienced girl who does fine taking care of the animal most ways. Josie Hand has kept an eye on her and says she does well. And I think Hannah and Dorie are way off base to suspect her being in cahoots with that Mane woman. Please, Meg."

I sighed. From the living room came the running

quiet rant of Ada's talking parrot, and here in the sunny kitchen, she nodded her head in his direction, smiling, as she stroked the curly black hair of her dog. Her face was still etched in worry, and yet every second of her life, Ada gave away more love than some people ever dream of.

"Danny and Janet will have their hands full with pet care while you're gone."

"Piece of cake," Ada said. "They're very capable. So will you come with me?"

I nodded as the phone rang. Ada had carefully replaced Sancho on the floor and was toddling out of the room. "Grab the phone, will you, dear?" she called. "I'm going to get into some barn clothes and join you in three minutes."

I shook my head at the transformation in the Queen of Women on Fire. She was barely limping now.

I answered the phone to hear Theo's calm and musical voice.

"You and Ada up to something?"

"Uh-huh," I said. "We're making the arrangements for Fitzgibbons to be shipped out a day early, and Ada wants me to accompany her to the stables. There was a suspicious character prowling around Fitzgibbons's stall last night, and she wants to see if Terry Bukowski will reconsider going to England with Gibby."

"But isn't there a chance the same Terry could be in on whatever killed the trainer?"

"Don't know. Ada doesn't think so. I'd be interested in seeing her questioned further myself."

"I wonder if the detectives have learned anything on their end."

"They haven't."

"Well, they should. They should expand their search. There are other... suspects, you see."

"How do you know?"

I drained my coffee and stared into the phone. It's always the ones you least expect who have the inside track, as Arthur used to say of seemingly withdrawn but shrewd faculty members.

Theo hesitated, cleared her throat. "Okay, I'll tell you. But don't upset Ada if she doesn't need to know."

"Theo, what? Not another run-in with Glenda Mane?"

"No, but just as scary. After you all pulled out of the parking lot at Lucia's yesterday, I was accosted by Gus Finch."

"Oh, Allah. How accosted?"

"He snuck up on me in the parking lot and grabbed my arm as I was unlocking my car. He was real smarmy, Meg. Threatened Siggy and me. Nothing specific, mind you, but very scary. He's still looking to find out where Ada got her horse, and said he'd be coming to visit Siggy with his daughter next time."

"Doesn't sound that bad, Thee. Except the grabbing you by the arm part..."

"But it's his looks, his anger, all roiling up and out of him that's so disturbing. I don't want him anywhere near Siggy. I tell you, it took me a good forty minutes to calm myself enough to call home. Then I warned Shannon to keep the doors locked and not let her sister know why."

"Impossible," I said. "I have a sister, we could never keep secrets."

"Well, you're exactly right. When Siggy heard about the part where I said I wasn't going with you all to England to help Fitzgibbons get rid of that EIPH, she went wild. Cried and screamed at me that I have to go, to take her place. As some sort of reparation, I guess. She feels responsible for the accident."

"Oh, Thee. I'm so sorry. It is kind of good you're going to be here to watch over things, though, isn't it?"

Theo's voice dropped a notch. "That's just it, Meg. I'm not telling anyone but you. I couldn't disappoint the child, so I checked with Wilson, and he agreed to take a few days off from work, so I *can* go. Siggy is beside herself with joy."

"You're coming to England with us?"

"Just for a few days. Please don't tell Ada. I want to surprise her, and don't tell her about Finch either. She has enough worries going on. Detective Cascone knows now about Finch accosting me. He's going to follow up on it. They'll also send a patrol car around to our house four or five times a day, too."

"When are we flying?" I asked. As the resident travel agent, Theo would have made the arrangements by ten this morning. The thought of returning to Europe after sixteen years away still gave my insides a run for their money, but not as much, I knew, as it must be worrying Hannah to fly at all. I held my breath.

"You're all leaving on Tuesday evening out of Logan. I have the e-tickets in my hand. You arrive at Gatwick at seven a.m., pick up your rental car—seats five, and with a tow for the horse trailer, and I've had the auto service map you out to Dover, and then over to Devon."

I let breath rush out of me. At least I'd be with my friends. And now, thank heavens, I had a U.S. passport. "Excellent. What about you?"

"Wilson's out of town until Thursday, so I'll fly out on Thursday evening, rent my own car and get to you in Devon Friday afternoon."

"Perfect. A sweet surprise. Ada will be thrilled to have you join us."

"Listen, Meg, I'm working on accommodations now. The list you gave me from the Equine Center? Three of the four are all booked. I've been in touch with the fourth, which is some sort of National Heritage site or something on the northern coast of Devon. Very ancient, eleventh century manor house with gardens. Sounds lovely. But the blurb talks about haunted rooms, and eerie legends."

"They have availability?"

"They do, two cottages open that sleep a total of six. All with kitchens, fireplaces, and a tea room on the premises. It's what the Brits call 'self-catering.'"

"Sounds perfect. I'm sure none of us is worried about a couple of thousand-year-old ghosts."

Theo laughed, but I detected a hint of trepidation in her voice. Maybe it was a residue of anxiety left over from her confrontation with Gus Finch. I couldn't wait to tell Hannah about that little episode, and hear Bernie's take on it, too.

"Oh, and Meg," Theo added at the end of her laugh, "Dan Javitts has already promised to help transport Siggy to therapy when it starts the week after if I'm still gone, but I extracted a promise from him not to tell his mother I'm following you over. Isn't that great?" We laughed together and closed the connection.

I was tickled to picture Theo surprising us at our little cottages in Devon. It was nice to have some good news.

Funny, it was usually Ada keeping secrets or having surprises for us. Come to think of it, on Monday she'd looked like the cat who had swallowed the cream, but never said why. What had someone said about Ada spending the weekend with Devlin Doyle?

Naw, couldn't be, I thought. Ada's so... so last century.

When I turned to see my friend approach in tight jeans and Reeboks, an Abercrombie and Fitch shirt tied at the waist, her make-up daytime perfect, big, golden hoops at her ears and her hair in a ponytail, I hooted.

"What?" Ada asked. "What's wrong?"

"Absolutely nothing," I said. *And welcome to the new millennium*. I glanced down at my own drab twill slacks and bulky tan over shirt. I could do with some self-improvement. Maybe I'd borrow Ada's NordicTrack or whatever it was. A ponytail was out of the question. But even Arthur deserved a woman with a waistline. Not that he'd love me any more than he did now.

Besides, I'd totally lost my waistline at the start of menopause and hadn't found it since.

Twenty-three

Ada

Fitzgibbons was not in his stall when we got to the stable. Something like fear caught in my throat and made me stumble, further irritating my aching knee.

Meg gasped and reached out to keep me vertical at the same moment I took in the view from Gibby's window and spied my horse already turned out in the paddock. I swallowed hard and took a deep breath.

"Honestly, Meg, sometimes I'm so klutzy I feel like I'm entering the 'pause all over again. I'm also getting paranoid over who's out to get my horse. Or us!"

Meg clutched my hand and shook her head. "It's natural to worry about Fitzgibbons and ourselves with all this crazy business going on. Let's check things out one at a time."

"Be scientific, you mean?" I asked, and we laughed, nervously on my part. On our way out to the paddock to look at my thoroughbred, we met Terry Bukowski as she was turning out a bay pony I was pretty sure was Charity

Finch's ride. We walked alongside her.

"Terry, did you hear what happened last night?" I asked.

The girl's eyes were round. "Yes, ma'am. But Ms. Hand and I checked everything out this morning and didn't see anything wrong with him or in his stall, either." The pale young woman studied her boots, which seemed huge on her petite frame, but were a lovely burnished and tooled leather in a medium brown.

Something connected in my mind but I couldn't put my finger on it. "New boots?" I asked, smiling.

"Mmm hmm." Terry's eyes darted up at me and she began to move away with the restless pony.

I put a hand on her arm. "Wait one second, Terry. Even though everything appears all right with Gibby, will you keep a special eye on him today?"

Terry nodded. "'Course, ma'am. I'm always careful of him. I told you I'm sorry about the bleeding thing. I just misunderstood someone is all."

I nodded, trying not to scream back that it had been a huge mistake, hard to forgive, and a threat to my horse's life. But Meg squeezed my hand and I squelched it. Instead I forced a tiny smile. "Listen, Terry, before you take Vixen out, just a quick question. Or two. That's the Finch's horse, right?"

Terry yanked hard on the lead and got the horse to stand, pawing occasionally at the concrete ramp and snuffling.

"Yes, ma'am. Ms. Hand tells me what to do, and I do it." She shuffled in her boots.

I gestured again to the boots.. "So. I never saw you in those. Kind of big aren't they? I mean, you could trip and hurt yourself..."

A forced smile broke the sad planes of Terry's face.

"Yes'm. They were, um, they were Mac's boots. He ordered them online, y'see, and they were a bit tight on him but he'd already run 'em down a little at the heels. So he gave 'em to me. I could never afford such nice boots, so I just wear an extra pair of socks with 'em. Is that all, Ms. Javitts?"

I blinked. Something still bothered me about the girl's footwear, but I couldn't get the errant thought into focus. I sighed heavily.

"Okay, one more thing," I said. "On Friday Fitzgibbons ships out to England. It's my last offer. I'll pay you top dollar to come along and tend him. When he's at the therapy facility, you could have time off to visit your fam—"

Terry's cheeks instantly colored pink. "No!" she said, her tone strident. "I mean, no, thank you, Ms. J. That's the last... I mean, I better stay and keep my job here." She looked wistfully out to the field where horses nibbled on the remains of summer's grass, and wandered around the penned corral.

"I'm sorry. I'm truly sorry. I hope Gibby does good, and I can work with him when you get back."

I wasn't sure, but there seemed to be a mist in the girl's eyes. I exhaled. "Okay, I won't ask you again. But please keep a very close eye on my horse until they pick him up on Friday."

Terry had already jerked the lead forward and kept herself hidden behind Vixen's bulk as she spoke.

"Full attention, Ms. Javitt. Good luck and all. I'll see him when you get back, then."

I heard Terry's boots clunk awkwardly on the ramp, and then she was gone. When I turned back to the stable, Meg's head was tilted to one side.

"I'm glad we're getting him away from here, Ade. By the way, I got Dr. Ingmanson. Shots tomorrow are a go. And Ms. Hand said she'll supervise Fitzgibbons's transport on Friday. The company's already been in touch with her."

"That's fantastic, Meggie. You're doing a bang-up job." As we strolled to the paddock fencing to visit my thoroughbred, I felt my worries return in a rush. "May I ask you a question? Coming from a hoity-toity background like I do, I sometimes don't understand the ways of, well, other people."

"That's me," said Meg. "I'm definitely one of those 'other people.' What's up?"

I gave Meg a gentle kiss on the cheek as we approached Fitzgibbons, munching away, his long neck stretched out and elegant. "Darling, you know I don't mean it in any class-conscious way. I'm just dumb about these things, like Dorie has her blank spot on words and expressions? I'm ignorant about people's, well, what they'll put up with."

We ended up at the fence and waited for the horse to turn our way.

"Shoot," said Meg.

"I'm just wondering. If people are, shall we say, economically pressed, would they actually stuff on extra socks in order to wear boots that are three sizes too big just because they can't afford a pair in their own size?"

Meg's laugh was a harsh ripple in the quiet among the soft neighing sounds around them. "Are you kidding? We handed down shoes in our family all the time in Bosnia. If we had any. And my favorite pair of ice skates was a few sizes too big. They'd belonged to my great-uncle Boris. I had to wear three pairs of socks not to slip around in them."

I gulped back my surprise.

"Don't knock it, Ada. I felt like an Olympic star gliding across the bumpy ice in our backyard pond when I wore those skates. Never even had the brains to know I was suffering from being underprivileged." She giggled, and my chuckle just encouraged her more.

By now Fitzgibbons had looked up and moseyed closer, eyes bright, jaw working on his lunch. When he came close enough, I nuzzled his head and stroked his face. He whinnied in recognition. The moment gave me a chance to sort out my thoughts.

"Okay, then. I can believe what Terry says about Mac handing down his boots to her. But there's still some pesky thought nagging at my mind and I can't quite pin it down."

Meg shrugged. "Forget about it for a while, and it'll come to you. Now. You going to feed Gibby that pile of carrots in your pocket before we go or are you going make carrot salad when we get home?"

"Ever the great forensic specialist," I laughed, tugging on my pocket and feeding Gibby the carrots one at a time, enjoying his funny faces as he chewed, then lipped my fingers and took another carrot.

Meg leaned up against the fence patiently. "Then," she said, to tease me I'm sure, "on the way home I'll tell you all about the ghosts and other things."

My eyes must have gone bug-eyed as I stared at Meg beside me.

"What?"

She laughed. "Later."

I nodded and said a reluctant goodbye to my chestnut thoroughbred, kissed his nose and hurried along to the Town Car, hardly limping at all, to hear the latest. I convinced Meg to drive, and we discussed the details of the housing in England, which I approved, despite the ghostly legends of Chambercombe Manor, which made me chuckle rather than grow fretful. I grilled Meg on the horse's transport.

"Are you sure we have everything covered? All the medications and shots Gibby needs?"

Her face soured a bit. "Trust me, honey. Both Dr. Ingmanson and the transport people came up with the same lists. They've done this a hundred times before."

"You explained Gibby came from England originally? And it's not going to be a problem to get him back into the states?"

"They know everything I know about your animal, Ada. And they've faxed all the paperwork to your vet so return entry will not be a problem. Depending on how long he needs to stay in England, he may need some shots updated. But Ingmanson will send us with a packet of papers for the return flight."

I breathed a sigh of relief. "That's good. Maybe I won't even bother going up into the attic to search for George's materials on Fitzgibbons. It's a difficult stairway for me to manage these days. And apparently, we're all set with paperwork and medical necessities."

Meg grew thoughtful. "Hmm. I don't know about that, Ade. I'd say wait until Dan gets home and have him help you put your hands on Gibby's provenance papers. Bring them along on the trip, just in case. We can't be too careful."

I groaned. "I was looking forward to a nap this afternoon. I don't know why it takes so much out of me every time there's a snooper or a threat or whatever, like what happened last night. My knee starts to ache, even with the injection..." I paused as Meg pulled the Lincoln into the driveway.

"Stress'll do that to you, Ada. Try to remain calm. Depend on others, for a change."

"I thought maybe I was doing too much of that," I said, letting my thoughts drift to Devlin.

Meg was too sharp for me. "Why? You're missing a certain new companion, eh?"

I felt myself blush to my gray roots. "Not such a new companion, Meggie. I've been seeing Devlin off and on ever since that dance at Golden Haven."

I drew in a big breath, recalling exactly how far that casual "seeing" had gone.

Meg read it on my face in an instant. "Wow, that serious? No wonder you miss him. And if I haven't said so before, I'm happy for you. But if he's away now, and you're going to be away for another few weeks..."

My grin must have crinkled my eyes and made my pointy nose wiggle. "Well, here's the truth. I'm not telling anyone but you, so keep it under your hat. Devlin plans to join us for a while in England. That's why I told Theo to get sleeping quarters for six. I think I'm just about ready to let the world of Women on Fire know: I plan to share a room with Devlin."

I wasn't too surprised at that shocked look grazing her laconic features. Maybe her built-in Bosnian morality standards had reared up, even if she did say she was happy for me and my beau. I laughed to myself. When they said "beau" in the old days, it meant the young fellow who came courting and sat properly a mile away from his desired.

Devlin and I were people of the new century; we'd never have to be apart for long anymore, sitting, standing or in any other position.

Twenty-four

Hannah

While I set out my bag to pack for my overnight trip to Mount Snow with Bernie, I decided to get a head start on packing my larger bag for England as well. But as I pulled out jeans and twill riding pants, dressy slacks and tops, long-sleeved shirts and sweaters and fleece for an English fall, I admitted to myself I couldn't feel excited about the trip across the Atlantic. Instead, I kept picturing Mac McClellan's body crumpled on the floor of the stable. How can Dorie and Lucia and the others be so enchanted with the idea of traveling to get Fitzgibbons restored to health, when Mac's killer is still at large? Were we wrong to leave West Parkford where the killer perhaps still lurked?

While I folded sweaters and tucked them into my roll-on bag, I suddenly realized I'd always been horribly paralyzed at the specter of death. From the time my mom died when I was a little girl, to the loss of my husband and brother in an airplane crash when I was in my twenties, something in me rebelled and mobilized in the face of an unexpected loss of human life. I needed to fix it, make it right, do it myself, like I was born for that purpose above all others.

Life was too precious, I was thinking as I packed, which is why I so feared flying, why I felt compelled to help children deal with grief in their lives, and why, too, I meant to live every moment to the full. Like this weekend with Bernie, trying against all odds to create love and passion with him again, even though we were barely speaking to one another. He'd been difficult, almost cruel, lately. And rubbed me the wrong way so often I wondered if our attachment could last.

But something inside—the loneliness abated, the new sexual fulfillment I'd been experiencing, hell, just plain caring about someone as deeply as I cared for that hard-headed Italian with the magnetizing eyes—made me think twice. No, three times.

I would try very hard to make a go of us, I thought, as I opened my overnight bag and slipped in a clean pair of slacks, some pretty undies and tops, and a particularly sexy nightgown Bernie always enjoyed slipping from my shoulders.

I shivered to remember the last time, and the time before. And the first time, almost two years ago now, when our lips and bodies had met hungrily after such a short acquaintance, and what had clearly been a long hiatus from love for both of us. Yes, life was too precious, and too short to waste on societal prohibitions and fear of gossip. I loved Bernie, and I didn't care who knew it.

Damn, this relationship was worth one good try.

I clenched my fists and moaned. I would not lose this wonderful, out-of-sight man. Even with his crooked nose, his two rambunctious teenage daughters, his flinty-eyed mother-in-law who kept tabs on him, and his aggravating, paranoid nerves about my getting involved in his cases.

Hey, they were my cases too, when I was writing about them for *The Courant*, especially when they involved friends. And even more so when I had something to contribute that might lead to an arrest. Which gave me a brilliant idea for spending my next two hours.

I enclosed my toiletries in my overnight case and zipped it closed with precision. Then I showered, put on fresh slacks and a long-sleeve jersey top and brushed out my hair. I poked around on my dressing table for a lipstick and some blush. Any ones would do. I wasn't fussy about such things.

But I was fussy about murder.

I decided to take a quick ride out into the country before I picked Bernie up at police headquarters tonight. Just for a gander at the barns and fields and any equine life that might be meandering there. I could stop at Dorie's for a quick chat to calm her down over her fears of staying in a haunted mansion, get to Rosemont Farms for a peek at the view, be back before six, and meet my sweet man on time.

It was only after all that that I might be in big trouble with the man I loved.

Dorie was breathless and full of questions, quite a

normal state for the willowy, violet-eyed blonde I called one of my very best friends. But there was a tiny stitch of a frown on her creamy high forehead I was trying to erase.

"Honey, they always say these old English houses are haunted. It adds to their touristic appeal."

"Not my appeal," Dorie snapped, pouting. "Really, Hannah, I think I have a very close connection to the spirit world—"

"But you're not even Catholic anymore, Dorine, you're a Unitarian," I said in exasperation.

"...and if that ghost is going to bother anyone, you just know it will be me." Dorie pushed the flyaway wisps of almost white hair from her face and shook her head. "My nerves can't take it. You know how flighty I get."

Get? No, panicked is what you get. Flighty is a permanent condition.

I tugged at Dorie's arm and led her to sit at the kitchen table where our diet colas were being diluted by the melting ice. Dorie sipped, and I jumped in for another sales pitch.

"I tell you, hon, there won't be any ghosts. What is a ghost, anyway? It's just a memory of someone who once lived there. But we don't and never did know anyone who lived there, so we won't be the least bit aware—"

Dorie placed her glass on the table with such a hard thump tiny droplets and bubbles shot out of it and sprayed her hand and face. "Oh. I'll be aware. You can bet your booty, or booties, or whatever."

I giggled. "I don't have to bet my booty, I've already given it away hook, line and sinker."

"So you've gotten back together with old Bern?" Dorie's face temporarily brightened.

"Well, for the weekend, anyhow. It's probably good we're taking a break from each other after this. I just hope he doesn't slack off on the case while we're gone."

"You can remind him by phone and e-mail, Han." Dorie's face had smoothed out, the frown fading. I hoped when menopause hit Dorine, it left her beautiful skin alone. And her innocence, and sweetness.

But Dorie wasn't done with her fears. "You're really pretty lucky," she told me. "If you run into a ghost over there you can always phone Bernie and cry on his shoulder. Who can I call? My doggie friends at the grooming parlor? Or my portrait subjects?"

"Maybe you'll meet someone over there, Dor, in England. Theo says the stables where Fitzgibbons will receive therapy are very close to Chambercombe Manor, where we'll stay. We can go riding, you and I. And there might fellows who ride, or big shots who own fancy horses, or something."

"Or fading white apparitions with only bits of protoplasm in them drifting around my bed. I tell you, Hannah, I'm scared. Besides we haven't ridden in years. Well, since you started having hot flashes every time you bounced up in the saddle."

I sighed. "No more scared than I am of even setting foot in that plane, Dorine. Brrr. And wait 'til you start getting your own hot flashes. You just might become more sympathetic." Thinking of stepping aboard the seven-fifty-seven did make my eyes water. Or maybe it was the turps and oils Dorie used on the painting that stood on its easel, nearly completed. I glanced toward it and oohed and aahed my approval.

"Yeah, Mrs. Warren's looking pretty good. Another long session tomorrow and I may be finished. I told her how we're going to England to accompany Ada and Fitzgibbons and she was so pleased. Said she'd tell the Board of Directors at the Polo Grounds at their monthly meeting last night." Dorie drank her cola, and I did the same.

"So are you feeling better, kiddo?" I asked.

"About the ghosts? Uh-uh. But I am sorry I forgot about your terrible fear of flying. And how you came to Florida that time to save me from the hostage takers even though you threw up all the way to Palm Beach."

She leaned over and squeezed me around the neck with one arm.

I figured it was a perfect time to say my goodbyes. I'd thought of inviting Dorie to come along on my ride out to Rosemont, but she was as skittish as an unbroken colt today, and I didn't need to nurse a nervous Nellie along on this particular outing. I promised to protect her personally from any evil spirits at the thousand-year-old Manor House in Devon, and she finally smiled.

"And find me a tall, handsome Englishman, with a pipe and a charming accent, and a tweed jacket, that I can run to when I'm scared."

I burst out laughing, and only quit when I was a half-block away.

Again my thoughts turned to the awful murder of

Fitzgibbons's trainer. And to the woman who so resembled a man and who may have been the last one to see him alive.

I took the entrance ramp onto I-eighty-four and tried to relax my grip on the wheel, smiling when I remembered my camera was in the glove compartment. If I was not greeted particularly warmly by Glenda Mane, I could always say I was here to do a couple of photos of Rosemont to accompany my free lance story.

Who could object to a little free publicity?

~ * ~

Although the barn doors were wide open, the fields around Rosemont Farms seemed quiet, and no vehicles stood in the wide yard behind the residence. I could hardly believe my luck. I took the camera from the compartment, slipped my keys in my pocket, and sidled out of the car, closing the door as softly as I could.

The October grasses were high and fragrant, and some summer roses still clung to their branches. In the north sky behind me, an ominous dark cloud marred the azure sky, but I knew it couldn't rain on such a perfect afternoon.

I snapped one shot of the wide open doors of Rosemont's barn, then headed for those doors and casually drifted up the ramp and into the darkened interior. I was met almost immediately by a chorus of whickers and whinnies, a couple of bold neighs, and a snort or two. There was a cluster of animals close by the rear doors, some very broad and sagging older animals, a couple of spotted ponies, probably Glenda's riders' horses. But in the stalls themselves, I saw only three horses, and though not an expert in horseflesh, these particular animals took my breath away.

They were probably thoroughbreds, all as gorgeous and well-groomed as Fitzgibbons always was. Expensive looking horses which, if they weren't renting space to live here, were a handy-dandy investment for Glenda Mane. Very interesting.

I aimed my camera at the first animal I came to, craning his neck to study me, and nickering softly. I snapped a photo and moved on. The second horse was as sleek and beautiful, a darker chestnutty brown with a white star in his forehead, and an intricately braided mane. The third horse seemed the largest of the three. He was uninterested in my presence, not even glancing up as I passed. But I took his photo anyway. And as I focused him in the lens, I was shocked to discover blood encrusted around his nares.

Wasn't that what Fitzgibbons had? And might not that blood be connected to Fitzgibbons's disease, that EIPH? I shivered, and looked closer. Something triggered a "humph!" but I wasn't sure where it came from. Suddenly out of nowhere, thunder shook the barn. The horses' fright was immediate, especially the ones clustered by the gate at the rear of the barn. These animals were panicky, pushing and shoving against each other, some rearing up in fear.

When the second thunder bolt sounded, accompanied by a flash of lightning not so far away, I panicked, too. Someone might be coming to get these animals to safety. Or if not, maybe I should do it, lead them in one by one. No, can't do that. My shoulders sagged. I didn't know in which stall each belonged, or if they'd stampede me in the middle of another blast of thunder. I felt totally helpless. But that didn't stop me from snapping one, two, three photos of the frenzied animals, with one ear cocked for the sound of a helper entering the barn or a truck driving up. Nothing.

Still, when out of nowhere it started to pour rain, beating like hail on the corrugated roof of the barn and sending the three gorgeous geldings into high alert with loud snorting and bucking up, I froze. I knew I had virtually seconds to get out. Someone would be here soon, and, in any case, I had just had my second brilliant idea of the day.

I tucked my camera in my pocket, whipped out my keys, apologized to the animals getting soaked and clustering madly in the rain, and ran to my car even as the realization totally hit me.

Glenda Mane had been hiding her best horses. And trying to get one of the best local riders to come on her team. If she was so desperate, she must have a past with some desperation in it, too.

Why hadn't I thought of it before? I'd hurry home and Google Glenda Mane.

If for nothing else, for my *Courant* story. I had the right to do it. In fact, I had a moral obligation.

About a mile down the road in the driving rain, the familiar black truck roared by. I obscured my face with an arm raised against the car window, but Glenda Mane or whoever was driving was too focused on getting back to their menagerie to even notice my classic Volvo squeezing to the right to let them pass.

Twenty-five

Ada

I dreamed of the green hills of western England. I hadn't been there in years, and yet the scenery around me in the dream was something I knew, remembered, deep in my heart. I saw myself approach a beautiful stone and timbered stable; I entered and began to look for Fitzgibbons. But in the dream, there was a huge hole in the floor of the stable and all the horses had slipped through, were falling still, braying horribly, while I screamed, reaching out my hand to help them, give them something to hold onto. And when they did reach back to me, their hooves had grown into hands grasping at me, until my own panicked howl woke me with a start.

There before me, my arm already reaching toward it, was the telephone screeching relentlessly for me to answer. My hand grabbed the receiver but I couldn't speak. For a second I was paralyzed, half in my nightmare world, reaching for the twisted, distorted bodies of desperate horses.

I finally jolted myself upward, wrapped my fingers around the handset and shouted "hello" into the mouthpiece.

Devlin Doyle's gentle voice came through clearly. "Hello, my dear. You seem startled."

I shook my head to clear it. "I'm so sorry for shouting, Devlin. I'd taken a nap with my leg propped up, it seems to help. I thought I was dreaming... but I'm so glad to hear your voice. So very glad. How are you?"

"Missing you," he said. I cherished the thought.

"Me, too. Are you getting some good pictures?"

"Yes, some preliminary ones." I could hear the conversation in the background, blended with the clinking of glasses or china.

"You're at a party?"

"Dinner with some old friends. I'm sorry I interrupted your nap, sweetheart."

"No, no, I'm glad you did. I was having the most awful nightmare. I think I must be afraid about sending Fitzgibbons off on his trip alone."

"Look, Ada, that's why I'm calling."

"About my nightmare?"

He chuckled. "No, about Fitzgibbons going off. I'm with Princess Sobieska and she mentioned something you may not be aware of. Have you unearthed those papers on Fitzgibbons your late husband tucked away somewhere?"

I was distracted: who was this Polish princess, and what did her presence have to do with shipping Gibby to

England? "No, it's on the agenda for this evening. Why do you ask?" For some reason I felt hurt, left out. Yet here was Devlin trying to clue me in. Why did I have to be so emotional in my attachments, so damned jealous?

"Darling, are you aware that since twenty-oh-five all horses arriving in the United Kingdom have to have passports?"

I giggled at the thought. Then a dark cloud settled over me. "What are you saying? An actual passport? Why? How? Where do I get one? Do you realize they're shipping him tomorrow?" Shocked, I realized my voice had turned to a screech in the upper registers. My heart raced.

"Ada, Ada, dear, be calm. Let's think this out. The princess says any horse born in England from around twenty-oh-four automatically applies for and has a passport marked with their silhouette, and most have an electronic chip implanted in them to verify their identity. She has a full stable, and race horses are her specialty. So she knows. Also, she tried to import a horse from Saudi Arabia into Northern Ireland a couple of years ago and had to go through the most awful red tape."

"But that's bizarre. I never heard—"

"I know, I had never heard either. But if Fitzgibbons was born in England,[,] he may be okay. When was he born?"

Devlin's voice was soothing, but I was having trouble with every word he said. Besides that, I could still hear the clink of glasses and the voice of the Polish princess adding details to what Devlin had told me. She must be standing close, very close to him.

"Ada?"

"Oh, oh, yes, let me see. George brought him home late in 'oh-seven, he wasn't yet three, I remember. But had such great promise..."

"Then he may already have a passport, Ada. Have you never seen it? George never mentioned it?"

I shook my head. "Sorry, no. Never. Oh, Devlin, we're all set to send him on his way tomorrow, and we women, five of us are leaving on Tuesday, have a house rented in Devon and all. This is going to hold us up, I just know it."

Devlin's voice seemed more hushed, closer to the mouthpiece of the phone he was using in Northern Ireland. "I'll be joining you in Devon, then. Do you have a spot for me?"

"Yes, and very close to my heart."

Devlin chuckled. "I should be through here in about ten days." I heard the princess' voice say something and laugh. I shuddered. Devlin went on, ignoring the interruption.

"E-mail me the address and telephone number where you'll be. It will be so good to be with you again. And before you panic about the passport regulations, my love, hunt for George's papers."

"He was a terrible packrat. Saved everything. And some of them may be in our deposit box downtown." I glanced at my watch. "Maybe I should check there first, since they close in an hour and will be closed all weekend. Oh, Devlin. I'm sorry to sound so helpless, but this is such a glitch in my plans. I can't bear it if we have to postpone everything. It may take days, weeks, months to get a passport."

Devlin's voice grew firm. "Don't even think it. Get down to the bank right away, then check your ex-husband's papers at home if need be."

"I was going to wait for Dan to get home this evening. But no, that's ridiculous. I'll do it myself if I have to."

"Where are these papers?" I could almost see Devlin stroking his chin.

"In the attic, and the stairway is tricky. But I can do it."

"Not with your knee bothering you, sweetheart. Call Hannah, or Dorie. Get your friends to help."

I sighed. I was not lying down on the job. Not totally helpless yet.

I thanked Devlin, relieved to hear the princess' and other voices chattering on at some distance from the telephone. "And thank Princess Sobieska for me. I can't understand why the transport people never mentioned the passport requirement. Or Doctor Ingamanson, either. They're going to hear from me, I'm so furious."

"Ada dear, don't be furious. It takes too much energy. You'll get Fitzgibbons to England eventually. I'll postpone my departure from Ireland if need be and still be able to join you in Devon. There's a lot I want to show you. It will be our time, while Fitzgibbons mends."

A softness and glow came over me so palpable I could almost touch it as I cradled the receiver in my hand.

"That's exactly what I needed to hear, you wise old fellow. You are a genius. Now let me go and do my job. And you go and have a wonderful dinner. Thank your friend for me."

I freshened my face and hair and snatched a hooded rain jacket from the hall closet against the downpour that had started during the conversation. I drove to the bank carefully in the sudden flood in the streets and the swishing of the windshield wipers. I got there with forty minutes to spare, and sat in the ante room of the safe deposit boxes, rifling through papers—stock certificates, bearer bonds I'd moved after our awful hostage assault. deeds to property, documents pertaining to my travel agency business, birth and death and marriage certificates, wills and other legal papers—but no passports.

In the car I phoned my lawyer and asked if he were holding any documents of mine and George's.

"Just your last will and testament, Ms. Javitts, and powers of attorney. You have copies yourself, but these are the originals."

"You're sure there's nothing else, Rob? Not any passports, or provenance papers for our horse, Fitzgibbons?"

"I'll have my secretary check and get back to you, Ms. Javitts, but I honestly don't think so. Is there something I can help with?"

"Not unless you have pull with the British Ambassador. I've got to export my horse to England tomorrow to undergo some rehabilitation, and suddenly discover I need a passport for him. Who knew? George never told me he had a passport, and I can't yet put my hands on any of the paperwork pertaining to the animal."

"George and I never discussed it, and I never heard of such a thing myself. Hmm. I can't think of any pull I might have in that direction, but do call me back if you get desperate."

I promised I would and continued on home. The downpour had let up, but sodden fallen leaves were masking puddles of water in the streets, and the way home was treacherous. I drove slowly, but once I parked the car in my driveway, I dashed out in the light rainfall and hurried to the house to continue the search.

It was on a single, wet, red maple leaf that I slipped on the front steps and went sprawling.

Twenty-six

Lucia

I whipped off my toque and lifted the corner of my apron to dry the perspiration from my face. My old sous chef was driving me to Naples in a hand basket! Twice he'd burned the finest cuts of meat, and now he'd sent out a filet with a sauce not nearly enough reduced. It looked like a hunk of flood debris floating in a river. I wondered if he were nipping the cooking sherry or could he be on drugs? Although the young woman I'd hired as co-*sous* chef was doing beautifully, turning out gorgeous plates with perfect entrees, plus baking up delicacies I had never even heard of, Nino was barely useful. I'd have to remind Tony to watch out for him while I was away, and feel free to let him go if he really was on the sauce.

Anger made me perspire even more than normally, so I kept swiping at my face with the apron, glad of the current phone interruption that sounded like it would get me out of the heat of the kitchen. Even if it was at the start of dinner service on Friday. I couldn't step outside, because it was pouring, but I squeezed into the passageway between kitchen and bar and clicked on my phone to see why Danny Javitts was calling. Maybe he wanted to cook up a farewell party for his mom, and I was the certified CEO of parties.

But Danny's voice didn't convey a celebrative atmosphere.

"Aunt Lucia, I don't know what to do."

"Dan, what's wrong?"

"It's Mom. She fell on the wet sidewalk coming into the house and she refuses to go to the emergency room. I know she hurt her knee 'cause it's all swollen up. I called the doctor's office but he's gone for the weekend."

I took a deep breath.

"Okay, tell her I'm on the way. Where else is she hurt?"

"Just the knee, I think, though she's moving very cautiously, like her back may hurt. She asked me for a bag of ice to put on her knee. Otherwise, she's pretty much all right but soaking wet, and Janet's not here to help her change or anything."

"Danny, why won't she go to the ER? She knows she's got to take care of that knee if she's going to make that trip to England."

"That's what this is all about, Aunt Lu."

Lucia could hear Ada muttering in the background. "Mom says Fitzgibbons won't be able to go to England tomorrow as planned unless she finds some papers my father left somewhere. She insists she's going up to the attic to hunt for them."

"*Madonna mia!*" I yelped. "Don't let her do that, Dan. Listen, pour her a half-inch of brandy and get her to lie down with that ice pack. Sit on her if you have to. I'm on the way over. Whatever she needs to do, you and I will do for her. Are you sure she didn't hit her head?"

Danny spoke to his stepmother away from the phone. He returned. "Aunt Lu? She says, 'Would my hair look so perfect, even if a little damp, if I had hit my head?'"

"*Bene*," Lu said, with a chuckle. "She's normal. I'll be over in fifteen minutes. Tell her I'm bringing soup, and not to move."

I shook my head and whipped off my apron as I returned to the kitchen. I fired orders at my chefs, all my assistants and whichever servers were in earshot. This was a test, I told them, to see if they could hold the fort while I was gone to Europe. I asked one of them to prepare a large takeout container of tonight's special soup, Umbrian Greens and Beans Minestrone, and explained to Tony *sotto voce* where I had to go. He said he'd meet me there after the rush hour to see if he could help. We kissed, I tugged on my slicker, grabbed the soup and was gone.

At the house on Mountainview, I felt a sock to my gullet when I saw how white and distraught Ada looked. I went up to her bedroom, found a sweatsuit and warm socks and brought them down and helped her change, then insisted we enjoy the hot soup before beginning the mysterious search. Danny had called Meg, too, and Meg sat herself down and stared, dumbfounded, while Ada explained the papers Fitzgibbons required before he could be transported to England.

"But no one, absolutely no one said anything about a horse passport. Not the veterinarian, not the transport people," Meg howled. "I'm so sorry I dropped the ball on this, Ada."

Renewed by the hot and hearty soup, Ada banged the table before her and told Meg she refused to hear another namby-pamby apology.

"This is absolutely not your fault. If I'd had a decent relationship with Danny's father, he would have told me all about the passport and electronic chip and everything else about where the papers were kept."

"But he didn't know he'd be dead of a heart attack within a month, Ada. Now let's you and I go into the den and let me check your injuries from this fall." Meg pressed her lips together.

"I'm not dead yet, Megan."

I led the laughter. All the Women on Fire still found it amusing Meg's doctoring years in the United States had been spent in post-mortem work.

Nonetheless, Ada accepted Meg's offer and they returned to the kitchen with Meg mollified. "Just an ace bandage and a steady diet of ice on and off that vulnerable knee of yours should do the trick. Call your doctor in the morning, though, and don't skimp on the anti-inflammatories tonight. We want to keep the inflammation down."

Ada gave Meg a kiss on the cheek and agreed to comply.

By then, I had rinsed the soup plates and made coffee, and asked Meg to make a list of places Ada and

Danny thought we should scour for these papers.

"His office," Dan said. "We've never really cleaned out his desk. I told Mom I'd do it, but I wasn't well enough until the last few months."

"There are loads of his books on the shelves, too, that we keep dusting but never have looked at." Ada renewed the ice pack on her leg, wincing.

"Good idea," Meg said, as she wrote.

"The attic," Ada said. "There are several boxes up there with George's belongings Chantal and I packed away for the day when Dan would be able to go through them."

I gave Dan a gentle punch on his bicep. "That day has come, my dear."

Dan nodded, hanging his head for just a moment or two in embarrassment because his drug problem had been such an issue.

"Anyplace else?" Meg asked.

Ada explained she had checked the safe deposit box and the lawyer's office. She shrugged in exasperation.

"Nothing in the game room downstairs, or your house safe?" Meg asked.

"I could check," Ada said, "but we've been in and out of both places and never saw anything."

"I hate to mention it, but could his nephew, could Judd have any idea?" Meg looked up apprehensively. Since Ada's step-nephew had gone to prison, his name was rarely mentioned.

Ada shook her head vehemently. "The last person I'd ask."

"Okay, then, let's get started with what we know," I said. "Ada, why don't you settle on the couch in the den, keep that ice pack back on your knee, and instruct Meg where to look in that big old desk? Dan and I will try the attic."

Ada nodded. "Bring the boxes right down here, honey," she told Dan. "I can go through them sitting on the couch or even in my recliner."

The search was on, paused after an hour for a coffee break and then continued. By then Janet was home, and she helped Ada go through cartons, through years of IRS forms and business papers, through suspicious looking photographs that seemed to verify George's womanizing, something that came as no surprise to Ada.

Meg had gone through the drawers of the desk twice, and was now examining every book on the bookshelves behind the desk. By eleven o'clock every box from the attic had been emptied, scanned and refilled. Ada was close to tears.

"It's less than twelve hours from the time Fitzgibbons will be picked up. Maybe you should call the company, Meg, and tell them the trip is off."

Meg shook her head with particularly staunch Bosnian vigor. "No way, Josè," she snapped. "They don't plan another group shipment for three months, and we can't let Fitzgibbons wait to get better. We'll find it. I feel it in my bones."

Ada laughed. "If your bones were as old as mine, Meg, all they'd be feeling right now is twinges of arthritis."

"Or osteoporosis," I joked, and Meg answered quickly that she took her calcium every day.

Dan shook his head in frustration. "There's something we're missing. Is there someplace like at the stables Dad might have kept Gibby's papers?"

Ada shook her head. "But he was pretty possessive about that horse. He claimed he bought it for me, but I had the feeling he was, I don't know, secretive or something about it."

I brightened. "Dan's right that we're missing something. We have to think like George. How did George think?"

Ada's snort of laughter was bitter. "Usually with a glass of scotch whiskey in his hand," she said.

My eyes widened. "Janet, go get the bottle of Scotch from the bar and some little glasses. Let's all have a dram, and reconsider this whole thing."

Meg scoffed. "You're crazy, my dear Lucia. Not everything can be solved with food and drink. I'm going to call Arthur and tell him not to wait up. I'll give this room another half-hour and then I really must get some rest. Ada, too."

Just as I was pouring them all a taste of whiskey, Tony arrived, walked into the den and saw the glasses held in each hand.

"A toast of celebration?" he asked. "You found what you needed?"

"No," said Ada. "But we're still trying."

Danny asked Tony to take his glass. "I shouldn't be drinking it anyhow on my rehab."

Ada smiled at him, clearly proud of his vigilance, and joined in the libation. "Hmmm," she murmured, as she relaxed back in her recliner. "Well, I'm not getting any bright ideas, but I do think my knee is hurting less and less."

"That's because I just changed your ice pack, Mrs. J.," Janet said.

"Brrr," I said. "I'd rather a glass of Chianti myself. But okay, now everyone relax and let your mind wander. If you were George..."

She moved in a three-hundred sixty degree turn and gazed around the den. Ada's botanical prints were so lovely and set the color tones for the softly lighted room. There were peaches and nectarines, ruby red grapes... And there, directly over George's desk hung a beautiful enlarged photograph of Fitzgibbons I hadn't noticed before. For some reason my mind switched to Italy, to the days spent there with my dying father last year.

We'd had a wonderful reconciliation, and how he'd cherished the photograph of our two sons we had framed for him. I could almost see his eyes fill as he examined the two grandsons whom he'd never met. He'd even asked me for a small piece of paper and a pencil, and wrote on it the boys' names, dates of birth, and that day's date, then he pried open the back of the framing and slipped the paper inside.

"For posterity," he explained to me. I'd cried silent tears, as I almost did now. Instead, I yelped.

"What?" Meg asked.

"Lucia, what is it?" Tony said as he came closer.

"Take that photograph down, Tony," I said, my face suddenly flushed and my fingertips dancing as I reached out.

I could hear Ada draw in her breath and Danny and Janet scramble forward to watch.

I pulled off the backing of the photograph, and slid out a stack of papers. I handed them with not a little ceremony to Ada, who bawled all over them, before she took them apart and gazed at the silhouette of a sleek, two-year-old thoroughbred on his British passport.

"Cheltenham," Meg read over Ada's shoulder. "He was born and purchased from a Van Dyne Stables in Cheltenham, England. And—"

Now it was Meg's turn to holler: "He has a microchip to prove it implanted in his right shoulder!"

~ * ~

In the morning I insisted on driving Ada to her doctor's, as it was my day off. He'd opened up specially to administer another injection, helping to calm the knee's inflammation from her fall, and for the upcoming trip. Then we drove to the Polo Grounds.

Snacks of carrots and apples filled her pockets, as Ada approached her dear Fitzgibbons. She spent a few quiet minutes with him, and then the transport people arrived. Ada turned over the special documents they needed, and of which I had made copies at the local library.

Ada stood by as tense as a rocket ready to blast off as the equine movers prepared Fitzgibbons for travel. Josie Hand and little Terry Bukowski helped. I left Ada standing alone as she insisted, braced up by her cane, and wandered off to talk with the security person my Tony had hired for Ada. Despite the lingering pain in her knee, she was determined to see her boy off, so she stood, and I could see she was getting more achy by the minute.

"Doc Ingmanson gave him all his shots yesterday, Ms. Javitts. He's all set. He'll miss you, but you'll see him over there soon enough." Slender Terry brushed her lank hair out of her face and patted Gibby's flanks as he moved up the ramp.

"I hope so, Terry. I hope so." Ada watched the two workers seal the trailer and mount the cab to pull away, the sheaf of documents in their hands.

I understood my friend couldn't bear to watch the departure. I stepped up close behind her and watched her cover her eyes, chanting under her breath a Hebrew prayer she'd probably known since she was a little girl. When the roar of the truck's engine died away, Ada opened her eyes and sighed, then used her cane to slowly and carefully walk alone toward the car in the stable yard. I trailed behind, admiring her growing sense of independence. Funny, I thought, that love can do that for you.

As we returned to my SUV, Ada's voice was hoarse and caught on a sob, "If only Mac McClellan had been as fortunate as Fitzgibbons, and were on his way home to England right now as well."

I sighed. Love can also make us less selfish and more concerned with others, I thought. All this murder and mayhem—could love help solve that, especially in far away England? I snatched my friend's hand and squeezed it, then turned the key in the ignition.

Twenty-seven

Hannah

I zipped up my hooded sweatshirt and tiptoed out of the apartment. Bernie had been gracious enough to settle for takeout pizza and let me do my Google search on Glenda Mane last night, leaving our time eclipsed except for the last hour of the evening when we fell, exhausted, into bed together. Fortunately we'd cancelled Mt. Snow and chosen instead a lovely old colonial inn in Wethersfield, about ten miles east of town, making my errand simpler. But when he discovered I'd gone to *The Courant* this morning for further research, he'd probably leave me to spend the weekend alone. Or maybe, for good. I swallowed hard, and gritted my teeth at the thought, letting my hand linger on the doorknob of the suite's door.

Still, after what I'd found, who could blame me for heading to the one place where old pictures might help to incriminate the person I was fairly sure had killed the

British horse trainer?

At *The Courant*, my old friend Lennie, the security guard, welcomed me in and even tipped his hat, as I made my way to the City Room. There were a few reporters I knew slightly who waved, but the editor I did free lance pieces for was not at his desk.

"Taking a well-deserved weekend off," one perky young woman said from a nearby desk.

I thanked her and headed down to the research library—what the newspaper people called the morgue, where reference files of back issues, many on microfiche, were stored. I referred to my own notes from my internet research, where I'd read partial articles about a most amazing coincidence: Mac McClellan and Glenda Manes knew each other, had been in each other's company over the last few years at least half-a-dozen times or more.

I needed to know what the relationship was about. Such information might reveal a motive for Mane to take Mac's life.

Or not.

I needed to know, and now, before possibly leaving the trainer's killer on the loose while we Women on Fire left the country in a few days.

The first item I found listed both Mac and Glenda as guests at an Equestrian celebration for local riders who'd qualified for pre-Olympic trials. Nothing ominous there, but if a picture had been included in the piece, I wanted to see it. I rolled up the fiche from the three-year-old *Courant* and my jaw dropped when a clear black and white photograph of assembled equine personalities showed the two side by side. McClellan looked fidgety and ready to bolt, standing beside Ms. Glenda Mane, who was eyeing him instead of the camera with a look of serious disdain, while everyone else in the photo appeared smiley and relaxed.

I took notes, got the names of the other personalities at the party, copied the photograph and hunted up the next event. There were no pictures of that one or the next I had copied into my notes, but finally, from a Charity Ball given by combined horse farms in the area were several photos, even candid shots of couples dancing. First I spotted Josie Hand actually dancing with that creep Gus Finch, and one of Mrs. Warren, Dorie's portrait model, standing at the side talking with a heavy man with his back to the camera.

Then I hit pay dirt. In the last photo on the page, I saw Mac dancing with Glenda Mane. His face was toward the camera, and again, he looked ready to bolt, his mouth twisted in an awkward smile, his hands barely touching Mane's body, as if he'd burn them if he did. I saw only the back of Glenda Mane, but what struck me was how large Mane was compared to McClellan. Oh, Mac was about the same height, and rangy, but slender and thin-faced in the photo, whereas Mane's shoulder and hip size dominated him, and her grasp, one arm wrapped tightly around him, the other with her hand clutching his probably to the point of pain for the poor fellow, seemed threatening.

"Worth the proverbial thousand words," I muttered to myself

I had to guess the man was somehow intimidated by Glenda Mane. She had something on him, and I doubted it was romance. I copied that one as well.

The last picture I found was taken at a horse show, last year's Polo Grounds show, and there, in the background, McClellan was leaning on the rail, his eyes lit up, clearly watching Sigourney Rutledge shine on Fitzgibbons, who was prancing up to a gate in the foreground. Two people to the left of Mac, standing rigidly away from the rail, hands balled into fists at her sides, Glenda Mane was clearly watching Mac, her beady, pig-like eyes with their straight, thick eyelashes, full of emotion.

What emotion, I couldn't say. But if I had to guess, I'd say jealousy, resentment, venom. Another great picture to preserve.

My heart racing, I checked the copies of all the photos I'd found, closed down the microfiche and stacked my notes together carefully. Were jealousy and resentment motive enough for murder? I'd ask Bernie. Oh, poor Bernie, waking to find me gone.

On my way out of the building, I flipped on my cell and called his number, barely remembering to wave goodbye to the security guard. When Bernie answered, I promised to be back in thirty minutes with fresh bagels for breakfast and a lead in the case.

What I didn't tell him about was the list of horse people I planned to locate and interview this very day. People at that first pre-Olympic celebration and the charity ball might be able to tell me—or Bernie and me—

something about Mac and Glenda Mane that would shed some important light somewhere.

~ * ~

"Driven," Bernie called me later when I spilled my plan. "You're a nut case, Hannah Doyle. I thought we were going to spend this weekend quietly together, forgetting about the case which is driving a wedge between us."

"Could we start that delightful time together this evening at dinner and through tomorrow? Really, Bernie, why couldn't we both do these interview checks? Or you do them, and I'll just meander along for the company. You'll be in charge."

Bernie roared. "Me in charge? Ha!" He dropped his cream-cheesed bagel and pulled me close to his chest from my chair at right angles to him. "If I were in charge we'd go back to bed, or take a shower together, or drive out to Lake Mogus and lie on the shore hand in hand in the sunshine. It wasn't the country I yearned for, y'know. It was you, woman."

I twittered. "I vote for all three. How about the shower first, and the other two later today? Don't you think I want to be with you? Bernie, you know I care about you, being with you, but I'm leaving for England in seventy-two hours."

Bernie shook his head, staring into his coffee cup. "All the more reason we should be focused on each other now, right now."

I longed to agree by showing all the signs of affection I could bestow on him, kisses, hugs, loving touches. But I felt somehow it would be manipulative of me, and I had to be true, be myself. I refused to be cagey, or pretend.

"I can't do it, Bernard. I've got to be real with you. Like you are, with me. You do remember the Osso Bucco, don't you?" I set down my coffee cup and felt my mouth turn into a hard line. I can make concessions, I thought, plan time away with you, love you till the end of my life

But, my God in heaven, there's a killer out there.

I thought of all the children I counseled at the Center who still grieved a loss and that made me grip the table to say what I was thinking. "How can you sit around making merry when the next person who dies might be someone you know, or a special horse, or, or even a kid?"

Bernie hung his head and buried his face in his hands. It was a long while before he spoke. "You're right," he finally said. "I'll go interview these people for you. With you. But I'd appreciate it if someday you remember I've had loss in my life, too, Hannah. Loss which taught me to cherish every day with those I love. To be with the ones I love. To hold you close!"

I felt myself melting. How could I be so careless with Bernie's feelings after he'd lost a wife, had to distance himself from his teen-age daughters, transfer from his high-powered job in New York City to this sleepy community? I reached one hand out toward him and bit my lip not to let my compassion carry me away.

Like a charging stallion, he was out of his chair in one jolting motion, and sweeping me into his arms. Almost like a romance hero in a love story, I thought, crumpling beneath his kisses, his touch. When I moaned at the flight of his hands on my body, he let me go gently, stepping back and watching for a smile on my face. When he got it, he returned to his breakfast and told me to finish mine.

"Let's plan our stops. And let's make Glenda Mane number one."

~ * ~

As I suspected she'd be, Glenda Mane again was missing from Rosemont Farms. Instead, all the horses were turned out, and even the ones who had been left to suffer the thunderstorm outdoors seemed unharmed. Two young men working in the barn told us Miss Mane had gone away, and some other lady was in charge but she was out today, and they were here to muck out the barn good and bring in the animals and set up the evening feeds before they left.

"What's the lady's name who's in charge?" Bernie asked.

Both boys shook their heads.

I suggested we return to town via the Polo Grounds and Bernie could re-interview the manager. I would explain, say I was along making notes for the article I was doing. In fact, taking notes was a perfectly normal thing for me to do. I was a journalist, writing a piece on the horsey set in the area, and Ms Hand knew more about that lifestyle than almost anyone.

Josie tucked her loose white shirt into her riding pants and refastened her ponytail while we talked. She had clearly been riding, and her cheeks were flushed.

"More questions, Detective? Okay, how can I help?"

"Just wondering, Ms. Hand. You know Glenda Mane over at Rosemont, and you certainly knew Mac McClellan. Any idea what kind of relationship they may have had?"

Josie lifted a shoulder and made an "I-don't-know" downturn of her lips. "Didn't realize they even knew each other."

I poked in my portfolio and yanked out the photograph from three years before, where Josie, Mac and Ms. Mane were posing with three champion riders. "Remember this event?" I asked. "You're all in the photo."

Josie waved an open hand at the paper dismissively. "Cripes, everyone who was anyone in riding circles was there. It was a big deal to have three kids in the trials. Nobody made it in, though."

I asked Josie to focus on the expressions on Glenda's and Mac's faces.

"Hmm. Don't look like they get along very well there. I still say that verifies they had no relationship at all that I knew of." She chuckled and started to turn away.

I pulled out the dance picture and shoved it under Josie's face. "How about this event.? I believe you were there, too."

Josie hesitated, glanced around her office toward the exit door and squirmed the tiniest bit.

"Oh, that," she said in a breezy tone. "We tried to set up a foundation for disabled kids to get riding time at all our stables. We still haven't collected enough to do it."

Bernie moved in closer and took the paper in his hand. "The pictures, Ms. Hand. What do you know about the obvious animosity in the faces of these two people?" He pointed a strong, long finger at the dancing duet.

Josie glanced up at him, and then at me.

"Look," she said, "Glenda Mane is a big person in show circles. A friend, really. Mac meant the world to me. But the two of them, okay, they were like oil and water. I don't know what their association was all about. But it wasn't pretty. He was never happy to see her, but she'd get him in corners, or out in the pasture, and yak at him to death."

She realized the word she'd used, and flinched.

"I didn't mean..."

"I know you didn't," Bernie said, while I hugged my notepad to myself trying not to shout "Bingo!"

Bernie kept at the stable manager. "But do you have any idea what it was all about? Why she chased him, what he had against her?"

Josie sank down at her desk. "I really don't. I wish I did. But the day Mac died, she wasn't anywhere around here. At least I didn't see her. None of her kids was competing. Believe me, if I could help you find Mac's killer, I would. But it would be a man, right? Someone strong enough to—well, to do what was done?"

Neither of us pointed out the obvious about Mane's size and strength.

Josie's eyes had filled with tears, and Bernie and I shared a look and eased our way to the door. "If anything else occurs to you," Bernie said, "call me. I think I left you my card?"

She pulled a card out from the margin of her desk blotter.

"I look at it every day and wonder who could have done this to Mac. The nicest guy in the world. Never had a problem with him, and I miss him a helluva lot. Thank God little Terry is staying on. She helps take up the slack. And I'm sorry I couldn't be more help. I just didn't want to see Mac's name get tarnished with something that didn't exist. Or anyone get wrongly accused."

We thanked her and left. I glanced into the stables as we did, seeing Fitzgibbons's empty stall, and the thin, mop-haired girl rubbing down a bay in the first stall. She met my wave with a wave back, daring a half-smile.

"Little Terry, huh?" I said to Bernie as they turned away. "About the only one not in those pictures."

"But you did put your finger on something, Han." Bernie wrapped an arm around my shoulders as we walked to his car. "I've been hesitant to push the Glenda Mane thing for lack of motive. But Mac clearly had something against her. Unless she comes clean we may never know what."

I sent him a smug grin as we got into our own sides of the vehicle. I fastened my seat belt and reminded Bernie I'd be in England in a few days.

"Who knows what I may find out over there, sweetheart?"

That dark cloud of disapproval descended on Bernie Cascone once more, and I clamped my mouth shut. He turned on the engine and drove us out of the Grounds and onto the highway once more.

"Investigating a murder on foreign soil? Don't even go there," he said, his voice gruff and unsympathetic. "I have a guy from Scotland Yard on it already." I didn't answer, so he softened a bit and shrugged his shoulders. "Where's this Warren woman live, anyhow? After our little chat with her, you have a date with a certain love maniac who absolutely needs a beer and a peaceful, friendly lie-down on the shores of Lake Mogus with you *toute suite*."

I laughed. "I brought the beach blanket. But I didn't know you spoke French, *monsieur*."

"It's not as good as my Italian, but it'll pass."

I felt my eyes go wide. "Bernie, Bernie, that's it. You should come to England, too. It's important to find out more about McClellan. You'd have the *mojo* to do it. Somehow we'll find out, perhaps from Ada or the stables where Fitzgibbons's therapy is going to be, about where Mac came from. You can hunt down people who knew him, what his background was, and what's the big secret Ada hinted at."

Bernie groaned and shifted his car into fourth as the highway cleared before him. "How'd I ever get hooked up with you, lady? You not only won't take 'No,' for an answer, you expand the 'Yes' farther and farther down the lane until it blows up into a European odyssey."

"And we could have a little time together in a new and romantic place," I muttered half under my breath.

He reached to the back of my neck and ran his fingers through my hair. "Honey, we've got continents to explore right here."

"It's really not a bad idea," I chirruped, starting over with new enthusiasm, "if it would help solve an unsolved murder in West Parkford."

He fired off another gruff, "No," and put both hands back on the wheel.

I exhaled noisily, gave him directions and prepared my notebook for Rita Warren's intimations.

It was Mr. Warren, wearing golfing clothes and just removing his cap, who opened the door at our ring. He led us into the family room.

"How can I help you, Detective?" he asked. "And Miss, eh, Doyle, is it?"

I explained I was doing a piece on the equestrian lifestyle in the area, and if he and Mrs. Warren didn't mind, I might ask a few questions on that score after Detective Cascone did his business.

He nodded, not quite reassured. "This about McClellan's death? So they're sure it wasn't suicide?"

Bernie gave as brief a nod as any human being could execute. At that point Rita Warren joined us, coming apparently from the kitchen or someplace else in the huge Tudor mansion.

She'd met me somewhere in town before, so smiled a friendly greeting. I introduced Bernie.

"Just a few questions," he explained.

Rita Warren led the four of us to two sofas facing each other on either side of a broad glass coffee table and nodded.

"No problem. Ms. Boulé and I speak of the accident and of Mac's death often. She's painting me," she explained to Bernie.

"It's a fabulous likeness already and she's not quite finished. I've seen it," I piped up, then settled back to let Bernie take over as Rita Warren smiled broadly, clearly thinking the kudos were for her beauty and not for Dorine's execution of the subject.

"Since you're on the Board of the Polo Grounds and you probably know most people in the equestrian community, Mrs. Warren, I wondered if you know what relationship there might have been between Mac McClellan and some of the others."

I smiled inwardly at Bernie's grace at approaching the subject. I'd have blurted everything out in one fell swoop.

Rita Warren sat back comfortably. "Yes, certainly. Like who?"

"How about Josie Hand? She seems to have been fond of Mac."

Rita nodded. "They got along famously. He was originally hired just to work for Ada Javitts, but Josie knew a good thing when she saw it and referred other stall renters to him. Ada didn't mind at all, since his upkeep would be shared by the several who paid for his services. Besides, Josie's stables would get a better name with an experienced, capable man like Mac bringing in winners for us."

"They never had any clashes?" I asked, pen poised for note-taking.

"Not at all. The only clashes on the Board were with Gus Finch."

I cringed at the name as Bernie took over again.

"Mr. Finch on the Board? What was the gripe?"

This time Mr. Warren got involved. "That damned Finch. I golf with the guy and I'm so sick of hearing how he plans to add horses to the ones he already has, how he'll buy up some thoroughbreds like George Javitts did with what's-his-name..."

"Fitzgibbons," Rita Warren answered. "And Gus pushes that little girl of his mercilessly. Of course, he has the money to buy. Married into an old family. His wife's off playing tennis and spending her millions in southern France while he tries to make a star out of Charity. I think he lives through her."

"A show-off," Mr. Warren muttered. "A braggart and a show-off. He prodded McClellan for the last few years about where to buy a horse like Javitts' thoroughbred. Wanted Mac to train his girl and his horses, too."

"Mac wouldn't have anything to do with him," Rita Warren said with finality. She asked if we would care for a coffee or cold drink.

"Thanks, but we're headed for a luncheon date," I said, smiling. "So that was the source of Finch's animosity toward Mac? That he wouldn't help him get a horse, or train Finch's daughter?"

"I'd say so," Mr. Warren answered. "He hated McClellan's guts, and moaned and groaned about his Brit ways when we were on the course or having a drink afterward. The other fellows in our foursome laugh at him, but he irritates me no end."

Bernie suddenly turned his attention to the irritated husband. "Would you say Gus Finch is a violent man?"

"Strong sonofabitch, sorry, ladies. Seen him snap a putter in two when he didn't get his shot—a shot anyone could have made." Mr. Warren settled back in his corner of the sofa and nodded gravely. Then realized what he'd said and leaned forward again. "Oh, I don't think he'd kill a man. Not over a stupid thing like horse eventing."

Mrs. Warren echoed his sentiment, greasing the air with kindness and solicitations. "He's just obsessed," she said, smiling.

I knew what obsession could do to a person, and sometimes it wasn't funny. "Any of the other parents like that, as obsessed and competitive as Mr. Finch?"

Rita Warren shook her head quickly. "Except for him, we're a pretty friendly bunch. All for one, one for all, you know." She glanced at her watch.

I nodded. "I heard what a nice thing you did for Terry Bukowski, putting her up in her cabin gratis for the next few months."

"Least we could do," muttered Mr. Warren.

"The child has no one else here," his wife said. "And Josie needs her at the stables. Besides, what we arranged isn't nearly as generous as all of you, Ada's friends, trotting off to England to support her while Fitzgibbons gets his therapy. And staying in an ancient haunted house in North Devon to do it." She shuddered.

I cringed; even Bernie didn't know about the ghosts yet. "Oh, you heard about that from Ms. Boulé?"

She shook her head. "Oh, everyone in town knows. Gossip spreads like the flu in West Parkford, my dear," she told me, giggling a bit.

Bernie brought us back to the issue at hand. "How about McClellan's relationship with other trainers, say, Glenda Mane?"

I could sense the shroud of darkness descend on the Warrens.

Mr. Warren just shook his head. "Heard of her, don't really know her."

His wife bristled. "I do, but I can't explain the terrible hatred, I'd have to call it, that seemed to exist between her and Mac. She was always at him over something. At first I thought she was trying to hire him away from Josie."

"But you changed your mind?"

"Well, yes, because he rebuffed her so completely. We were at a dance once, a charity ball, and she dragged him out on the floor against his will. So embarrassing."

Her husband nodded. "I remember. She's a big woman, too, probably stronger than McClellan was. And bossy."

"And we danced by them once, remember, dear?"

He did.

"She kept saying some odd phrase, that he'd 'better not come clean'... was that it, Ron?"

"Yes. 'Better not come clean.' And the poor bastard kept staring at her and saying, 'Don't do it, don't do it,' with his mouth clenched tight together, in a fury like.'"

"Yes, that's it exactly," Rita Warren verified. "'Don't-do-it.' Over and over. Almost like a mantra, he kept repeating it, spitting it, right into her face."

I saw Bernie's eyes narrow. Something had occurred

to him. A lead. Something helpful. And I'd never even had to pull out my pictures.

"Thank you," Bernie said, rising. "You've both been very helpful. Of course, if you think of anything else, please give me a call."

As he stood and stretched, I asked a couple of innocuous questions about Rita Warren's involvement with the Polo Grounds.

"How's that Foundation coming, the one for disabled children getting free riding time at area stable?"

It was the perfect thing to close on. "I think we finally have enough money to go forward," Rita said, her eyes sparkling. "If my husband's pockets loosen up a bit, we'll be over the top. We hope to start in the spring."

I smiled broadly. "That's wonderful. I work with a group of children who could so clearly benefit from that kind of experience. Please keep me informed, would you?"

Rita Warren agreed, and even hugged me as we turned to leave. There was light laughter around the group. I congratulated Rita once more on her efforts, and her portrait, and wished the Warrens well.

Out in the car, Bernie gazed at me in wonderment. "You make a damned good partner, Doyle. Sure you don't want to sign up at the Academy as a recruit?"

"Just to spend time with you? Heck, no," I said. "But that was masterful, your questioning, too."

"They're an easy pair to question."

"Too innocent? Or that rare breed, totally honest people?" I asked as we drove away down the long sloping drive.

Bernie shrugged. "Dunno for sure. I'm not God. But right now, they look like perfect witnesses to put on the stand. We've got to find Glenda Mane. Let's give her one more try before we go to the Lake."

I punched his bicep lightly, then rested my head where my fist had been. "You're a pushover, Cascone. Ever tell you that?"

"Only in bed," he said, his head tipping toward mine and his lips brushing my hair.

Twenty-eight

Ada

I was so tired I couldn't help but limp down the driveway of the old Manor House in North Devon when we arrived in late afternoon. We'd met Fitzgibbons at the holding stables in Dover at noon, then delivered him in his deluxe horse van to the stables where he was well received, turned out for some brief minutes of freedom, then fed and watered before we left him for the evening. Once I'd seen he had made the trip without injury or upset, I felt I could breathe easily again, and I was so pleased with the director at Amber Hill Equestrian Center I nearly cried with relief. Tomorrow at noon I'd meet with the whole staff and hear them plan my thoroughbred's therapy program.

Now, surrounded by the white-washed limestone buildings of Chambercombe Manor, I drew on my ebbing strength to instruct the cottage manager, Heather Ringold, about the arrangement of luggage and the assignment of rooms. Ms. Ringold was exceedingly agreeable, a sweet and sturdy young woman who had rounded up two men just leaving their work in the gardens to help with the luggage.

But we were all so exhausted, dehydrated and ravenous for food we had a hard time concentrating. Lucia kept dragging Dorie back from her enraptured wanderings around the gardens in the courtyard, and Hannah had made her way up the driveway's slope, trying to access cell phone bars to call the states, to Bernie Cascone, no doubt, for an update on whether he'd got his hands on Glenda Mane who seemed, at last word, to have mysteriously disappeared.

I had to admit what Hannah and Bernie had learned over the weekend certainly cast both Ms. Mane and that awful Gus Finch in an even more notorious light; either one may have killed Mac, and Bernie was on the job, though he'd had his wrists slapped by Captain Ketry for involving Hannah in his investigation.

The best news was that within days we'd all be breathing easier, we hoped, with the guilty party in jail. That knowledge had made the transatlantic flight a little easier to bear, and my knee had behaved with its extra dose of cortisone, until this very minute.

"Heather, dear, I'm taking the Rose Cottage here, to the rear. I need that peace and quiet. Put the other four in the two large bedrooms over in Lilac Cottage."

Heather nodded and went to work dividing the luggage. "Who will room together in Lilac?" she asked. Lucia came by in time to answer.

"Let's put Dorie and Hannah together. They plan to rise early some mornings and do some riding from Amber Hill Farms. I like to sleep a bit later so I'll room with Dr. Dautrey, who's as quiet as a mouse." Meg guffawed to make a liar of her, but Lucia cheerfully helped divide the luggage for the men waiting nearby.

Dorie heard the plan and nodded.

"But won't that leave Ada all by herself in Rose Cottage? Too lonely for you, Ada dear. And don't forget, the..."

"Ghosts. Yes. I know, Dorine, but I'm not worried about the ghosts. If I can handle the lot of you, I think I can manage some thousand-year-old spirits on their last legs, so to speak." I tried not to laugh, because Dorie was so serious.

Meg pitched right in. "It's a perfect plan. Ada's used to living alone, and needs the quiet. She has that nice large living room in Rose Cottage for us to gather in when we have group meetings, too. And a bathroom upstairs beside her bedroom, so no stairs in the middle of the night."

Inwardly, I chuckled. Only Meg knew Devlin might be joining me in a few days. No point in housing one of the other women in my tiny cottage. I'd need the second bed in the one bedroom, if I dared—for Devlin Doyle. Yes, I thought, I will sleep with the dear man in full view--well, not exactly full view—of all my friends but Theo.

Which was probably fine, I thought in a flash, as Theo was the one who'd hold me to higher standards, and that dear lady was stuck in West Parkford with her recovering daughter.

I smiled at Meg, who offered back a funny, twisted grin, but the exchange quieted the others down, and even Hannah, who returned shaking her cell phone and growling in frustration, agreed to the arrangement.

"I can't get a signal," she moaned.

"Oh, sorry," Heather said. "We're so far down in the valley here. You'll need to go to the center of town, out in front of the Tourism Center, where you'll be up on the cliffs, and with the Atlantic right out in front of you, you'll get brilliant reception."

Hannah thanked her, then checked out the possibility of getting our evening meal nearby.

Again, Heather came to the rescue, suggesting three different restaurants, one of them a pub, where we could find adequate and reasonable food for tonight.

"And when you want to stock up on your groceries, there's a lovely brand new SafeCo right up the hill from here. Just bear left, at the top of the driveway and take your first sharp left at the intersection."

"How about other kinds of shops, you know, hairdressers, notions, books?" Meg asked.

Heather turned to her. "Absolutely. On the High Street, in town, you'll find all of that and more."

I thanked Ms. Ringold, and headed to my own apartment at the back of the Manor House. The other women would be a few yards away, at the front of the Manor House, and both units were along the northern edge of the ancient house. Imagine, I thought, walls that were three-feet thick that had stood for over a thousand years!

"So no one stays in the Manor House itself during the night?" I asked as I stood poised to enter my "cottage."

Heather shook her head. "It's already locked up. Tomorrow, starting at ten a.m. we have tours, and you're each entitled to a tour, since you're renting here. It's quite lovely and nicely kept inside. And with some pretty nervy stories of the past."

"I can't wait for that part," Dorie lied.

Hannah patted her friend on the back. "I *really* can't. This is just an amazing place. Thanks for your help."

Heather nodded and walked a few steps away before turning back to me as I stood in my doorway. "Just call me on the night number if you need anything. The phones in your bedrooms are a direct line to me. And remember the tea shop, just there," she pointed across the driveway, "opens at nine a.m."

She left us, then, and the rest of the Women on Fire made their way to their home away from homes.

"Let's unpack, friends. We meet in half an hour to find one of these supper places," Meg said. "Before we all die of starvation."

I waved, and firmly closed my door. I wouldn't even make the trek upstairs to unpack. Instead I drew a glass of water in the unit's tiny kitchen, swallowed it along with a pair of anti-inflammatories, then threw myself down on the sofa in what I was sure was called the sitting room.

"Here at last," I said aloud to the old walls. "Where Fitzgibbons will get well, and we'll all have a fine, restful vacation." My eyes slitted open to survey the simple surroundings, white-washed walls with dark walnut-stained trim, bunches of dried flowers in jugs, and thick carpet on the floor—no doubt to keep out the winter cold.

"Oh, Devlin," I heard myself whisper. "We'll have our little cottage to ourselves." I'd meant to phone him, but it would have to wait until we found better reception. Instead, I closed my eyes and fell into a deep sleep.

Twenty-nine

Dorie

I just adored the white-washed Manor House with its dark wood trim and curly tiled roof, and once I got indoors I loved the slight musty scent of age in the building itself, and the brilliant patches of autumn garden visible out every window. From my bedroom window, I caught a glance of the long garden path twisting and turning out of sight alongside a babbling brook behind Rose Cottage. Every margin of grass was studded with plantings of one kind or another. Shade plants like impatiens and hostas there beneath some large trees, sunny patches with summer roses and black-eyed susans and Canterbury bells still blooming in brilliant blues.

I was so glad I'd brought my watercolors as well as my camera. I could spend hours—weeks!—doing sketches of the different vistas here at Chambercombe. And surely there were more stunning sights yet to be seen. I could hardly wait until morning to wander the grounds.

Meanwhile, I started unpacking my bag, saw Hannah had already taken the upper drawers and a few inches of closet space. I cheerfully fit my things in, leaving nightclothes and slippers by the bed, trying the mattress and then pausing, cautiously, to tap the wall which separated our apartment from the main portion of the manor house. My knuckles made virtually no sound.

How real were the rumors of ghosts? How true were the legends that had built up around this thousand-year-old dwelling, so old that in the times of the Norman conquest, was one of the finest houses listed in the Doomsday Book? I could hardly imagine how a house could stand for a thousand years, or what kinds of secrets its thick walls held. Again I pressed my palm to the wall of my bedroom, the very wall adjoining the British Heritage manor house. If only I'd been a fly on that wall even a few centuries ago.

What kind of life would I have observed? What kind of happiness, or terror? What kind of people? Loving? Sad? Evil? No, not evil, I couldn't believe that. I wouldn't even go there.

I shivered as I went downstairs to meet with the others, eager to plan our dinner and escape the chill I'd suddenly felt deep in my bones.

No one raved about their dinners later, but no one had any harsh criticism either. Those who had fish did smile as they commented on its freshness, and everyone loved the variety of firmly steamed veggies on every plate. Those who had yearned for dressing on their salads had been somewhat disappointed, but anyone who loved french fries or huge baked potatoes running over with butter and sour cream was surely sated.

Despite their tiredness, Hannah and Ada insisted we drive to the waterfront to make our phone calls and perhaps find an ice cream shop for dessert. We were disappointed in neither, and totally overwhelmed by the geography of the place.

The town of Ilfracombe, where the manor house was located, dipped down abruptly to the shoreline, so as we traversed the angled roads that led us to the Tourist Board we came upon a wide view of the Atlantic, and a strange double-domed white concrete building that flaunted itself on the shore.

Everything else we had passed in this quaint city smacked of Victorian times, and Hannah, especially, had been enthralled, then stunned.

"It's like a walk into a hundred years ago," she said, "every dormer and dentil and the gingerbread frosting in wonderful colors and with fine gardens. Wow. But those cone-shaped thingies on the shore! What on earth—"

"Looks to me like Madonna's bra when she did that famous, outrageous video of hers," Lucia said as she angled the van downhill.

All I could do was stare and giggle.

"Ilfracombe Tourist Bureau," Meg piped up, reading the sign that soon met our eyes. "Those spires are modern art, my friends. They're trying to tell us they're not still ensconced in the-nineteenth century."

As Lucia slowed the car, my eyes scanned the wide lawns and colorful flowerbeds that greeted visitors to these abstract-looking, ultra modern towers.

"Someone has a sense of humor," Lucia muttered as she followed signs to parking spots around the back of the building.

There, the steep, rocky coast and pounding waves of the Atlantic below took our breath away. I for one forgot the strange concrete cones at our backs as we pulled into a parking space just as the sun, moving off to the left, painted the waves with its last glints of red.

We were speechless, and the troubles back in West Parkford seemed distant and small.

While Hannah made her call home to the States to interrogate Bernie on the case's progress, Ada stepped away from the car, too, to dial up Devlin in Ireland. Meg, Lu and I dashed first right and then left along the embankment, captivated by the rock formations of the cliffs that formed a half-circle dotted by caves. The seabirds catching thermals to dip and rise all around us enchanted me, and I wasn't alone.

"I have to see more of this," Lucia shouted over the noise of the surf. Even a hundred feet up above the crashing of waves on rocks, we could feel the tang of ocean spray on our cheeks.

"I love it. Better n' Maine," I called back.

Meg laughed. "You two! You'd think you'd never left your staid little New England town before."

"I haven't been that far away," I admitted. "But see that huge green hill rising from the cliffs across the little bay?" They did. "I'm going to climb it before we leave here, I swear."

"I'm with you, Dorie," Lucia promised, her melodious alto keeping pace with the crash of rolling waves. "If these old legs hold out, I'll start training for it tomorrow."

I pulled out my camera and snapped shots of the cliffs and caves so picturesquely arranged on the other side of the curving bay. Down on the beach, or what I later learned the Brits called the shingle, children skipped stones into the roiling water, then ran backwards, laughing, as their shoes got soaked with an incoming flood.

Hannah joined us and snapped pictures of her own, capturing first the three of us in the foreground, then one of Ada, hugging the phone in the crook of her neck away from the wind and surf as she completed her call to Devlin. When she returned to us, she was aglow.

"I may as well tell you all now that it's final."

They hung on her words, cupping their ears to hear her gentle voice.

"What?" Lucia asked. "Speak up."

Ada blushed, swallowed hard and grinned. "It's Devlin. He's completing his work in a few days. He should be able to join me by Sunday or Monday."

"Say what?" asked Hannah, glancing at the other faces around us when the wind whipped Ada's words away.

"Your father," Meg shouted. "He's coming here from Ireland to be with Ada."

Ada reached a quick hand out and covered Hannah's with her own. "You don't mind, do you?"

Hannah chortled. "Why should I mind? The UK is also a free country, if I'm not mistaken, and these days..."

I bit my lip when I saw the tumult on Hannah's face. I jumped in to try and make things seem normal again but knew as soon as I spoke that things were not normal. "Oh, how lucky, we have extra space for him. Oh..." Meg knocked against me, her right hand balled into a half-fist. I got quiet, trying to figure that out.

Ada studied her shoes, as we stood there in a half-circle, the Women on Fire, clinging to the fence, our hair being whipped and lifted by the sweep of wind from the ocean. Hannah leaned across the space and gave Ada a one-armed hug.

"How can I blame you? He's a lovable guy. I've known that my entire life."

When the chuckling died down Lucia prescribed Devon frozen custard.

On the way to our just desserts, Hannah told us Bernie had finally located the woman substituting for Glenda Mane at Rosemont Farms.

"Terry Bukowski. Who claims she has no idea where Mane is, just hired her on to supervise the grooms and monitor things at the farm. She's sleeping there, too, to be a presence if anything is needed with the eight horses Mane keeps, her own and others."

"Terry Bukowski," was all Ada could murmur.

"Well, at least now she'll be able to afford boots that fit her," I said, so light-heartedly that everyone laughed.

It covered up their fears, I thought. It wasn't that funny.

~ * ~

Back at Chambercombe Manor, where bright outdoor lights lit our way from the parking lot on a higher level down to the deserted courtyard and our two cottage-apartments, we said goodnight and watched as Ada let herself into Rose Cottage, and the rest of us piled into Lilac. I was glad, when I finally climbed into bed, that I was too tired to mull over my fears of sleeping in a haunted building. My body ached from all the travel of the day, especially the long ride from Dover to Devon, from the excitement of settling into our home away from home, and from even the tensions of the evening, which had dissipated in the afterglow of strawberry, chocolate and vanilla.

I slid into my twin bed, not surprised to see Hannah already asleep on her back and snoring lightly a few feet away. Even a loud snoring wouldn't keep me awake tonight, though. I curled up on my side toward the wall and let my body relax into the latent curves and bumps of the mattress, vaguely wondering how many people had slept here before me.

That's when it woke me, shaking me to the core.
Thump-thump. Thump-thump.
The wall just above my head vibrated in a steady rhythm. I spun around in bed, reaching out toward Hannah only to find Hannah reaching back and muttering. In seconds, we had the lamp on between us and I knew my face must be devoid of all color. The thumping repeated itself.

"You heard it, too?"

"Of course," Hannah said. She was just about to condemn our roommates across the hall for playing jokes on us in the middle of the night when our door flew open with a clatter, and a flashlight shone in our eyes.

"My God," Lucia bellowed. "What are you two up to?"

I squeaked and Hannah guffawed. "Us up to?" she said. "You woke us—"

At that same moment, the sound partly muffled by Hannah's words, arose... another pair of thumps, and another.

"Where's Meg?" I asked in a tiny voice, flinging myself onto Hannah's bed and nestling against her.

"Meg's sound asleep," Lu said, flicking off her flashlight and scooting onto the edge of Hannah's bed, too. "Nothing wakes that Balkan but a bomb. Ooh, I shouldn't have said that. Don't tell her."

"Shh," said Hannah. "Let's see if it happens again."

We listened in silence for a full three minutes but no more thumping came from beyond our apartment wall—the main rooms of Chambercombe Manor.

"Should we tell someone? Call that Miss Heather?" I asked.

"Sure," Lucia said. "Let's drive down to the seashore where there's a signal and ask her if it's safe until morning?"

"No need. She said this phone is a direct line," Hannah answered sleepily. "But, look. There's got be a logical reason why the building goes 'thump' in the night. A, a heater or something turning on, or floors settling."

"Cripes, Hannah," Lu snapped. "If the damned building hasn't settled in nine-hundred-fifty-three years, it ought to give up by now."

"What could it be?" I asked through my shivers.

"I don't know. And maybe I don't want to know, but I'm going back to bed." Lucia flicked on her flashlight. "We'll talk about this in the morning. Wonder if Ada heard it from Rose Cottage."

"She must have," Hannah said. "Her room is adjacent to this same wall." She made a fist and started to bang the wall. I grabbed her arm and pulled it back.

"Don't, oh, Hannah, don't. Just... let it be. Maybe it's gone to sleep now, and we should, too."

But as I crept back to my own bed and Lucia returned across the hall to hers, I knew I wouldn't fall asleep for a long time. And tonight I'd think up some old schoolgirl prayers to say, too. Hoping the crick in my neck and chill in my body would go away, I curled up on my side toward Hannah's bed, reassured by the shadow of my friend's flung out arms and relaxed form beside me. Ada's gift of this trip had been such a wonderful blessing—but now I was freaking out about the price we might pay. I prayed, I did breathing exercises, I tried to relax.

Hannah was right. It was nothing. In the morning we'd all laugh about it.

Maybe.

Thirty

Ada

As soon it was open, I stepped across the alleyway to the Lady Jane Tea Shops and met the manager, a vivacious blonde woman of my own age bracket who knew how to pour a full cup of American coffee and didn't have an attitude about it either. Shelly had been in the hotel-restaurant business for decades, and her smiling, friendly eyes and contagious laugh were obviously part of her success. As we hadn't yet shopped for groceries, I asked for a breakfast table for five to be set up on the patio on the crisp but sunny morning, then went to haul my sleepy crowd over for their breakfast.

"I have an early appointment at Amber Hill," I reminded them.

Only Meg was in a full state of dress and ready for the trip. "Just us, though, right, Ade?" Hannah piped up, "Dorie and I'd like to come along. It's not that far, and if we get bored we can hike back."

Dorie nodded enthusiastically. "I'd love to get out for some air this morning."

Lucia, stirring cream into her coffee, balked. "Not me. I'm more interested in getting in some provisions. Find that famous SafeCo Market."

"But we don't have a second car," Dorie moaned, smiling up at Shelly as she arranged plates of scones and whole wheat toast on our table.

Shelly had overheard. "I have to run over to Safeco later," she said, her smile beaming at Lucia. "Drive along with me. If you're not finished when I am, I'll send one of the men over for you later."

Lucia nodded. "Thanks, that would be perfect."

When Shelly had left the table and everyone was munching and fighting over the luscious strawberry preserves, I set my mug down and placed my fingertips in a tent before my eyes, a sure sign to my friends, I suppose, that I had something important to say. I couldn't wait any longer. My heart hammered in my throat as I began.

So I began very quietly. "Look, everyone, last night when I went to bed I could think of nothing but Devlin. We really are very close. I hope no one is offended by my saying this. We feel we, well, have a future. I didn't think last night it was in any way wrong to bring him here to stay in Rose with me."

While others made murmurs of agreement, I cleared my throat and put up a well-manicured hand to stop them.

"But then I woke during the night, having practically been hit over the head, and I decided it wasn't fair to all of you who came along on this trip to help me get my thoroughbred well, and maybe," I said glancing at Hannah, "try to get more information on Mac and who might have killed him."

I paused to take a large swallow of black coffee and went on before anyone could stop me.

"I had a real wake-up call, believe me, and I've made a big decision. I know my darling Devlin will understand. I'm going to call him this morning and ask him not to come." I tilted my head back to gaze at the blue canvas of the sun umbrella above our heads, hoping the squeezed back tears might not fall.

A choral gasp fell across the entire patio.

"But Ada," Meg began.

"My dear..." Lucia started.

I put out both hands in "stop" positions. "It's okay, I've made up my mind. I imagine missing him will add more excitement to our reunion back in the states when I get there. So," I concluded, managing a smile, "I now have room for another person in Rose Cottage. I hope one of you will join me, as it's very lonesome, and a bit scary, over there."

A heavy silence fell over the group, and only Lucia kept munching, staring all the while at me, as I began to spread jam on my toast.

Then several people spoke at once. Hannah's voice could be strident when she chose it to be, and she dominated the melee.

"This is absolutely bizarre. Dad wants to be with you, you want to be with him, and he's only an hour or two away by ferry. You're consenting adults, for God's sake. I insist you change your mind again. You're not yourself right now, you're—"

"A little bit crazy," Dorie said. "I for one am not going to pack up all my things and keep you company when a perfectly nice, handsome and lovely man is practically on his way here."

Being the closest in the wide space around the circular table, Lucia put a heavy hand on my arm. "What on earth do you mean, you had a 'wake-up' call during the night?"

Dorie's eye caught Lucia's, and Hannah piped up, "Yeah, exactly what was this call? And how did it change your mind?"

I felt myself blush to my roots. Thinking of roots, I wondered in that moment if I needed a color job while here. Just in case Devlin came, of course. I looked around the group at three pairs of accusing eyes, and some slightly slanted exotic ones which were also flitting in a wild survey of the group. Meg looked confused, but everyone else seemed accusing.

I sighed, and gave it up. I glanced behind me to be sure the lovely Shelly was not nearby, and then drew in my breath. "Okay, all right," I said. "Here's what happened. I had fallen asleep, dreaming about my sweetheart, I think, when suddenly right on the wall above my bed—"

"Aghh," said the multiple scream of three women at the table. Arms fluttered, faces fell, coffee cups rattled in their saucers.

"Oh, my God," Lucia murmured.

"She heard it, too," shrieked Dorie.

Hannah squared her shoulders and hit the table with her fists, jarring the coffee pot and causing the jam to slide to the edge.

"Ada, no. Really? You heard the thumps? You heard the thumps in Rose Cottage, too?"

"I, I, yes. Oh, you mean you did too?" The wind was completely knocked out of me. "Four times, in pairs, and then a bit later another four times?"

"I thought... oh, Lord, I thought of Mac's death, and that maybe someone had tailed us here and was trying to frighten us to death," Dorie piped up, "Like that awful Glenda, or Mr. Freaky Finch."

Meg laughed cynically, but the others nodded in affirmation.

"It passed my mind," Lucia admitted.

"Eek!" Dorie cried again, sliding her chair closer to Hannah. "I don't know what's worse, being pursued or, or... haunted!"

Shelly had come running at the burst of noise and activity. She stepped back, arms folded across her ample bosom. "You've been 'visited'?" she asked.

I stared up at her. "So this is normal, here at Chambercombe Manor?" I hadn't realized my voice was trembling.

Shelly nodded, making orchestra leading motions with her hands. "Don't worry about it, luv. No, really, it's all right. Okey-dokey as you Yanks say."

Meg sat speechless, trying to gather what the rest of us were talking about.

Shelly went on in soothing tones. "Surely you read the Manor House has been considered haunted for many years? But of course you haven't had time to have the tour yet, have you?"

We shook our heads.

"Will that help us understand what happened last night?" Hannah asked.

"Absolutely. And even if there are ghosts here, they're not dangerous ghosts. I mean, you really don't have to worry. There's never been... a bad episode or anything. No one hurt, or anything bizarre like that. At least in my time here."

I reached up and took Shelly's hand. "Thank you. That's all I needed to hear."

"But, wait," Hannah said. "Is the thumping real, or did we imagine it?"

Shelly chuckled. "It's been real enough for lots of people who stay here."

"Then there's got to be some logical cause," Hannah persisted. "What's causing it?"

"You'll have to each decide that yourselves, m'dears. I'm no expert on the haunting, or the legend. Ask the tour guide. And do go soon. You'll love it. Unless you scare easily."

Dorie shuddered aloud.

"Now, stop, all of you," I said. "You're here to help me, not fall apart over some ghost stories. Let's trust Shelly here, and learn more about the story of Chambercombe later."

"That's pretty trusting of you, Ada," Lucia

commented, "considering you fell apart yourself a few minutes ago".

"Well, okay, but now I'm trusting enough to be glad I didn't call my, uh, boyfriend and ask him not to come," I said.

We pulled ourselves together, sighing, shaking our heads and pouring more coffee and tea. Eventually they all congratulated me on my decision to still have Devlin come to Chambercombe, and babbled to Meg about how she had slept through the commotion from the other side of the wall at midnight.

"But, but, but..." Meg said. No one would let her speak. Everyone seemed suddenly lighthearted about the unexplained noises in the dark. Or just being queens of "de-nial," as Hannah herself often accused us.

I pursued my toast. I knew they would all feel guilty for complaining further about the thumping in the night, feeling I'd take it as a sign Devlin wasn't to come lest the spirits (and my friends) become annoyed. Whispering to Lucia beside me, I said, "Wait 'til they hear the bumping and thumping after he's gotten here."

Lucia spat out a chortle and rolled her eyes.

~ * ~

As four of us pulled up a half-hour later at Amber Hill, everyone was full of chatter. Meg said she was disappointed she hadn't gotten to hear the curious sounds in the night, but insisted she was too skeptical by nature to believe our nonetheless matching accounts. I assumed Meg merely felt like a new citizen to the country being teased by the veterans around her, and noticed she decisively kept her mouth shut from that point on.

The Director of Amber Hill met us in the parking lot and walked with us into the stable where Fitzgibbons nickered noisily and tap danced against the bedded floor at our arrival. We spent time at his stall, me sneaking him an apple I'd bribed from Shelly, and the Director explaining the schedule.

"I'd welcome just you into the meeting, Mrs. Javitts, to hear exactly what our plans are for Fitzgibbons, now that we've had a chance to assess him," he said, glancing around the large group. "Our methods are quite confidential and we like to limit the number of people who hear about them."

I shook my head firmly. "I've brought Doctor Dautrey along—she's my right arm person, understands all these technical terms better than me. I'd like her in with us."

His eyebrows lifted. "Veterinarian?" he asked, looking toward Meg.

"Retired human pathologist," Meg snapped back.

The director bowed. "Very well. You physicians take oaths. No problem." He turned toward Hannah and Dorie, who were alternately eyeing the several stalls of fine horseflesh nearby and trying to get a glimpse of someone long and handsome in tan riding pants at a far stall.

"Would you ladies like to walk about the farm, or perhaps—do you ride?"

"We do," Hannah answered, "though not in some years, in my case."

"I'm a former eventer," Dorine said, her pretty lips

turning up in a smile. Even I had never known that.

"Brilliant," the man said. He motioned to a groom midway down the stable currying a dappled gray Dutchblood. "Hamish, give these ladies some nice gentle mounts." He winked at Hannah and Dorie. "Until you're used to our trails, anyhow."

The boy mentioned two horses' names and the Director smiled an okay. Just then a tall, good-looking fellow slapped a saddle on the back of his large chestnut.

"Fenn," the Director called out. "Out for a ride?"

The looker nodded and waved, smiling, and was about to finish tacking up his mount.

"Come meet these American ladies. They're out for a walk-trot as soon as Hamish prepares their rides."

The chisel-featured rider abandoned his horse after buckling the bridle, and came closer, smiling in a reserved, British sort of way, I thought.

"Please permit me to accompany you. Our trails are many, and we wouldn't want you to lose your way and find yourselves facing some unexpected hurdles."

Dorie covered up a giggle and Hannah tilted her head. But when they were introduced formally to Fennimore Layton and the blue-eyed Brit with the shock of dark blond hair and movie star looks had mastered their names, they both seemed quite at home and I relaxed. Smiling broadly now at Dorie, he touched her elbow so she'd follow along. I sucked in some extra air when I saw her face brighten as she turned her chin up to face him. He was tall even for her five-feet-nine inches.

Over her shoulder, Hannah winked back at me as she

trailed what was clearly a couple about to happen. Meg and I went into our meeting with enthusiasm. Although I was concerned Dorine would forget her prize-winning dressage moves in the face of such sudden infatuation, I considered that Amber Hill Equestrian Centre was already turning out nicely for at least one of our fiery women.

Thirty-one

Dorie

In the afternoon, at my urging, all five of us took the tour of the Manor House together. Eve, the most experienced guide, was patient, full of knowledge and anecdotes, and let us ask questions to our heart's content, or distress, depending on the answers.

I had not been able to erase the glow in my cheeks, and now felt strangely unconcerned about any possible ghostly dangers in Chambercombe Manor. I'd explained earlier to the group that Fenn had invited both me and Hannah for an early morning ride the next day. And my heart stumbled in its rhythm when I thought about our next meeting. That was what filled my head with woozy thoughts as we trekked across the stone patio toward the house's main entrance.

"I shouldn't come. Let you two get to know each other," Hannah said quietly.

"Please don't say that, Hannah. Sometimes I can't

even understand him when he speaks with that, that Eton accent," I whispered. "I need you there."

Earlier they'd all teased me without mercy, but in the end Hannah had agreed to go along, saying that. Fenn did seem very knowledgeable about the equestrian world in England, and also quite open and honest. Who knew what we might learn from him that could help our case?

Ada smiled with gratitude. Her friends hadn't forgotten their mission here.

Plans made, I could hardly stop grinning, and the sumptuous soup and salad lunch prepared by Lucia for our return added to my happiness. When we gathered for the tour, I tried to pull my thoughts away from the attractive, interested Englishman, and inspect all the architecture and appointments in the Manor House with a curious artist's eye.

Like the others, I was thrilled with the antiquities we were allowed to see but not touch—a copy of the Domesday Book, circa ten-eighty-six which listed Chambercombe Manor as a "baronial holding," a fragile and original "Britches" Bible, old pottery, glass and hammered metal cooking implements.

Dried herbs and flowers, along with some convincing spider webs, shrouded the rafters of the large limestone kitchen with a sense of days past. Black iron cauldrons hung in the woman-size fireplace, and bowed timbered beams, likely something off an old ship, held up the aged ceilings. I saw Meg shiver with a chill more than once, but had no idea why. When the group climbed the stairway and paused in the hall for a lecture by the guide, I myself began to shiver uncontrollably for no apparent reason. I tugged my sweater closer and saw Meg doing the same thing.

I started to ask a question, but the group was staring into an ancient alcove listening to Eve's tale of the legend of the Manor. I poked my head into the circle, squeezing between Ada and Lu, and soon became as speechless as they were, as we heard about the land pirates that had operated off the rocky shores, the young woman and her child who had died in a shipwreck on that shore, and the discovery of the woman's body in this tiny boarded-up secret room over a hundred years ago.

Gulping, and noticing how pale we all looked in the diffused light of the hallway, we groped toward the next room and stepped through the undersized doorway into a well-furnished nine-hundred-year-old master bedroom. I tried not to feel anything at all as I stood there, but the room seemed filled with odd vibrations. Then I realized this room was the one adjacent to our bedrooms next door in the apartments.

Ada leaned against Hannah, who bit her lip, while Lucia covered her mouth with her fingers and tried to look nonchalant. Meg and I kept shivering. The guide was still talking about the ancient hangings on the wall, the four-poster bed, the once magnificent but now decrepit silk spread. Then she turned to the piece of furniture beside the bed, a long, narrow, wooden platform cradle.

"They say this cradle still holds the spirit of the infant who died on the beach, but who knows?"

I was about to turn away, when I heard it: "Thump-thump, thump-thump."

I shrieked without meaning to, grabbing at Meg's arm. I turned back to see that the guide had merely tapped the cradle so it bounded from one side to the other, then back and forth again. Thump-thump. Thump-thump.

As one, our group pulled together in a tighter circle.

"We... we heard that, in the night," Ada said. "Was someone in here? Did someone rock it like you did?"

Eve smiled wanly and tried to calm us. She shook her head.

"There's no one in here at night at all. It's locked and secured. You all heard it?" she asked.

We greed in cacophony.

"That's unusual. Sometimes one or two people will hear it, but never a whole group."

Meg stuck out her chin. "I didn't hear it. I was asleep," she said "Someone must have been over here fooling us."

"I'm afraid not," Eve said again. "It just happens. We don't know why. Sorry if you were frightened."

Of them all, I knew I was the one most convinced of a spirit's presence. But now I didn't feel so alone. As Hannah examined the cradle's shape and the floor it rested on, I looked away. Perhaps someone or something was trying to send us a message—I didn't want to know. I tried not to think of the time hundreds of years earlier when perhaps a child had died on the beach, and his mother's remains discovered in the secret room years later.

I edged to the only window in the room and gazed out at the garden below, feeling the muscle ache in my gluts as I bent toward the low window. Yes, I hurt from riding for the first time in six or eight years. I could tell Hannah did, too. It helped me forget the spirit, focusing on going riding again tomorrow. I found myself picturing my new friend, Fenn Layton. How beautifully he sat in the saddle, strong back straight, hands gentle on the reins. Those hands, long-fingered, hands and wrists topped with a curly blond hair—how I'd stared at them. My weakness, hands and wrists. I remembered Fenn's voice, low and rumbly, and anticipated with a quickened heart beat tomorrow's meeting with him. That's what I'd keep on my mind.

This was no time for hysterics and I was determined to beat them. We had too much to solve in today's mystery to dally in the sixteenth century and curious sounds in the night.

I told Hannah so as we exited from the building and emerged into a suddenly cloud-covered day. Jetlag was undermining our enthusiasm, but there was no stopping the chatter of the five of us as we took Devonshire tea with strawberries and clotted cream on Shelly's flaky scones.

"So the 'Jane Grey' name of this establishment comes from a young woman who slept here at the Manor hundreds of years ago," Lucia ruminated.

"And then went on to marry Henry the Eighth—until her early demise," Meg said. We all shivered again, even while huddled in the warmth of the cozy tea rooms.

Hannah's eyes grew round. "A thought jiggled my brain when we learned about the cradle," she said. "I've just remembered what it is. To solve Mac's murder, we must learn about his cradle days, his background. Otherwise, it's worse than hunting for a needle in the hay.'

"Stack," I said, proud of myself.

Meg shushed me. "What do you mean, Hannah?" Meg asked.

"I'm just saying, to hell with old legends and seeing sights. We're here to help with Fitzgibbons, yes, and if he needs exercise, Dorie or I are your girls. But this is our chance to help solve Mac's murder by learning about his background."

Ada clapped and looked up with cream-dabbled lips. "Yes!"

"So tomorrow we give this Fenn Layton a chance to help us locate Mac's family, if any exist, and then, I don't know about you, Dorine, but I'm going up to Cheltenham where Fitzgibbons came from. Besides, my thighs and backside muscles might welcome a break from actually sitting in the saddle tomorrow."

I laughed, understanding.

"Great idea," Lucia said around a mouthful of scone. "You can perhaps at least hassle the people who sold George Javitts the horse."

"And that we'll do, if we have to. Are you on board, Dorie, or have you been too swept off your feet?" Hannah looked fierce, and I knew not to cross her at this moment.

"I'm with you, Han. Especially if Fenn is agreeable to skipping the ride. He did say he'd take us anywhere we'd like to go in that Jaguar of his. Poor Mac died without a chance, and I agree, there's got to be a rocking cradle or something in his background that will help us find out why." I tapped the table twice with the side of my clenched hand.

Everyone applauded. Ada pounded the air with her petite fist and suggested we take a break from the Manor House and drive down to the seafront where we could gain a cellular signal. But the rain from the ominous dark clouds had begun to patter on the shade umbrella over us, and thickening curls of fog were starting to descend into the little valley. We decided en masse to take naps instead. All but Lucia, who wanted to start dinner.

"This tea break was fantastic," she said. "We need even more comfort tonight—how's mac-and-cheese and meatloaf sound?"

At that very moment, Heather, the manager, passed our table and called out, "Sounds just fine to me."

Everyone grinned, but it took Lucia to jump up and issue a real invitation. "Do join us, Heather. You can give us some inside tips about what to see in the area."

"In addition to the Manor House," Ada added.

"And about certain people over at Amber Hill Equestrian Centre," I murmured with a lift of my shoulders.

"You should know she's a professional chef," Hannah piped up, standing and stretching her legs out. "And her mac-and-cheese and meatloaf are gourmet all the way."

Heather accepted, beaming. "What a brilliant idea! I was just joking, but I was going to be alone tonight in any case."

"Then come to Rose Cottage," I added. "It will be fun."

~ * ~

Heather insisted on pitching in during the meal, helping Lucia set out plates and bringing the food to the table where we squeezed together for our meal. While Meg and Hannah cleared and Ada rested her knee under an ice pack, and we all oohed and aahed over Lu's cooking, I sensed there was enough trust between my friends and the lovely, ingenuous Heather to say a little bit about our purpose for being in Devon.

"So while Ada's horse is being rehabilitated over at Amber Hill, we'd like to learn more about the poor British trainer who was killed," I explained.

"Oh, my," Heather exclaimed. "Sorry about your loss. Do you have any idea where the man was from?"

Ada shook her head. "His name was Michael McClellan, and he had worked up at Cheltenham as a trainer for some years. We don't know if he lived there, though. He never mentioned family either."

"Hmmm. You've asked the Director over at Amber Hill?"

Dorie said they had, and they'd even asked Fenn Layton, who showed them around the trails that morning.

Heather made goo-goo eyes at the mention of Fenn's name. "Woo-hoo, he's a looker, in't he? Nice chap, too. Fenn lost his wife in an accident some ten or more years back and never remarried, more's the loss."

Hannah stuck her face in from the kitchen. "He's asked our Dorie for a date. I'm to be the chaperone."

I objected, embarrassed and waving Hannah off, but Heather giggled. "You gals work fast. Lucky you."

"We're hoping he'll take us up to Cheltenham to track down someone who could perhaps help us in our search," I explained. "So you think he's, well, reliable?"

Heather sipped her coffee and then nodded. "I'd trust him completely," she said simply. "He knows his way around a steed, for sure, and probably knows plenty of the horsey set up there. Sounds like a good lead."

I grinned. I hadn't needed an excuse to see Fenn again, that thick shock of hair finding its way out of his riding helmet, or those luminous blue eyes drawing me in. Why me, I didn't know. I was on the verge of hot flashes and osteoporosis, and here I was letting myself fall head over heels with a man I'd probably never see again after this week.

I sighed, glad to be forgetting the topic of former residents of the Manor House, and the sounds in the night.

The whole group kept Heather engaged in conversation for hours, and when she'd left a little after eleven, we decided to stay up together for another hour just so we wouldn't be around any thumping walls at the witching hour. Meg was a little soured by the idea of taking everyone into our confidence, but didn't lecture me too much. Instead, we made lists of all we had to do on the next day, and kept our minds off of our present real estate.

I needed little encouragement. In bed I dozed off dreaming of the tall, slender fellow we'd ridden with twelve hours before, and nothing marred my sleep but the steamy sensations in my lower body and the rising itch I didn't dare scratch.

Thirty-two

Theo

I rolled my baggage into the Virgin Atlantic queue, relieved the hectic day of packing and driving to Logan was behind me. I still had two hours before boarding, and a cheese sandwich in my pocket for late lunch, which I'd missed at home by having to depart before the commuter traffic began. Sigourney's therapy would begin soon, and my family was safely ensconced at home under Wilson's charge. He'd promised to keep the house locked up, in case that nasty Gus Finch should prey on us again. And Danny would be available any afternoon for chauffeuring.

I lifted my rolling bag onto the scales, smiling, imagining Ada's reaction when I arrived at the Manor tomorrow. How good it would be to see everyone, and how terrific to be part of Fitzgibbons's recuperation and maybe even the search for Mac's killer. I showed my documents to the clerk, received a boarding pass and baggage check, and picked up my carry-on, receiving a friendly "*Bon Voyage* and cheers," from the clerk. Bag over shoulder, snapped together with my purse, I began the hike to my gate.

People rushed pell-mell around the lobby, and as I turned down the appropriate passage toward the gates, I glimpsed among them, or thought I did, the sight that made me stumble, catch myself and look again.

What I saw washed the blood from my cheeks and sent goose bumps racing over my skin. I stumbled again, but righted myself. My carefree hours came to an abrupt end. This time I picked up the pace, feeling the slam of carry-ons against my hip as I raced helter-skelter toward my gate.

The horrifying face of Gus Finch was in that crowd of people. My peripheral vision told me he'd separated out from the crowd, that he'd seen me. Was headed my way. I ran straight on, pushing my fairly fit but quickly fading body as I hadn't pushed it in years. I didn't dare waste time to glance backward. I tried to tell myself maybe he had some other business here. Maybe it was a coincidence he was at Logan when I was. Maybe...

Pump those legs, Theo, I ordered myself. You know that's all a crock. He's after you. He knew somehow when you were leaving the country, when and where, and he...

He what? What did he want of me? I had no idea, but I ran harder, gripping my bags tight against my side. *Get me to some people,* I screamed in my head as I passed through a lonely part of the corridor, not daring to turn back.

When I clearly heard the hastening footsteps behind

me, I picked up the pace again. *Thank God for the mountains of Bolivia that strengthened my legs. Now if only I had some breath!* I prayed without thinking then prayed some more. When I passed a shiny bank of stainless steel elevators, I dared to move my head a fraction to the right and saw reflected in the shiny surface, as I knew I would, the audacious Gus Finch, gaining on me.

If only I saw a security guard, an employee of some kind, but yards of corridor stretched ahead, unpeopled for the moment. I thought to grope for the cell phone in my purse, but no, I'd lose time. I gritted my teeth and raced on, feeling my stomach tumble when I heard him call my name.

"Mrs. Rutledge. Wait. Wait up."

No mistake then, it was my pursuer from West Parkford in the flesh. Mac's killer, no doubt, only yards away and coming closer.

I flew, totally out of breath, nearly losing my bags, and my footing, as a few people came into view on the fringes of the security area. I dashed toward them.

Then, like a bolt striking out, just when I thought I'd made it to safety, he reached me, grabbed me by the arm and pulled me to a stop. Panting, I tried to yank free, and back away, but he snatched at my bags. I lost the tug for them, and hollered.

"Hey, someone help me!" I couldn't lose the tug for the carry-ons or the trip was off. Passport, tickets, money, everything I'd need in England? No, I wouldn't let it go.

Unbelievably, even in the flurry of activity, no one

seemed to hear or notice me. I'd have to fight him off myself. Throw him a shoulder block and run again.

Between short breaths he spoke quickly.

"I'm sorry. Mrs. Rutledge. Really sorry. I didn't mean... to frighten you."

I squirmed. "Then let go of me... this instant."

He did, backing away a fraction of an inch. I breathed, backed away myself, and breathed again, my ample chest heaving, tears ready to flood my eyes. An older man standing in a line not far away glanced up and studied my face. Tears of panic, or tears of relief, I didn't know, covered my cheeks.

Around us, everyone else kept moving, coming and going to the gate area, only vaguely aware of the arguing man and woman in their way. I caught the eye of the gentleman in the blue blazer, let him know I saw him.

"I had to catch you before... you left. Tell you something."

"You might... have phoned."

He smiled. A good sign. But was it real?

The old gentleman cleared his throat and moved sideways away from us, less concerned now.

I still trembled, out of breath. I was about to turn and hasten to the clerks standing at the departure desk but curiosity stopped me. "What... the hell... do you want?" I asked the husky man shadowing me, his face scarlet and perspiring, his comb-over blown to the wrong side, his eyes dark and fierce and pleading.

I imagined how I looked, and didn't care.

"Sorry, I just wanted to give you this." He reached

into his pocket and I froze—a weapon? A knife, a gun? I prayed again, made a small, whimpering noise. The blue blazer turned slightly, paused. Went on.

Finch handed me a folded slip of paper.

"What?" I asked, imagining poison, anthrax sprinkled on its white surface. A threatening message.

"Look," he said. "Really, I wouldn't hurt you. I'm sorry about how I treated you in the parking lot that day in town. I was just—" he cast his eyes downward, "—so frustrated I couldn't get what seemed like the simplest bit of information. But I realize now I was wrong, this determination, obsession, to get a new horse."

"You are wrong," I snapped. I glanced at the paper I'd unfolded in my hand. No powder. Flowered edges, a girl's stationary.

"That's a note," Finch said, still panting, too. "From my daughter. For you. Please, read it and forgive us. Forgive me. I was way off base. Charity helped me see that, her and that girl groom over at the barn."

I paused, thinking that would be Terry Bukowski. Why was she still involved? What was her part in all this? Sighing, I set my carry-on bags down on the floor but kept a hand on their straps, wiped perspiration from my forehead with the back of my hand, ripped open the envelope and flattened out the paper.

Dear Mrs. Rutledge,

I am really sorry we have not been very nice to you and Sigourney since the accident. I know now Sigourney doesn't want to be friends, and I won't bother her. Dad and I tried too hard to get me a horse I probably wouldn't be very good at anyhow.

I'm really sad my father wasn't nice to you, and to lots of people, all over trying to get me a better horse.

I hope Fitzgibbons gets better real fast so Siggy can ride him again. And I hope they put Mac's killer in jail for a million years.

Thank you for always being nice to me, cookies and cocoa and everything. Please don't be mad at my father, because he promises he won't be mean again.

Sincerely,
Charity Finch

I was glad the note wasn't any longer. The words had begun to blur through my tears.

Finch's words came out trembly. "I couldn't write it, like she could, so I had to say it in person. I'm sorry."

More people were scrambling past us. I hoisted my bags but couldn't nod.

"It will take time, Mr. Finch," I said, "to forget how brutally you've acted toward me. And maybe to others. I just don't know. Time will have to tell. Now I have to catch my flight."

The man bowed his head, swiped a hand across his pate to replace his errant hair, and seemed to shrink into himself as he spoke. "Thank you at least for listening. Have a good and successful flight."

I turned away. I couldn't risk getting any more involved with this man, who still might, as I well knew, be involved in the death of Mac McClellan. I shook my head as I took my place in the security check line before the gates. Absolutely refused to watch and see where he went or what he did.

I was becoming quite a cynic.

"Forgive me, Lord," I muttered aloud, as I pushed my hair off my forehead, then lifted it from the back of my neck while a lingering hot flash mingled with the sweat from my face and ran down the passage to my breasts, nearly melting me where I stood. "I don't do these speeded-up exercises so well anymore. And I don't forgive so easily, either." I muttered the words aloud and the blue blazer turned to me for one last look. I gave him a weak smile and a little wave and mouthed the word, "Thanks." He smiled back.

I folded Charity's note and tucked it into my jacket pocket. After I checked in, I'd phone home and tell Wilson. And Bernie Cascone. Maybe the threat from Finch quarters was over.

Or maybe not.

Wait 'til I told the Women on Fire.

Thirty-three

Hannah

I drove the van over to Amber Hill in the morning, hoping Dorie and I would arrive before Fenn Layton had a chance to tack up for our expected trail ride. We were both still saddle sore from the day before, and would be happy to postpone the next ride, fun as it had been. Besides, our investigation into Mac's murder came first with us.

Ada and Meg went along with us to spend time with Fitzgibbons, as the director suggested they do every day during his treatment to keep him from getting out of sorts in his new surroundings. Ada couldn't stop raving about the roomy box stall, totally open to the outdoor paddock, in which Fitzgibbons now reigned. He'd be spoiled by the time he got back to West Parkford and his much more modest quarters.

Meg would drive the van back to the Manor House later, and I would phone the tea rooms when we were ready to be picked up, though I was convinced Layton would gladly drive us all the way if it meant more time with Dorie.

"Do you have those photos of Mac?" Ada asked before going into the barn. "Mr. Layton or someone he knows might recognize Mac."

"Mac with Glenda, Mac with Josie Hand, even one of him with Terry Bukowski." I patted my backpack purse. "A good journalist's always prepared."

Dorie had spotted Fenn parking his dark green Jag and I could sense her go wobbly with anticipation. I shook my head, then thought of my own first reaction to Bernie Cascone, and knew even a woman on the down slope of middle age could be a school girl when the pheromones were flowing.

Ada and Meg stepped away, grinning, and wished us luck.

"Be careful," Meg advised, her stern face gathered into frowns and pursed lips.

"We will," I whispered. "Now off with you. I want to hear how our divine Dorine handles this."

Dorie and Fenn were walking toward the barn, his arm casually draped around her shoulders, and Dorie's violet eyes sparking with something other than a plea for help.

"We didn't tell you the whole story yesterday, because it's a lot to convey to a new... friend," she was saying.

Fenn grinned and paused to brush lengthy wisps of hair away from the face of the tall, very female woman beside him. "Then tell me, now," he said. "Hi, Hannah. Glad you could make today's ride, too."

"We hope you'll take a different kind of ride with us," Dorie said quickly. "Could we sit somewhere while we tell you all about it?"

Fenn nodded, and led us to the tack room, where vending machines and vinyl sofas offered hospitality.

Fenn bought us all coffee, and, since it was so early in the day, we sat in an undisturbed group while Dorie and I told of Ada's horse's accident, his EIPH, and our hopes at Amber Hill.

"That's why I started coming here, too. My Zephyr was diagnosed, and I'd come down from Lancashire to have him fixed. It worked. And I stayed close by in case I ever needed their services again. The Director's a genius."

"Great news," I said, then told him about the rider who was injured when Fitzgibbons crumpled, and the tragic aftermath, with the trainer found dead.

He expelled breath in a rush and his eyes darkened. "Bummer, that."

Dorie's eyes had filled, as they always did at the memory of Mac's loss. "At first they thought suicide, but Hannah's, um, fiancé is the detective in charge, and he, well, he's convinced it's murder. We know nothing about Mac, and it's our hope, Hannah's and mine, to find out here in England something that might point to his killer."

"Because he's from here somewhere. We don't even know exactly where, or if he had a family, or anything about him." I drained my coffee and crunched the cardboard cup.

"Wow, big responsibility," Fenn said. He glanced from one to the other of us, and his eyes suddenly brightened. "I get it," he said, laughing a bit, "you want my help in some way."

"In lots of ways," Dorie said, blushing belatedly, I guessed, when she realized how insinuating that could sound.

He made a little bow from his sitting position. "At your service, Mesdames," he said, his eyes brightening. "How can I help?"

"Well, you know so many people in equine circles," I said. "We know the horse was bought in Cheltenham, we even have the name of the stable where he was housed, but our friend's husband, who bought him, died soon after, so we're not sure how he happened to hire Mac to train Fitzgibbons."

"Or the young girl groom who assisted him," Dorie said. "Who for some reason won't tell us anything."

"Hmmm. Mystery, all right," Fenn said as he tossed away his own empty cup and stood. "I gather you ladies want to sack our planned trot and take a runner in my Jag up to Cheltenham."

We nodded in unison. Dorie patted her curvy behind. "We could actually use the rest after yesterday's ride."

Fenn chuckled. "Gotcha. First time in the saddle again, eh?"

"Is it too much to ask? Or too far to go?" Dorie spoke as if fearful of seeing a negative expression appear on his long, sculpted face.

Fenn grinned from ear-to-ear. "Are you joshing?

Most interesting offer I've had in years." He reached out an arm to us both and pulled us up out of our seats. "Two lovely ladies, one exciting trek up a very scenic road onto the M–five, and a mystery to solve. How can a fellow resist?"

"Then, you'll take us, today? Right now?"

I could tell Dorie was trying to ignore the butterflies in her gut.

"Shall indeed," was Fenn Layton's answer. "Give me ten minutes to muck out my horse, and we'll be off. In fact, if the stable people here can't help, I know the very individual up Cheltenham way who can probably put us on the right path. What's the trainer's name?"

"Michael MacClellan, known as Mac," I answered.

He nodded. "Got it."

"Oh, thank you, Fenn," Dorie started, taking a few dancing little steps toward him in an emotional burst of I didn't know what. Or, rather knew quite well what. I yanked Dorie away in a different direction and said we'd meet Fenn by his car.

"We have to take care of some business first, as well."

After he'd waved and left, I whispered fiercely in Dorie's ear. "Down, girl. Save the emotion and romance for tonight or tomorrow. We're all business today. And this is important. I think we're on the right track."

Dorie sighed. "But he's so hot, and so sweet to say yes to our crazy request."

I shook my head. "He's investing in the future, Ms. Beaulé. He thinks you're hot, too."

~ * ~

The hundred-plus mile drive to Cheltenham, home of the famous race track, went by like a blur in the Jaguar, me perched in the back seat playing guardian to Dorie's bubbling feelings as she sat beside the handsome horseman. Fenn told us he'd checked with the people at Amber Hill, and though folks had heard of Mac, they'd no idea where he came from. The couple up front exchanged a little autobiographical material, then Fenn quizzed me on my own work as a journalist.

"Just free lance now," I said. "Quit my very fine job for Connecticut's best daily paper because they insisted I fly to Afghanistan to interview a local doctor who's working with the women there. I'm pretty terrified of flying."

Dorie glanced over her shoulder and nodded. "But then in an emergency she, uh, well, she flew to Florida to save my life," Dorie said.

Fenn's quirky eyebrow lifted as he turned his straight, stone-cut profile to Dorie. "Sounds like television, or a film," he said.

We women laughed. "Too long a story for a hundred-mile trip," I said. "Let's say I'm somewhat reformed."

"Though she nearly vomited all the way from the U.S. to Gatwick," Dorie piped up. "And she is finally off to Afghanistan after this England trip."

"Enough, Dorine. My bodily functions and scary future plans are off limits today. Oh, look," I said, "the sign for Longmere. That's the home of Van Dyne Stables, who sold Ada's husband her horse."

Fenn slowed the car competently and turned left. Before long we were pulling into a long drive marked with the stable's name. The yard seemed deserted, an old truck and an abandoned-looking car were all that was parked in sight. A dozen or more horses, all beautiful, all sleek and burnished in the mid-day sun, were turned out behind the barns.

When we'd parked and found our way into the barn, the only live person we found was a young girl groom, mucking out stalls.

"The owner about?" Fenn asked. The young lady shook her head.

"Know when the owner'll return?" The slender girl kept shoveling.

I stepped forward, a bit impatient with British formality. "Excuse me. You worked here long?"

The girl paused in her work, intrigued no doubt by the American accent. "Naw, a couple years."

"You must have been twelve when you started," Dorie muttered.

I stepped closer. "Okay, since you've worked here, ever heard of a horse named 'Fitzgibbons'?"

Something flickered over the girl's face, and she pushed a greasy hank of hair out of her eyes before she answered. Hedging for time?

"Naw. Hardly ever know their names. Just their business ends, if y'know what I mean. That's m'job."

Before she could start shoveling again, I thrust the picture of Mac and Glenda in front of the girl's face. It was the clearest, largest print I had.

"So?" the girl asked.

"Know either of them?" Dorie snapped, before I could, probably trying to sound official. "Seen either of them, ever?"

The girl shook her head and lost the battle with her rancid looking hair, which she allowed to cover half her face.

"How about these people? Know who they are?" I slid the other two pictures in front of her one at a time.

The girl seemed slightly interested but kept her main attention on the shovel in her hands. Then in a flash, she put her back to us and pursued the bits of debris in the corners of the stall. "Dunno. Never seen 'em." There was more than cockney in her accent, but I couldn't figure out what.

Fenn growled under his breath and I worried about his irritation level. I had no idea if his British reserve had a high or low cracking point, and we didn't need a fight here.

"Listen, miss, you the only one around right now? Where're the Van Dynes?" he demanded. "We have business with them." His voice had an air of authority, a good, baritone voice with an Eton accent that made you listen.

The girl shrugged. "Just doin' m'job." Her voice was weak, almost trembly. "I work for my pa, and he don't tell me anythin'."

I drew Fenn away with a hand on his elbow and Dorie followed, shaking her head.

"Let's check out the farmhouse. No point in

frightening her. She's obviously not talking,"

"Or not knowing much either," Dorie said as we crossed the yard, seeming glad to breathe the fresher air out here. "Something about her—almost feel I've met her before."

"Another life?" Fenn joked. Then, "Look, there are cars behind the house, half-a-dozen or more. There ought to be people." He circled and scanned the horizon three-hundred-sixty degrees as we walked.

"They could be riding," I said.

"Sure, morning exercise I presume."

We were standing now at the elaborate, paneled oak door of the large Georgian brick house with its old-fashioned knocker of a horse's head. The brass could have used polish and the yard some landscaping, but it was the slapdash look of people who rode out of very finely kept stables. I guessed horse lovers rarely had the money and time to keep everything spic and span, and chose horse work over housework.

When no one answered the ring of the bell or Fenn's firm knock of the horse head on the door, I nodded at Dorie, who sidled over to the nearest window on the right front of the house and cagily peered in.

She reported quickly. "Nice sitting room, leather couches, fireplace, no human beings. Ooh, a big, wooden desk in the corner, absolutely covered with papers and folders and things. And a light over it still on."

"So there probably is a business still running here," I said.

Taking his cue from Dorie, Fenn ambled over to the

left of the building and did the same through the multi-paned windows there. "Dining room. No one at lunch. Kitchen in back looks deserted, too."

"They've got to be out riding." I glanced at my watch. "Surely they'll be back for lunchtime. Let's wait."

We leaned against the car in the shade, draining the few bottles of water Fenn had in his boot. Once I made a casual amble around the entire house, even calling out, "Halloo!" to the upper windows, some of which were open to the day's soft breezes. No one answered, and no one returned to the barn area from the trails that meandered into fields and woods.

When I returned from my round trip, Fenn and Dorie were mixing it up. He'd wrapped both arms around her and she was beaming up at him, though barely holding him off at arms' length.

I figured my interruption was well-timed. I needed Dorie's full attention. She was excellent with details, noticing things other people didn't. Trouble was, those details currently revolved around six feet-two inches of glorious manhood.

"Sorry," Fenn muttered. "Trying to get this lovely lady to have dinner with me."

Dorie jumped away and rearranged her clothes, the filmy orchid top over black riding pants having stuck to her overly warm body.

"I told him maybe tomorrow," she said. "It kind of depends on what we find out today." Although she'd backed away from Fenn's embrace, she'd grabbed his hand as she did, as if to say, "I'm not going far."

I'm sure I grimaced. I knew Dorine, and she meant that bit about not going away.

By one o'clock, no one had appeared, except the skinny girl groom who'd come out exercising three of the horses, one at a time, then cooling them down and returning them to the barn.

Now it was Fenn who checked the time. "Listen, if we're going to find a lunch place still open we'd better get a move on. We can always return later to check if they're here."

"Good plan," I said, heading for the back seat of the sports car. In twenty minutes we'd found a gussied up pub, not far from the famous Cheltenham track, which to Fenn meant it was mostly a tourist trap now and not a good ole' neighborly place featuring gossip and bitters. But the clock was running, so we stopped.

Fenn introduced both of us to Ploughman's Plates, which seemed an improved sort of horizontally-arranged chef salad, and included a huge chunk of the best Stilton cheese, greens, tomatoes, pickles, beets, hard-boiled eggs and a coarse whole grain bread Dorie adored. We women each managed to share a pint of bitters, though Dorie had to pinch her nose to get it down, while Fenn stuck to Coca Cola since he was designated driver of the day. As we drank up, I tried out one of my particularly bright ideas.

"They must have a public telephone. Do you think they'd loan us the phone book, so we could look up any possible McClellan's we might call? I mean, in case the VanDynes are still not at home?"

Fenn got on it right away, and we put our heads literally together over the slender book while Dorie took notes and recorded the eight listings in the Gloucestershire area. Out in the Jaguar, Fenn called the first three on his mobile with no success, two no answers and one, "Never 'eard of 'im."

Dorie tried the next three and struck out. "Wrong number," said one. The next didn't answer. The third, a Muriel, was no longer a McClellan, due to a divorce and never wanted to hear from the scum bucket again.

On my first turn, I spoke with an elderly gentleman who asked just who wanted to know if he was related to Michael E. McClellan.

"I'm a journalist from the United States, sir," I said. "I knew Mac there and I need to reach someone in his family. Are you related?"

The old fellow paused a very long time. He asked my name. I gave it. What did I want to know? he asked. I had a hunch I'd lucked out.

"Actually I have some information for his closest relative."

Another long pause.

The man's voice seemed to grow feeble. He coughed. "Call me tomorrow," he said. "Might find someone."

I hung up and drew a big circle around the name. "I'm sure this fellow knows something. He was emotionally involved with my questions. Scared, maybe. Not ready to talk. Wants me to call tomorrow."

Dorie checked her list. "Seventeen Longridge Close, Cheltenham," she said. "I copied the addresses, too."

"You're a genius," Fenn said. "Want to take a drive-by?"

We both nodded. Fenn disappeared back into the pub and returned with directions scribbled on a post-it note.

"Now you're the genius," Dorie crooned.

We laughed and headed for the part of town beyond the horse track. As we passed the entrance with hundreds of cars queued up to go in, Dorie asked what on earth was happening.

"It's their usual October Showcases," Fenn said. "A whole schedule of races. That friend of mine I said might help us will probably be there later today in the Centaur Bar. We could stop by then."

"Not too much later, after he's tasted the wares too much," Dorie said coyly.

"Nah," Fenn said, shifting his car into high gear as we passed the track. "Actually she'll be better, in her cups. Restores long term memories, she told me once."

I nodded, hardly listening. I couldn't stop thinking of the old man and his nervousness on the phone. Was he the relative of Mac we were seeking? Could he be Mac's father? Did he even know his son was dead, murdered in the United States so far away from home? I shivered.

Fenn slowed the Jaguar on Longridge Close and Dorie searched out the numbers on the buildings. "Thirteen, fifteen, oh, there, seventeen," she said pointing to our left. From the back seat, I leaned left and my eye caught the movement of a white curtain on the ground floor. Fenn actually pulled to a stop until I squirmed with guilt washing over me.

"No, no, Fenn, do ride on. I can't believe I upset that poor old man's life like this, so that now he's peeking out the window in fear. Let's get back to the stables, and then try your friend if we get nowhere. Tomorrow I can call the old McClellan gent, from Devon if we need to."

Fenn gave a little wave and drove around the block and back toward the Van Dyne stables. The afternoon sun slanted into the car and warmed us all, making us drowsy after our adequate lunch and certain beverages. Only Fenn stayed wide awake, whistling as he drove.

As I shifted to a more comfortable position, my eyes opened and I saw Fenn wrap a gentle hand around Dorie's neck, fingering the drifts of pale, white-blonde hair that had settled there from her pinned up do. He glanced at her with such a fond gaze I myself quavered and found my thoughts riveted on Bernie, on his tenderness with me, his love, despite his current irritation with my involvement in the case.

I shook myself and closed my eyes again. Fenn Layton seemed an incredible find, and he was incredibly interested in Dorine.

I hoped they'd have time and opportunity to develop their interests.

When we slowed, I sat up straight and saw we'd turned down the drive for Van Dyne's farm. There was another car in the yard, an expensive-looking one, and ambling toward us from the barn was a middle aged man with a beer belly just held in by a sleeveless tee shirt, with a halo of gray unkempt hair framing his pudding-soft face.

"Doesn't look much like of a rider," Dorie muttered, coming out of her nap.

"Give me a shot at him." Fenn was out of the car

before the hum of the motor quit. We followed in time to hear the exchange.

"He's not Van Dyne," Fenn told us. "Doesn't speak much English. Works here and doesn't seem to know when the owner will return. He drives the owner's car to keep it in shape, and stays in the house a few nights a month for the same reason."

Dorie smiled her usual charming smile and stuck out her hand. The workman kissed it. Her eyes opened wide.

"No English," the man said, smiling petulantly.

He pointed toward the barn and said something in another language. Czech? Polish?

I gave it a try. "You have horses here? You ride?" I pantomimed rein-holding motions with my hands and bounced up and down.

The man shook his head, pointed again barnward, made a baby-rocking motion and smiled more broadly.

"Your daughter?" Dorie asked?

He nodded vigorously. "Daugh-ter," he said. "Sophie. I work, too."

He made shoveling motions.

Fenn stepped closer. "So you work for the Van Dynes, and the groom in there is your daughter?"

"*Toch*, yah," the man said, nodding and pointing to the car. "Van Dyne's," he said with a heavy accent.

"We need to talk with Van Dyne," Fenn said, pointing to the house and making hand gestures to demonstrate talking.

The man shrugged. "U.S.?" he asked, indicating Dorie and me.

We nodded back "But we must talk to Van Dyne," I said again, getting nowhere. As we spoke, a few scrawny chickens appeared out of barnyard corners and pecked around our feet.

The man took the opportunity to start backing away, shaking his head and shrugging his shoulders. "No Van Dyne. Not here."

Fenn reached out and tapped the man's elbow.

"Wait," he said. He tapped his chest and said, "Layton."

I caught on, tapped my own chest and said "Hannah."

Dorie quickly followed with tap and pronouncement of her name. "Dorie."

The man in the undershirt grinned, understanding. He tapped his own chest with a work-worn and grubby hand and announced his own name.

"Bukowski. Me Bukowski."

"Mr. Bukowski?" Dorie gulped and gestured toward the barn. "And she's your daughter, the girl?"

"*Toch, toch.* Sophie." He was still gesturing toward the barn and smiling.

I couldn't help it. I took two steps toward him, my teeth clenched and fists clutched at my sides. "What about Terry then, sir? Is Terry your daughter, too? Teresa?"

As soon as he caught the name in question, the lumpy old guy's expression changed from sugar to vinegar. "You go," he said brusquely. "Van Dyne not here." He took a few determined steps toward the barn.

When we hurried after him and Fenn reached for his arm, this time the flabby-looking fellow braced himself and shoved back, proving the strength in those old arms. Fenn's slender form went flying backward.

"Go now. I call police," Bukowski said. And although his English had improved over the last few minutes, the man clearly was done talking. We got the message we may have missed when he reached the barn, entered briefly, then came out with a rifle in hand.

We stood there speechless until he cocked it and aimed it in our direction.

"The car, ladies," Fenn called out, already en route to the driver's seat on the right-hand side. "Discretion being..." he muttered as he slammed his door shut.

"...the better part of valor," I finished for him as our two passenger doors swung closed and Fenn u-turned out of the yard at a clip challenging even the Jag.

We didn't fasten our seatbelts until we were back on the public access road. By the time we'd caught our breath, Fenn opined the Centaur Bar was looking pretty good to him right now.

Thirty-four

Dorie

"You okay, Dorine?" Fenn asked.

I finally caught my breath to answer as he turned the Jaguar into the racetrack parking lots and put us as close to the entrance as possible. We made our way in, following his long strides, and though I tried to pick up details on the décor, I was far too flummoxed to be doing it well. It was rich looking, full of chrome and glass, and people chattering in suave British tones.

"It's a major convention and meeting center for all England," Fenn said. Everywhere groups of people gathered in chummy conference, or hurried by on their way to somewhere.

"Nice," Hannah said, gazing around at the twenty-first century structure and decor. I nodded numbly, still seeing that big, long gun pointed our way.

Fenn led us into an elegant bar area and stopped, his glance covering the room in a flash and then landing on a table perfectly positioned to see the field, the grandstands and surrounding attractions. There sat an older woman wearing a purple-plumed cloche over flyaway gray hair, framing the thinnest face and most beakish nose imaginable, with its translucent skin stretched across mercilessly, her hands like gnarled claws grabbing at air and moving incessantly while she spoke to a gathered crowd.

I sighed with relief. Obviously, my observational powers had returned. Hannah and I followed Fenn but stood a few feet away as he established his reacquaintance with the lady before him. He leaned forward and kissed her cheek. Her thin, poorly painted lips parted in as broad a smile as she could probably manage.

"Haven't seen you in a yearling's age," the woman cackled. "Who've you got there?" she asked, peering around him to study Hannah and me.

Fenn bowed toward us, graciously presenting us as his special American friends, and the woman's lips compressed tightly. She waved her painted talons at the three men sitting around her and they tipped her a wave and stepped away from her table, making room for Fenn and us.

As we sat, a waiter loomed over us.

"Gin and tonic—a tall one—for me," Fenn said. "Can I freshen your drink?" he asked the old woman, and she nodded. "You ladies? Tea, perhaps? Or sherry?"

Hannah laughed. "Thanks, but gin and tonic sounds perfect to me."

I nodded. Perhaps it would settle my nerves.

"My aunt Clairie," Fenn explained as the waiter departed, "knows more about the equestrian scene in Great Britain than any jockey, trainer or inveterate fan you could find anywhere."

The woman Clairie let a bubble of laughter escape her compressed lips after the generous introduction. "I've probably forgotten more than any one of them will ever know, too."

Fenn laughed back. Then grew serious. "We need some information, Auntie. You're probably the best bet to give us an answer."

"Oh, I am, am I? That because I'm so old I've been around since horse and carts?"

"Look, Auntie, no. Everybody knows you haven't truly forgotten a thing since the crown made racing the royal sport and the state sanctioned its shoring up."

"Wasn't that in the time of Henry the Eighth?" I asked.

Clairie cackled and slapped the table with her hand. "I like that one. Look at her eyes all violet and innocent."

Fenn laid his very warm hand on my arm. "I like her, too, Auntie. In fact I hope to take her to dinner at Foxsmith tomorrow evening."

Aunt Clairie tilted her head for a better look at me, then shifted her gaze to Hannah. "What's your story, birdie?"

Hannah winced. "Well, Ms. Clairie, a friend of ours in the United States died, and we're trying to find his family, or someone who might know why he was killed."

"You police?" the old woman asked.

Hannah shook her head. "Journalist. But Mac was a decent fellow and he didn't deserve..."

"Mac who?" the old woman asked, tapping her fingernails on the table's surface as the drinks were passed around.

"McClellan," I answered. "We don't even know where he came from, or if there's anything sordid in his past." I sipped my gin and tonic still trembling from the incident at Van Dyne's farm, and watched Clairie's dark eyes harden into agates.

"You know the name, then," Fenn said, after a huge slurp of his own drink. His hand shook as he replaced his glass.

His "auntie" sipped the last of her previous beverage and pushed it aside, angling the fresh one in front of her.

"First let me ask you why you three are so nervous. You're all quaking. I don't know these American birds, but I know you, Fenny, and scared isn't in your lexicon. What's going on? Tell me quickly because the first race is going to start in a few minutes and I've got a hundred quid on a bay with high odds." She tapped the binoculars at the center of the table.

"Well, I've never been shot at before," Fenn told her.

"Not exactly shot at, Fenn," I corrected him gently. "Just shown the bad end of a gun."

"A very large gun," Hannah added, keeping her glass close to her lips and sipping continuously.

Fenn explained how we'd gone to Van Dyne's where a friend of ours had bought a horse a few years back and found no one at home but a girl groom and her father, who threatened us and told us in no uncertain terms to get the hell out.

"Huh," the old woman said. "You wouldn't find the Van Dynes. He's in prison and the wife died when the whole... mess came out. Bad heart. You remember hearing about them, don't you, Fennie? Three or four years ago it was, the year what's-his-name, Quint's nephew, took the Gold Cup?"

"He's in prison? The owner is?" I grabbed onto Fenn's arm and his other hand covered mine to comfort me. I felt its warmth and breathed a sigh of relief.

Clairie noticed the interaction between us and nodded.

"I remember when the young fellow won. But not the scandal. Maybe it was the year I spent in Mumbai, my missionary year?"

Clairie nodded. "Be careful. Boy's a veritable priest at heart," she told us. "Cares too much about other people. Doesn't know how to have a good time himself." She eyed me with a glance sharp as nails. "Perhaps you can help fix that. And he does need help."

I felt my face warm to either a full blush or a hot flash. Or both.

Fenn twisted in his seat, clearly irritated. "Just tell us about Van Dyne, Auntie. Leave the sermon out."

She slapped at his hand and stuck her tongue out at him. A man passing by had leaned close and asked a question of her. She whispered back an answer and then told him aloud to get lost.

"They always want to know my pick. That doesn't

come free, I tell 'em. If you ain't buying, do your own research."

"Does that go for us, Ms. Clairie? Because we'd be happy to buy you a steak, or a whole side of beef or something if you could say more about the Van Dyne farm." Hannah had leaned far forward in her seat, clearly anxious to get some answers.

Clairie cackled again. "Like that one's sense of humor, too," she said, then coughed to clear her rheumy throat. She sipped her drink again.

"All right. Lesson number one. Van Dyne wasn't all to blame himself. Seems it was becoming a tempting practice for small owners to unload horses that had promise, won some races here and up north, even, but then had a tumble, or were found to be ailing in some way. Thoroughbreds, mostly. They realized they could unload these animals on unsuspecting Yanks or others who were so thrilled to be buying their kids a mount with an English pedigree they'd pay anything, and trust any signature on the horse's record—health and otherwise."

Fenn Layton looked aghast. I thought of Gus Finch, and nodded.

"And someone found out?" Hannah asked.

"Surely did. The racing commission. By then some of the owners had disappeared, changed their names and relocated or taken up residence in Ireland or somewhere, and Van Dyne wouldn't talk. Only one owner came forward, and his sentence was minor, compared to Van Dyne, whose name was on the all the bills of sale. They even offered to lighten his sentence if he'd incriminate more, but..." She shook her head.

"He took the blame and went to prison alone? Bugger the system, then." Fenn drained his glass and waved to the waiter for refills for all of us, club soda for himself. Hannah and I declined.

Clairie chuckled. "Don't kid yourself. He had deals with those owners that'll pay off when he gets out in a few years. Meanwhile, he's lost his wife, his kids emigrated to Australia, and I'm betting he'll join them there when he's free. Pulled the wool over everybody's eyes for a while, though. Smart guy."

My last gulp of gin and tonic threatened to choke me. "You surely don't approve of what Mr. Van Dyne did, do you, Aunt Clairie?"

The old woman laughed and shook her head. "Got to admire the brains and spunk, though."

"What about his farm? Who's running it now?" Hannah asked.

The old woman shrugged her thin shoulders, then turned slightly in her swivel chair and picked up the binoculars, aiming them for the field beyond. "Seems some foreign fellow who used to work for him is keeping the place going, him and his wife and their brats."

"Would it be the Bukowskis?" Hannah asked. "That name ring a bell?"

"No idea. I seem to recall there was a hush-hush problem with one of the girls. He rides them hard, won't let them waste water bathing or even eat much. Look, the first race is going to start. They're in the parade ring." She adjusted her binoculars.

"You've been very helpful, Mrs., uh, Ms. Clairie," I said. "We promise not to take up too much more of your time. But perhaps you have also heard of Mac McClellan, the one we mentioned earlier."

Clairie put down her binoculars, but her claw-like fingers played over them as she spoke.

"Everybody's heard of McClellan. Lots of people knew him. Nobody will admit it, though. A nice, honorable boy, clean-cut. Good trainer, too. Made plenty of money on his horses. Just let us all down that one time."

Hannah and I were almost too speechless to ask what Mac's "one time" had been about. And when Fenn asked, Auntie wasn't telling.

"Time for the race. You three skedaddle out of here."

Fenn put a hand on her shoulder. "Auntie, these women have comes across the big pond to figure out who might have killed McClellan. To them, he was a good sort, did his job well over there. No marks against him."

Aunt Clairie set down the binoculars again and drank from her second glass of gin and tonic. "Don't you go making me sick, boy. I don't like remembering how disillusioned I felt after Mac—did what he did. There just isn't anyone you can believe in nowadays. Now go. I got to pay attention to this bunker so he'll win me some money. Nice meeting you ladies. Cheerio," she said, her voice quavering as she turned away, her crabbed fingers gripping the binoculars, which were quickly moistened by stray tears running down her cheeks. I gulped.

Fenn paid the tab, shaking his head and gathered us

closer as we stood. "She gets like this. No use asking anymore." He leaned over and placed a gentle kiss on the old woman's damp and withered cheek.

As we said our goodbyes and stepped away from the window-side table, Aunt Clairie shot out one last piece of advice. "It never got into the papers. He's one of the ones got away, because of friendship, they said. Loyalty. That's hogwash. But who knows? Aah—they're off!" The back of Clairie's hat shook so much the feather threatened to take off.

I gripped Fenn's arm as we left the Centaur bar, filled to the brim now with aficionados of Showcase racing, intent on their cocktail glasses and binoculars.

Mac had done something really bad. But what? I felt so shaky I was afraid I'd trip. Fenn wrapped an arm around me and my insides shuddered, too.

"We were so close, Hannah" I murmured. "She's got to tell us."

"She won't," Fenn said. "I could try calling her at home, or see her alone, but..."

Hannah told us it was okay. "It seems Mac might have a connection to the Van Dyne scheme. Somehow, we'll find out which seller Mac protected, if that's what he did. When we do, we may know who killed him. At least we have a context now."

Back in the Jag, we summed up our discoveries, trying to decide if we should attempt any more investigating, although the day was growing late.

"We found out Van Dyne is in prison for selling defective horses for his owners," Fenn started.

"And that Terry Bukowski's father and sister work the Van Dyne place. Either alone or with someone." I was feeling way better now, ensconced in the Jag next to the tall blond man who'd so tenderly helped me make the trip to the car.

Hannah whistled. "That's a lot in one day."

"And don't forget Mac," I couldn't help but pipe up. "We know he was somehow involved and people were very distillusioned with him."

Hannah sighed. "Disillusioned, Dorie."

"That's what I said."

"And we know a frightened old man is expecting a call from me tomorrow that may resurrect all his saddest memories. I don't know, guys, I've got a bad feeling about that one. I'd love to forget the fellow at Seventeen Longridge Close and let him be."

Fenn guffawed. "How could you? You said you want to find out about Mac's life, reach his family. This is our best shot so far."

Hannah pouted. "Oh, what do you care?" she asked. "What does anybody care? Damn old lady didn't. Had to watch her race. Mr. Bukowski certainly didn't. Damn him, putting a gun to us to get rid of us. We should have called the police on him!"

I shrunk back in my seat, staring straight ahead, hoping Hannah wasn't getting into one of her menopausal furies. She could be really unpleasant when she did. Although they never lasted long, and always ended up with her seeming stronger and brighter than ever.

"I care," Fenn said, but it was me he encased in his

angled arm on the back of my seat.

I jumped to his defense. "Of course we care, Hannah. It's not Fenn's fault we didn't solve everything today. What do you think we are, detectives like your Bernie?"

I could tell Hannah bristled in the back seat.

"Okay, so maybe I could get Bernie to harass some more information from sweet little Terry," she growled. "She had to be involved somehow, to have known what went on."

"Yes, try your American sources, Hannah," Fenn offered as he turned onto the M-five. "Sorry it didn't work out better for us, but I think you two are well on the trail, as they say. And I will call Clairie later. Try her again."

Hannah's voice dropped a decibel or two. "Sorry I jumped all over you."

"No problem," Fenn said.

"So will you be able to drive us again tomorrow, Fenn?" I'd been studying his lovely profile and the shock of straight blond hair drifting down over his forehead, and I couldn't resist asking.

He coughed, pressed his lips together and sighed. "Dorie, I do care how this turns out for all of you, believe me. But I can't make it tomorrow. It's one of my few work days of the week."

"Oh, what do you do? I mean, what is your job? You didn't seem to keep any schedule, so I thought..." I turned to him, hoping my cheeks still bore some blush and my lips some color. I had a hunch he approved of me, even if I did despise my own bumptious behind.

"I could understand how you might think so. I'm in

radio," Fenn said. "I work a morning show out of Exeter."

"How exciting," I said.

"Not really. It's just a horsey little reporting of the latest in competition, hunting and other racing news. Sometimes I interview celebrities in the field, or festival managers looking for publicity. Which is why it's so funny I should miss that whole Van Dyne thing when I was in India. I do remember rumors of it, but never caught the names of people involved. Figures Auntie would have it down pat. She's obsessive about eventing of any kind and especially steeplechase racing."

"She's quite a character," I said, trying not to show my disappointment he wouldn't be free.

"And she's really not my aunt but my second cousin. Hard to believe she's ninety-six, isn't it? And that I dated her granddaughter for a while way back when."

"Before you were married?" I spoke softly. Probably shouldn't have brought that topic up, it was too bold, too American of me. I slumped in my seat.

But Fenn Layton nodded, and reached around to smooth back the wisps of hair across my cheeks.

"We are on for tomorrow night, then?" he asked. "There's a whole lot more to learn about one another."

I glanced back at Hannah's grinning face and nodded yes, then settled back when I realized we were getting closer to Devon.

Fenn studied the highway and got serious. "Just be careful if you decide to go back and hunt around for clues tomorrow. You ladies are a bit too brave. American superwomen, as they say."

From the back seat it was Hannah's turn to guffaw. "I can hardly wait to call Bernie and let him know what we've discovered. He'll be impressed. Angry, but impressed anyhow." She must have been weary, because she sank back into the leather nest of the Jag's upholstery, and closed her eyes. She didn't wake until we'd passed Lynmouth and were headed west on the shore road toward our English home.

I was already worrying about how bold she'd be in our search for information tomorrow, and how I could manage to be strong and independent, without Fenn to catch me if I fell.

He and I exchanged grins as we sped along, and I realized no one could help me up from the fall I'd already taken.

Thirty-five

Ada

I had done way too much walking at the farm and I knew it. Fitzgibbons was taking well to the herbal concoctions mixed for him, and when he was exercised today there had been no sign of bleeding in the nares. Of course, the tempo had been slow, the ride short, and the rider very lightweight. But I'd happily moved from one position after another to keep Fitzgibbons in my sights, and Meg hadn't been there to nag at me, since she had taken up the director on a trot on one of his gentlest steeds.

Despite the tragedies she'd experienced in her life, quiet, sometimes dour Meg was surprisingly always ready for adventure. Maybe that's what drew me to her as a friend when Hannah introduced us four years ago. That never-say-die spirit also was my biggest personal quality—sometimes leading me smack into trouble. Except for the death of my first husband and the philandering of my second, my worst battles had been with hot flashes, insomnia, mental instability and the other crazy symptoms of menopause. I'd fought my way through, with a little pharmaceutical assistance, never giving in, and I was the same with my arthritic knee. I'd be damned if that one twitchy joint was going to put me in a rocking chair. Never, never, please, God.

Once more, I'd let my passions lead the way coming over here to England. But was that such a bad thing, really?

I thought of Devlin and couldn't help but smile.

When Meg and Lucia left to do some shopping in town, I decided to rest my leg to prepare for the weekend. I hobbled up the stairs with an ice pack and lay across the bed, positioning myself to nestle my knee into the cold pack.

Heavenly—what relief.

Now my memories of that last night with dear Devlin filled my mind. What a hottie, what a tiger!

I shocked myself, remembering how bold I'd been, stripping before him with a dim lamp still on in his room. And he'd shocked me when he seemed overwhelmed at how I looked in the lamplight, apparently not so bad even at my age. No quick scurrying under the covers for me to hide my post-middle-aged body. Devlin wouldn't hear of it.

And I had to admit the sight of him, startlingly erect yet vulnerable in his nakedness, had spun wild imaginings in my head. Almost every one of those fantasies had come true, a thread of his breath mingling with mine, his tongue describing my dark nipples, his passion, rousing me beyond where I would have dreamed ever to go again. Now I anticipated the rest of the package.

I squirmed on the bed, tantalized by the thought that tomorrow evening he'd be here, scooping me up in his strong arms, begging me to let my release come as his fingers played in my depths and ordered my heights.

"Hallooo!"

I jolted upright. I heard the voice, knew it to be female, but could think of no one but Devlin. Could it be he, joking around? Come a day early?

I leapt from the bed, limped out into the hallway and called down. "Yes, who is it? Who's there?"

At the top of the stairs I caught the newel post to hold myself up on shaky legs, utterly shocked and confused at the sight of Theo Rutledge down below, wrapped in her colorful poncho, mouth stretched in the widest grin I'd ever seen on a nun, and baggage lying at her feet.

"Surprise!"

Thirty-six

Meg

By the time I returned with Lucia from our perusal of local shops and a purchase of fresh clams and plaice for her to whip up for dinner, Theo's rental car was parked beside Rose Cottage and Heather was waiting nearby to ask if we would move it to the parking lot.

"More guests coming in to the cottages," she explained. "They may want to unload here."

"But whose car is at Rose Cottage, Meggie?" Lucia asked, straining to see around me.

I nodded sweetly to Heather and poked Lucia in the ribs. "You really don't know? I can't believe I managed to keep the plan so secret even you didn't guess." I roared, laughing, as we gathered up the bags.

"Who, then? Is it Devlin, here early to romance his girlfriend?" She hustled her two big bags of groceries toward the door.

"No," I said, toting up the smaller packages and

protecting my saddle-sore buttocks with short, light steps as I followed. "Aren't we missing someone in the Women on Fire department?"

Lucia went wide-eyed as the door opened quickly at the sound of her steps.

"Theo!" she gasped. "But how, but when, why..."

The woman herself came forward. "My Sigourney said she'd never forgive me if I didn't get my behind over here to help out with Fitzgibbons. I spent twelve years on horseback in the hills of South America," she said, "and I'd be thrilled to exercise Gibby if I'm needed." Theo winked at Meg and distributed hugs all around, then went back to Ada, who was smiling, but with a look of puzzlement on her usually composed features.

Theo caught the look and grinned. "She told me about Devlin and she's worried about where I'm going to be put up in her little love nest."

Ada objected with a noise in her throat, but I gave Theo a little poke and she landed on the sofa beside Ada. They stared at each other.

"That's where you're going to sleep, Sister T," I teased. "Or I'll take that spot and you can share the room in the next apartment tolerating Lu's snoring. Besides, I'm a little hard of hearing and I won't know a thing going on three feet beyond my cradle. Oops."

My boldness broke the tension. Now it was Ada's and Lu's turns to laugh. While they were excitedly filling Theo in on Fitzgibbons's progress and the ghostly happenings at their Manor House, Hannah and Dorie returned, looking peaked and worried. But they bolted straight-backed and open-mouthed when they saw Theo ensconced on Ada's couch.

They rattled off questions about her presence, but the sound of Fenn Layton's sports car roaring away also brought quick questions from Theo. In the midst of the jibber-jabbering back and forth, Ada mentioned it was tea time and asked if someone would put on the kettle.

"Better idea," I said, slipping out of the room. By the time everyone had the answers they needed, I was back with tumblers of Pimm's for everyone. The local liquor-iced tea mix, floated with slices of cucumbers and strawberries, brought oohs and aahs and then awed silence from the group as we imbibed.

I toasted Lucia across the sitting room with a lift of my glass.

"Told you it would work to calm us all down if things got dicey," Lucia said, "even if Pimm's is out of season during the fall in England. Excellent job mixing it up, Meggie. If you ever want to hire on as bartender at Lucia Mia, you're on."

"Yea, Meg!" Hannah toasted to me. "This stuff should be in season all year 'round."

"Fantastic libation, dear," Ada complimented.

I scowled into my glass. "Well, there was a lot of chemistry in my work, you know. I come naturally to my mixology skills."

"Euw," groaned Dorie, no doubt recalling my former occupation. Everyone else held up their glasses for refills.

That's when Hannah and Dorie gave up the serious information they'd discovered in Cheltenham.

Ada nearly fainted when she learned Fitzgibbons already may have been a maimed horse with EIPH and sold fraudulently to her deceased husband as healthy.

"But he has papers, statements from veterinarians that he was fine." She shrugged and waved her free hand helplessly.

Theo comforted her. "Sounds like a serious crime. It should never have happened."

Hannah explained the man responsible had gone to prison. But that Fitzgibbons's actual owner was unknown, as everything had gone through the Van Dyne name and stables.

"But you'll never guess who we met there," Dorie said. She didn't make them suffer the suspense long—she never could bear to keep secrets. "The sister and father of little Terry Bukowski."

There was unified gasp around the circle.

"I knew as soon as that young girl-groom spoke, I'd heard that combination of Cockney and Eastern European accent somewhere before. They look enough alike to be twins, too."

"And you all know how good Dorie is at noticing things like that," Hannah reminded them. Dorine beamed and took another bite and sip of her drink.

"But how are the Bukowskis involved? Did they know Mac, where he came from or anything?" Ada stirred her Pimm's with a delicate forefinger, picked out a strawberry and munched on it while she listened.

Hannah and Dorie let out a twisted chuckle. "Let's just say," Hannah said, "our questioning was abbreviated when the father pulled out a huge hunting weapon and aimed it in our direction."

Dorie nearly lost a mouthful of her enhanced iced tea as a laugh bubbled out. "You should have seen Fenn toss us into the car and get us away from there pronto-quicko."

This time the gasps in the room were in a lower register.

"Horrors," Theo said, waving the air in front of her and mumbling, "heat flash."

"But we also did find some things out about Mac," Hannah explained. "Dorie's right, Fenn was extremely helpful, and this old equestrian-obsessed aunt or cousin of his, whatever, told us Mac was a great trainer, a real gentleman but got mixed up somehow in a Van Dyne deal to sell unhealthy horses. She won't say exactly what he did, but that's apparently when Mac emigrated to the States, Ada. When you got Fitzgibbons."

"We're still on the trail, though." Dorie drained her glass and pulled out a cucumber slice to munch. "Hannah's supposed to call an old man with the same name as Mac whom we reached by telephone today."

"But I don't really want to, if there's another way..." Hannah eyes were damp, to my surprise. She usually hid her emotions better even than Ada and me. I sometimes wondered if she had any. Or just a few. Then again, Bernie Cascone had discovered some, hadn't he?

"Why not, Han?" I asked. "If it will help lead us to Mac's killer, anything's fair, isn't it?"

Hannah said she supposed so, but the old fellow seemed so frightened. And if he were related to Mac, how awful to bring back what must be painful memories for him. And, worse, to give him the bad news of Mac's death if he didn't already know.

The group reflected on Hannah's scruples. Ada was nodding. Lucia compressed her lips and closed her eyes, as if thinking it out. I just shook my head. Finally Theo set down her empty glass and cleared her throat.

"It's all in the way you do it, I think. Mac deserves justice. Don't we all, with what we've gone through? And surely you wouldn't be harsh with the man, Hannah. Isn't it merciful to let him know his relative, if Mac was one, has passed?"

"I thought of that, too," Hannah admitted.

"Besides, guilt seems to be pointing in one direction now, toward these evil horse traders, although the ramifications are not quite clear yet. Still, we must pursue it if only to clear the innocent." Theo set her glass down on the book and magazine-covered coffee table.

Five curious faces turned her way.

"Let me tell you about my day yesterday, my hectic departure from my ailing daughter and the rest of the family, and my arrival at Logan Airport. It's quite unbelievable. So much so I've talked to your detective twice already, Hannah, and I'm supposed to call him back tonight."

We sat in mystified suspense as Theo recalled her sighting of Gus Finch at Logan Airport, his pursuit of her, his apology and Theo's eventual pacification. "Though I still don't know whether to believe him, or maybe he protests too much and is truly guilty after all."

Some of us, myself included, cleared our throats and made "Don't-be-simple" eyes at poor Theo.

"I know, I know, you think I'm so spiritual and peaceful I couldn't believe evil of anyone. But you're wrong. Detective Bernie has talked to Mr. Finch at length and checked out his alibi for the time of the attack on McClellan, and at least twelve people vouched for his presence beside his daughter as she cooled her horse in the paddock ring after winning the Blue Ribbon."

"But why didn't the police check that out before?" I asked.

"Because Finch was being so ugly he managed to make himself look quite guilty, though in a phony way. He says it was Charity who finally made him ask forgiveness of me, and also of you, Ada, for bugging you all these years for Fitzgibbons's background. He's promised to lay off pushing his child into competition in future, and to let her own interests be his guide, not his self-centered desire for glory."

"Whew!" It was Lucia who expressed the most amazement at the change in Finch, but we all felt it, judging from our expressions. I congratulated Theo for coming to terms after the man's attack on her.

"I was so happy to be alive and out of harm's way, it wasn't so hard after all. Not that it didn't take me an hour or more to catch my breath from that sprint down Logan's endless corridor." She studied her hands and then looked around the group. "Being friends with all of you has given me more courage and more faith than all those years in the missions and the convent."

Somewhere in the tiny cottage living room more than one person sniffled, and all of us raised our glasses to Theo. She grinned broadly, and then asked for an explanation of who this "Fenn" was. "On to romance," she toasted.

"Oh," Dorie said, blushing "Ada has that corner covered."

At that moment, Heather knocked on our door, opened it and peeked in. "What a lovely, gay group," she said. "I'm so sorry to bother you, but someone needs to go through and this car..."

"Oh, sorry, sorry," I said. "We forgot about it completely. C'mon, Theo, I'll go with you as you park in the lot above and we'll walk down together while I tell you about Mr. Layton."

Dorie jumped up, dropping her tumbler on the kitchen counter. "I'd better come, too, to make sure you tell the complete truth, Miss Megan. He's quite nice, Theo, kind to others, and good-looking, and well, I think he likes me a bit."

Hannah guffawed. "A bit? Don't believe a word. They're both smitten, as the Brits say. Meanwhile, I'll fill the rest of you in. There are big plans afoot for the charming couple. And, oh, yes, Fenn's going to be on the radio, and is hoping to field some answers to questions we have about aspects of the case. Putting it on the air could be helpful."

Theo picked up her car keys and went to move her rental. I followed, and Dorie stood watching us go down the doorstep, making a little gasp in her throat.

"Meg, hon, why are you limping? Have you caught Ada's terrible knee disease?"

I groaned going down the steps. "No, m'dear, I took the director up on his invitation to trot out a gentle filly at Amber Hill and gave myself an arse-battering like I haven't had since girlhood in Bosnia."

"Oh that," Dorie tried to keep from laughing. "It'll pass, right, Hannah?"

Ada shook her head. "You gals are amazing. What you sacrifice for me and my horse and my lost friend."

Energized by her Pimm's, Lucia reminded everyone she wasn't preparing dinner alone tonight. "I need help."

"And I need to drive to the cliffs to call Bernie and fill him in," Hannah declared.

Lucia was quick to respond. "Okay, I'm starting with you, Ada. Come cut up some cabbage for slaw while I bread the fish."

"Could I set the table instead? I'm not much good with a knife," Ada whined

I popped my head back in at the front door. "I am. Save it for me."

"Yea, Meg," Lu answered, laughing. "How could we forget?"

Thirty-seven

Hannah

I reached Bernie on the first try. It paid to call in the evening, since it was still work day hours back home. We took the first few minutes of the call to reconnect on the personal level.

"I've missed you so much I'm not even functioning rationally," he told me bluntly. "For example, thanks to your friend Theo, I finally managed to clear Finch from the whole deal. He was too snotty and violent to even talk with me much before this. But Theo seems to have transformed him."

"I think it was his daughter Charity, aptly named," I said. "Hey, I'm missing you, too. And envying both Dorie's sweet infatuation with a Brit who's been very helpful to us, and Ada's palpable yearning for my father's arrival tomorrow. Guess there's still hope that romance can bloom in future decades as well as the one I'm in."

"Never doubted it. I want to grow old with you,

sweetheart. But I also want you to stay alive for the event. You haven't been chasing anybody dangerous around the moors or anything, are you?"

I gulped. Thinking of the *Osso Bucco* of long ago, when he pretended to cook for me then admitted, to keep himself honest and our relationship "more intimate," that someone else had done the cheffing, I had to come clean, and so I spilled the day's adventures, as casually as I could. I also tried not to let his outbursts offend or disturb me.

"Held at gunpoint? Good God, Hannah!" he screamed back at me.

"Not really held. We got the hell out of there fast. Did you know a Jaguar can take a corner on two wheels?"

"Hannah! You say you're going back tomorrow to see this mysterious old man? Don't you dare!"

"No, no, Bernie. We're going to see the old gentleman who may be related to Mac. Not the guy with the gun, Terry Bukowski's father. But I want you to probe Terry about it. We feel certain she knew Mac over here, as he probably worked at the same farm. Why did Terry go to the U.S. with Mac? And does she possibly know who the owner of Fitzgibbons was before he was handled by Van Dyne and sold to George Javitts?"

He calmed down at last. "I'll try, but she doesn't seem to like me much. You and Dorie she likes, and misses."

"Well, get her on the phone to us tomorrow at this same time and one of us will speak to her, if you can't get anywhere."

He thought that was a plan. "I'm also going to give you the number of the Scotland Yard guy who's on the case over there, Hannah. You must call Phillips and get him to accompany you if you are even imagining going back to Bukowski's place, or questioning that old man who might be related to McClellan."

I took down the necessary info on Phillips and thanked him. "I wish I could hug you right now, feel your strong arms around me," I whispered into the phone.

"Me, too," Bernie said, though the pounding of the waves below made it ever more difficult to hear his softening voice. "Come back soon, okay, honey? And stay safe. I promise not to bark at you anymore. Just stay safe."

~ * ~

The next morning Theo and Lucia took a quick drive to locate the charming local Catholic Church in preparation for Sunday Mass, and after a simple breakfast of scones and toast at the tea rooms, Theo and Dorie tagged along as I drove to the seacoast under scudding grayish clouds to telephone the Scotland Yard man. I reached his voicemail, and was instructed to wait ten minutes and call again. While I waited between calls, Theo borrowed the phone to call home and assure them she was well and hear the latest report on Sigourney, who was thrilled her mother was there and helping.

"She didn't even seem to mind I was calling at five a.m." Theo shook with what seemed to be chills, and I wondered why, since even half-covered, the sun was already warming the interior of the car.

Dorie had been thinking likewise. "Is something

wrong, Theo? You seem, I don't know, not yourself."

Theo fussed with her clothes, buttoned her corduroy jacket up farther and tucked her hands into the cuffs. She shook her head, but too rapidly to be believed.

"C'mon, Thee. Give it up. What's wrong? Did you not sleep well your first night at Chambercombe. Did you... oh, no, oh migod, Theo. Why didn't you say something?"

I grabbed Theo by the arm and shook her.

"What?" Theo asked. "Did I what, for the Lord's sake?"

Then I let go and laughed, bouncing up and down in the driver's seat until Dorie joined in and Theo screamed at me.

"What on earth are you two talking about?"

Dorie said, "Got to tell her, Han."

I caught myself and stopped, patted Theo's cheek. "You poor thing, and none of us warned you."

Theo looked enraged. "For God's sake, Hannah, about what?"

"Why, about our ghost," Dorie said, "our Manor House ghost who rocks the cradle late at night to keep her ghostly baby quiet so the new tenants can sleep."

Theo's eyes darted every which way and came fiercely to rest on mine. "She's kidding, right? Ada told me briefly something about spirits, but I thought... It's a joke, you were all joshing with me, you set it up." She tried to laugh but it wouldn't come.

I shook my head. "Theo, no, we all heard it our first night here. I tell you, I'm the biggest skeptic of the lot, well, except for Meg who slept through it all. But even I heard it, and saw, on the tour the next day, where the sound came from."

"From a cradle being rocked," Theo said, her voice dull and flat.

Dorie and I nodded.

"When no one was there."

Another twin nod.

"Right on the other side of the wall from our rooms."

We sighed.

Theo breathed, and looked away, into the distant waves getting choppy out beyond the rocks. "I heard it twice, around midnight. I prayed to God it was nothing that would hurt us and tried to forget about it."

"I heard the same thumps, hon, but I'm used to them by now. You weren't scared, were you?" Dorie said.

Theo shook her head. "Well, I know there's a spirit world, Dorine. I have faith, lots of it, as you know. I believe in the Holy Ghost, so why not others, why not poor misplaced spirits that can't find their ways home?"

Dorie giggled. "So you wouldn't be scared to take the tour of the rooms and see where the noise emanates from?"

Theo again shook her head. "I'm looking forward to it." She nudged me with a poke in my side and grinned. "As long as you hear it, too. I think it's all a good sign. We've got numbers on our side. I'm pretty sure it's not Gus Finch scaring me out of my wits way over here."

I whacked the steering wheel with the flat of my hand.

"You amaze me, woman," I said. "Thank heavens you're part of our group. We could all learn a little something from you."

Theo shrugged and pulled out a small prayer journal from her pocket. "'Scuse me a minute, ladies, while I do my morning prayers." She stepped outside the car and gazed around at the cliffs, the tiny beach coves, the froth of waves in the Bristol channel. Dorie walked around the car and let the breeze destroy her pinned up hair so she looked more normal and came back inside.

Meanwhile, we listened to the radio, a little morning music, some commercials, then a deeper voice announcing a new program. Theo nearly jumped out of her pretty floral print shirt over her trim jeans when Dorie screamed aloud. "Ladies! He's on."

Theo leaned into the opened window.

"Oh my God! Theo, this is him, my, uh, it's Fenn Layton."

"Her man of the hour," I hollered. "Listen!"

The voice on the radio, its Eton accent intact, its baritone smooth and velvety, was asking for the listening audience's help in their search. Fenn explained that visitors from the States were seeking any relatives or associates of Michael McClellan, well-known horse trainer possibly formerly of Gloucestershire. McClellan was famed for developing some huge winners in the hunting class, jumpers as well as flat racers, and any small detail about his background would be likely to assist the American friends who sought the information.

Theo slid back into her seat, Dorie still bouncing up

and down. All three of us were bent close to the radio to hear the description of his plea. I choked a bit when Fenn went on to say a reward was likely in the event of substantial help. Then he covered us by saying he himself was offering the reward.

Theo and Dorie clapped their hands and grinned madly.

"Contact me at this station," Layton said, "or call the tea rooms at Chambercombe Manor,"—he gave the telephone number—"and ask for Ms. Beaulé or Ms. Doyle."

"Yikes!" Dorie yelped again, and Theo's face went dark with worry. Fenn went on to discuss the current Showcase being held at Cheltenham, suggesting which jockeys were in good shape, which not, and discussed the likely winners. It was good talk radio, but we continued to gape at each other unbelievingly.

"He's given us away. He's practically told people where we are." I felt my jaw clench.

Theo coughed back a knot of alarm in her throat. "Anyone could find you, that Bukowski man, or someone else who could be responsible for Mac's death. Anyone! Why didn't he just give a cell phone number, yours or Ada's?"

"Probably because we can't receive cell calls at the Manor. No reception in the valley."

The strong shifting baritone tones on the airways interrupted us. "This is Fenn Layton reporting on the equestrian scene in horse-loving England. Do your part to keep racing, hurdling and all eventing safe and fun. We're here today for this two-hour jumbo agenda. Call us at... Now for a message from our sponsors."

"Yikes, Fenn. Wait 'til we see you tonight. How totally irresponsible," Dorie snapped.

I started the car with suddenly clumsy hands and ground the gears, then remembered my second call to the Scotland Yard man. Again, the voicemail. I left another message, hung up and pouted.

Theo harrumphed and eyeballed Dorie who had vacated into the back seat. "But I thought you liked the fellow."

"When we thought he was smart," I chimed in.

"You, you don't think he's involved in some way, you know, against Mac or Ada or something?" Dorie asked.

I shook my head. "Yesterday I would have said absolutely not. Now I'm not one hundred per cent. We better get going and head up to Gloucester while we can still move about without someone shadowing us."

Dorie, trembling, questioned whether she should still go out with Fenn tonight.

"You have to decide that one, girlfriend." I tried not to sound too glum. Dorie easily lost her nerve, and I knew this dinner with Fenn had really excited her.

Theo shivered, but nodded. "Let's see what we find out today, Dor. Speaking of that, I'd like to come along. And I was thinking, since Mr. Bukowski doesn't speak English so well, why don't we bring Meg up there? She can make herself understood in practically any Eastern European language, from what I've heard tell. And she has that unflappable manner. She'd be brilliant."

I shifted gears and started the steep descent back toward the Manor House. "Wonderful idea, hon. But maybe you should stay with Ada. We shouldn't leave her here alone, and she's still pretty gimpy to be running around with us."

"I could do that, take her in my car to Amber Hill for her visit with Fitzgibbons, and have a ride there meanwhile on some gentle beast like Meg did yesterday. I haven't ridden since Bolivia, so Sigourney would be thrilled to hear I'd done that. Maybe eventually they'll let me ride Fitzgibbons."

We drove along in silence for a few minutes, then Theo heaved a sigh. "You know, I didn't mind at all sleeping on the couch in Ada's living room last night. But tonight maybe I could switch to your couch? I'd be kind of *verklempt*, as Ada would say, sleeping in that cottage with your dad just arrived from Ireland and getting cozy upstairs with my friend."

"Not my subject to discuss, Thee. Talk to Ada about it. She's the leader; I'm just one of the girl scouts."

Theo laughed. "Neutral like Switzerland, huh?"

"Anyhow, don't be put off by Devlin. He puts his pants on one leg at a time, in case you didn't know."

"Never considered it. But I'm sure Ada knows," Theo said, shaking her head and blessing herself.

~ * ~

While Lucia, more used to a big car, drove the van, I took shotgun seat, and Dorie and Meg, who had agreed to visit the Bukowskis to try and translate, encamped in the rear. I directed Lu to the M-Five, held cell phone in fist hoping for a callback from Scotland Yard, and predicted rain. "Only the second time it's been overcast since we've been here. And to think they say it always rains in England."

"The sun may break through as we go north," Meg suggested.

Lu huffed. "Whatever the weather, we'd be a lot safer with the British detective along. I'm not prepared to drive us into a shotgun blast before we've even started the day," she said. "Besides, I picked up some beautiful napoleons in that cute little bakery on the High Street. We could bring them as a peace offering."

"Why don't we go to see the old man first, then?" Dorie asked.

"I hate to involve the old fellow," I started, but Dorie interrupted.

"She's got this thing for the old Mr. McClellan."

Meg lectured me on thoroughness in the investigation. "Let's not allow emotions to get in the way, dear."

"You're a reporter, for golly's sake, Han," Dorie spouted. "You always say you'd get the right facts even if you had to third-degree your own grandmother."

Lu, too, shook her head. "It's Mac's death we want to solve. If this man knows anything, and it seems like he does, I'd say that's our first destination. Besides, I didn't let Tony tuck his pistol into my luggage this trip, and I'm not facing that other wild-eyed, gun-totin'—"

I let out a great raspberry of air and succumbed. "Okay, okay. You've got it. Continue on, Lucia. The old guy first. I won't call him until we're on his street. Then we'll try the personal approach and bombard him with the charm of Women on Fire."

Meg sounded morose in the backseat. "I think it will take a lot of charm to soothe him, if he really is a close relative of Mac's and doesn't know yet Mac is dead."

There was a lull in the conversation. Eventually, Dorie, who had a problem with silence unless she was painting, recalled to us how upset she'd been to hear Fenn had outed us on the radio. "I tried to call him from the tea rooms to ask him why on earth he practically gave out our address but he's still on air. Could we turn on the radio?"

I agreed that we could.

"I talked to Heather and Shelly at the tea room before we left, and asked them to take special note of anyone who seemed to be looking for us." My fingers twisted the dial looking for the right frequency.

"Good idea," Meg said "And I brought my camera, thinking it might come in handy. Especially if this non-English-speaking fellow won't cooperate. He might be encouraged if he knows we have his picture."

"And Bernie's going to talk with Terry Bukowski first thing today. She's bound to know more than she's said so far. I'll call him after we see Mr. McClellan."

"You mean you hope we see Mr. McClellan," Lucia interposed, taking the entrance ramp for the M-Five North.

"Don't make me hit you, Lu. I know it's hard enough to drive on the left hand side of the road as it is," I snapped.

Lu put up an arm as if to defend herself.

"Yeah, let's be cheery and hopeful," Dorie said. "Like, I can't be real mad at Fenn for giving away our location on the radio until I know why he did it."

"Maybe he's one of the bad guys," Meg chimed in.

"Not!" Dorie yelled back, unusual for her. "He even took us to see his auntie yesterday who gave us lots of good information, right Han?"

I hesitated. I didn't want to dash Dorie's hopes for a romantic interlude with the rich, handsome Fenn. But I couldn't ignore my doubts. "Still, Dorine, that woman refused to give us the final, most important details. Like who owned Fitzgibbons, and what exactly Mac did that she can't speak of it."

Dorie made blips of noise in her throat and held a hand up to her face.

"Oy," cried Meg. "You're not car sick are you?"

Dorie shook her head, and I craned my neck to watch from the front seat.

"What, Dor? What's wrong?" I asked.

"Nothing, I... oh, Hannah. I thought of the very same thing about Fenn Layton. Maybe he's, well, in on it. But still, why would he help us, and take us to lunch and then tea later on the way home, and buy drinks at that Centaur thing and all? Why did he invite me out tonight for dinner?" Dorie was edging toward hysteria.

"That last question I can answer unstintingly. Because he cares for you. And no, I don't think he's in on it. I saw him while you were sleeping up front, Dorie. He'd glance at you with eyes of well, definite attraction, it looked like to me. He touched your face, moved your hair out of your eyes, and generally looked besotted."

Meg and Lucia made "woo-woo" noises. Dorie blushed.

"So the only funny thing he did was give our location over the radio," she said.

I nodded and Meg patted Dorie's shoulder.

"So then, I should still go out with him."

"You go, girl," Lucia bawled from the driver's seat. "Did you bring something girlie to wear?"

Dorie blushed again. "Feathers."

Now it was Meg's turn to howl. "What on earth are you talking about, little one?" Dorie towered over tiny Meg, so everyone laughed at her phrasing.

"I'll explain. I have a couple of different boas, right? But I only ever wear the pink one anymore, because it's my special Women on Fire garb."

"Right, right," Lucia said. "So?"

"So, I couldn't afford a new dressy dress or anything right now, but I wanted something sort of, well, sexy just in case we went somewhere. Well, it being a trip far away, even though it has a serious purpose and..."

"Go on, Dorine," I tut-tutted from the front seat.

"So I took this white jersey scoop neck tunic I have, and stitched two white boas to it all the way around."

"I'd look like an entire chicken coop if I wore that many feathers," Lu exclaimed.

"But on Dorie's slender upper body it will be gorgeous," I added.

Dorie grinned. "And balance with my bigger bottom half, right?"

We all booed her en masse.

"Oh, stop. Let's be real. I even glued on some of those white sparkly things to add bling, and brought a black skirt and also some black velveteen pants, whatever will make my lower half recede a bit. What do you think?" She turned to Meg, not the group's *fashionista*, but the honest one, for sure.

"I'm jealous. You have the most artistic knack I could ever imagine. If I wore feathers, given their biological source, I'd expect to either lay eggs or fly," she said.

"Oh," I said, looking directly out the windshield with a hand holding up my chin and keeping me from smiling, "she will, I'd bet on it. I think she might be beyond the egg part, but trust me, Dorie will fly."

~ * ~

In the end we could not pick up reception for the radio station where Fenn was dealing out equestrian news and probably making all of us more vulnerable by repeating his request for information on Mac. I worried aloud old Mr. McClellan might have heard the announcement and grown more anxious about speaking to me.

When we reached his block on Longridge Close, however, I dialed his number and the old gent answered on the first ring.

"Knew you'd call," he said quietly, calmly.

"Do you have any information for me, Mr. McClellan?"

He paused. An unidentifiable throat noise preceded

his answer. "Yes, yes, I'll tell you."

"Thank you so much." I tried not to sound overwhelmed. "Sir, I'm in your neighborhood with three of my lady friends. I wonder if we could come in for a brief visit."

Again a pause. "All from the United States, sir. They could wait in the car if you—"

Meg frowned at me and Lucia waved away the idea while shaking her head briskly.

"No, no, that wouldn't be very hospitable. I'll put the kettle on. Bring along your American friends. You know the flat." He hung up before I could say more.

Lucia beamed. "Told you he'd offer us coffee or something."

"Bringing those napoleons was a terrific idea, Lu. Leave it to you," Dorie said, picking up the white bakery box. "It'll probably be tea."

"Too early for sherry?" Meg asked and made a grumpy face.

We pulled up across the road and made our way from the van to number seventeen.

Dorie poked Meg to go in front of her up the steps. "Don't be nervous, Meggie. The guy's sweet as icing and definitely more scared of us than we are of him. White hair, gentle face."

"So was Mendel," Megan snapped.

Lucia rang McClellan's doorbell, and we were buzzed in. The old fellow had the inner door open as we came down the hall. He was exactly as Dorie had described, and also tall and slightly bent forward as he shook hands with us and urged us in. At once he seemed flustered.

"Huh, I-uh, never entertained so many ladies before," he said, and covered his mouth to chuckle softly.

Dorie handed him the white box, saying, "To go with our beverage."

His pale eyes, the same blue as Mac's, brightened and he smiled. "With the tea, yes. Very kind of you."

In turn he put the box on a plate and handed it all to Lucia, as if knowing she'd be the one to best arrange the sweets. While she did, he poured five scant cups from the kettle, apologizing that it didn't hold more. We sat around his enameled kitchen table, which was scrubbed clean, as was the work area and floors of the room. The lights had been off in the sitting room or lounge, I wasn't sure what he called it, so we'd landed in the kitchen. A pot of geraniums on the window sill brightened the cream-white room despite the heavy day outside.

I barely took a sip of tea before speaking up, fearing I might give up the whole enquiry if we didn't start right off.

"It's good of you to meet with us, sir. You said yesterday you might know someone who knew Michael McClellan."

"Aye. Did, didn't I?" The man sweetened his tea, and, as he took a full sip, I saw his pursed lips tremble.

"I'm sorry if this is difficult for you, Mr.—"

"Won't be, if I don't let it. And don't call me mister. My name is Boonie, that's what they always called me. 'Cause I wore a fur hat at times like that Daniel Boone of yours. Boonie and Mac, they'd say. Mac was my nephew. We were close. Well, until recently."

Dorie, it seemed, couldn't hold back the clicking sounds in her throat. She reached for a napoleon, broke off a piece and stuffed it down to smother her reaction.

"Not sure what you mean," I said. The others were gaping, drinking tea and munching on the sweets so they could remain respectfully outside the questioning. No point in making the old fellow feel inundated.

"The boy's dad, my brother, died when he was a teenager. Lived with me until he made himself a little career in training horses. Our whole family was into it, had a breeding farm of our own, once."

I tried to show my interest and approval, then put my mug to my lips.

"A good fellow he was, too." Boonie's eyes picked a spot out the window and latched on to it for a half-minute.

"We knew him," Dorie couldn't resist saying. "We thought so, too."

"Mac's a gem, I always told my friend who hired him over in the States," Lu jumped in, maybe hoping to cover what Dorie had put in past tense. Great idea, I thought, as the man may not even know of Mac's death yet.

Boonie rose, made a wait-a-minute sign and shuffled off to the sitting room, returning with a framed photograph of himself and a younger Mac, standing on either side of a flower-draped thoroughbred. "Trained and rode that one, he did. Took plenty of ribbons for him. For The Gib, too. Great eventer, jumper. You probably know that."

I exchanged glances with Lucia and Dorie. Only Meg nodded.

She took a breath. "You know he's sick now, though, don't you? The Gib, er, Fitzgibbons. That's why we're here, mainly. To get our friend's horse rehabbed."

Boonie was nodding, and moisture accumulated on his eyelids. "Yes, that's my fault, y'see."

Tension rippled like a lightning strike across the room. "Your... fault?" I asked.

The old man waved his crooked-fingered, bony hand at us. "Let me tell you 'bout Mac first. People blame him, but it wasn't his fault. My prospects were down, had to sell the farm long ago, Mac still young and growing to a fine trainer. He took a job over there at that newfangled stable. Golden Mane they called it. You know, after a horse with a golden mane. Claimed they'd had one of those, must have been a palomino from the States or Spain or somewhere, that had a mane and tail same color as his hide."

Boonie paused to break open a napoleon and wolf down a piece, then another. I wondered if he'd had breakfast.

"Folks liked the place over there. They added on, had a good thing going, lessons for the pony clubs, good horses coming out for competition. Huge effort. They hired on Mac, gave him one of those gypsy trailers to live in. Said he didn't mind. Had it good, he said, and made a name for himself training lots of winners. Riding some of 'em, too. What a jumper! He'd take on anything." He cleared his throat and dabbed at his rheumy eyes with a paper napkin. Asked if he should put the kettle on again.

Lucia thanked him for his graciousness and declined, for all of us. The story was too gripping.

"So, these Golden Mane people, were they at all associated with Van Dyne, and that scandal about selling sick horses?" I couldn't breathe until the panicked look in McClellan's eyes softened to resignation.

He nodded slowly, pressing both his hands to his face for a moment before he could speak. "Behind it all. Their idea. Meanwhile, it was a bad time for me... I'd been sick, the cancer you know. Mac tried to help when I came out of hospital, but we had to hire people, specialists he arranged for, then home nurses. I... I couldn't lose the council house, y'see. And he couldn't take me in, living in that tin can of his."

Breathing seemed to stop around the room. Lucia rattled her spoon beside her mug and we all jiggled in our seats. No one but Dorie would look at the old man.

"What did you have to do, Mr. McClellan, Boonie?" she asked.

He stiffened his shoulders. "I knew Mac wouldn't approve. He was devastated about what they were doing at Golden's. Right ready he was to report them to the Jockey Club—that's the big shots of racing here. Said it was a damn shame they'd lie about a horse's health and could still sell him for big money if he had any sort of winning record."

He paused, then a twisted cry came from his mouth together with the words, "Not me, though. I fell for it."

I reached out a hand and laid it on his trembling arm.

"You mean you sold..."

"The Gib. Yes. Mac had found out the poor horse had that pulmonary thing when he was pushed hard, said he should never race again like he had. And not even three years old. I made a private arrangement with them at Golden Mane, so it wouldn't have my name on the Bill of Sale. They sent him to Van Dyne who made a small fortune, like they did themselves. I picked up pennies, enough to pay my bills and live here rent free for the last few years." He tried to pick up his mug but let it clunk back on the table, popping the liquid out in a puddle which Dorie mopped up without a word, leaning around him.

He nodded a thank-you at her, blinked a few times to refocus himself.

"Mac was in a rage. Said he couldn't even stay in the same country as me. How could I do it, and all."

"Why did you do it, sir?" Meg asked, no emotion in her voice.

The old man looked her in the eye.

"Not to ruin Mac's life, of course. So he wouldn't have to take care of an old man for a couple of decades. Much as it hurt me to let that beautiful horse go, I thought he could make a pretty good eventer for a kid. Not racing, easy stuff. He was worth nothing unless we lied about his lungs. I thought to spare Mac. And I ruined him instead."

McClellan buried his face in his arms and crossed them on the table before him. We glanced, panicky, at one another as the harsh, throaty keening of a man in deep mourning thundered out. For what he'd done, and for what had happened to his loved one.

I rested a cautious hand on the man's shoulder as the room grew quiet, so quiet we could hear the tick of a clock somewhere, and the first scattering of raindrops at the window.

"We're so sorry you had to go through that, you and Mac, too," I said at last.

"It wasn't my way," Boonie said. "It wasn't Mac's way. He was so broken up, he took on the job with the American who bought the horse. And you know the funny thing?"

We nodded as a chorus to encourage him. "He wrote me a nice letter about a month ago. Said he couldn't live anymore with not turning himself in, since he'd known what those people were doing. Said someone over there threatened him, told him not to repeat any of it, or I'd be the first one hauled in. He apologized, said he had to do it."

Boonie reached for his cup, and Dorie placed it closer to him. He drained the remaining tea.

"Do you have any thoughts on who that might be?" I asked quickly. "The one who threatened him?"

"He never said. But I was glad for him, if the threat helped him decide to tell. I knew he'd get some peace if he finally reported it about the Van Dynes' and the others. I didn't care if it meant jail for me. This little flat is a jail sometimes anyhow. Living with your memories, and your mistakes."

Lucia tried to console him by murmuring and gently stroking his arm, but he waggled his fingers at her and she pulled back and clamped her lips shut.

"I was told he died, and it was suicide. Perhaps because he was going to tell, and hated to do it—couldn't live with himself. And that's why you're here, isn't it?"

I nodded. "We're so terribly sorry it may mean implicating you, Boonie."

"No, don't be. You're good people, and you're trying to help my boy—get him justice, anyhow. Just get that horse fixed, if you can. And let me know."

"Horse?" Dorie asked.

"He means Fitzgibbons, don't you, Mr. McClellan?" Meg said.

The man nodded. "We called him The Gib because he was the thing that made everything possible, the form, the piece you couldn't leave out. Mac followed him to America to keep training him, gentle-like, so he'd stay healthy. He even was trying some medicine was supposed to help..."

His voice had weakened and he became still, pulled in on himself.

"Fitzgibbons is, was, your horse?" Lucia asked.

He barely nodded, and gently removed my hand from his shoulder with a smile.

"You better go," he said. "Know where Van Dyne's placed is?"

I nodded. "But not the other one, the Golden Horse."

"Long ride out to Golden Mane's. Go toward Leicester, take the second road to the Industrial Park. You'll come across it on your left after a few miles."

We thanked him, each hugged him, and I had to ask

one more question. "Who told you Mac was, well, that he was killed, sir?"

The old man shrugged. "Everybody knew but me. Then a young girl, worked over at Van Dyne's stables, she called. Said her sister worked with Mac. Broke my heart he was that hurt over the whole thing. I might's well've killed him with my own hand. She said to let her know if I set up a memorial thing for Mac, but I wanted nothing to do with it. Keep it quiet, that's what I figured. Now I've gone and told you everything."

I bit my lip. This time it was I who reached for his hand, his quaking, dry old hand, the fingers crabbed and bony.

"It's not true about the suicide, sir," I said softly. "The police found out someone... well, hurt Mac..."

His eyes opened wider. "Murder?"

I nodded. "That's why we're here, trying to find out who killed him."

The old man nodded, looking relieved but horrified all at once.

"Thank you," he said, his solemn glance sweeping all four of us. Then, from where he sat, eyes focused a million miles away, Boonie swallowed hard and waved at us to show ourselves out.

Thirty-eight

Dorie

I cried halfway to Leicester, while Megan cluck-clucked over all the ironies in Boonie's and Mac's tale. Hannah dabbed at her nose a few times, and Lucia kept muttering prayers under her breath. The rain had let up, but dark clouds still lingered, ready to pour out their bad tidings any second.

"At least we know a lot more than we did," Lucia finally rationalized. "No matter how sad."

"I hope it helped the old guy to get it off his chest," Hannah said. "I have a hard time condemning him. Sometimes the line between one decision and its opposite is so fine it can blow away in a breeze."

"Let me understand this," I pleaded after the fourth or fifth tissue got wadded up. "Mr. McClellan sold Fitzgibbons to the people we're going to see now, because he needed money to live without destroying Mac's life."

"Yes, and then to Van Dynes'," I said. "This stable is

the one where Mac worked."

"And," Megan concluded, "the ones who seemed to have started the whole scheme. Fitzgibbons would have been worthless sold as a horse with confirmed EIPH. Mac never revealed it, but clearly he was treating Fitzgibbons on his own, probably with Lasix before every workout and every race. Apparently it mostly worked, until that last time, when the poor horse's lungs just couldn't take anymore."

"Mac had already told his uncle he was going to tell Ada and others the truth, that they'd been swindled on the sale of Gibby," I mused. "Whoever was threatening him back in West Parkford knew that, and figured when the horse collapsed that day at the Polo Grounds, Mac would do it pretty quickly. Guilty conscience and all."

Lucia moaned a series of non-verbal shocked noises. "Why, what, who? I remember Ada said Mac had scheduled a meeting with her for the Monday after he died. Why, I wonder. What was it about? And who? The big question is who, who threatened Mac?"

"Because," I said, a light bulb going off in my head as I twisted and bounced up and down in the back seat, "that's the person who killed him!"

The others clapped and I grinned smugly. "Oh, sure, like you already figured it all out."

"No, sweetheart," Meg said, patting my denim clad leg, "we're putting it together just now like you are. It's just who did it? We can't know yet for sure. We know Mac had a rough relationship with that woman over at Rosemont, and Terry Bukowski said he was mean to her."

Hannah joined in. "It still could be Gus Finch, even though tried to make peace with Theo."

Meg nodded. "Supposedly. What I don't understand is what we hope to discover at this next horse farm, and the one where the fellow has the shotgun already loaded."

I shivered. "I don't know, either. But I think there'll be bad people there, so now I'm the one who's a Nellie-nervous."

"Nonsense. You're very brave, Dorine," Lucia argued from the front seat.

"I've seen you in action down in Florida with that creepy relative of Ada's," Hannah added, "so I can prove it."

I thanked my friends for bolstering my courage, but I had to quiet down, make myself think of Fenn and our date this evening and forget the gun. I watched the dark, heavy clouds swirl and dip in the sky as we passed other horse farms and pretty countryside, hoping the weather wouldn't spoil my time with the strong, sweet and handsome Fenn.

Where had he said he was taking me? Fox-something? Was that a restaurant, or a horseracing thing, or a, a... *ohmigod, maybe it's his ancestral home.* He implied he was independently wealthy, had a big estate to manage, and the radio job was just a fun thing. Also, he rode at Amber Hill every day. So he must live close to where we were staying.

My mouth hung open for a second. *He must be a millionaire.* I couldn't give him a call on Hannah's cell phone, despite what I'd planned because now it would feel like chasing his money, when in truth it was more his tall, rangy but slender body, his tenderness toward me, his indigo eyes, that I could be accused of chasing. Anyhow, Hannah had just told Lucia to turn right into the Industrial Park, and I knew The Golden Mane Equestrian Centre wouldn't be far.

Even on this dark day, I spotted it from the back seat before they did upfront.

"There, on the left, see the golden horse painted on the brown sign?"

They had. We turned into the drive and soon came to a locked gate. Lu and Hannah stared at each other and Hannah waved at Lu to go ahead, push the button.

An unintelligible, staticky answer burred back at us.

"Understand you may have horses for sale," Lucia yelled into the microphone beside the speaker.

"Buzz you in," a man's voice said, more clearly now. The black wrought iron gates swung open and Lucia advanced the van down the drive. Trees overhung the roadway for about a half-mile, then it twisted and turned and opened up into a clearing. A small brick house stood on an elevation to the right, and straight ahead were two large horse barns. Small outbuildings were scattered around the property, and from one of them came a large, hulking man with a broad face, wearing jeans and a gray flannel shirt that made his face and his once dark hair look gray, too. He wore fine riding boots and an annoyed expression, and carried his gray Stetson in his hand.

Lu pulled up to within six yards of him and swung to the left to park beside some old farm equipment.

For a big man he moved quickly, and was leaning into Hannah's open window, his broad leather belt with a brass horse-head buckle in her face before the motor rumbled to stillness.

"Help you?"

I could hear Hannah gulping, taking a big breath and see her pointing toward me in the back seat. "Her girl needs a horse. We were told you might have some decent horseflesh for a reasonable sum. Got anything you can show us?"

The big man nodded and his face seemed to brighten. Then he glanced back in the car. "American?" he asked.

"Yes," Lucia said. "That a problem?" We all followed Lucia's lead and were exiting the car. All but Hannah, who had to wait until the jeans stepped back from her door and let her step out, too.

"No, naw," the man said." No problem." He stuck his hand out. "Goldie," he said. "You know, for Goldwin."

Each of us shook hands with him. Hannah called herself, "Debbie," and we each followed her lead, giving ourselves false names. Meg became Misha, Lucia MaryJane and Dorie "Bunny." The man smiled. He was more attractive when he smiled, I thought. His teeth weren't too bad, and when the heavy planes of his face lifted in a smile he didn't seem as old as I'd first thought. There was something familiar about him I couldn't place, something about the meter of his voice and his inflection of certain words.

Of course, I'd never met him, but he reminded me of someone or something.

"So what kind of horse you looking for, Bunny?" he asked as we walked lazily toward the second barn.

"Oh, you know, a decent jumper. An eventer with a solid record. My daughter loves to win."

"And she's good," Lucia added for flavor. "She's just outgrown her pony."

"She's young?" he asked.

"Twenty," said Dorie, at the same moment Hannah said, "twelve."

Dorie giggled and grabbed at the man's gray-sleeved shirt. "Yes, she's twelve. I meant my budget is twenty, you know, thousand."

"She's divorced," Lucia added, disguising the rumble in her throat. "Big settlement."

Meg nearly choked, but coughed instead. "You okay, Grandma?" Hannah asked, and the coughing continued, harder.

Goldie's eyes brightened. "That can buy you a beauty. Let me show you a couple of possibilities in that range."

We entered the semi-darkness of the barn, and I was vaguely aware Meg had lagged behind us, slightly bent over a dark object in her hands. I realized with a shock that she was taking pictures.

Inside the stable, though, where she'd have to use a flash, she put the camera in the pocket of her navy blue cotton sweater. Goldie had stopped at a large box stall, where he was pointing out the qualifications of a Dutch Warmblood who'd performed well in all kinds of eventing, he said. Hannah suggested politely he looked a little long in the tooth and she wondered how many jumps the horse had left in him. She reached into the stall and scratched his ears, and he rumbled rhythmically from down deep.

Goldie acted insulted and gave the horse's age as eight. "If the girl's still riding in ten years, and most don't stay in competition much longer, he'll still be jumping, believe me."

Far down the aisle of box stalls, there was movement, a clatter and the nickering of another horse and his caretaker. Dorie peered in that direction but could see nothing but the bobbing of another western hat.

"How about a thoroughbred? My daughter's slender, it seems she might look better on a thoroughbred," I said when I looked back. Lucia cooed in agreement. Goldie took us to another stall, and another. We were getting closer to end of the barn where, from the jangle of buckles and leather someone was tacking up a horse to ride it.

Probably a groom, or one of the renters, I thought, and I inhaled the air around me. I frowned and glanced at Hannah, who also was frowning as her nose wrinkled in a sniff.

Goldie noticed and commented as how we ought to be used to barn smells if the daughter's had a horse for years. Hannah and I choked on fake coughs, but the man went on, growing impatient. "What d'you think of this little filly? She's as graceful as a ballerina, but strong. Only two. Responding real well to the jumps in her first tries. Lots of good years in her."

We looked up when we heard a woman's voice, low

and husky, then the roll of a barn door opening to the outside, the clink of stirrups and the slap of a body landing on the horse's back. The crash of the horse out the doors left a whoosh of air behind him.

From more of a distance now, we heard the hurried commands of rider to horse.

"So what do you think of the horses you've seen? These are the best I'm offering today."

Goldie stood with his legs wide apart, hands on hips, his chin jutting in a menacing way.

"I'm not so sure they're all that healthy," Hannah said, leaning toward our guide.

"You wouldn't sell an injured horse without giving the buyer the appropriate warning, would you?" I asked, coming closer.

"What the hell are you talking about?" Goldie exploded, his voice dug down in bass range now. "Who are you anyway?"

"I'm a physician," Meg announced curtly. She didn't say what kind. "And I also am not happy about the health of the animals we've seen today. That Warmblood is swayback, this filly looks like tendonitis personified. You think we're idiots, and we don't know questionable horseflesh when we see it?" She stuck her own chin up close to Goldie's. He began to back away.

"Hey, these horses are treated by the best vets in Leicester. They'll have veterinary confirmations. They're bred of champions, all of them."

"Yeah," Lucia said, stamping her foot and crossing her arms. "Champions on their way to the glue factory."

Goldie had had enough. He started poking and pushing us toward the barn doors. "I don't know your game, ladies, but I'm telling you to get the hell out."

We let ourselves be hustled into the yard, giving Meg the perfect opportunity to snap his picture with that wild-eyed, furious look on his face as I poked at his lapels and he shoved me away.

By the time we'd reached the car and started to climb in, he was swinging his arms at us, ready to land a punch if we dawdled one more second.

Meg was the one to dawdle. "I imagine The Gib was not quite in such bad shape when you bought him and then arranged to have Van Dyne get rid of him for you."

"Hey!" he shouted. "What the hell—"

She slammed her car door shut just as he swung at her, and screamed. He'd caught his finger in her door.

He began swearing, ranting at us as Lucia started up the van and backed out.

"I'll call the police," he hollered, holding his wounded hand and hopping up and down.

"I'll bet," Lucia yelled. "We'll wait for them at the gate. Thank you very much."

She roared away, but I saw her staring into the rear view mirror and glanced behind myself to look. Roaring down the trail toward the wounded man was a figure, turning her mount around in a tight circle, heels moving in and out around the horse's belly, dark hair flying out from under her western hat, big shoulders braced and a whip snapping in her hand. The figure gave me a sickening sense of dread, but I wasn't sure why.

"Let's hope we can get out the gate," I whined.

As we raced down the curving driveway, Hannah dialed the Scotland Yard detective and was relieved to hear him answer. She explained who she was, the connection to Bernie, and said they'd like to meet with him. He asked where they were.

"Escaping a madman," Hannah said. "On our way to Van Dyne's in Cheltenham. Can you meet us right away?"

"Gads, I'm in London right now. With the traffic I can't get up there in less than an hour-and-a-half."

"That's okay," Hannah said, as Lucia zoomed through the gate which had automatically opened when she pushed the exit buzzer.

"We'll get some lunch and meet you there. This one might involve firearms, and it would be nice to have you along." She quickly gave him Van Dyne's address.

"Firearms," the Brit said. "Leave it to you Americans. More guns than biscuits over there, I always say. Right, then. See you. Cheers."

"Yeah, yeah, we're full of cheer," I yipped.

We began to breathe again around the time Lucia found what looked like a popular place for Saturday lunch, off the main road, far enough away from Golden Mane, and, according to Hannah, well on the way to Van Dyne's. There were umbrella-shaded tables in a side yard, though due to the impending torrents, they were lightly populated. Dorie said the fresh air would be great after smelling that awful, sweet, sickening odor at Golden Mane.

"I love eating out here and seeing the quaint cottages

with their thatched roofs, though I can't believe you're not used to the scent of manure and hay by now, Dorine," Lucia said.

"It wasn't just barn odor," Hannah said, searching in vain for a cigarette in her purse. "Dorie means that perfumey smell, like, like..." She seemed to struggle for a connection, but lost it even as her fist tapped her chest over her heart.

It was only after our first round of beers she could finally laugh and hoot and stop trembling. Out of the blue, I grabbed the edge of the table with both hands.

"...like Musk, Han," I said. Lu and Meg stared at us.

Hannah's eyes enlarged and her lips pressed together in shock. "Dorine. That's it. That was Musk perfume in that barn!"

I looked at Meg and Lucia to explain. "Musk is the scent that awful Glenda wears, the owner of Rosemont who's trying to steal Siggy away from Ada." I felt pleased with myself, then wobbled my mug of beer as Hannah jumped up.

"She means Glenda Mane, folks. Glenda of Golden Mane. Get it? That's not the name of a horse, for Chris' sake. That's the family name, and that brooding, hulking guy we just met is practically her twin."

I picked up the thread and ran with it. "A brother, at least. That was *her* racing down the path to the woods. No wonder Bernie can't find her in West Parkford. We were a few yards away from Glenda Mane and didn't know it. Right here in England. How stupid can we be?"

"Not stupid at all," Meg said, her face forming the

slightest smile. "You may not have seen her but you smelled her. And now we can figure out the significance of her being there."

"I saw her perfectly well in the rearview mirror," Lucia added, her cheeks pinked by the exciting news. "I was thinking I want to concentrate on that figure flying toward us, but we were in a bit of a rush to get away. I've met the woman at Chamber meetings, I'd recognize that wild, dark hair, that mannish physique anywhere."

"She might have killed Mac," I squeaked. "She won't like that we're poking around her horse business."

Meg glanced at her watch. "The day is young, my friends. I'd say Ms. Mane's making her plans this very moment."

"We'd better call Ada on her cell and fill her in," Hannah said, taking her own flip-up phone from her pocket. "If she's back at the Manor and we can't get her, we'll call Shelly at the tea rooms and ask her to give a message."

"Tell her we're on our way to Bukowski's, too, Han," Meg said. "And we'd better leave soon, since Scotland Yard should be there shortly."

Hannah tried but couldn't reach the tea rooms. The line was busy, so we paid our bill and clambered back into the van.

"Anybody nervous?" I asked, squeezing in close to Meg.

"Just you," Meg said, chuckling. "Don't worry about this guy, Dorie, he can't shoot all four of us."

"Yeah, but I'm the tallest with the biggest tush, so I

make a great target, especially running away."

They all laughed, maybe glad to break the tension, I thought. That was when I got the great idea that could help save Ada and her horse.

"I've got to call Fenn," I announced. "He should be off the air by now. Hannah, will you lend me your phone? And stop the car."

"Here's the phone," Hannah said as she passed it back. "But why do we have to stop the car?"

"Because I think they have a no-hands law here, too."

Meg groaned. "That's only for the driver, Dorie. Make your call and we'll all pretend not to listen in."

I felt like pouting. But Women on Fire had long ago taught me that gets you nowhere in a hurry. I found the scrap of paper in my purse with Fenn's cell phone number and dialed. He answered after two rings.

"Cheers," he said.

"It's not cheery here, Fenn," I said. "In fact it's pretty dangerous, and I think I hear thunder rumbling in the distance."

"What's wrong, darling?" he asked. "I put out a call for information on my radio show and got a few responses. Course, they could be bogus. People do like to speak on the air and pretend to know something. But I'll give you the list when we meet, and we can check them out tomorrow if you like."

Damn him! I meant to be angry with him for giving away our location, but when he called me darling and suggested we'd be spending more time together, it was hard to keep my focus.

"Yes, okay. Thank you. Fenn, the old man is Mac's uncle and he's the one who owned Fitzgibbons and sold him to have enough money to live on, even though he knew the horse was sick."

"No," Fenn moaned. "And your friend, Mac, knew it, I suppose."

"Yes, and threatened to expose the whole scam just recently, which is..."

"Probably why he was killed. Right?"

I nodded, forgetting he couldn't hear me nod. "Old Boonie led us to a stable that did the deed for him, and, oh my gosh, Fenn, we saw this woman riding toward us, and we think it was maybe the one who threatened Mac."

"The one who killed him, then? My Lord, Dorie, where are you now? I don't want you out there sporting with evil people on your own. Sweetheart, please take care."

I grinned and slouched down in my seat. "Don't worry about me. There are four of us now, on our way to that Van Dyne farm, and a Scotland Yard fellow is going to meet us there. And one of us can speak the language."

Megan groaned. "Let's hope so."

"Darling, sweetheart, don't do it. Let Scotland Yard handle it all. What if you ladies somehow bungle it and the madman comes out with his shotgun again? I'm not at all sure Scotland Yard dicks even carry a weapon. It's not the States, you know."

"But," I said, "but..."

"Dorie? You ought to come back to the Manor and stay safe and get ready for our date tonight. Do it for me, lovely lady. You've touched me," he said, his voice growing softer but somehow more intense. "You've touched me as I haven't been touched in years. I don't want to, well, I can't lose you."

I nearly dropped the phone. Meg poked me and I sat up straight.

"You're very sweet to say so. I... I like you, too," I said. "But we can't stop the ball from rolling now, Fenn. Trust me. We're on fire. We're women on fire. Now I really need you to do me a favor."

"All right. What?" His voice flattened like the bubbles on a pint of beer.

"Well, I know you didn't think of it that way, but you practically told people on the radio where we're staying. Our friends Ada and Theo are alone there now, and I think the tea rooms are closed on Saturday, and their cell phone won't work in that area. Will you go to them, make sure they're okay and tell them we discovered how Fitzgibbons was sold, and Mac was being blackmailed, and Glenda Mane, from our own town, is here in England? No telling what she'll do or say when she finds out we've uncovered her and her brother's nasty plot from three or more years ago."

"Jolly will. It sounds like you've broken this case wide open, love. 'Course, I'll get right on it. I looked up the directions yesterday so I'd get to you on time tonight. I have them in the car. I'll head up there right away."

"Tell them to lock the doors, Fenn," Hannah shouted.

"And to have someone at Amber Hill keep an eye on Fitzgibbons. That Glenda woman is so crazed she might try to hurt the horse, do away with the evidence of their wrongdoing, or something" Lucia yelled.

Fenn said he would cover all bases, and begged us to be careful. He'd be waiting for me, he told me.

I was too moved to respond, and hung up the phone at once.

"I think I'm in love," I blurted.

The moans and groans in the car were a cataphony of sounds—is that the word?

"Don't make fun of me." My cheeks were flaming.

"Honey, we're not, it's just, it's not a good time to fall in love," Lucia said. "Can you put it on hold?"

"Until we get back to the Manor House and the safety of all those strong arms waiting for us?" Hannah said.

"Or at least 'til we escape from Van Dyne's in one piece?" Meg begged.

I giggled and wiped away the perspiration from my neck. In my heart I knew I was in love and it didn't matter what my Women on Fire friends said. I could no sooner shove this rush of feelings to a back burner than I could leap over menopause unaffected, and I knew it.

Come to think of it, that was the second hot flash I'd had in two days. I just prayed the famous "pause" wouldn't affect my relationship with Fenn, no matter how short or how doomed we might be as a couple.

The cell phone rang before I could hand it back to Hannah, so I answered. It was Bernie Cascone, looking for her.

"She's right here, Bern. I'll pass the phone to her.

She's not driving so it's okay, they told me."

"That's great, Dorine. Just put Hannah on, driving or not."

"But..."

"Please, can I speak with Hannah now?"

"Mm-hmm," I passed the phone to Hannah and, snuggling down in my seat, considered how everybody but me had a boyfriend or husband. Now maybe I had one, too. It was nice. I didn't feel so alone anymore, even if it was my turn to go crazy.

Thirty-nine

Meg

Allahu Akbar, I prayed silently, the way we did at home in Bosnia in times of trouble. Allah be with us. I watched, and listened, alert and a little anxious about the role I was to play at our next stop. Sometimes, I thought, my dear husband Arthur was right, and Women on Fire should take up golf or quilling or something more sedentary and leave the detecting work to those who get paid for it.

Still, it was challenging, and fun. The best way to spend retirement. Just look at Hannah's growing excitement and emphatic, long scream at Bernie over the phone.

"We know, we know she's here, Bernard. We just saw her. Yes, at her brother's farm near Cheltenham. That's where the big racetrack is." She cupped her hand over the phone and turned toward her friends.

"Bernie's calling to tell me he just tracked down

where Glenda Mane is."

"England," our trio sang out in a chorus.

Hannah punched the air with a fist. "Yes, okay, sweetheart, we will... No, she wasn't threatening us, just racing toward us with her whip raised... Oh, that qualifies? Okay, we'll tell Phillips the Scotland Yard guy. He's meeting us in a minute at the Van Dyne Farm."

Hopefully at the gate before we enter, I thought.

Hannah whispered something at the close of her call, then said aloud she would call Bernie as soon as we left VanDyne's. She clicked off the phone and the questions flared up all around her at once.

"How did he know, Hannah?"

"Who told him Glenda was in England?"

"Does he think she's the one who killed Mac?"

"Whoa, whoa, ladies! You're like skittish horses at the gate." Hannah put her phone in her pocket, directed Lucia to turn left, and sighed. "I miss him so much." Her voice sounded like Dorie's in its plaintive little wail.

We began to taunt her and she growled at us.

"All right, all right. Here's the scoop. Bernard questioned Terry Bukowski again. He told Terry we'd met her dad and sister. She went to pieces and cried. Begged him to tell us they're not bad people. It's the only job her father could get that paid enough to support his sick mom and the other four kids, etc., etc. Bern promised to give us the message if she'd come clean."

"Clean? What did he mean, Hannah?" Dorie asked.

"Where in Hades were you brought up?" I snapped. "Even I know what that means."

Lucia shushed me.

Hannah took a breath. "He meant, Dor, like who was behind this sale of sick horses, who was responsible for Mac's death and why he was killed. When he'd told Terry we were all in England looking for answers, she turned white, absolutely ghostly white."

"I wonder if the Chambercombe ghost is like that, all white and misty..."

"Dorine, hush up," I said. "Go on, Hannah."

Lucia was suddenly applying the brakes and rattling on about the black Mercedes parked on the edge of the wet and narrow road ahead. "I can't squeeze past him," she complained.

Hannah yelled.

"Wait, it could be him, it could be Phillips."

The man in the black car lifted a hand in a wave and pursed his lips as he surveyed the four women in ours. When Lucia did squeeze by him and pulled over, he got out, stretched and locked his vehicle. He came toward us. Lucia rolled down her window.

The slender, gray-haired man tipped his hat and stood there getting whipped by rain and sudden winds. "Ms. Doyle?"

"That would be me," Hannah said, leaning across Lu and asking if he were Phillips.

He nodded, opened the rear door, gave me a gentle shove to sit alongside me. He tipped his hat and gave us a thin-lipped grin. "Best we arrive together, I would think," he said. "This Bukowski fellow has a record of violence. Has been known to lay a hand on wife and children, once arrested in a barroom brawl. Nothing major though, like shootings."

"How about selling sick horses?" Lucia asked.

"And he does have a large gun, Officer," Dorie said. "He held it up and pointed it at us."

"Rifle," I corrected, "Sixteen gauge."

Phillips asked to be introduced to each woman, making sure it would be okay to call us by first names. We all agreed.

"Who's the linguist?" he asked.

I raised a hand, then put it down and laughed at my own silliness. "I'm no linguist, but I come from Eastern Europe, Bosnia to be exact, and I've had to communicate with plenty of other Eastern Europeans," I explained.

"For example," Hannah said from the front seat, "she can speak Hungarian, Russian and Polish quite well."

"And muddle along in Romanian," Meg added.

"She's also a forensic scientist," Dorie added, beaming as if at her little girl.

I slapped at her hand and mumbled something negative.

"Shall I drive on," asked Lucia, "or do we want to have a plan or something first?"

"Plan? No plan," Phillips said. "You just explain to the man why you're all here, see what you can find out about the horse-selling scam, Meg, and when necessary I'll move in. Drive on, Madam." He was no double-oh-seven, but he had a certain air about him I liked. Calmness, dignity—always in short supply in our group.

Hannah directed Lu to the turn, and she slowly drove

the van around the ruts and bumps, though I was sure I heard Lu's teeth chattering a bit, and it wasn't that cold a day despite the rain that fell steadily.

"You are armed, right?" Hannah asked, a frown puckering her usually clear forehead.

Phillips smiled mysteriously. "Let's put it this way: if you hear any gunshots, hit the deck."

"Wait," Dorie yelled so hard Lu stopped the car. "No, I don't mean to wait the car, Lu, you go ahead. I just meant, I never noticed they had a deck. Where is it, exactly?"

Phillips laughed heartily. "Good one," he said. I apologized for Dorine's silliness and watched as Phillips shrugged, gazing ahead now, as the woods opened up to clear spaces.

He pointed to a spot where he wanted Lu to park. She did, and he opened his door and yanked me out. "C'mon, then, let's find this rat."

I pretended my very intense heartbeat was the drum of someone walking behind me, but in reality the only ones behind me were Lucia, Hannah and Dorie. Phillips had attached himself to my left elbow and I had no choice but to skip and lunge along beside him with my very short legs, getting pummeled in the downpour.

"This is the house we reconnoted, right, Han? Or is it connoitered?" Dorie said, as we passed the brick residence Hannah, Dorie and Fenn had skulked around the day before—still no activity there—and came closer to the first stables. There was not a chuckle in the assembly.

Hannah's phone rang and I could sense her fumbling

in her huge secondhand Versaci bag as we crept along.

She spoke quickly and quietly into the phone. "Yes, Fenn. We're here now. We have Scotland Yard with us, yes. ...Oh, I see... No, you cannot talk to her. Why? Because we're busy, Fenn. We'll call you back. Okay, you call us in a half hour." She clicked off and shoved the phone back in her bag.

She spoke *sotto voce*. She'd taught me that word once at a play we were watching.

"Folks, Ada's worried about us. Fenn went over to be with her and Theo, but Ada insisted Fenn and Theo get back to Amber Hill and stay near Fitzgibbons. She's more afraid Glenda might want to harm him, the evidence of her misdoings."

"Shut up, please, Ms. Doyle," Phillips snapped under his breath. Dorie whimpered. We kept walking, like some kind of march to Bataan or somewhere. Suddenly there was a crash of metal and wood, a variety of horse nickerings and screams. We all gasped as Stanley Bukowski appeared in the doorway of the stable, hatless, shirtless except for an armless undershirt and drunker than a dog in a dish of vodka, as I said later.

As he came forward, we realized he was dragging the rifle at his side.

Phillips pulled me forward. Thundered rumbled in the distance.

I yelled "Hello," in Bosnian. Then tried something in Polish. The wild-eyed man stopped in his tracks and glowered at me, answering in Polish, then English "What you want? Who are you?"

"Friend of Terry," I answered. The man staggered forward and reached out his empty hand to show he didn't understand.

"Terrushka!" he cried. "My daughter. Where is she? How is she?"

He turned and called into the barn. "Hautch tuti." *Come here.* The girl groom ran up to him.

"Papa? What is it? Is Terry here?"

She turned to gape at the array in the yard, Phillips and me only a few yards away, Hannah, Lucia and Dorie a couple of yards beyond that.

"Oh, it's the ladies from the other day. You have seen my sister? You spoke to her?" the slender young woman asked. "Please. How is she?"

While the tipsy man wobbled behind the girl, Dorie answered and eased up closer to me.

"She's sad because her friend Mac has been killed. But I helped her keep the place where she lived, and she is working very hard. She's a good girl."

Phillips waved at Dorie to be quiet and drew the old man's attention to him. "Sir, would you please put down your weapon?"

The detective nodded at me and I translated the plea into Polish. Bukowski looked up, startled that someone here could speak his language. He glanced down at the gun as if he had forgotten he held it. He started to raise it as if to study it further, while a chorus of gasps crept out on the air.

"Papa, no!" the young girl cried and ran smack into her father's chest, trying to wrestle the gun away.

I shouted a command in Polish for him to stop, but the man looked confused, and grew more belligerent. "*Nie,* he cried. "No."

Before Phillips could make a motion toward him, Bukowski swung his daughter around and grabbed her around her waist, clutching her to him with one beefy arm and swinging the gun out at his side with the other. She kept throwing her body from side-to-side, jamming him with her elbows, and stomping on his feet.

"Young lady, I beg you, stay still," Phillips said, pleading with both his hands palms out. She quieted, but I could see it wouldn't be for long.

Phillips' voice deepened and grew more intense. "Mr. Bukowski, these women want to help you. They already helped your daughter in America."

The drunken man screamed obscenities back at us. "My daughter in America no good," he hollered, and then added something more in Polish, something that made Meg draw in breath and gape.

"Terry mixed with a bad crowd, got pregnant," she whispered to those around her. "He threw her out, sending her to America with Mac when he left."

Bukowski continued, his voice turning sorrowful, tears pouring from his eyes. When he paused, I filled them in further.

"They left when the horse was shipped to America. Teresa was to keep an eye on Mac, so he would never tell about Van Dyne and the 'others.' And Mac, in his guilt, was to give her work to support her."

"She was the insurance policy for the ring," Hannah

said, nearly choking.

"And she knew it, that little—" Dorie snapped.

Terry's sister Sophie pushed backward against her father, nearly toppling his out-of-control body.

"No!" she screamed. "Terry knows nothing about what those people did, the Manes, the Van Dynes'. They made her go to have the abortion. She hated it, she cried for days. Now she hates us all. She never writes or calls because she is so sad. Mac was good to her, but he won't let her go either because he promised Papa to look after her. I tell you she didn't know..."

"But you know, Miss? How they sold sick horses?"

The girl nodded. "We see the papers, Papa and me, after Mr. Van Dyne go to prison. He thinks we are stupid and leaves us to take care of his farm. He pays Papa good so Matka can get treatments and my little brothers can eat. Papa doesn't mean to hurt anybody. He's just scared of Goldie and his sister. She came by on her horse today and was very mean. Warned us to tell nobody about the horses, or she would hurt Terry. Papa goes so crazy he drinks a half a bottle vodka until I throw the rest on the ground. I know he's scared because we miss Terry, and we hate to keep this secret from police."

"Teresa, my oldest girl. She made big mistake, but she's good girl," he said, clearly moaning in emotional pain. In one sudden movement of surrender, he pushed his daughter away from him, dropped the gun and fell on his knees.

Phillips ran forward, grabbed the gun and dislodged the bullets. I pulled the girl to my side.

Bukowski collapsed into the mud and wept, his eyes reddened, distraught Polish words flowing out of him like a river of despair. Dorie came close and offered him a hand up but he wouldn't look at her.

I explained. "He's embarrassed. He says he was stupid to take on this job when Van Dyne went to prison. But he had banished Terry by then and was afraid his family would starve, his wife would die without the extra income for special treatments. He's ashamed."

"Will he help us now? Will he show us the records in that house of what Van Dyne and the Manes have done?" Phillips said.

I asked in Polish. Both Bukowski and his daughter nodded yes, yes, they would both help.

"I don't understand why the police didn't find these papers at the time they investigated Van Dyne.

Once more I spoke rapidly in his language and Bukowski covered his eyes and muttered an answer.

The girl translated. "Van Dyne hid them in our cottage. He told us take them back here after the boss went to prison. It's Papa's job to keep the books now. They still sell sick horses, but not from here."

Hannah's eyes sparked. "I'll bet Ms. Mane transported some fine looking horseflesh to America not long ago—and was looking to make good money on it there."

I explained in Polish to Bukowski, who sighed and shrugged, head hung low.

"That's what she was hiding from us, Hannah," Dorie said. "That's why she wouldn't open the barn doors the day we visited her." She stamped her foot in anger and disgust.

Lucia led us to the front door of the residence, pointing out that the rain had dwindled to a fine mist and the distant rumblings vanished.

"You have the key?" Phillips asked the girl. She did, and handed it off to Lucia. He asked the girl to make coffee, saying they would pour it into her father if they had to. "Then, if Bukowski's still willing to take responsibility, we'll all come in and take a look."

The girl answered. "I'll make the coffee. I am Sophie." She managed a small smile around the group. "You sit on benches if not too wet," she told the women, pointing to two garden benches in the front garden. "I call you when ready," she told Phillips. "Papa, stay with the man. He is police. He will help us get out of here for good. Now we know Terry is okay, we will get different work. Our family can be together again."

Lucia stepped forward and hugged the girl as she went toward the front door, stuffing the ring of keys back into her barn jacket pocket.

"You're a strong young woman," Lu said, her eyes bright and her voice warm. "I am proud of you, I would be proud to have a daughter like you."

Sophie smiled, and Meg recalled Terry Bukowski's smile, so rare and unexpected in her wan face. But there, always there under the surface. "He can't be all bad to have raised such daughters," she muttered to the detective, who nodded back to her, giving up a small grin.

Now he watched over the damp wooden bench where

the old man had collapsed. "Nonetheless," he explained, "I'll have to call the local branch of the police to be part of the search of Van Dyne's books and the taking of Bukowski's statement. As soon as we've sobered him up a bit."

While they waited, the sun gradually wore its pinkish way through the thinning clouds. Dorie poked Meg and whispered they should probably let Fenn and Ada know they were all okay.

"But are we all okay?" Hannah asked, overhearing. She came and stood by Dorie, handed her the cell phone and gazed down the foreboding driveway they'd traveled twice in the last two days. "Glenda knows we'll be here at some point. She also knows where we're staying, thanks to your boyfriend, and probably where Fitzgibbons is, too. I don't trust that woman..."

"...ever since she stuck that hay fork in our faces," Dorie added, shuddering.

She quickly dialed Fenn, told him about the results of our confrontation with Mr. Bukowski. We could all hear him exhale with relief, say he was on cloud nine and couldn't wait to see her.

"The director has called in some extra security people for the night to keep an eye on Fitzgibbons, and as soon as they arrive, we'll get back to the Manor house. Ada says her friend Devlin will probably be there when we get back."

Dorie sighed with contentment and handed the phone back to Hannah, who of course was unable to reach Ada on the cell phone. She also tried the tea rooms to warn her about Glenda but got no answer there and we all grew more fidgety wanting to start the long drive back.

After Bukowski's second cup of coffee, the local police arrived and Phillips led them into the VanDyne residence. Bukowski and Sophie showed them the imprisoned horse trainer's desk and pulled out the papers they needed to see.

We all cheered, asked a hundred questions, and were soon dismissed by the befuddled local authorities who were happy to see us go.

Phillips gave me a wink and thanked me for my translation services and said, as he shook my hand, "I had the feeling, though, that half the time you were making things up somewhat different from what I'd said or he said."

"Very perceptive, sir," Meggie answered with a blush. "But we were a good team in any case."

Phillips shrugged his shoulders and held out empty arms, offering a hug. When Meg took him up on it, Dorie made raspberry noises and settled into the back seat of the van. As the sun came out full blast in time for its evening ritual of setting, we set off for Chambercombe Manor.

"I'm fagged out, as the Brits would say," Hannah said, taking her post in the shotgun position. "Glad I don't have a date for this evening."

Lucia hmmed. "I need to cook. How about some simple comfort food? I have all the ingredients for *Fettucine Alfredo* with a lighter sauce than usual," Lucia proposed.

I sighed from the back seat. "Definitely a lighter

sauce. My nerve endings are so shot I couldn't pick up a plate of anything heavy tonight."

Only Dorie was bubbly and wide awake. No one had to ask her why.

Forty

Ada

Alone and fidgety, I waited for Devlin. I'd changed into neat, pressed gray slacks and a short sleeve white angora sweater with a scooped neck and looped a gauzy lavender scarf around it. I wore gray pearls at my ears and minimized my eye shadow and blush—after all it was still daylight hours. I wanted Devlin to see me in my best light, trying to overcome the effects of that silly cane and the fact I hadn't yet found an adequate hair stylist.

That done, I took my cell phone and thought I'd wander around the Manorhouse gardens to try and pick up a signal. But the soft, recurring rain changed my plans. I hurried back, as much as I could hurry, for my all-weather powder blue jacket and an umbrella, and slipped into the tea shops for a hot cup and chat with Shelly. They weren't officially open on Saturdays, but she was there to do some supply-checking and clean-up, and would be glad to make me some tea, she said. Together we watched across the driveway as the guides to the haunted house locked up for the day. Now the place seemed deserted. Even sitting in the cozy shop, I quaked a bit.

Not a good day for Devlin to be late, I thought to myself. I'd have to show him the haunted house tomorrow. He'd make fun of the whole idea, perhaps, except his own, intelligent, skeptical daughter had heard the evidence, too, and hadn't yet pooh-poohed it. Thinking of Hannah and the others on the trail of Terry Bukowski's father and all the other guilty parties behind Fitzgibbons's accident, a sudden chill of fear rode up my back.

I watched Shelly shine up her counters, and asked why it was so deserted today at Chambercombe.

"Not a day for walking about the gardens. I expect most folks are involved with a rainy day activity someplace," Shelly said, with a cheerful smile. "The films, maybe, or some museum or other. Your friends coming back soon, luv?"

I nodded. "I sure hope so. My, uh, my fellow, too. Coming over from Ireland."

Shelly tilted her head and smiled, more with her eyes than her mouth. "Jolly well, then. Here's to you both." She lifted her own mug of tea, drank it and rinsed the cup.

I thanked her and finished my Earl Grey.

Shelly surveyed me, hands on hips, and smiling. "Sorry, dear, but got to be closing up now. I see Heather's just locked her office and she's giving me a ride to town. Shopping for guests for dinner, I am."

"Oh, of course. I've overstayed my welcome." I stood slowly, remembering not to put too much weight on that damned right leg, zipped up my jacket and went to the door with Shelly.

"Not at all. You're welcome 'round here anytime, darling. And if you're staying in for dinner, with that great chef friend of yours cooking, you'll be a bit crowded over at Rose Cottage. Suppose I leave you the key to the tea rooms, and you can bring your dinner over here and set up real nice for the crowd."

My eyes warmed with tears. Whoever said the English were cool and unwelcoming? I'd never met a nicer group of people than the ones at the Manor House.

"I thought of the very thing, myself, how nice that would be, with seven of us here. Though I wouldn't have asked. Too pushy, we Yanks are called."

"Not you, Ada." She laughed and winked.

"Thank you, Shelly. We'd be certain to clean it up as spotless as you have it."

"I know you will," Shelly said, snapping the tea rooms' key off her ring and handing it to me. She got a big American style hug for my gratitude.

I followed her out, locked the door to be sure I could manage it later, then with my cane playing a major role, clambered up the steep hill to the parking lot with her and Heather, and waved goodbye as the two women climbed into their car.

"You get nice and dry in your little cottage, luv," Heather called out.

"I will, for sure. It's so quiet here tonight. A little spooky."

Heather leaned out her car window. "Oh, not at all.

There'll be folks around. There's a new family in Laurel have just gone out for some shopping, and the old couple with the terrier went to dinner early. Your friends'll be here soon, too, eh?" She smiled, and I tried to smile back, but couldn't find one in my repertoire just then.

We waved to each other, and they drove off, their fading taillights making me acutely aware how quickly the darkness was settling. Bits of fog drifted out of the gardens, and a sense of gloom pervaded the little valley that had always seemed so cheery and friendly in the past.

Sure, with five marvelous yakking friends around, plus the other tenants and the sweet staff people, it was like Disneyworld for the old and decrepit like me. But now...

I shivered as I surveyed the white, dark timbered, Tudor style buildings still glowing with a sort of incandescence below me at the bottom of the road, the fog creeping along the lawns. How amazing these same buildings had been part of the area's finest home, the Manor Farm, almost a thousand years ago. No wonder there were stories of ghosts and strange noises in the night, tales of pirates and half-buried skeletons and worse. It could all seem pretty bizarre and daunting in the lengthening shadows.

I could just imagine Dorie shivering beside me, terrified of what lurked in those shadows. But I had never been controlled by a fanciful imagination, or by headless horsemen in my dreams, or monsters hanging from trees. So why now?

The rain had finally stopped, and I made an effort to buck up, breathed deeply and reminded myself I was Ada

Javitts, a woman who'd always succeeded at making her own way. Yes, I depended on the men around me, my father as a little girl, then my first dear husband Jake, and, I'd hoped once, on George, who turned out to be less supportive than last year's pantyhose. Since George, and his selfish, sly nephew's part in my life, I'd learned more and more to manage my own life, my own small but adequate fortune, my future. Even my stepson.

Now, with Devlin Doyle in my future, I mustn't depend wholly on him. I was my own person. This was my chance to prove it.

With determination to ignore ghosts of all kinds, as well as the descending darkness, I turned my back on the buildings far below and tried the cell phone. I turned in three different directions, but "No Signal," was the only response in my LED window.

If Devlin got lost, he'd have no way to contact me. He must have Hannah's number, though God only knew where she was, she and the others on the trail of the killer. I could hardly believe all they'd accomplished so far: meeting Mac's uncle and learning that sad story, finding out Glenda Mane and her brother might be behind the murder, and now Terry's family somehow involved, too

How lucky Fenn and Theo had been with me and could go to Amber Hill Centre to keep an eye on Fitzgibbons. No telling what someone as cruel as that Mane woman might do to the poor horse, my baby, my... self!

Wait.

I stopped dead on the roadway leading farther up the hill toward the town road.

The idea cut into my reverie like a serrated knife on butter.

Would the killer come after me? Maybe Glenda Mane or her brother?

But why? Simply because my husband had bought Fitzgibbons through them? The papers, I thought, goose bumps riding over my skin, maybe they feared the papers I had which had sealed the deal, papers which could be used as evidence against them. Maybe they'd want to hurt me to get those papers!

A powerful flush coursed through me, a sign of aging and anxiety together. The mother of all hot flashes. This was far worse than deepening shadows in a strange place. I was alone, alone here at the haunted Manor House, and Glenda Mane—the whole world—had as much as been invited here to this address on the radio.

In the deepening twilight, I gazed down at the main house and attached cottages where we were staying. Noises in the night, ghosts rattling around. Perhaps I should go and lock myself in. Or stay away from there altogether. Chills ran down my back.

Look, here in the parking lot sat Theo's jaunty little rental Austin. Sitting idle, splattered with rain and mud from the day's inclement weather.

But available.

Down in Rose Cottage was Theo's purse, probably with her car keys inside. I measured the distance down to the cottage and back with my eye and feared it was more walking than I could manage right now, even with the cane. I turned and gazed uphill at the road which curved off into light woods until it met the town roads at the top. If I listened carefully, I could hear a dog barking, voices talking, laughing, boys' voices, no, young men's voices. No ghosts.

Not that far away. Better.

And the rain had suddenly stopped altogether.

The only human beings anywhere near me were at the top of this private road.

Young men who could shield me from harm. Young men who'd respond to my neediness as an older woman, surely.

And up there, from the top of the Manor House road, I'd be able to see Devlin arriving.

Or the murderous woman, the one who'd possibly killed my trainer and nearly killed my horse and his young rider.

I had to choose. Now.

I took another deep breath and hobbled upward, praying for the strength to get there, to the voices, to safety. And away from the danger.

With each step, my knee screamed out. I refused to baby myself. I kept moving, trying to place most of my weight on my left leg, keeping to the side of the road in case a vehicle came swerving down. I cringed at the thought of being assaulted, but didn't let it slow me down. Perhaps Devlin would get to me first and keep me safe.

No, no. I shook my head, barreling along faster... it was up to me to save myself. To put that Mane woman down for all she'd done. In my mind's eye, I saw myself waving the cane over my head, like that English princess from long ago waving her sword as she rode against the marauding Romans. What was her name? Bodi... boad... Boadiccea?

Okay, tonight I'd be a Boadiccea. Me, Ada Harrison Javitts, who was so anti-violence I'd never swatted a mosquito or stepped on a beetle! I would be the one to chase away the attacking hordes, the Romans, whoever. Yes, yes, it was payback time. Time to save myself. If Glenda or her brother came at me, I'd hit them with my stick, pummel their heads, kick at their knees. If only I had a horse...

I would—what?

I slowed down a bit, feeling the perspiration bead on my face, and laying my umbrella down by a tree to save carrying the extra weight. I could do this, not much further to go.

The voices were clearer now. Young male voices, all right. Coarse, shouting voices, laughing maniacally, and loud, twanging, hard rock music...

As I came around the last curve in the upward snaking road, my eyes were level with the road across from Chambercombe's driveway. I saw the sneakered feet and blue-jeaned legs of a group of boys, just teens, really, jostling one another, having fun. I thought to yell out to them, but decided to make it to the top, cross the road and come up close, where they gathered around a junk of a car—a car—a car was good, they could drive me away, take me to safety. Another "no" formed in my mind and tightened a band around my heart.

First I had to make sure the street was safe, that there was no Glenda peering around corners. No danger imminent among those young fellows catcalling and teasing.

I stopped and pressed my back against a tree to catch my breath. The sounds of the boys' horseplay made me think of my stepson Danny, the few years of struggle we had after I'd married his father, trying to bring him up and turn him straight. I whisked strands of spider webs and dampness in the brush from my face and thought back to Dan's days as a wild and noisy young teen. Despite what he'd put us through, with his addiction, his outrageous behavior to get hold of drugs, I loved Danny as a son, and always would. I loved his sweetheart, too, the Innuit girl Janet. And trusted that someday I would be as a grandmother to their child.

An upsurge of joy fluttering in my stomach almost made me smile. How I would love to be a grandmother, and with Devlin as Granddad. How he completed my picture of the future.

The boys erupted in caws and catcalls, sounding something like Ramon, my cockatoo, who was such a genius at putting sounds together to make words, "Goodnight, Sweetheart," he'd sing to me. I pictured Sancho, my Labradoodle puppy, always so ready to nestle on my lap and seek my comfort.

Then, always looming in the background of my mind was Fitzgibbons, my valiant, injured but recovering thoroughbred. My pets, and Danny had filled my life these past years. And except for Fitzgibbons, whose needs had gotten me to England in the first place, I had given them all so little time or thought or energy. Even my friends, the Women on Fire. They'd been wonderful to me and sometimes I neglected them, bossed them around instead of listening to them!

That would change, I decided. As even my friends had said, I had plenty of love to give; instead of hoarding it for when it was convenient, I'd never hold it back again. A yip-yapping across the street startled me to attention, and I realized the boys had a dog with them. A medium-sized brown dog on a leash who suddenly sniffed my presence, shook off his owner and came bounding across the road huff-puffing at me where I stood, cramped, tired, soaked from the wet brush, leaning on my stick.

"Foxy, you punk. Get back here," a boy's voice called out. Then they saw me, I knew they saw me come forth from the rim of the woods and bend toward the little brown dog. His face was a perfect triangle, his ears pointed straight up, and his full intent was play. Play with me, play with me, he seemed to say through his barking. He circled me, tail wagging furiously, and stopped to lick my fingers, then circled me again, barking and beside himself.

The boy who'd followed him across the street grabbed at his leash and stared up in surprise at the woman in the wood.

"Who're you, then?" he demanded as he rescued his dog, snatched it up off the ground as if I would hurt him. "Hey guys, look-it the old hag hiding in the woods here. Wot, are you one them ghosts from the Manor down there?"

My laugh was feeble, but not as feeble as my overtaxed body after the hike up the hill.

The other boys had come running and gathered around me. I was so relieved I wanted to hug them, but they were clearly not as happy to see me. They were all smoking, but hid their cigarettes behind their backs, making me wonder what flavor they were. One of the older boys blew smoke in my face, the young one gawked. Obviously they were going to try and make a fool of me, badger and bully me. Try to scare me.

I squelched a little laugh. If they only knew how much worse a scare I was expecting from Glenda Mane...

"I'm from down there, yes." I gestured to the little valley that sheltered the Manor House and tried to seem confident and unafraid. "Um, your dog is a sweetheart. What's his name?"

One of the other boys, his hair cut a quarter-inch from his scalp, got in my face. "Wot you care, then? American, eh? S'pose you're loaded, lady, staying down there." He turned to the boy with the dog and the smaller, brown-faced lad who laughed hysterically at everything the other two said.

"Loaded, yeah?" said the boy with the dog. "Where's your purse, then? Let's say you treat us to a little something from the packie."

I angled my way around them and headed toward their car, hoping they'd come with me. The car gave me someplace to hide if Glenda Mane came up the road, a place to spy from.

"I... I don't have any money on me, but I could use your help, and I'll pay you later."

"Yeah, when's that?" the browner boy asked.

"When my... uh, man gets here. I came up to look out for him. I'll pay if you help."

"Yeah, like what d'ye want us to do, eh?" The boy with the dog set him down and the nameless pup dragged his leash over to me, sniffing my legs, tilting his head one way and then another, hungry for attention. I bent and petted him.

"That'll cost ye," the dog's owner said. The brush-cut fellow leaned close and pinched my cheek. "Little mama likes to pet things, eh? Hey lads, I think she's looking for some pouf, meself. C'mon, mother, I got something you can pet."

I cringed, while the three laughed hysterically, the dog running in circles and his yipping adding confusion to their racket.

Now I was anxious, glancing down the street and into the side yard of the house where they'd gathered. No one else around, houses shadowy, no street lamps lighted and it was getting so dark I could barely see their faces.

"Be quiet, will you?" I said, playing the stern grandmother. "I'll tell you what I want. A nasty woman is mad at me. She's coming here to do me harm."

"Oh, woo woo! Do 'er harm," one boy said. They all giggled. "We're so scared."

"She's already killed one person and wrecked a horse and nearly killed his rider."

Suddenly the boys grew quiet. The brown-faced boy edged closer. "That straight? This perv hurt a horse and killed someone?"

I nodded, leaning on my cane with almost my full

weight. I couldn't stand much longer. Both my knees were about to buckle, and my head spun. I gestured, asking if I could sit in their car. The dog's boy nodded and opened the passenger side door. I slumped into it, and took several deep breaths, while the boys held a meeting blocking my exit from the door.

"I think she's in big trouble, lads," one boy said.

"Maybe she'll really pay us if we help."

The tall boy was the angriest and loudest of the group. He lit a second cigarette from his butt while he studied the situation, then growled in my face. "Naw, she's on the bottle. Had a few too many, din't ye, miss? You saw how she walks. Nothin' wrong wif her a night's sleep..."

"No!" I shouted. "I am not drunk." I turned toward the house. "Now listen, is anybody home in there? Your dad or your mum?'

Laughter all around. "Yeah, and the King of Siam," one of them said.

I waved them off and reached in my pocket for my cell phone. Maybe up here, way at the top of the hill, I could get coverage. I glanced at the face of the phone: three-four—five bars. Yes!

"She's got a mobile," the brown boy said.

"We c'n use that," the tallest one said, and grabbed the phone from me.

"Hey, give that back, you crook." I hustled out of the car and took two steps toward him, the dog running wildly around me and tangling my feet in his leash. I slumped backwards.

At the same moment, a vehicle approached slowly up the road, headlights glaring, up higher and higher, up the hilly road it came. I suddenly realized it was not a car but a truck, a vintage Ford truck, driven by a long-haired cowboy-hatted person—man? woman?—with a dazed expression. Brakes squealed and the truck stopped.

"It's her," I hollered. "The one I told you about. Run!" I tried to move myself, but froze in panic.

Without a word, the three boys surrounded the driver's side of the truck. "Get out, bitch," one of them said.

"You been a bad girl, we heard."

I gaped, icy with fear as Glenda Mane slipped down from the Ford's seat and stared around her.

"You idiots, stand back. Get away from me." Her words pounded the air with rage. "Get back, I say, or I'll kill you."

She reached into the truck and I screamed. "Watch out, she could have a weapon." I was so terrified they'd be hurt I felt energy bound through my veins. "You!" I shrieked, and came running at her with the cane, swinging it wildly in her face. "Don't-you-hurt-these-boys." My blows at least caused the startled Glenda to lose her balance and fell against the truck as she warded off the attack of the cane.

The two bigger boys shuffled around aimlessly, paying close attention now, glancing back and forth at each other, but stunned, too, maybe, by my unexpected outburst. The brown-faced lad shoved us all out of the way and ran into Glenda, butting into her with his head bent down. He spun her around by her arm, then managed to get hold of both arms and twist them behind her back.

"Hey, good 'un, Brownie," the dog's boy shouted.

"Get somethin' to tie her with, you eejits," Brownie ordered.

Her fury rose, insulted as she must be to be manhandled by a much smaller person. "Get off me, you idiot. I killed a grown man singlehanded, you think I can't hurt you and hurt you bad?"

That was all I needed to hear. I snatched up the foxy little dog, unbuckled his leash and tossed it to the boys. They looked up in surprise, saw what I'd done, and finally joined in the battle. Shouting obscenities at Glenda, they helped their friend subdue her while one of them tied her wrists together with the leash and lashed it to the steering wheel of her car. They made such a racket that lights went on in houses up and down the street, doors opened and people streamed out.

"You bitch!" Glenda screamed at me. "Get them off me. You think you can get away with anything, but others can't?"

"You're the bitch, bitch," the tall boy yelled. "The lady din't do nuffing."

The dog's boy backed him up. "Yeah, you hurt a horse. You took down a helpless animal."

"Sold us a sick animal and blackmailed Mac, too, didn't you?" I wailed. "Then killed him!" I lifted my cane again, so pent up I'd have liked to slash it across her face. The littler boy drew me away and I sobbed beside him.

Glenda kept muttering but the gathering crowd joined

in to shut her up when they'd heard she had harmed a horse. I choked on a laugh, thinking how odd people were to be more horrified at an animal's mistreatment than the death of a man. I kept gasping for breath. I was so exhausted and so staggered at the threat from Mane and at how the gang had helped me I could hardly speak.

"Police," I said to the first adults who arrived on the scene. "Call. Please."

The youngest boy held onto my arm, his face ruddy with color and his eyes shining. "I did it, miss, I got her for ya."

"Thank you, thank you so much," I cried. I reached out and grabbed the boy's hand.

He blushed with embarrassment.

"A hero," I said. "You're a hero."

He hung his head and grinned, a shock of black curly hair hanging forward to cover his blush. "Naw, not me. Weren't nuffin'."

But I knew it was something. Something I'd never forget.

At the same moment the first police vehicle swerved around the corner, another car, a modest Mercedes with its bright headlights beaming, pulled slowly into the fray and blocked any possible passage of the big old Ford truck stuck at an angle in the middle of the road..

Could it be? Was it...?

The tall, white-haired figure who emerged seemed as calm as the Irish sea between storms as he came forward.

"Ada?" he called. "Dear God, Ada, is that you? Are you okay?"

Although I didn't have the strength to answer, I was okay. Very okay, and suddenly in Devlin Doyle's arms.

~ * ~

The big red van couldn't make its way around the collected police vehicles and a certain Mercedes, nor could the dark green Jaguar swerving up the hill and veering into someone's driveway like he owned it. Fenn emerged, spotted Dorie and ran to her, clasping her to his chest.

It was hours before the crowd could untangle itself and the police take the necessary statements from the necessary people. At first they thought the gang of boys was somehow to blame, but I made heroes of them in the telling of my story, and the way I handed each a reward of several folded bills confiscated from my friends. They grew wide-eyed and exclaimed about iPODs and cell phones. I grinned.

At last, the lead detectives, mostly dependent on Fenn Layton's clarifications, though charmed by the many lovely ladies and their babble, took Glenda Mane into what they called the Barnstaple gaol, for what the Women on Fire hoped would be the beginning of a very long and secure stay.

Later we'd talk about issues like extradition, and making bail, which we prayed would not happen, and keeping Mac's sweet old uncle informed and making all the calls to the States which would wrap up our package in a pretty bow if we had anything to say about it.

Forty-one

Heather and the Women on Fire

By eight o'clock, after checking from one cottage to another several times, I discovered the Women on Fire who'd needed to change clothes from dampness or certain other obligations had done so.

When Miss Dorie came floating down the stairs of Lilac Cottage in fluffy white feathers, fitted to her lovely, feminine shape from shoulder to hip, Mr. Fenn Layton had to hold onto the banister to remain upright.

Next door at Rose Cottage, the natty American Devlin Doyle had gotten hugs out of everyone, especially his daughter and then turned to see Miss Ada, upright, without a cane, and perfectly coifed and made up in a long swishy blue skirt and tight little silver sequined bodice and dangly sapphires earrings. He drew a big gulp of air and swept her off her feet, and enthroned her in the biggest armchair in the room, where she grinned and pulled him down to kiss his lips and muss his hair.

I sighed at all this romance and turned in time to see Miss Lucia come popping through the door, looking radiant herself in a red crushed velvet tunic and clingy black skirt.

"We will now be crossing the yard to spend the evening at the Lady Jane tea rooms, my friends." Her voice was authoritative, and, as manager, I helped lead the way as I explained.

"Shelly told me she'd given you the key so you could spread out, Mrs. Javitts, and after I heard from the neighbors what you went through with that awful horsewoman, I thought I'd add to your merriment by collecting some champagne at the packie as well as the champagne flutes we keep in storage. I also want you to feel free to use the tea rooms' land line to make all necessary calls home to your loved ones, who must be terribly worried about you."

Miss Meg burst into the tiniest of tears, then smoothed out her deep gray sheath dress and blinked. Her hair shone like silver, and pearls at her ears brightened her very serious face. "Why, thank you so much, Heather. I'm dying to speak with my Arthur, and hoofing it over to the seafront and screaming into the waves didn't seem like the handiest thing to do right now."

I gave her a thumbs up, smiling wide, and nodding with understanding.

Lucia helped explain, too, as we walked over in the soft night air, the rain having gone and the sky now filled with brilliant stars. "The meal I've put together wouldn't have been worth serving in such lovely ambience, friends, but Shelly heard about our dilemma, too, and gave me a buzz as I set the tables. She had a lovely prime rib in the oven since she was expecting guests for dinner. But they changed plans to a lighter meal at the last minute, so she's bringing the whole medium rare beauty over here, popovers and all, to add to our feast."

"Shelly's a professional cook, like you, Lucia. She's good!" Miss Hannah and Sister Theo, as I'd been asked to call the late arrival, cheered aloud, then laughed at themselves.

"Time for phone calls first, I hope," Theo said. "Siggy will be so thrilled when I tell her we and Fitzgibbons are safe. And we've solved the crime. Remind me to tell Ada, too, the director at Amber Hill says Gibby is making wonderful progress—better than expected."

"I've already called Bernie, and he says Terry finally opened up to him, when she heard we had found her father and sister. The reason she came to the States was to keep an eye on Mac, so he wouldn't reveal Gibby's ill health. But he was basically very kind to her, knowing she'd suffered from the enforced abortion, and at her father's hands. Not mean at all, which confused her no end. And she wouldn't have reported him for anything, she said."

"Oh, how difficult that must have been for her," Theo said.

Hannah nodded while the others stood spellbound to hear her continue. "There was another reason, too. She got herself pregnant by some stable lad who sold her a bill of goods and then took off. Trouble was, Glenda Mane was in on the crude sale of unhealthy horses and hounded

Terry who had a hunch about it, to keep her quiet. Made her life miserable."

Dorie had just come in with Fenn, and she exclaimed in pity and sadness. "I just knew there was some deep sadness in that child."

"But, Dorie, she feels you especially have helped her see she has a future, and she is so grateful, according to Bernie."

I joined Hannah in clapping hands and cheering, which made Dorie dab at her eyes and grin up at Fenn. They beamed at each other, and Hannah said Dorie looked so happy and bubbly she might float away in those feathers if she weren't hanging on to Fenn's arm.

The gentleman spoke up. "I think we'll all be a lot safer when the police get Mr. Bukowski sorted out, and Mr. Goldwin Mane in jail, too," he said. "I've already talked to my friends on the Devon and Gloucester forces and thanks to you ladies and a certain Mr. Phillips from the Yard, they're working on it."

"But it's so complicated a story, Fenn wants me to be with him tonight when he gives the rest of the racing authorities the details," Dorie added. "You all know how good I am at details." There was a moment of mad hysteria, then gentle mirth, as Dorie explained. "The festivities Fenn's taking me to tonight are something for the horseracing industry."

"The Jockey Club, like the racing association groups I imagine you have in your country. It's their annual bash at the Foxsmith estate, and all the big names in equestrian circles will be there. Once Dorine explains how you all have unraveled that scandal of the sale of sick horses, they'll be on our side."

"Dorie knows the facts as well as any of us," Ada said, with a nod of approval.

"They shan't be able to resist her," Fenn added, his eyes wide as he drew her close against his chest. Dorie beamed. Everyone clapped.

"But may I encourage you to stay and have dinner with us first," Devlin said. "There's plenty, from what I've heard. And I think it's important that all these lovely Women on Fire be together for a short while this evening to bask in their glory, so to speak. Besides, I've got a camera just itching for some beauties like these."

There was a spreading murmur of agreement. "As long as we make it in time for the speeches, coffee and trifle," Fenn whispered into Dorie's ear, and, having overheard, I called the group to order.

"You Americans are wonderful," I said. "And to think I've always heard you're all heartless, mercenary and noisy."

"We'll admit to the noisy part," Hannah said in nearly a whisper. "But only if you agree, Heather, to being our guest in your own rooms this evening. Our motto is 'make new friends but keep the old,'" she said. Her simple black party dress and jet chandelier earrings were not wasted on her friends. Hannah said she took the wearing of both as practice for the next time she chose to vamp Bernie, whom, I understood, was someone waiting for her back home.

Then she stuck her tongue out at Theo and muttered,

"Told you I was only a girl scout."

The rest of us didn't comprehend, but Theo, statuesque and understated in a crepe silk pants suit in taupe, with topaz studs at her ears and a glorious primitive bronze pendant at her throat, made motions of surrender. Cheers all around echoed the festive tea rooms as the troop assembled around the candlelit Jane Grey shop, so transformed for the evening.

Meg had grabbed Lucia's arm as they walked over. "I have to admit, I felt awfully bad for the Bukowski family. Once I understood what the poor man was saying, how valiantly he fought to keep his family off the dole and to be a good provider for them—after what they went through in Poland during the earlier years, wow."

Lucia hugged Meg's arm. "I could see you were touched, Meggie. What could we do to help them, do you think?"

From the doorway, I watched Meg stop on the cobblestones and look up—way up—to Lucia's warm brown eyes.

"I'm so glad you asked. "What do you think of my taking Sophie home to West Parkford for a visit with her sister while her dad works things out with the authorities here? They miss each other so badly, and I don't think either one of them had anything to do with selling sick horses."

Lucia hugged Meg tightly. "Fantastic idea. And one less mouth for poor Mr. B. to feed. Of course, if she likes it there, and can get papers, maybe she'll hang out a while and work at the Polo Grounds, too. Josie can always use an extra hand. Or..."

"What are you thinking, Mother Catamonte?"

"Well, just that she's the perfect age to train for the restaurant business. I mean, if she'd rather be a bus girl, and later a waitress. I could always use someone... In fact on my phone call home Tony begged me to hurry back. My mother-in-law and her sweetheart are making it official, and becoming engaged next month since they're already sharing a room at the nursing home. It'll be a big bash. Everyone invited. And of course, I get the job of catering the shebang."

Meg inhaled with a loud gasp. "You are a woman of endless opportunities," she said.

"And you, of endless surprises."

Devlin and Ada come up behind them and joined in. "I've already given that title to my sweetheart here—Queen of surprises," Devlin said. "Those boys told me she had Glenda down on the ground with that little cane of hers."

"We always knew she was a fighter, deep down inside," Lucia said.

Meg shook her head. "You did surprise me today, Ada. Always avoiding conflict, or hurting others, that sort of thing. Yet when you had to break ranks you did so, and magnificently, I heard tell."

Ada grinned, and in the candle light from the tea rooms sparkling in her eyes and on the jewels on her ears, nodded. "I've always been known as a very good little girl. But sometimes, my friends, one is forced into all sorts of measures not sanctioned by temple, church or state." She looked up shyly at Devlin, who held her close by his side. "And I have to admit, often the results of such activity are most worthwhile."

"And lead to more and more life..." Devlin said, standing on the threshold and looking back toward the night, a hand lifted as if in greeting. We all sensed the words floating on the air and echoing around among the thousand year old buildings and up the long alleyway into town and over the cliffs and out, over the sea.

More life. More life. Life...

Meet

Eleanor Sullo

Eleanor Sullo writes a food and spirituality column and gardens voraciously all-year-round. Between traveling and writing, she directs programs for families and adults and spends enough time with strong women to feel their inspiration and support, along with that of her terrific husband and extended family who all live on a self-sufficient family farm in rural Connecticut. Her ongoing commitment to help others face life's trials and grow has evolved from her training as teacher and spiritual guide. As with the besieged characters in **Moonrakers**, and in **Menopause Murders**, so often love is the answer, says Ms. Sullo, while faith and trust, and a sense of humor, put the frosting on the cake!

*VISIT OUR WEBSITE
FOR THE FULL INVENTORY
OF QUALITY BOOKS*:

http://www.wings-press.com

*Quality trade paperbacks and downloads
in multiple formats,
in genres ranging from light romantic comedy to
general fiction and horror. Wings has something
for every reader's taste.
Visit the website, then bookmark it.
We add new titles each month!*